THE CERDO GRANDE CONSPIRACY

By Jimmy Jacobs

Copyright © 2014 James Lamar Jacobs
All rights reserved. No part of this book may be reproduced, scanned or distributed in any printed or electronic form without permission. Please do not participate in or encourage piracy of copyrighted materials in violation of the author's rights. Purchase only authorized editions.
Published simultaneously worldwide.

This is a work of fiction. Names, characters, places and incidents are the product of the author's imagination or are used fictitiously, and any resemblance to actual persons, living or dead, businesses, companies, events, or locales is entirely coincidental.

Although great care was taken in editing the text, perfection is elusive. Please report any typographical errors to jimmyjacobs@mindspring.com.

Special thanks to the supporters
that read the early drafts and encouraged the
completion of the book.

Polly Dean
Brent Jacobs
O. Victor Miller
Debbie Thompson

Chapter 1

Riley Bright sat in the blue sofa, sucked into the plush depths of its softness. As with the rest of his present surroundings, he was aware of the piece of furniture's grasp on him, but only vaguely so. Late summer, afternoon sunlight sliced between the slats of the partially open blinds that hung vertically over the picture window, stretching the entire length of the facing wall. The slivers of light played on the potted jade plants that cluttered the room, while some beams wavered across the cloud-gray back of a plaster Siamese cat standing before the hearth to his right. The movement of the light was caused by a section of the blinds shaking from having been brushed by the fur of a fat, genuine feline slipping through them to plop down in the sun's glass-enhanced warmth.

At best Riley's attention was unfocused. Behind his glazed eyes a hodgepodge of unrelated snippets and flashes streaked through his mind. He ran his hand over the slick surface of the Sunday newspaper magazine laying to his left, thinking how different it felt from newsprint. And, did that mean you could not put it in the same recycle bin? There were also two bottles of white zinfandel and a case of tennis balls just purchased at the buyers' club warehouse to consider. The balls would obviously be used, but was the wine a mistake? He had noticed she often drank other types of wine lately. Though his brain was in hyper-drive, outwardly there was no motion, not even a blink.

Riley's eyes locked their lifeless stare on the ivory and rust slices of the cat's coat, visible where the animal sprawled behind the blinds. Just a couple of hours ago he had been languishing in the sun, half watching her tennis match, then stopping off for the shopping on the way back to the condominium. The word that kept popping into his head was "unreal." He raised his eyes from the cat and locked them with Jillene's.

He met Jillene Calder about a year and a half after his divorce had become final, but she had worn the label of divorcee for more like a decade and a half. Wrapped in a cocoon of depression from what he perceived as having lost his real life, Jillene was like a gust of cold wind sweeping into his world. She was blunt, world-wise and had no time for the past. She lived in the present only, and resurrected Riley from his long funk to join her in the moment. Their romance had been hot and steamy at first, with frequent terms of endearment bandied about. As he became more and more embroiled in her sphere, he slipped from his old one. Her friends, her tennis and traveling became their pursuits. His old hobbies and acquaintances were reserved for times she was not available. All the while as he ascended into this new realm, he felt more like a prized curiosity rather than a partner. He had to admit that even he considered them a bit of an odd match, but she did seem to take pride in having him present in her circles. Yet, through the entire time it was a bit annoying that she introduced him only as her friend. The times when the possibility of living together had come up, it had been dismissed outright as impractical. Still, they fell into a long, pleasant period of comfort in which they basked almost constantly in each other's company. In retrospect, beginning even then the professions of affection had become less frequent on both their parts.

But, the last several months had presented yet another scenario. He had tried to ignore the new silences that crept between when they were together. He assumed it was always because she was preoccupied with her business - though her career had predated their meeting. Despite complaining mightily about being obligated to work in the corporation her father had founded, business took precedence over everything, including time with him.

At first he was understanding about the situation, then indifferent to it. Resentment was never one of his reactions. She had her responsibilities and priorities, which she had made clear, though never in spoken form, did not include his input. Unless, that is, listening to her moan about them could be construed as sharing the burden. On the rare occasions when he did feel a compulsion to speak out, he was struck dumb with what he considered his "grade school" syndrome. A quarter century after leaving elementary school he could still recall how he sat in class, listened to the teacher's question, knew the answer, but simply could not bring himself to shove a hand into the air. Oh, he wanted very badly to answer and prove himself, but could not force himself to carry through on the desire. Then after another kid had answered, he loathed himself and his timidity.

"I said I've been seeing someone else."

He saw her lips move, heard the words and understood them. Still, at some level they just did not register. It did not help that he felt himself wither under her glare. That look always made him feel as though something was being demanded, even if unaccompanied by words. He had seen that look often from her. In this case, however, Riley had no idea what, if anything was being demanded.

"Is it serious," he asked, already regretting the sheepishness in his tone

"It's been going on since spring," she replied, surprising him with the indifference in her voice.

It was time for action, he knew that much. But trying to gain release from the mushy grasp of the sofa sapped all dignity from his effort to get to his feet. Pushing up, wobbling and teetering, Riley finally rose, slipping a hand into his pocket and producing his key chain. Removing the thick silver key from the ring, he thrust it forward.

"Guess you'll want this back then?"

"Unless you want to come over and feed the cat when I'm out of town," she replied, trying to inject levity in her voice.

Still, he was not sure if it was a joke. There was enough evidence in what he knew about her personality to make it within the realm of possibility that she actually thought he might provide the service.

Passing the key over, he stared into her face. He remembered when she had told him of leaving her husband prior to getting a divorce, and how she would have relented on walking out, just by being asked to stay. Perhaps that was what was hiding behind her stare. She wanted a plea from him to reconsider. Reconsider what? She had not said their relationship was ended, just that she was dating someone else.

Suddenly, Riley yearned mightily for an out-of-body experience so he could kick himself squarely in the butt for even considering such a foolish notion. And for knowing he might even put up with such a situation. Did she find him as pathetic as he saw himself at the moment? He shoved the key into her hand.

"It was fun," he said with no real conviction. "I'm going for a walk."

As the screen slammed behind him, he saw the plastic vase sitting on the carport. Jutting from its mouth were the dead stems of a half dozen withered carnations he had presented to her a few days earlier. Now he found himself on the outside staring down at a metaphor of which he was a part — just one more bit of debris being discarded. The muscles coiled in his leg, but just before kicking the vase and its contents across the concrete, he checked the urge. What was the point?

Riley walked out into the heat of the afternoon.

After three years together, it was the last time he ever saw her.

Chapter 2

Hands buried in his pockets up to where his sleeves were rolled to the mid forearm, Riley stood at the window, his tie loosened, shirt open at the neck and peering out over the Atlanta skyline. He had heard somewhere that the city had more trees than any other urban area in the country. Maybe, maybe not, but in spite of all the glass and steel in sight, a tree line formed the close horizon. His eyes were glued to that dividing point between green and blue. That line held the promise of something better, not that he knew exactly what that might be. But whatever was beyond the rim it seemed to be beckoning.

"Man, you've got to snap out of this. You're even beginning to get me down," snapped Charles Malor, who was draped in a chair in front of the office desk.

Riley half turned to look across the desk at the man that most of the office staff knew as Chick. They were about the same age and held similar positions with Amax Publishing Company, but there the similarities ended. Riley's fastidious nature was diametric to Malor's rumpled appearance, shaggy hair and stubble face. His clothes had the proverbial look of having been slept in. Riley guessed that his co-worker probably had slept in them, but it had been while sequestered down the hall in his own office all morning. Which was, no doubt, the result of Chick having not slept much the night before. No, Chick was not striving for a look or a statement with his appearance and demeanor; he was just a slob.

"You're better off without her. I mean, name one thing you actually got from that woman?" Malor asked, then added. "Sex doesn't count. You can get that anywhere."

Riley turned back to the window.

"OK, tell me I'm wrong then," Malor renewed the assault. "Explain the big picture to me."

"Just drop it, will you?" Riley said, having returned his gaze to the horizon. "How do you know that's bothering me anyway?"

"Because you don't have anything else in your life. Unless you're holding out on your old buddy, you haven't been consorting with women and you avoid the rest of us after hours. Jesus, it's been six weeks since she cut you loose," Malor continued. "What little I was around her I could see you were just a trophy."

"Just like a trophy blonde, huh?" Riley said, managing to stifle a smile.

"No, my friend, her prized intellectual, her writer, her man of letters," Malor chided.

"Yeah," Riley scoffed. "Only, I edit instruction manuals for ovens, bicycles and hair driers. Hardly a job calling for sterling prose."

"But for the unschooled rabble of her world, who have nothing but money and can't construct a complete sentence, you were an impressive oddity."

"Chick, you are so full of crap," Riley said with conviction. "You only met Jillene twice. For that matter, you've known me less than a year. Your insights are baloney.

"Not to mention that advice on women from you is a real hoot. What have you gone through since we met? Is it a dozen women, with four or five irate husbands still looking for you?" Riley added.

"That's exactly my point," Malor said. "It's my curse. If there is one thing I can read it is women and I love them all for a few weeks until I know them inside and out. Then they lose their mystery for me.

"I'm telling you, either your sheen wore thin in her circle of rich folks, or she stumbled across an even better trophy. Either way, you're better off. Sort of like a circus monkey released back into the wild. Just means you've got to find peanuts on your own now," he concluded.

Riley turned from the window again and briefly studied Chick Malor. The man was in his late thirties, slender and light skinned. His face was thin with cheekbones and chin chiseled sharply on its edges. Light blue eyes and a tuft of sandy blonde hair completed the countenance that women seemed to find so appealing. The silence between them held for only a moment.

"Tell you what," Chick resumed, "after work come on down to Manuel's with me and have a beer. It'll be a good jumping-off point for reentering the world."

"Maybe," Riley mumbled with little conviction and more from his habit of hating to flatly turn down a request from anyone.

"Heads up gentlemen! The boss wants to see us in his office in five minutes," the announcement coming from a baldpate sticking through the office door and belonging to Benson Carter III. "We don't like to be kept waiting."

Riley saw a sly smile flit across Chick's face.

"What's on the big guy's mind, Bennie?" Malor asked.

"My name, as I have reminded you many times, is Benson. I suppose we will find out in his office. That is, after all, the reason for business conferences."

With that Carter withdrew, his crane-like frame continuing down the hall making similar pronouncements at several other doors. His position with the publishing company was senior assistant editorial director, but the title outstretched the accompanying responsibilities. Other than acting as the office crier as he was at the moment, his job was the same as that of Riley, Chick and their counterparts.

"Business conference, my butt. What a prick," Chick smirked as he arose. "Don't sit next to him. He's so full of it, it'll be flowing out his ears."

"No argument from me," Riley agreed, heading for the door.

As they entered the hall, Chick turned back to the right, the opposite direction from Riley's lead.

"I'll catch up to you," he offered over his shoulder.

Riley glanced back to see him turn into Carter's office, which differed from the rest in that it had a window facing on the hall. Taking a couple of steps back in that direction, through the corner of the window he could see Chick hunched over the keyboard on Carter's desk. With a shake of his head Riley turned toward the office of Seth Wheeler, editorial director of Amax Publishing.

As expected, Riley found the meeting to be a colossal waste of time - 40 minutes of oration that could have been dispensed instantaneously in a five-line e-mail to Wheeler's electronic address book of underlings. The only breaks in the director's monologue were from Benson Carter's questions that peppered the session. These too grated on Riley, since Carter simply took the last statement made by their boss, turned it into a question, and tossed it back at the man. They served no purpose other than producing more rhetoric and punctuating the meeting with Carter's need to highlight his meaningless position in the hierarchy. Riley managed to kill some of this down time pondering the apparent need that men in control had for surrounding themselves with extraneous, but appreciative subordinates.

When the meeting finally broke up, Riley was the first on his feet, but was prevented from bolting for the door by the rest of the herd of editorial staffers lumbering for freedom. Though Chick had given the appearance of being nearly asleep throughout the event, he was also quickly standing. As they neared the door, Seth Wheeler spoke.

"Bennie, could you hang on a moment, please."

"Of course, Mr. Wheeler," Carter replied, falling out of line.

As they made the turn into the hall, Chick reached forward to grab Riley's arm, bring him to a halt, just out of sight of the men within.

"Now Bennie, looks like I have to talk to you again about your computer," Wheeler was saying. "The ladies on the cleaning crew have complained again about pornographic screen savers showing up on it after hours."

"Mr. Wheeler, I assure you that someone must be tampering..." Carter stammered as his face reddened.

"Bennie, we've discussed this before. You have passwords. Don't you use them?"

"Yes sir, but..."

"My God, Bennie, women with goats? What you look at on your own computer and own time are not my concerns. This office, the operation and our computers, however, are my concerns. I'd better not have to cover this ground again."

Out in the hall Riley was trying hard to suppress a laugh, as he and Chick started on down the passageway.

"How'd you get his password?" he asked Chick in a whispered tone.

"Professional secret, old buddy," he grinned back.

"I don't want to know how you knew about the website with the goats."

"That falls under the category of rampant curiosity," Chick observed with a studious, but mock seriousness. "I expect to see you walking through the door at Manuel's exactly 17 minutes after we leave here this afternoon."

"You've even timed the drive over there? That's a bit anal, you know."

"I savor the important stuff," Chick pointed out.

Riley sat in the driver's seat of his small sedan, waiting for the traffic light on Ponce de Leon Avenue to cycle through its colored ritual. It was just after 5:30 and Friday afternoon congestion was already snarling the old thoroughfare that is often referred to simply as Ponce. At each change from red to green the cars bolted forward, to immediately queue for the next light. It was a metaphor for life in Atlanta. Though it seemed the entire country was determined to move to this city for the lifestyle, to Riley that ambience seemed nothing more than mind-numbing days in a brick and steel edifice, followed by snail-paced creeps on the road system. So much for Chick's 17-minute timetable.

At the crossroad with Glen Iris Avenue, he idled at the light, wedged between the towering omnipresence of a couple of sport utility vehicles. The height of those conveyances, coupled with their width, produced a claustrophobic effect in the narrow lanes of the avenue. Along its course into mid-town the street had been extended to six lanes, but they were shoehorned into a space envisioned to hold four. Such engineering called for special attention to keep the commute from turning into a contact sport. Still, coupling the lack of attention the creeping engendered, ears glued to cell phones, a dose of road rage here and there and a general neglect of basic driving skills and courtesy ensured that a few of the participants in this daily migration would end up bending fenders.

To the south of Ponce and the intersection loomed the massive fortress-like walls of the building that was once the bastion of retail activity along the strip. The six-story structure had housed a Sears, Roebuck and Company store on its ground floor and the organization's southern mail-order warehouse above. He had been in the building a few times as a kid, when an uncle had worked there. He had watched his mother shop and even gotten a bit of a mini-tour of the place from her brother. Wide-eyed he had followed his uncle down to the basement of the building's powerhouse to look through a grate at dark water moving below. The stream was coming from Ponce de Leon Springs, which had first attracted Native Americans to the area to camp as they hunted or traveled along the Peachtree Trail between the Creek and Cherokee nations. Much later, long after the red man had been banished from the area, entrepreneurs had built a resort around the springs, complete with horse-drawn streetcars to bring folks out from the city. By the time of the tour in the 1970s all that history was buried beneath the building, commemorated by a single plaque near one of the doors facing on Ponce. Riley gazed at the place, which now was called City Hall East, housing city government offices and a police precinct.

A piercing bleat welled up from behind Riley's car, demanding attention and resurrecting him from his musings. It sounded like an annoyed animal, a young piglet being poked in the ribs maybe. He glanced up into the rearview mirror at the reflection of a woman in a nondescript car that may have been designed in Japan, Korea or Europe. They all looked the same to him, and a far cry from the finned, land barges that plied Ponce during his boyhood. Now, those had been real cars. Each model so changed annually that even folks who were not auto buffs could readily identify the new Imperial or DeSoto. It was the demise of such cars that had quelled all his interest in vehicles long ago.

As he pulled forward into the intersection, the impatient shoat-like squeal continued to urge him onward. Riley obliged the restless driver behind him by moving forward through the light for perhaps 50 feet, then rejoining the milling herd of traffic. Just how much of the lady's valuable time had his inattention cost her? Or had he provided an unintended service? Maybe the momentary relief of blasting the horn, and the verbal abuse that probably accompanied the action, had been just the outlet she needed. Now when she finished today's commute, rather than pouncing on husband, lover or kids, she could recall for them that idiot driver holding her back on Ponce de Leon.

The next light was in front of the old retail buildings main door, where the Peachtree Trail plaque was placed. There was no cross street, the traffic light only accommodating cars entering the avenue from a parking lot on the opposite side of the street. This spot also offered reminders of Riley's long links to his hometown. A complex of single- and two-story offices and storefronts surrounded the parking area. Behind and just visible above the buildings on a slight slope, stood a single, incongruous magnolia tree, claiming a share of the hillside. Riley's father had regaled him with stories of this place and Ponce de Leon Park that had occupied the site of the shopping area. It was the home of the Atlanta Crackers in baseball's old Double-A Southern Association. The park had been peculiar in that it had no centerfield fence. The signs reaching out from the left and right field foul lines stopped at the foot of the hill in center, where a much smaller version of the stately magnolia stood even then.

Often he heard his dad recount the tales from the late '40s when Ralph "Country" Brown had owned centerfield for the Atlanta team and raced up the slope to grab fly balls from the low limbs of the magnolia to the amazement of the bleacher crowd and disgust of opposing batsmen. Though Riley had no recollection of the old field, he had been assured by his father, as a toddler he had gazed upon its facade, which remained standing into the late 1960s. Inching farther down Ponce on the next change of lights, he glanced down the railroad tracks to his left for a fleeting view of the full stature of the magnolia tree.

It seemed there was no place around Atlanta that Riley Bright could go that did not provide some kind of link or memory. Those bonds were not particularly surprising, because he had spent his entire life in the metro area's confines. At an intellectual level, his own lack of mobility was bothersome, but in practice it had served him well, providing a measure of comfort found in specific boundaries. Staring at the invisible grandstands of the old Ponce park, Riley pondered the idea that in exchange for harmony and a sense of security, he repaid the city by being part of its memory − a flesh and blood connection to a past that Atlanta had no time to remember otherwise. It was far too bound up in change, always eyeing the future, and seeming determined to stampede headlong into at all cost.

Finally reaching the junction with North Highland Avenue, Riley turned right around the corner past the strip mall holding the ancient Plaza Theater, which remained open offering bills of foreign and cult classics. On the corner itself, was a food market in the space formerly occupied by Plaza Pharmacy. During his childhood it had been Atlanta's only 24-hour drugstore and at the center of then ribald, high-school tales of condom purchases by under-aged Lotharios. More landmarks whose history he was charged with maintaining, he thought, as he crawled by them. A couple of blocks farther down, he passed in front of Manuel's Tavern. In approaching the building he stared at its brick side facing North Avenue, painted with a Coca Cola advertisement incorporating the bar's name and Est. 1956. Beyond the structure he peeled out of the traffic and into the parking lot.

Crossing the narrow side street from the parking area to the tavern, Riley made his way along the smaller parking lot behind the building, opting to enter through the rear door. For all but first time visitors, this was the main entrance. The glassed doors facing the sidewalk on North Highland were rarely used by any of the bar's regular clientele. At the end of a short hallway he passed through a second door, this one with glass frames like the ones on the front of the building. As he approached, he could see through the glass to the long wooden bar to the left, lined with bar stools filled virtually to capacity. To the right the wall was lined with wooden booths. Above them hung a painting of a former Governor of Georgia, but the centerpiece was another painting of a nude woman reclining on a sofa. It was supposedly the wife of a regular patron who had fallen on economic hard times. The bar owner had offered the man a couple of hundred dollars for the painting as a gesture of support. Over the years the tavern had expanded from this single room and now was composed of six rooms of various sizes that filled three former storefronts.

Riley turned to the right, entering a space filled with freestanding wooden tables of different shapes. Some were round, others rectangular or square, but all surrounded by wooden chairs. The odd mixture of furniture suggested the decorator enjoyed browsing in yard sales and flea markets.

Across the dimly lit room, Riley spotted Chick ensconced at a rectangular table against the far wall. Occupying another of the four seats was a man who appeared to be in his early 50s. As Riley approached, the man rose as though leaving.

"So you did find your way here," Chick offered up as greeting.

"Traffic was its usual," Riley replied. "You must have left early."

"It wasn't early enough," Chick grinned. "Have you met Jack Thornton?"

The other man at the table was on his feet now.

"The pleasure is undoubtedly mine, sir," he said, but not extending his hand in greeting.

"Nice to meet you," Riley offered.

"I would love to extend the camaraderie, but as I was telling Charles, I have to get to the theater."

"What are you going to see?" Riley asked.

"I am performing," was the curt return, tossed out with a touch of ruffled feathers, and mixed with disappointment for not having been recognized as being in the profession. "Perhaps we shall cross paths in this oasis at a later date."

He then wheeled and headed for the door.

"He always talk like that?"

"You guessed it. Totally full of crap and grand illusions," Chick stated. "Only reason he acts is to keep from having to work. But he can be entertaining to have around."

"Is he a friend of yours?"

"Not really, I've talked to him a few times. In here it's easy to find actors, politicians and other pricks," Chick explained. "You'd know that if you ever got out of your gopher hole."

"Don't start with that again."

"Only thing I'm starting is to order you some drinks," he said, waving to a waiter. "Bring us a pitcher of draft and a shot of tequila for my thirsty friend. He needs a fast start."

That order set the tone of the evening. The conversation began with grousing about work, but then wandered in many directions as a steady stream of acquaintances, bar regulars and complete strangers were lured into the web of sociability that Chick wove around his fiefdom against the tavern wall.

As additional pitchers were delivered to the table, along with occasional rounds of shot glasses filled with the fiery Mexican mescal drink, Riley reached that stage where his hearing seemed to kick into neutral, leaving him with little control over the sense. He would find himself, with no effort on his own part, clearly hearing a conversation coming from three tables away. Yet, someone sitting across from him was totally indecipherable, and try as he may, words coming from that person's mouth seemed to escape before he captured them. Based on the few phrases he did hear, he tried to nod, smile or laugh at the right times to hide his befuddled condition. At the same time, it was a bit comforting to gradually feel the loosening grasp of the talons of other people's perceptions that ordinarily gouged his flesh. The constant fear of erring or offending was tossed off for a while. Riley Bright was not responsible for appeasing, placating or attending the needs of everyone with whom he came in contact. By the time afternoon had fully turned into night among the stately oaks of Midtown and along the garishly lit strip of Ponce that sliced through the neighborhood, he had shed all culpability for the destruction of polite and civilized society.

Sometime after reaching this state of freedom – or was it insignificance – Riley found himself tagging along behind Chick and another man he did not know, out into the parking lot and into the back seat of a car. Short moments later he was clambering out into another parking area. They were below street level and at the back of a multistory brick building – a hotel or apartment house he guessed. Entering through two sets of doors, his senses were accosted by music, plus the din of voices mingled in speech and laughter, all fronted by a thick veil of cigarette smoke. They took seats in the corner to the right of the door, at a horseshoe-shaped bar, where Riley was immediately attacked by a tinge of claustrophobia. There was scant space between their backs and the wall, while that surface's dark hue suggested even closer proximity. The entire place seemed barely lit. But was that the effect of somber decorating, or dingy, smoke-stained years of use and neglect? At this point he could not tell because his alcohol-dulled senses were not functioning well enough to focus on any question.

  Their newfound acquaintance and driver was sitting in the middle, apparently directing comments his way, when Riley became aware of a raised stage in the inner sanctum surrounded by the bar. A heavy-set, dark-haired woman mounting the platform prompted his discovery. She was dressed in a shear cover of some type, through which a G-string and bra were clearly visible. As she began strutting to the music, Riley's gaze locked on the high, black boots with red-flame patterns that swallowed the woman up to the knees. In them she was perched at the apex of nine-inch heels. He picked up the shot glass that had been placed before him and knocked it back, hoping it would clear his head. The woman looked like a dancer, but her bulk and massive, drooping breasts suggested to Riley that he was now seeing the world reflected through a fish-eye carnival mirror. He struggled for some clarity as he scanned the rest of the surrounding, shadowy domain. The room stretched to the left, becoming even gloomier in the distance, but leaving another stage against the front wall visible. Toward the back was a double row of small table-and-chair arrangements, a few of which held one or two men seated before partially clad, dancing women.

A sharp crack, akin to the report of a small-caliber handgun snapped Riley's eyes back to the stage. Again it sounded as the women slapped her gyrating and prodigious rear with an open hand. She now wore only the G-string, her bust cascading, not with proverbial jiggling, but more the inexorable force of molten magma flowing downhill. Riley was transfixed. It was like the time he had come upon a semi-truck load of pigs that had overturned on Interstate 285. It had been an ugly, bloody scene, but one from which he could not turn his eyes. For just a moment he revisited the actual pity he had felt for the animals squealing on pavement.

"Close your mouth, sport!"

Riley realized that Chick was grinning and literally yelling at him through the noise from two bar stools away.

"Place like this, somebody's likely to try to stuff something in it," Chick added, as he and their companion guffawed.

"Where are we anyway?" Riley slurred, never taking his eyes from the stage, while finishing the contents of another glass that had appeared on the bar in front of him.

"I'd say you're in hog heaven," the stranger between them said.

Riley wondered for a moment if the comment was coincidence or if he had been doing more than thinking about the wreck he had witnessed on the interstate. The question went unanswered and was also the last coherent thought he would recall about the evening.

Chapter 3

The small moving van kicked up a cloud of dust as it traversed the sandy, south Florida road. Having just exited State Route 70 in Highlands County, a little southwest of the town of Lake Placid, it passed a couple of double-wide trailers and now coursed between fenced pastures that were punctuated by occasional palm trees or live oak hammocks. Beneath the hardwood trees small knots of Brahma cattle clustered in the shade to escape the still blistering heat of early October.

From the passenger's seat Tommy Arcada scanned the muted green-hued tableau of the passing ranch land, with its tired, sun-scalded grasses seeming to yellow before his eyes. The boy's dark features hinted of his Latino heritage, but his gray tee shirt emblazoned with a Shorty's logo, baggy, low-riding jeans and court shoes could pass for suburban, ghetto cool anywhere in the country.

"Welcome to cracker land, nephew," the driver tossed across the cab.

"*Es enfierno*," the kid observed.

"No place to use that skateboard out here, huh?" Enrico Gutero snorted back with a laugh.

"Let's just get it over with uncle," the boy growled.

Gutero guided the van onto a dirt drive, running to a cluster of sheds positioned behind a mobile home. In front stood a middle-aged man in overhauls, no shirt and a baseball cap, along with a boy about the same age as Tommy Arcada. This youth wore the omnipresent baggy jeans, but with a white tee shirt and sported a buzz cut. Lean and sinuous as the older man he stood beside, the boy squinted at the approaching truck, perhaps because of the Florida sun, but Gutero wondered if the countenance was mirroring something from within. Rage perhaps?

"*Hola, amigos*," the man in overalls drawled as Gutero and his nephew exited the truck.

"*Habla espanol*?" Gutero returned.

"Naw, just trying to be sociable," the man said with a grin.

The two youths exchanged a glance conveying no greeting. An air of distrust hung heavily between them.

"Is our pickup ready?" Gutero asked, and then added with a smirk, "My nephew seems in a hurry to get back to concrete. He's not used to all this greenery and nature."

"We got it all set," the overalled one replied. "Come on back to the shed."

The party walked around behind the trailer in silence. Tommy Arcada scowled as they neared the shed, raising his hand to his nose. The man in overalls noticed the gesture.

"It does get a little ripe in the heat," he offered as they reached the mouth of the open-ended building.

Gutero looked into the shade at the large, pale-colored domestic hog lying within. The creature lay motionless on its side, its large eye open and curiously watching the small knot of spectators.

"*Es un cerdo grande*," Gutero said to his nephew with a smile.

"*Hede como mierda*," the boy stated flatly, provoking a disapproving look from his uncle.

"Y'all speak American," the youth in the white tee shirt barked.

"Don't mind my boy," the older man offered, shooting a look at the youngster. "He just don't get on with strangers.

"He'll go near 300 pounds," he continued, turning his attention back to the pig in the enclosure. "Mind if I asked what you need with a boar hog in Key West?"

"Stock Island," Gutero corrected, and then added, "It's for the holiday."

"Which one?" the farmer said quizzically.

"October 10, the anniversary of the beginning of our 30 Years War - our War for Independence from Spain."

"Some kind of Cuban holiday, huh?" the man noted.

"A very big one in our family," Gutero assured. "We roast a pig for the entire family. One day it will be that cerdo Castro that we also roast for the holiday."

"Well, that's one thing we can see eye-to-eye on," the overalled man agreed.

At the mention of roasting, the hog let out a muted grunt and readjusted itself on the dirt floor of the shed.

"*Vamos, sobrino*. Help me get the hog in the truck," Gutero said, as the overalled man opened the gate.

Late on the same evening just north of Atlanta, Hound Dog, the house band at a small club called Crystal's On The Square in the suburban town of Marietta, was pounding out a vintage Rolling Stones song. The tiny bar, wedged in what had been a carriage house 100 years earlier sat just off the old town square and was filled with a late-night crowd that wandered in from nearby eateries and other entertainments. On the cramped space that passed for a dance floor in front of the band, a couple, plus several unattached women, were writhing to the music.

At the end of the bar beside the door Bart Skier was on a stool, leaning back to rest easily on the chiseled chest of a cigar store Indian, which stood between the bar and jukebox. Eyes shut, he relaxed in the buzz brought on by having sipped a variety of adult beverages throughout the evening. It had begun on the deck of a Mexican place with a pitcher of margaritas on the rocks with salt. He could still see the blue eyes that had been across the table from him, sheltered in a slender face framed by shoulder length, sandy-blonde tresses. From there he had taken her to a blues dive, where they sat at the bar, drank cold beer, watched the crowd and swayed with the beat.

Then he had taken her home. He knew he could have gone in and had her, though he was not certain that was what she wanted. Still, he sensed she would have had a hard time saying no. Tall and supple, she had tempted him greatly, but it was her wandering eye that caused him to leave with just a peck of a kiss on the lips. It was only their second date, but Bart recognized that she was looking, having already decided that he might provide some companionship but they would never connect. From there he had come to Crystal's and a rum concoction to finish off the night, all of which left him drained and depressed.

Opening his eyes, Bart looked at the Indian headdress that hung on the wall above the tiny stage, just a part of the bar's Native American motif. As he stared, the urge for a road trip swept over him.

"Time to head south for some fishing," he muttered, tossing some money on the bar, and then heading out the door.

Chapter 4

Riley was aware of a humming sound that enveloped him, but could not focus on it enough to tell what it was or where it was originating. The slight spin in his head also told him that opening his eyes was going to be painful, so he lay slumped in a pile listening to the droning from behind closed eyelids. The taste of the night before welled up into his esophagus, biting bitterly, then sinking back down the gullet toward his sour stomach. To say he was hung over would be incorrect. Rather his condition was the closing stages of intoxication, with the hangover yet to come. Wherever he was at the moment mattered little, for the near future promised only discomfort. At least he was laying down and from the texture of the surface he was sure it was not in a gutter or alley. Also, he felt dry all over, which led him to believe that he had not thrown up — at least not yet.

As he floated through this half-conscious state, a throbbing behind his left ear became more pronounced. He would have rubbed it, had movement been possible without awaking the demon that promised to split his skull should he open his eyes. Instead he yielded to his situation, listened to the hum, and slid in an out of sleep, stupor or some related condition.

Finally, and almost involuntarily, one of Riley's eyes opened slightly. Dull light shown through glass above him, punctuated occasionally by a brighter, but still dim, illumination. There was also the sense of movement. He realized the droning sound that had lulled him through his fitful sleep had been the hum of tires on the highway. His body was splayed in the back of a SUV with the first glow of morning slipping in through side windows at an angle that suggested the vehicle was traveling southeast. The brighter lights were on illuminated billboards, streetlights and security lights that were flitting past at the roadside.

Riley was no virgin with regard to feeling the morning after, but it was an experience he had not faced often; perhaps just enough to know when to quit drinking in order to avoid the whole affair. Obviously his safeguards had failed him this time. He could remember having a number of beers, then doing some shots — no doubt those small glasses tossed back were the source of his downfall. The rest of the night was a blur of music, noise and vaguely perceived conversations with people he would not be able to pick out of a line up now. He lay for a long time in his misery, not even caring to figure out who was driving, where he was or where he was headed. Still, the left rear of his head hurt even more than the rest of his throbbing skull? At some point he was sure he would have to force a hand up to search that region, but not quite yet.

Finally, as the light grew brighter, he pulled himself up to peer over the backrest toward the driver.

"You look like a sick chipmunk peeking over the seat."

It was the voice of Chick Malor, who was steering the SUV along an interstate highway toward the barely visible sun cresting the tree line.

"Where are we?" he managed to mutter through the gathering pain.

"Off to seek adventure, Chipmunk," Malor retorted in a tone much too invigorated for the early hour.

Riley slumped back to his former resting place, feeling that any further clarification of the situation would have to wait until his body decided whether it would live or die. Momentarily he again tried to retrace how he could have arrived at his present location and condition, but again found it an impossible task. Inching a hand up he finally felt behind his left ear to discover a very tender knot protruding a full half inch at the hairline. Its tip was crusty with blood confirming the skin had also been broken. Curling into a fetal position against the back seat in order to block out the growing light, Riley Bright soon blacked out again.

When he revived, the SUV was sitting at a gas pump, with Chick filling the tank. Riley slowly managed to slither over the back seat and get into a sitting position. From there he progressed to opening the door to step shakily from the vehicle. The air seemed to swat him squarely in the face, providing a measure of refreshment, but the feeling quickly passed.

"Ain't nightlife a bitch?" Chick observed. "You still don't look so well, my friend."

"Where are we for real?" Riley managed.

"Just east of Macon."

Riley stood wobbly trying to absorb the situation and pick out his next question. And, there were plenty of them to choose from swirling in his aching cranium. What were they doing in Macon? Where were they headed? What had happened to his head? Where had they been? Had Chick lost his mind? At the moment, however, none of them seemed important enough to pursue and he instead headed inside to find the restrooms. Returning to the car with a bottle of water and foil wrapper from a couple of aspirin, he plopped heavily into the front passenger seat, the tender spot behind his ear now throbbing. Momentarily, Chick was behind the wheel and turning past an I-16 East sign on the way to the expressway.

"What happened last night and how did I get the knot on my head?" Riley asked.

"Well, I'd say you proved yourself less than a gentleman and earned it," Chick snorted. "I assume you remember we were consorting with dancing women down on Ponce?"

That drew only a nod from the suffering passenger.

"I believe you imbibed a bit too much in the process, then made the mistake of calling one of the more mature ladies a 'dancing granny,' which she took offence to and slapped the fool out of you. You were just about to slug her back when the bouncer pole-axed you from behind. Being an innocent bystander, I offered to drag you out of that pleasure den."

"Now explain to me why I'm not at home in my bed?"

"Simple, we decided that the only cure for your misery, both mental and emotional, was to head for the beach for a while and get your shattered love life out of your system," Chick explained.

"We decided?" Riley said, shooting a skeptical look at the driver.

"I asked and you didn't argue. So I called the office to leave a message on the boss' machine that we were taking a week of vacation. In the process we decided to make it two weeks. Then you grabbed the phone and announced what an innocuous son of a bitch you consider Seth Wheeler to be and that we were taking an indefinite leave of absence. And here we are," Chick concluded with a grin.

"Tell me you're making this up as you go," Riley pleaded. "I've never done anything that stupid."

"First time for everything, buddy. But not to worry, we'll smooth it out when we get back or find new jobs."

"Just great," Riley groaned, still hurting and not wanting to think anymore.

"Lean back and relax. We'll be in Dublin in about an hour, have some breakfast, pick up a wardrobe for the coast and begin reconstructing your life," Chick offered.

The hour passed with Riley napping fitfully through the misery of a soured, hung-over stomach, lingering headache and bruised head. In his more lucid moments he was surprised that he felt no panic regarding the phone call Chick had recounted to him.

Once in Dublin the pair stopped at a Cracker Barrel. At first Riley anticipated only drinking some coffee, but ended up eating as well. Chick, showing no ill effects from the previous evening, ate heartily, all the while tossing out possibilities for the coming days. Riley could tell, however, that his companion's only real plan was to maintain a flexible itinerary and follow the moment. Their breakfast was protracted over more coffee, since the waitress informed them the local Wal-Mart did not open until 9:00 a.m.

Finally vacating the restaurant, they stopped by an ATM and, as Chick put it, cleaned out both their checking accounts. After a short shopping spree they were soon back on the road, now bedecked more casually in shorts. Riley wanted to get some athletic shoes, but Malor was adamant that he needed to have flip-flops for their destination.

"And where exactly is that?" Riley countered.

"Any place by the water that has sand," Chick replied, "but let's start with Tybee Island because it's closest."

By the afternoon, they had parked at a meter on the end of a side street to the east of Butler Avenue and were walking down the beach toward the fishing pier at the area known as Savannah Beach.

"We really should have a plan," Riley offered.

"Way ahead of you, buddy," Chick shot back. "I propose that we release our Caribbean souls and make our way south to Key West."

The idea was intriguing to Riley, but left him with concern for the details. Those concerns did not surprise him, but the fact that he was so easily signing on to the venture did feel rash.

"Won't that get pretty expensive?"

"Not the way we're going to do it," Chick replied.

"Have you been there before?"

"Only in my mind," Malor continued as they paced along the hard-packed gray sand of the beach. "Read about it a lot and heard Jimmy Buffett sing about the place. Seems like the right time to check it out for ourselves, seeing as how we have time on our hands and a little cash in the pockets."

"Emphasis on little," Riley interrupted.

"You worry too much. How many tanks of gas can it take to get there?"

"What about a place to stay once we get there? Maybe we'd better call ahead," Riley badgered.

"Jeez, I may have to send you back to Atlanta on a Greyhound. No wonder women run you off," Chick mused. "Just let it flow for once. We're following instinct here. We all sprang from nomads, hunters and gatherers. Try releasing the genes you got from the Cro-Magnon branch of the Bright family."

"OK, your point is made, but can I have some insight into shorter term thinking. Such as what we're going to do after this beach stroll?"

"Thought we might check out River Street, grab some dinner and then drive down to Brunswick. Should be able to get a cheaper room there. Then we once again play it by ear. I've never spent any time on the Georgia coast and want to get a feel for it," Chick said.

Like most early fall evenings on the Georgia coast it was still hot and extremely muggy when Riley Bright and Chick Malor ambled eastward down River Street along the Savannah River, the last rays of the dying sunset streamed over their shoulders. The sidewalks were not very crowded, appearing to hold mostly local folks headed to and from restaurants or watering holes. The musty river-smell of an inland port city hung over the thoroughfare, though the only commercial vessels at the wharfs were sightseeing tour boats. The main cargo facilities had long since moved farther upriver, leaving the old harbor to tourists and entertainment.

The out-going tide sent the river rushing in muddy brown swirls down toward old Fort Pulaski and the Atlantic Ocean beyond. In the distance, down the street on the river edge, The Waving Girl statue was highlighted in the angling sunshine. The bronze sculpture of a young woman facing the river, waving what looked like a small blanket over her head as a collie heeled beside her, reflected a greenish sheen as Riley eyed it.

At the corner of River Street and the Lincoln Street Ramp, the pair entered the Boar's Head Grill and Tavern. The hostess led them to a table near the back wall.

"How're you ladies doing?" Riley asked as they neared the table, his question directed at two women seated at the adjoining table.

"We're good," the redheaded one replied with a slight smile crinkling her freckled face. Her dark-haired companion glanced up, but not recognizing the two men, quickly cut her eyes back to her menu. She struck Riley as a bit mousy.

"Would have rather been on a deck somewhere, but it is just too humid," Chick offered, after the men took their seats and ordered beers. "Is it always this steamy down here?"

"Pretty much this time of year," the redhead replied.

"I'm Chick and this is my buddy Riley," he said. "We're gentlemen of leisure from up in Atlanta. You ladies live here?"

"I'm Janice," she said, glancing at her companion and seeing no indication the woman was about to speak added, "This is Ellie. Lived here all our lives. And what exactly is a gentleman of leisure?"

With that she and Chick began a steady banter, of which Riley only caught snatches as he looked over the menu. He also noticed that the mousy one was still glued to her menu.

"Never mind the menu," Chick directed at Riley. "Janice says crab cakes and she crab soup are the specialties. Let's try them."

"You'll like them," mousy Ellie said, eliciting slight, surprised turns of the head from her friend and the men.

"She speaks," redheaded Janice mocked.

Riley nodded his consent to the proposed order.

"Hey ladies, since we are going to talk, why don't we share a table?" Chick suggested, already rising to begin the move.

"Why not?" Janice agreed, while Ellie offered a tiny smile.

Janice turned out to be a receptionist for an insurance agent and NASCAR fan. Riley was a bit surprised at Chick's ability to talk about different tracks, races and drivers, since he had never heard the man mention auto racing before. As for Ellie, she worked for the Chatham County voter registration office and provided no hints as to what else comprised her life. After the meal, which turned out to be as good as billed, the four of them exited the restaurant and walked east down River Street, Chick and Janice carrying on a playful conversation, only rarely joined by Riley or Ellie. Near the Waving Girl statue they sat down on a pair of park benches, but moments later, Riley realized that Chick and Janice had risen and moved off into the shadows near the surrounding hedge, while he and Ellie mutely shared their bench.

"You look at the statue like it's the first time you've ever seen it," Riley finally broke the silence.

The girl shot a thin, self-conscience smile his way.

"I guess I'm afraid that I am going to be her."

"Who was she anyway," Riley asked, detecting the first clue to any of Ellie's interests. He also had the thought that this girl had a slim, but somehow archaic figure like the statue. Maybe it was just the way she dressed, not accentuating her shape.

"Her name was Florence Martus," Ellie said, still staring at the bronze sculpture. "She lived with her brother at the old lighthouse on Elba Island just downriver of the town back in the late 1800s and first half of the 1900s. One of my aunts met her when she was an old woman and crazy as a loon."

"And you think you're going to end up crazy too?"

"Who knows?" she began again. "They say that when she was in her teens, a lieutenant in the Navy from a ship docked down at Fort Pulaski visited the lighthouse, met her and swept her off her feet. He vowed to come back to her when his tour of duty ended and she promised to wait for him.

"For years she would go out and wave to every ship entering and leaving the harbor with a scarf the sailor had given her. She hoped the sailors on the ships might run into her lieutenant somewhere and tell him she was still waiting. Eventually she began waving a lantern at night as well. That went on for 44 years, until her brother retired from the lighthouse. She died during World War II. By then she was completely demented and, of course, her sailor never came for her."

During the tale, Riley had shot glances toward where Chick and Janice were secluded and could just make out their figures wrapped in an embrace.

"It makes me sad to even think of her," Ellie added.

"So why do you think you're going to end up like her?" Riley asked, cutting one more glance to the bushes.

"Because I may be worse off. At least she knew what she was waiting for," the girl concluded.

Riley was relieved to see the other couple walking back toward them, arm in arm.

"Y'all going to be around for a while?" Janice asked.

"Afraid not," Chick said, "got to head south."

"Not even for a day or two?" the redhead quizzed, affecting a look designed to portray hurt and make an offer at the same time.

"Love to, but business calls," Chick replied.

"Then we had better head home, Ellie," Janice said, perhaps a bit miffed, but more likely disappointed.

The four exchange farewells and the girls started back up River Street.

"What was that all about?" Riley asked.
"What?"

"Looked like a wrestling match in the bushes."

"Yeah," Chick laughed, "I got my hands on everything she had to offer. Janice is just a good old girl. She'd be fun to spend a weekend with."

"She didn't seem too happy about us not hanging around," Riley observed, as the two began walking back up River Street in the direction the women had gone.

"She didn't come right out and say it, but she has a boyfriend. Sort of hinted that he's not around right now," Chick surmised. "Like I say, she would be fun, but not enough to make up for the trouble it could cause both of us."

"What is this," Riley kidded. "Am I detecting a conscience here?"

"More likely survival instinct," Riley smiled back.

Up ahead at the entrance to the River Street Inn a young black man was holding a flat top acoustic guitar, hastily grabbing his tip hat, case and a valise. He was dressed in dark slacks, a white dress shirt and slender dark tie. Finishing off his attire was an old, crumbled jacket from a dress suit. As he struggled to corral his gear, a stocky man in a white shirt and tie, who apparently worked for the inn, was verbally bombarding him with encouragements to speed up, punctuating the barrage by kicking a small folding stool off the sidewalk and onto the cobbled surface of the street. The young man, his old fedora now sitting crooked on his head, scurried after the seat, adding it to his load before fast stepping down the sidewalk toward Riley and Chick. Half way to them the black man turned to face his persecutor and began walking backward.

"You have a nice evening too," he yelled sarcastically, "and thanks for the help."

When the hotel employee feinted a move to pursue him, the musician spun quickly and plowed into Riley and Chick, spilling his load onto the sidewalk, to the obvious amusement of his tormentor.

"Not much of a music fan, I take it." Chick stated as he picked up the black man's fedora and watched the hotel man retreat into the inn. "I thought they encouraged street music down here?"

"They do," the young man said while placing the guitar in its case. "But that cracker's just got it in for me and don't like the blues, I guess. Not the first time he's run me off, but probably the last. Time to be moving on I think."

"Chick Malor's my name and this is my buddy Riley Bright. We're from up in Atlanta," he offered, passing the hat to the musician. "And you are?"

"Rosman Boscoe Mann is what my daddy christened me, but everybody else calls me R&B."

During the exchange Riley noted that the younger man's elocution did not seem quite right for a street-corner blues man. It sounded very little of the mumbled-jive-drawl heard on the streets or in blues clubs around Atlanta. In fact, it struck him as being rather refined. He appeared to be in his early to mid-

20s, and despite his old clothing seemed too well groomed for a down-and-out street musician.

"Where you from, Arbie?" Chick asked.

Riley detected a slight wince from the young man at Chick's mangling of the moniker.

"Columbia, South Carolina originally," was the answer. "But I been on the road since I got out of school. Mostly the street corner is my home now."

"What school was that?" Riley asked as the three reversed course, again walking east toward the Waving Girl.

It was obvious from the black man's manner that the conversation was on a subject that R&B Mann did not relish discussing.

"Clemson," he mumbled almost indiscernibly.

"As in university?" Chick asked. "How'd a college man end up on the streets?"

"Better question's how'd a brother end up in college," R&B replied. "Trick of fate, man. I was born into a family with no soul. Bunch of doctors and lawyers that forgot their roots."

"So you dropped out of college to escape to the streets?" Chick quizzed with a twinkle in his eye.

"Not really," R&B said sheepishly. "I graduated with an art history major. At least it was a degree that disappointed my old man, the surgeon."

"Best riches-to-rags story I've heard today, Arbie," Chick snorted jovially, wrapping his arm around the man's shoulder. "So where you headed now."

"Name's R&B," the black man squinted at Chick. "I'm on a quest. Looking for my crossroads."

"Just you, the devil and Robert Johnson, huh?" Chick offered conspiratorially.

"You making fun of me?" Mann asked, as he turned to face Malor.

"Excuse me," Riley said, "I hate breaking into your private world, but what exactly are we talking about?"

"Hey, I believe," Chick said apologetically to Mann, then added gesturing toward Riley, "but you better explain to our culturally deprived companion."

As they again started down the street, R&B Mann began a rambling account of what he considered a painful life as the only child in an upper-middle-class African-American home and his battle to overcome such a handicap. During the middle school years, his rebellion found its voice in his music - with the emphasis on "his." Once he discovered the blues, with all their raw and reckless energy spilling out of the Mississippi Delta country, a spell was cast over him, calling him to plunge headlong into that culture. Unfortunately, his parents had no such affinity for the sound, and they considered its founders to be nothing other than they had appeared — low-rent tenant farmers or skid row bums. As for current practitioners of the art form, they were a pack of ne'er do well alcoholics, dope heads and disgraces to their race.

Faced with such an obstacle to his creative endeavors, R&B found himself held captive in prep school and the university for much longer than he liked. About the only thing he could find for which to show gratitude to his father was the bestowing of a pair of family names — Rosman and Boscoe — on him. In fact, he considered it an omen of sorts, pointing to his eventual transformation into R&B.

Through his college years he spent long hours, relentlessly attacking his guitar, sitting in dark bars listening to local blues acts and developing his own vocal style. With graduation he knew it was finally time to take his guitar — and the annuity his father had set up for him beginning on his 21st birthday — and hit the mean streets.

During the period in which he was hanging out in blues dives, he had been particularly taken with songs of Robert Johnson. Born in 1911 in Hazelhurst, Mississippi, Johnson grew up in Memphis. In his teens he began playing the harmonica, but later switched to the guitar. Soon he was playing in jook joints, lumber camps, community socials and brothels around the Delta region. His talent for writing, singing and playing the blues soon developed to such a state that it was considered down right unnatural. In fact, another well-known bluesman of the era said of Johnson, "He sold his soul to play like that."

Pretty soon it was accepted knowledge that Robert Johnson had met the devil at a crossroad and sold his soul in exchange for his prodigious talent. The idea that such a transaction was possible was deeply rooted in traditions dating from African folklore. During his life Johnson did nothing to dispel that notion when he wrote and performed songs like *Hell-Hound On My Trail*, *Me And The Devil Blues* and *Cross Road Blues*. He also developed a penchant for travel, never staying long in one place, preferring to be on the road boozing, gambling, chasing women and, of course, playing the blues. Like a modern rock idol, Robert Johnson's star was bright, but short-lived. In 1938, while playing a two-week gig in Greenwood, Mississippi at a jook joint called Three Forks, Johnson died mysteriously. He was probably the victim of poison administered by a jealous husband.

At 27 years old he had produced 42 recordings on a dozen 78-rpm records. Though little known at the time, over the years they became a pillar of the Delta Blues and Robert Johnson became a legend.

"Now I'm looking for my own crossroads," R&B reconfirmed.

"Aren't you a little off with your geography though?" Riley asked. "It's a long way from Savannah to the Mississippi Delta."

"Way I figure, any delta should work," the black man pointed out. "But it seems the one on the Savannah River may not be mine."

"If you're looking to move on, you can catch a ride with us," Chick offered. "We're just about to head south to the Altamaha Delta country down around Brunswick. We got room for some stuff if you need to pick anything up."

"Everything I need or own is right here," R&B said, lifting the valise and his guitar case, "and I got no reason to stay here."

"That'll work," Chick grinned, then added, "of course there's a price to pay. You got to play something by Robert Johnson for us right now."

The suspicious look that had first appeared on the musician's face faded into a smile when he heard what the ride would cost. He quickly had his guitar out, seated himself on the low stonewall beside the ramp leading up to Factors Walk and dove into a rendition of the *Dead Shrimp Blues*. The fingers of the musician's left hand danced smoothly among the frets of the flattop, while his other hand employed a four-finger picking style. Unfortunately they rarely seemed to be in sync. To the performance he also added a guttural growl, passing for vocals. Much lower in timbre than his speaking voice, it was reminiscent of the sound emanating from Linda Blair's mouth in the old movie *The Exorcist*.

Chick and Riley stood listening, at one point joined by a passing couple that was walking arm-in-arm up the ramp, though they paused for only an instant.

"Let's hit the road," R&B said as he finished and put his guitar in the case. He then began the climb up the cobblestone lane away from the river.

"Can you believe that?" Riley whispered to Chick as R&B started up the hill.

"Worst I've ever heard," Chick said, smiling after the black man lugging his belongings ahead of them.

Chapter 5

Just off the southwest coast of the island of Hispaniola and the Dominican Republic the U.S. Coast Guard Cutter Sapelo was cruising at 10 knots headed north by northwest. The sea, though not slick, was moving with only quite mild rollers of less than one foot, as the bow of the sleek ship knifed through the water. The glow of the sun glanced off the surface, but the reflected sheet of light was broken in many places by a veritable junkyard of floating debris. Besides being present in large quantity, the flotsam was composed of more than the usual refuse tossed or lost overboard by shrimp or pleasure boats. Much of it was of a terrestrial variety, both natural and man- made. Palm fronds, planking with roofing tiles attached, tree limbs, a plastic lawn chair and a wooden door with hinges still attached, slipped past the cutter to bounce in the wake created by the vessels twin diesel engines.

The ship was one of the earliest versions of the Island Class patrol boats to join the Coast Guard fleet, having slid into the water at Bollinger Machine Shop and Shipyard at Lockport, Louisiana in 1987. At 110 feet and 154 tons, with regard to size she was in the mid-range of the fleet, able to operate quite close to shore with a minimum draft of 7 feet, but equipped with active fin-roll stabilizers for handling even heavy weather in open ocean seas. Based on the Vosper Thornycraft patrol boats developed by the British, the Sapelo had proven its metal long ago with operations from the Aleutian Islands to the Pacific coast of Panama. Like all 48 of her sister ships, the vessel was named for an island — in her case a barrier island off the Georgia coast. However, her homeport for the last year at Coast Guard Station Key West was as close as she had ever sailed to her namesake isle.

The tower created in the middle of the ship by the bridge with all of its antennae was flanked fore and aft by the boats two conspicuous features. Toward the bow was mounted a 25-millimeter rapid fire cannon that represented the teeth of any command issued to a vessel the Sapelo approached, though it was backed up by a complement of heavy, .50-caliber machineguns. Amid ship and just aft of the bridge tower stood the other feature, a large winch used for launching a 19-foot, ridged-hull, inflatable boat by swinging it over the side.

To the port side of the winch Chief Petty Officer Foster Bork leaned his stocky body against the railing, watching the parade of debris pass the ship. Beside him, dwarfed by this 6-foot, 2-inch frame, a slender feminine figure dressed in work trousers and light blue shirt, hair tied back and folded up under a ball-type cap, scanned farther out toward the horizon with binoculars.

"See anything interesting, Livingston?" Bork asked.

"Nothing, Chief, and it'll suit me if I don't," came the reply. "If the monotony is going to be broken, I rather it happen with something besides picking up a corpse at sea."

"I wouldn't worry too much about it," the chief replied. "It'd be a one-in-a-million shot if we stumbled onto one of the poor bastards. It just makes for good public relations to say we're keeping an eye out for survivors while we're headed home."

"I can't imagine what they must have thought," Seaman Andrea Livingston mused, with eyes still glued to the glasses. "One minute you're asleep in bed, the next minute you and your house are headed out to sea in the storm surge. Must've been scary as hell."

"But not for long, I'd imagine," Bork said with the hint of a dark smile. "The kind of shanty you describe as a house would break up in a hurry and they probably drowned within a minute or two."

To the east of the cutter the shore of Hispaniola was clearly visible. A week earlier Hurricane George had swept across the island with maximum wind speeds of 176 miles per hour and pushing a storm surge of 10 feet of water. In the process the storm had killed more than 500 people, some of whom had been washed out to sea during the night. From there the hurricane hit Cuba, brushed Puerto Rico, then its eye passed directly over Key West, Florida. As the storm had built, the Sapelo had put to sea, skirting south of the main turbulence to fall in behind it, offering what assistance it could as it steamed back toward its home port.

"Not much different from the last time we were through here," Seaman Livingston observed.

"Except for all the crap floating in the water. Maybe not quite as boring either."

To that the chief offered only a nodded agreement that the sailor did not see, since she continued to scan the sea with binoculars. Earlier in the year the Sapelo had coursed along this same coast, but usually making only 5 to 6 knots, on station as part of Operation Frontier Lance. At that time they had also endlessly scanned the horizons, but looking for the sleek, go-fast boats of drug smugglers. That had been tedious, labor-intensive duty. The speedy, go-fast "cigarette" boats provided virtually no radar signature, and even in daylight were difficult to see at a distance. As a result the crew stood constant watch at the rails for days on end, while the cutter crept around the island. In the course of the drug interdiction operation the Sapelo did not stop a single boat, but still the presence of it and other Coast Guard vessels had caused the smugglers to divert their runs to the west to Puerto Rico. In turn that move launched Operation Frontier Shield in which the Sapelo did two tours off the Puerto Rican coast. Those ended with the month of June, allowing the cutter to return briefly to base in Key West, before heading out to trail George across the Caribbean.

All told, Chief Bork was thinking, it had been a spring and summer filled with interminable tedium. But, since Livingston had only joined the crew in the spring, she was yet to discover that was part and parcel of being on station in the Coast Guard.

"Think we'll get any shore leave when we get home, chief?"

"You never know, Livingston," Bork replied. "We're due, but it'll depend on what the hurricane did to the Keys, who decides to get lost at sea and whether any of those dope heads try to make a run to shore. I'll be surprised if it happens before the end of Fantasy Fest."

"I've heard about that. Pretty wild party?" she asked, finally lowering the glasses for moment.

"One of the many reasons the local folks call it Key Weird," the man answered. "Usually not any real trouble, but with about 50,000 drunk tourists on an island that size, seems some of them invariable fall off into the water. That's why we'll probably be on duty. Past years the lieutenant has let us know a couple of weeks early, as soon as he finds out."

"How long have you been on the Sapelo, chief?"

"Been on board since just before we brought her through the canal from San Diego in '97. Before that I did a tour on the Mellon out of Seattle."

"What's it like to serve on one of big boats, chief?" Livingston asked, looking up at him.

"Not much different," he offered. "We spent most of the time looking for the bad guys and their drugs. Up there we did have to chase Russian and Japanese fishing boats out of our waters. Mostly though it was more people on a bigger ship in a bigger pond, getting just as bored.

"What's that at 10:00 o'clock?" the chief said, pointing in that direction.

The seaman raised her binoculars and scanned the area he indicated.

"It's a floater, chief," she said, a smile spreading beneath the glasses. "But it appears to be the carcass of a goat."

The cutter Sapelo continued on course, headed north by northwest for Key West.

Chapter 6

The morning sun was slanting in off the Atlantic Ocean and through the screen walls of the porch, promising the heat of another early October day. Riley was slumped in a wooden deck chair, coffee mug in hand and gazing blankly to his left past the row of beachfront houses in the direction of the surf that he could hear, but not see.

The porch was attached to a low, brick, ranch-style house set on a paved street between two very similar buildings. Though paved, the street running perpendicular to the unseen ocean had enough of the islands gray sand blown over it that only the very center proved it was topped by asphalt. The lane intersected the waterfront road, and then turned into a pathway leading down to the beach. Through that gap, the ever-present breeze streamed off the water and up the street. Cloaking the enclave of houses was a canopy of live oaks, which allowed only a measured amount of sunbeams to slip through at an angle beneath their crowns. In the yards, morning dew still sparkled on the green palmetto fronds scattered around the houses, while gray squirrels chattered and scurried about the ground, intent upon their morning foraging.

The scene would have seemed idyllic to Riley, had his head and stomach not been conspiring to make his existence miserable. In what had become all too much a fact of life since leaving Atlanta, he found himself recovering from the previous evening. Still, sipping his coffee, he appreciated being able to recover in such surroundings. The small three-bedroom house sat an easy walk from the beach, a bit north of the midpoint of Jekyll Island, and just offshore of the city of Brunswick, Georgia. Chick, R&B and Riley were into their third day of a week's rental of the place.

From Savannah they had driven south and spent a night at the Days Inn near the Brunswick waterfront, all crashing in a single room. In the morning the trio headed across the long causeway to Jekyll. To either side, the prairie of Spartina grass stretched to the horizon, alternately glowing green or gold as the breeze rustled it beneath the emerging sun. Midway to the island, they paused briefly in the parking lot on the small enclave of land that housed the Georgia State Patrol station, walking to the picnic tables overlooking the panorama.

Tidal water sparkled amid the stalks of grass, while the sand and mud in bare spots seemed alive as tiny fiddler crabs meandered in mass. Then the shadow of a passing sea bird sent the entire herd scurrying for the burrow holes that dotted the surface of the mud. During the mad dash the males brandished their single claw in the air, whether for protection or to intimidate other crabs with which they were competing for hole space was not clear. Though the pincer equaled the rest of the creature's body size, it was unlikely to intimidate anything but another fiddler. The panic reminded Riley of old Godzilla movies, when the streets of Tokyo bristled under a similar, jostling blanket of humanity.

Once across the bridge over Jekyll Creek, onto the island, and past the toll kiosk, they next stopped at the visitor's center at the highway's dead end at Beach Drive on the ocean. After browsing the available information, Riley and R&B opted to be tourists, but Chick would have none of it, instead agreeing to drop them at the historic district while he explored the rest of the island on his own.

Riley and R&B rode the tram through Jekyll's Millionaire Village, spending some time in the Jekyll Island Club, chapel and Rockefeller Cottage. Riley soaked up the history, while the blues man exhibited quite a knowledge of architecture — no doubt another legacy of his misspent youth in college. It was the perfect site for both their interests.

The island had been purchased in the 1880s by a group of the nation's wealthiest industrialist and operated as their private Jekyll Island Club and a sanctuary from northern winters. In the process the elite had built "cottages" that would qualify as mansions elsewhere and opened the clubhouse to accommodate their guests. This grandiose lifestyle continued until World War II when the military evacuated the island to make sure that all the leaders of the U.S. economy could not be kidnapped as a group by marauding German submariners. After the conflict, the club, which was already on hard times due to the Great Depression of the 1930s, never returned to the island. In 1947 the club's holdings were purchased by the state of Georgia, the causeway was constructed connecting the island to the mainland and a quasi-public state commission had taken over management, turning much of Jekyll into a vacation playground. Some private holdings still existed, but 65 percent of the island was also mandated to remain undeveloped.

Finally at lunch on that first day Riley, R&B and Chick had reunited at Zachry's Seafood Restaurant in the little strip mall that is Jekyll's commercial hub on Beach Drive. Over the family diner's signature speckled trout sandwiches, Chick presented his plan of action. Hanging out at one of the local marinas, he discovered that they could rent a house on the island for a week during this off-season for less than motel rates, and had already concluded the transaction.

Thus, Riley found himself sitting on the porch of that house in the late morning, a bit bleary, but recovering by the minute.

"Mind some company?" R&B tossed the question as he entered the porch from the house, also nursing a steaming mug and taking a seat.

"Not as long as I don't have to think," Riley croaked.

"Y'all over on Saint Simons again last night?" the black man asked.

"Yeah, at Murphy's. You need to come over there with us," Riley replied, and then continued. "Find you a place to play in town?"

"Not yet. Been all over Brunswick and there's not a lot of clubs. Some real bad juke joint dives, but even they're not looking for a blues man."

Riley stared out through the mist rising from his cup, wondering where the truth lay in R&B's explanation. He suspected that anyone who allowed his new traveling mate an audition would not be impressed with his playing and probably appalled by the vocals.

"Chick already gone out? Saw his door open."

Riley was glad for the change of subject.

"Yeah, left just as I was getting up. I don't know how he functions so early. Took off on that bicycle he rented. I'm supposed to meet him around lunchtime over at Jekyll Harbor. Want to grab a sandwich with us?"

"Guess so," R&B said rising. "But first I'm going down to the beach and get inspired. Come by and get me when you leave."

As the young man shuffled back into the house, Riley pondered whether any of the legendary Delta blues greats were likely to have created their music sitting on the beach at an ocean resort.

Moments later R&B exited through the kitchen door, passed the porch and walked down the lane toward the ocean, looking out of place in his black sport jacket and carrying the guitar case. Riley stared after him, enjoying the morning more as his head cleared. This was a good place they had settled, and Chick's insistence that they move on at the end of the week seemed unnecessary. They were just getting a routine going, the island was beginning to feel comfortable and Riley saw no reason to rush away. It was not like they had any timetable. Even if one were established Chick would undoubtedly change it several times in the course of three more days anyway.

For just a moment the prospect of eventually getting back to Atlanta slipped up on Riley. It was not a pleasant prospect. Uncertainty always had a debilitating effect on him. Considering whether he would even have a job to return to was bad enough, but in this case, dwelling on the subject only convinced him that the worst-case scenario waited back in the city. Any fate seemed better than walking into the Amax offices and facing Seth Wheeler. It would be easier to get a pink slip through the mail. No doubt, he would have to start looking for a new job — trying to sell himself to strangers. The idea reawakened vestiges of the nausea remaining from last night.

Stay here or move on, at the moment Riley was not about to jump ship regardless of how hair-brained Chick's sabbatical became. What they were doing was not very logical, but it sure sounded better than the alternative. Besides, not bucking the waves and just going with the flow was not only the simplest, but also usually the most practical route to take. Besides, something might come up to make heading home easier.

A little before noon, Riley ventured out into the heat of the day, dressed in a portion of the tee shirt, shorts and flip-flop wardrobe he had acquired on the way down from Atlanta. At the dunes separating the end of the lane from the beach he surveyed the sand in search of R&B. He spied the black man sitting on a big 8-inch by 8-inch piece of lumber that had washed up during an extreme high tide and was deposited at the foot of the dunes. Bare-chested with his slacks legs rolled up and the guitar across his lap, the sea breeze carried most of the sound away from Riley, leaving only occasional collections of miss-plucked notes to escape upwind. Through cupped hands Riley shouted to R&B, who looked up, then encased the guitar, gathered his cloths and trudged back along the sand.

"Let's get some lunch," Riley said as R&B neared; an offer acknowledged by a nod and grin.

After depositing the guitar in the house, they drove south along the shore, past a couple of motels, then the public beach area. On the inland side of the road a thick wall of wind-swept trees leaned to the west, hiding the fairways of the islands complex of golf courses from view.

On the other side, construction workers and their equipment covered a stretch of land between the road and the beach to the east. Rather than throwing up yet more ocean front hotels, however, they were obliterating an asphalt plain, and returning it to natural areas dotted with cabbage palms. It was an effort to reclaim a bit of beauty from earlier ill-conceived convenience.

During the 1950s, in the first flush of ownership, state authorities constructed several miles of parking lots to accommodate vacationing beach goers. Over the years these lots had formed a virtually empty, sweltering black desert along the dunes, so aesthetically ugly that even transient snowbirds avoided them. In place of the disappearing pavement, smaller parking areas and connecting drives of gravel and crushed shell were being woven into the landscape.

"Paying for our sins," Riley mused.

"Huh?" R&B grunted, turning a quizzical eye to the driver.

"Fixing what should have never been broke," Riley said with a sweep of his arm toward the construction site.

"Oh, yeah," his passenger agreed disinterestedly, then returned to staring straight down the road.

At the island's main intersection, where the road from the mainland formed a dead end into Beach Drive, Riley steered right, heading back toward the bridge over Jekyll Creek. Before reaching that span, however, a left turn put them on the road paralleling the inland side of the island and again heading south. At the Jekyll Harbor Marina, they kicked up a white dust cloud on the entrance drive, before pulling to a stop in front of Sea Jay's Waterfront Café & Pub. The white frame building nestled beneath moss-draped limbs of live oaks. The trees seemed to be sheltering the café, striking postures like tree-herding Ents from J.R.R. Tolkien's Middle Earth. Around the perimeter of the building beds of palmetto fans formed a vegetative moat. A veranda littered with plastic tables and chairs ran along one side of the structure and wrapped around to the back, to front on a small swimming pool and the marina docks and creek beyond. At the corner, a live oak protruded up through a hole in the deck and on through the ceiling.

R&B and Riley strode across the sandy parking area and up the veranda steps, taking seats at a table looking out over the marina. While awaiting their lunch order, the pair sipped Corona beer from long-necked bottles, with the liquid filtering around a slice of lime on its way through the constricted opening.

The sun was now blazing down on the marina, and the surrounding water reflected the beams up toward the porch, causing Riley to squint as he scanned the single t-shaped dock that ran for several hundred feet along the shore. On the inside an array of small fishing boats and medium-sized sailboats hugged the wood planking, riding on the wake of passing vessels. Along the outer edge of the quay several more sailboats sat in line, dwarfed by the huge motor yacht moored near the south end. The traffic on the creek was not heavy, but steady. Since it formed a portion of the Intracoastal Waterway, even on weekdays it was rare to have no boats in sight.

The low tide revealed a black, mud flat stretching about 50 yards out from on the far side of the creek, hinting at the extreme tides for which the Georgia coast is noted. During the course of their three days on Jekyll, Riley had already seen two pleasure boats sitting high and dry on that bank, with their passengers whiling away the four-hour wait for enough water to returned and allow their escape. Once grounded, that was the only choice save for slogging through thigh deep muck to the highway.

His cursory inspection of the docks revealed no sign of Chick, so Riley turned his attention to the gray squirrel that had descended through the hole at the corner of the veranda roof, creeping down the live oak trunk to forage for crumbs beneath the tables. It was obviously not the animal's first foray onto the deck, for it showed no fear even when R&B shifted his chair to keep from staring directly into the glare coming from the marina. Eventually the rodent mounted the table next to the men, reared up on its hunches and stared expectantly in their direction.

"Damn tree rat," R&B said as he looked about for something to use as a weapon against the squirrel.

"Not much of a nature lover are you?" Riley jibed.

"Wild animals are fine as long as they act the part," the black man replied, maintaining a wary eye on the gray clump of fur, "but when they start acting too much like people it spooks me."

"Spooks you?"

"Yeah," he began again. "Probably from some of the stuff I heard down in New Orleans. Knew a girl down there that dabbled in voodoo. She said critters acting like that were controlled by dead spirits. They're always hanging around because they got some unfinished business before they can make peace in the spirit world."

"You believe in that stuff," Riley asked, a bit amused by the way R&B's usual crisp inflection had shifted to more of a guttural, mean-streets slur that was usually only evident when the blues man was performing or talking about his music.

"Not really, but that squirrel ain't natural," he said, concluding the remark by throwing a waded paper napkin at the animal.

Rather than retreating the squirrel hopped off the table in pursuit of the paper when it bounce past. Realizing the wad was not food, it again turned back toward the men, but this time R&B sprang up, stomping the floorboards loudly. The squirrel sprang back onto the tree trunk and disappeared up toward the roof.

"I think you put the fear of God in that zombie," Riley smirked.

"Damn tree rat," R&B muttered again, as he sat back down.

Just before the sandwiches were brought out, Chick appeared, walking in off the docks, though neither Riley nor R&B had noticed from which boat he had emerged. Already well-tanned by just a couple of days on the shore, Chick wore cargo shorts, a loose, floral pattern cotton shirt with tails hanging out, while announcing his approach with the slapping of his heels in his thong footwear, demonstrating how the sandals gained their name of "flip-flops."

Approaching the table he yelled to the waitress at the door.

"Chelle, how about bringing me a Corona and a double cheeseburger, hold the mayo," then as she disappeared through the door and he flowed seamlessly into a chair, he called after her, "Thanks, honey."

"And what have you gents been up to?" Chick fired away immediately.

"On the beach," R&B offered.

"You really should think about the *Sand Dollar Blues*," Chick said, switching instantly to an earnest mood. "It's a great song title. Kind of thing that can cut you out of the herd, set your music apart."

"Probably be a good idea to wait until I get into the herd before trying to get out," R&B countered.

"Just trying to be of service," Chick continued. "How about you, Chipmunk."

Riley grimaced at the name. Chick's affinity for such monikers was the one thing that constantly rankled him about his traveling companion. Particularly when he tossed out the nicknames around new folks, they provoked questions regarding their origins. Chick never provided those, leaving Riley to answer or endure uncomfortable silences. Even worse, on some occasions there simply was no history or explanation to go with the tag Chick picked out of the air. In this case, Riley just avoided the issue and answered.

"Nothing at all," he said, "and it felt good."

"Well, I've been hard at work this morning greasing skids for future adventure," Chick stated.

This time the faces of both his companions revealed a hint of resignation regarding the revelation that was inevitably going to follow.

"See that 63-foot Jefferson Marquessa tied up at the dock?" Chick asked, as he gestured to the motor yacht moored in line with the sailboats. "I talked to the guy that owns it and he's headed down the Intracoastal Waterway to Key West."

"And?" Riley squinted in the glare.

"And Briscoe Feldman, who owns the boat, is meeting us at Murphy's tonight. You need to come with us too," Chick said, aiming the last statement toward R&B.

In mid bite the blues man paused, just staring at Chick, but all the same, asking for an explanation.

"We just may be making an important connection for the next leg of our adventures."

R&B continued to stare wordlessly.

"Squire Feldman is sailing on his annual pilgrimage to Key West, timing his arrival to coincide with Fantasy Fest," Chick offered.

"Which is exactly what?" Riley asked, still wondering if Chick's earlier identification of the boat indicated another of his friend's hidden fields of interest, or if he was parroting the owner's description.

"Bunch of girly boys flaunting it in the streets," R&B scowled.

"You got it all wrong," Chick countered. "You obviously don't spend enough time surfing voyeur sites on the Internet. It's their version of Carnival, Halloween and a frat party in the street all rolled into one, complete with crowds of women wearing just body paint!

"The town is trying to kick its image as the gay Riviera," he continued. "It's more hetero-family friendly now."

"Hetero-family?" Riley repeated quizzically.

"Yeah," Chick said. "Pet shows and kids' stuff in the daytime and at night it's parades and drunken women in body paint on the streets."

"I gather your new buddy provided the description," Riley noted.

"I'd heard of Fantasy Fest before. Briscoe just updated me," Chick replied.

"I'm beginning to sense where this is headed," Riley offered toward R&B as an aside.

"Still a bunch of sweet boys, I'd bet," the black man shot back.

"I take it you're not overly fond of guys that are light in their loafers?" Chick asked.

"Don't bother me at all, as long as they don't bother me at all," R&B said.

"Sounds like another song title," Chick chimed. "Better write that down. You need to reserve judgment here. Let's talk to Briscoe tonight, then we can decide."

With that Chick grabbed his newly arrived burger, took a bite and followed it with a drag on his beer.

"Don't you love the sun on the Spartina?" he concluded, smiling as he gazed out across the marsh.

The shadows were gathering heavily under the ancient live oaks on Mallory Street in downtown Saint Simons Island. Several small knots of tourists meandered along the sidewalks, staring into the windows of closed gift shops and boutiques. They trudged bovine-like, burdened by the weight of an active day on the beach or water, topped off with seafood in portions too large.

Past them strode couples in beach attire, but less garish than the members of the herd. These duos headed decisively toward one or another of the bars or restaurants that bordered the pavement, suggesting the familiarity of local residents.

On benches or on door stoops, teenagers both black and white, but all dressed in drooping, ghetto chic fashion slouched, obliviously absorbed in their conversations and seemingly unaware of the passersby.

The buildings framing the street scene lacked the polish of modern beach resorts. Rather than glass and steel they offered a hodgepodge of varied brick designs sharing common walls. Each facade hinted of previous utilitarian commercial uses, now forgotten in the effort to attract and service visitors with vacation money to spend.

As the day faded quickly, Chick, Riley and R&B flowed with the creeping human tide, moving northward along the thoroughfare. A slight evening breeze was just beginning to well up, bringing with it the smell of salt air and pungent aroma of over-ripe bait from the fishing pier that stretched out into Saint Simons Sound at the foot of the street behind them. Crossing the intersection where Kings Way changes names to Ocean Boulevard, the threesome came to a brightly painted green and yellow store front, above which a sign proclaimed Murphy's Tavern. The freshly administered paint job on the wooden facade was the only thing new about the appearance. Like the other buildings along the street, it too suggested incarnations under other names and guises.

Through a tiny hall the men then entered the main room of the tavern, with the bar to their left and a pool table on the right. At the near end of the pool table, a small alcove opened with one wall formed by the windowpane beside the entranceway. The other two walls were bookshelves, filled with dusty hardbound volumes, none of which appeared to have been opened in years. At the other end of the pool table, the wall facing the bar held a fireplace, with a couple of dartboards above it. A low railing cordoned off this area; no doubt to keep errantly tossed darts from puncturing wandering patrons. Farther back in the rear of the room were two more pool tables. Every detail of the place spoke of long use and minimal maintenance. The room was populated with some folks dressed a bit more upscale in polo shirts and shorts that could be vacationers or more affluent locals, but the bulk presented a more working class jeans-and-tees nonchalance.

The trio headed to the rear, where the bar made a 90-degree turn to the left to meet the wall. As they moved down the row of stools, Chick exchanged nods and shook the hand of an elderly, heavy set man with flowing white whiskers and sporting a straw Panama hat. He then familiarly grabbed the rail thin man on the next barstool by the shoulder.

"What was biting today?"

"No-see-ums and skeeters," the thin man, who was dressed in khaki shorts and a vented angler's shirt, grinned, "plus a few speckled trout and some spottail bass."

"Enough to keep your anglers happy?" Chick asked.

"Couple of Yankees from New Jersey," the fishing guide replied. "Nothing made them happy, except telling me how great their arm pit of a home state is. Didn't get much of a tip either, after I told them they ought to get their asses back up there if they love it so much."

When Chick and the bearded man had rewarded the remark with guffaws, he joined Riley and R&B in taking the three seats that ran along the short stretch of bar from its dog leg to the wall.

"You have any idea when this Feldman guy is going to show up?" Riley asked after they had ordered a round of beers.

"In his own time," Chick offered. "Just kick back and soak in the ambiance. He'll be here."

At the moment that ambiance consisted of a friendly argument at the bar regarding whether the Atlanta Braves would hold on in the pennant chase to claim their eighth straight National League division title. Meanwhile a couple of women, appearing to be in their mid-thirties were shooting pool at one of the back tables. Each time the short, chunky one of the pair leaned over to take a shot, her worn sun dress skirt rode up, and from his grimace, Riley guessed it was more than R&B really wanted to see. At the other rear table the game was more serious, judging by the intensity of the players and custom cue cases laying on the drink stand.

The wait proved to be a short one. When Briscoe Feldman came through the door Chick did not have to point him out. Virtually every eye in the tavern cut at least a cursory glance in his direction. Short, pudgy and heavyset, the man looked like a spoof from an early 1960s sitcom set by the sea.

Attired in deck shoes, white slacks, and an open-necked, collared shirt topped with a blue blazer, his ensemble was completed by a white, billed captain's cap. With no hint of embarrassment, the man rather seemed to bask in the attention he garnered as he scanned the room. A smile spread across his face when he spotted Chick at the bar and he began traversing the crowd toward him. As he approached, Chick grabbed a recently vacated stool and pulled it around the corner of the bar, as Riley and R&B edged their seats over to make room for it.

"Chick, my fellow," Feldman greeted, while again sweeping his gaze around the tavern. "This is quite a rustic setting."

The comment was delivered with a hint of approval, which allayed some of Riley's initial fears regarding the man's appearance. At least he could appreciate a good watering hole.

"Glad you made it," Chick returned. "Briscoe, these are my buddies, Riley Bright and Arbie Mann."

"That's R&B Mann," the blues man corrected, while shooting a stern stare at Chick.

During the introductions Feldman shook each man's hand in turn, presenting a flaccid grip. Riley instantly disliked the flare with which the man presented his hand. It was reminiscent of royalty offering a hand for subjects to kiss.

"So these are your seafaring friends," Feldman next noted, to which Riley and R&B exchanged a puzzled glance. "It's good to get off the cramped quarters of the ship. I love the sailing, but life at sea can get dreary."

"You'll like Saint Simons," Chick assured him. "Unlike Jekyll, it has some character. It's a real island town. In fact, the only one I've found in Georgia."

"I'm sure it is, but unfortunately time is short and we sail soon," he stated, as if a cruise ship schedule were forcing him along.

"Chick says you're heading for Key West," Riley said.

"Yes, I make it down to the island every year at this time. I find their Carnival quite entertaining."

"Where's your home port," Riley asked, noticing that R&B was sitting side saddle on his stool, grimacing again as the stout woman studied her next shot quite close beside him.

"I suppose I'd say Boston, though the crew and I generally follow the winds and tides."

"By this point Riley had pretty much decided that Briscoe Feldman was a pretentious buffoon. Though he hated to make such snap judgments, his instincts rarely failed on such matters. Still, by nature he felt obligated to give everyone more than the benefit of a doubt. Riley always assumed that folks were more talented, more intelligent or gifted than he. That was one reason he tended to be a bit reserved around strangers, giving them the opportunity to reveal themselves. Usually, though, his first impressions proved true, as the pedestal he put them on gradually crumbled under the weight of their own personalities, dropping the individuals down from the heights to the level at which Riley's initial take had placed them.

"Chick tells me that you are quite the musician and have an appreciation for art as well," Feldman said, turning to R&B. "Quite impressive."

"Just a street musician," the blues man replied, affecting his street drawl.

"Perhaps you could play for us sometime?"

The look on the faces of both Riley and Chick said, I hope not, though both smiled and nodded.

For the next couple of hours, the talk centered on Briscoe Feldman, his recounted adventures and the people he knew, which seemed to be the man's favorite topics. In the process the trio of listeners nursed beers, a steady stream of Manhattans flowed across the bar to Feldman, and some of Chick's newer acquaintances from the bar drifted in and out of the conversation. The more he drank the more boisterous the yachtsman became, and his condescending comments were at the heart of why the locals exited the group after short interludes. Even R&B bolted for freedom, striking up a conversation with the rotund billiard lady, probably as a way of not ending up behind her shots any longer.

Around 10 p.m., Feldman was slurring his speech, laughing way too much at his own perceived wit and had become a sloppy drunk. Fortunately, he stared for a long moment at his watch and announced he had to meet his ride, which he then confided he had no idea how to find. When he stood, Riley feared the man might topple over onto the nearby pool table.

"Not a problem, Squire. Let's get him outside, Chipmunk. You want to help us here, Arbie," Chick called out.

Once out the door, they steady Feldman at the curb.

"Somebody bringing a car over for you?" Riley asked.

"Of course not," the drunk snapped. "I'll be going by boat. Just help me to the main quay."

"I guess he means the fishing pier?" Riley said to Chick.

"Might just want to chunk him off the end," R&B observed. "Might sober him up."

"I do like your sense of humor, Arbie." Feldman slurred.

"Now you got him doing it," R&B complained to Chick.

As they talked the foursome made their way down Mallory Street, which was now mostly dark and deserted. A small knot of people were congregated in the light streaming from the front of a bait and tackle store that sat incongruously in the midst of the gift shops and restaurants. It was near the end of the street and the entrance to the pier, obviously keeping late hours to supply bait to the fishermen visible under the lights out on the structure.

Once on the pier, Feldman and his entourage followed a weaving course beneath the portico covering the main stem of the T-shaped structure. Turning right they emerged onto the uncovered right wing, walking to its end. Riley became uneasy as they approached the dead end where the railings bordering the rest of the pier stopped short. Rather, the brink here was edged by a three-foot drop to a sort of deck running the width of the end.

At the left corner a metal ladder descended to water level. But, even with the present high tide, the pier was still 30 feet above the black surface.

"Ah, this is it," Feldman stated. "Captain Mays should be along at any moment."

"He's drunker or crazier than I thought," R&B muttered softly to his companions, with his back to the still weaving yachtsman, then turned to Feldman. "Is this how you got here?"

"But, of course," was the reply.

At that moment a beam of light swept across the base of the pier, projected from a small boat approaching out of the darkness from the south.

"That would be her now," Feldman slurred approvingly.

"Chick, how are we going to get him down to the water?" Riley asked while scrutinizing the ladder. "There's no way he'll get down there without breaking his neck."

"Just hang on a minute, Squire," Chick said to Feldman, then flashed a smile at Riley and retreated back along the pier to where a single fisherman was tending the lines of a couple of stout boat rods that had been cast out toward the shipping channel of Saint Simons Sound. Momentarily Chick and the angler began drawing in a rope with which a plastic minnow buck had been lowered into the water below.

Meanwhile, Riley peered out toward the approaching boat. It was the small dingy they had earlier in the day seen hanging at the aft of the Marquessa cruiser at Jekyll Harbor Marina. Despite the blinding spotlight effect of the hand-held light directed at the pier, the glow of running lights revealed a single occupant in the rear, handling the outboard motor.

"Mr. Feldman?" called a feminine voice from behind the spotlight.

"Yes captain, my dear," he shouted back, "I'll be right down."

R&B reached out, grabbing the yachtsman's arm and steadying him as he leaned perilously close to the brink.

"Here you go, Briscoe," Chick announced, returning to the group with a length of rope coiled in his hands. "Let's get you in harness for the descent."

Chick proceeded to put a loop in the end of the rope, which was slid down over Feldman's head and secured beneath his arms. The other end was tied to the last post of the railing running along the dock.

"You boys want to give me a hand with the cargo," Chick grinned, then all three men took hold of the rope and Feldman began lumbering down the ladder.

The rope was kept just tight enough to steady the man's descent to the boat that now sat directly beneath him against the pilings. Half way down Feldman's cap tumbled from his head, sailing slightly to the side to splat unceremoniously in the drink. The figure in the boat put down the hand-held light on the back seat, leaving it trained forward, then leaned over the side in the beam of light to retrieve the errant hat. Chick released a stream of air in an almost silent whistle that caused Riley and R&B to both glance his way.

Finally at the water's surface, Feldman wallowed into the dingy and was helped out of the sling.

"I bid you good evening gentlemen," he shouted up to the dock with a drunken flourish. "Will the three of you please join me for dinner on board at the marina tomorrow evening?"

"Count on it, Squire," Chick called down without consulting his companions.

"Thank you boys for the help," the female voice added, then the motor on the dingy came alive and it pulled away from the pier.

"Did you see the figure on the captain?" Chick offered from beneath raised eyebrows as the boat faded into the darkness.

Chapter 7

An afternoon wind originating far offshore in the Atlantic Ocean swept over the breaking waves of the reef, then rushed across the shallow aquamarine grass and sand flats to eventually flutter the leaves of royal Poinciana trees and palm fronds that shaded Stock Island. Separated from Key West by Cow Channel, in pioneer days the isle had earned its name by playing host to the cattle, goats and other livestock that fed Florida's second oldest town. In a similar way, its rundown trailer courts and ramshackle neighborhoods still propped up the city's life style. Only now the commodity was cheap manual labor for the services that kept tourists happy in the American tropics. Stock Islanders are dockhands, waitresses, taxi drivers and janitors for the slice of paradise sitting at the southern end of U.S. Highway 1 and often referred to as the "end of the line." Without these folks, this bastion of writers, troubadours and vacationers would grind to a halt. And just as the animals of yore were isolated out of sight and scent range, Stock Island now housed the necessary human herd.

Wedged on a sliver of land between U.S. Highway 1 and McDonald Drive, which angles off to the southeast, a patch of sand and sparse grass hid beneath the trees from the drenching Florida Keys sun. To the east was the last in a row of mobile homes, while the other side of the clearing was formed by a convenience store and its parking lot that linked the two roadways. Though the brilliance of the light flooding down toward the clearing suggested conditions akin to a solar blast furnace, the temperature hovered only in the low 80s, about average for the string of tropical isles that extend from the mainland to the southwest of Miami. When the palms and Poincianas interrupt the sun's rays, the resulting shade can be quite comfortable. That is, if it were not for the humidity and mosquitoes.

Beneath the trees Enrico Gutero used his free hand to swat a biting insect on his sweat-drenched arm. In the hand of that arm he held a rope, with the opposite end looped around the neck of the large hog. Also standing in the shade was a woman who appeared to be in her early 40s, with dark complexion and jet-black hair pulled back in a bun. She was dressed in a light green uniform dress that hinted of housekeeping at a chain motel.

"I don't know," the woman said in English, thickly clouded with Hispanic tones. "What will the neighbors think?"

"It will be fine," Enrico replied. "As if I care what the nosey ones say."

"But, *mi esposo*, a pig in the yard in plain view? The animal control will come for it. You will humiliate me and bring the authorities to our home."

"It is for a short time, woman," he countered. "In a few days Arturo and I will be butchering *el chancho*."

"It will be a week! At least you could build a pen or fence to keep it hidden."

"Enough," he commanded. "We will have our celebration and I will have my peace. With all the mess from the hurricane to clean up, no one will pay attention to the hog."

Gutero's wife stood by sullenly as he tied the end of the rope around the trunk of the Poinciana tree, then stepped back to consider his effort. The hog tugged at the rope, seemingly to test its situation, then with a soft snort, collapsed on its side in the shade.

She was a goddess. The thought raced through his mind as she slipped from his arms and sank onto the sofa. Her sandy blonde tresses draped down, lying over the left shoulder of her white blouse. She slid her feet from leather sandals, and then swung long, denim-clad legs around to stretch out, face up on the settee.

Bending beside the woman, he pressed his lips to hers, and then dropped to a kneeling position. He stared into soft blue eyes, irises flecked with hints of gold and black that seemed to dance before him. Without breaking their visual connection, he pulled the tail of her blouse from the jeans and ran his hands up along the smooth warmth of her torso until meeting the resistance of her bra. Fingertips burrowed beneath the fabric of the cups, like a gang of convicts digging under prison walls, their final desperate lunge for freedom pushing the bra and blouse upward. He felt the softness of her body retreat slightly as he squeezed. His fingers literally trembled as they explored, followed along their path by his thirsty eyes drinking in the vision.

Now his hands retraced their path down to her stomach, passing the depression of her navel to the metal button at the waist of her jeans. Awkwardly he released the button, and then pulled the zipper downward. A sense of awe mixed with euphoria swelled his chest, impeding the heavy breaths now escaping from him. The fact she did not protest or resist him in any way seemed incomprehensible; she was allowing him to explore at will.

Pushing onward he felt the satin, slickness of her panties. The long traverse to reach that border suggested a very skimpy bikini cut, which sent blood boiling through his arteries to burn in the capillaries of his fingertips.

At that instant Joey Smatt felt a crushing jab to his rib cage. It knocked him off balance, leaving him momentarily stunned. His eyes squinted at the light flooding in as they opened.

"What'd you do that for?" he stammered. "I was so close."

"Cause they throw you out of places like this when you fall asleep and start snoring," Elsworth Score laughed. "Only thing you were close to was falling in the floor."

The two men were seated with a woman on a bench at a rough wooden table, surrounded by equally crude, unpainted lumber walls and floors. On the opposite wall, in a nook that served as a stage, a trio with guitar, bass and drums pounded out a country rock rhythm.

"Don't see how you can fall asleep with the music blaring anyway," Score added, as the woman giggled.

The two men were a contrast. Both were dressed in black tee shirts with leather boots, pants and jackets, but all resemblance ended there. On his head Score had a red and white Budweiser bandana tied into a ghetto rag covering his hair, topping off his 6-foot, 3-inch, heavy set body, complete with emerging gut protruding over his belt. The lower fringe of his face was ringed with a heavy stubble, well on its way to becoming a beard. Smatt, on the other hand, was short with a rail-thin physique, topped by an equally slender face. Sunken eyes framed a sharply pointed nose, providing an appearance vaguely suggestive of a rodent.

"It was a long ride down here," he defended. "Wore me out."

"We got a longer ride ahead of us," Score said, then turned toward the woman to add, "We're meeting up with the rest of the gang I was telling you about down in the Keys. Going to raise some hell then."

Unimpressed the woman smiled thinly. She looked to be in her forties, probably a good decade older than the men. Brittle blonde hair with dark roots puffed out over an abundance of rouge and mascara, layered on as a defense against encroaching maturity. But, her tank top and tight, low-slung Capri pants revealed a figure that was fighting a successful rearguard action against the onslaught of years.

"Uh huh," she murmured. "I'm going to the ladies room, then why don't we head down to the beach for that taste you promised."

"Sure thing, babe," Score grinned, and then watched her gyrate, unsteadily away.

"What gang are we meeting, Ellie?" Smatt asked. "And what is she going to taste?"

"Damn it, Joey, I keep telling you not to call me that. We ain't kids anymore," he scowled.

"I'm Big El, or maybe Bad El, now. Haven't made up my mind yet which sounds best. Anyway, I got her convinced we're bikers. Even hinted that we're joining the Hell's Angels. Only I may have given her the impression that we got a little something she could snort up her nose for pleasure."

As he completed the sentence he had cut his eyes suspiciously around the room, making sure his pronouncement went unnoticed at the other tables and benches along the wall.

"What'd you do that for?" Smatt asked blankly.

"Cause I'll be getting a little something in return, if you catch my drift," the big man noted with a smirk.

"But we ain't got no — stuff," Smatt stated, dropping his voice conspiratorially on the last word.

"I know that," Score rasped impatiently. "But hell, she's so drunk she won't know the difference. While I walk her down to the beach, you go out to the bikes and bring me a little of that powder you're always sprinkling on when your jeans chafe you."

"I can't help that, Ellie — I mean Big El," Smatt said indignantly. "I ain't used to straddling that big seat."

"Just do it," Score demanded, as the woman approached the table, and then added as he rose, "and bring us both another rum and coke down to the beach."

"I got to go to the john first," Smatt called after them.

"Just do it," Score glared over his shoulder at the smaller man.

Rising from the bench, Smatt picked up two cups from the table and began wandering through the jungle of rooms that composed the Flora-Bama Lounge & Package. There was no floor plan to its construction. It seemed as though whatever building material washed ashore after a hurricane was slapped together to add space to the structure. In the process it had grown into a maze of rooms, several featuring bandstands. There was also a kitchen that dispensed food through windows in a wall. Several bars, including one with a deck looking out over the Gulf of Mexico, completed the motif. The claim to fame of the establishment is that it straddles the state line between Alabama and Florida, making it possible to drink in both states without leaving the lounge.

"Where's the bathroom anyway," the little man mumbled aloud as he wove his way from room to room past knots of tourists and what appeared to be real bikers. "Didn't give me any money for drinks either."

Eventually Joey Smatt found his way to the parking area in front of the bar, which fronted on the highway skirting the seaward shore of Perdido Key. To the west it was Alabama Route 192, while its eastern incarnation was labeled Florida Route 292. Smatt's 250 KLR Kawasaki bike sat next to the new Harley-Davidson Sportster 1200 that Elsworth Score had purchased just before they left Fort Payne for the trip. The big motorcycle had been on order for more than a year and awaiting the arrival of the "hog" had given Score plenty of time to plan, while both men carried over vacation time to accommodate their road trip.

Smatt liked the feel of riding a two-wheeler, being free on the road with the wind rushing past, but found his friends fascination with biker life puzzling. It was good for weekend fun; a break from showing up at the factory every morning and fashioning aluminum into "mobile housing units." But, why did Ellie have to drag him off to Florida with all that talk about gangs, bars, bitches and brawling? And now Ellie wanted to sleep on the beach tonight! Fact was he would rather be back home, building doublewides and watching television in the evening. He just had a bad feeling about this road trip.

At the bikes, Smatt dug into his pack, fumbling through it to produce a bottle of mouthwash and a plastic bottle with a flip-top shaker lid. He poured a shot of the yellowish liquid in each cup.

"It's all alcohol," he muttered aloud, and then shook out some white powder from the plastic container into his hand. Cutting back through the lounge, he stopped at the bar to have both cups filled with Coca Cola, taking a sip from one to see what it tasted like.

"Close enough," he said to the bar tender, then paid for the cokes.

Descending the walkway out onto the beach, he struggled with a drink in one hand, the powder in the palm of the other and the additional drink pinned between his forearm and chest. It was difficult not to slosh the drinks over the edges of the cups as he moved on the uneven sand that shifted beneath his feet. Peering into the dark, the backlit glare from the lounge made it tough to pick out anything more than vague silhouettes on the beach. With a shrug, Smatt started to this right, heading west into Alabama.

"Over here, Joey," he heard after several dozen paces.

As he drew near he picked out the shadowy shapes of Score and the woman. She was standing in front of his partner, appearing to have just backed up from the big man. At closer range he could now see that her tank top was draped over his friends forearm. The pale white of her breasts reflected what little light was streaming down the beach, framing them in the darkness. As Smatt stared at them, the mounds seemed to sit unnaturally high on her chest, almost chiseled onto her body.

"Has he got the stuff?" she asked.

"Yeah, you can count on by buddy Joey," Score said as he drew a lock knife from a leather, snap-top holder on his belt and popped the blade free.

"Put it in my hand," he directed at Smatt, who dutifully complied, never taking his eyes off the bosoms levitating in the dark before him.

Once in possession of the powder, Score used the knife to rake it into a neat line in his own palm, then put the hand forward toward the woman. Smatt continued to hold the two drink cups, eyes glued to her movement and mesmerized by the fact her boobs did not jiggle; hardly seemed to budge as she moved. The woman bent forward over Score's offered hand and Smatt heard the sharp rush of air being sucked into her nostril, followed instantly by a dry hacking cough.

"What the hell was that," she finally managed to demand as she grabbed one of the cups from Smatt's hand. "Tasted like talc."

She then took a swallow from the cup and in a single motion sprayed the liquid out of her mouth onto the front of Smatt's shirt.

"Damn," she screamed. "You trying to poison me, you piece of crap little weasel!"

She threw the cup onto the beach and her right leg jerked violently upward, guided with malice and precision directly into Joey Smatt's crotch. The remaining cup of soft drink and mouthwash flew into the air, splattering down onto the little man as he folded. His eyes bugged out as he sank to the sand with a guttural groan and assumed a fetal position, hands cupped between his legs.

Grabbing her top from Score's arm the woman stomped off in the direction of the Flora-Bama, the sound of spitting emanating from the darkness that closed in behind her.

Elsworth Score stood on the beach looking down at his fallen companion who had now rolled over, allowing his wet clothes to pick up a heavy coat of sand. A low moaning sound streamed up from Smatt.

"Tell you what, Joey," the big man said, an amused look on his face as he put his knife back in its case, "you sure got a way with women. Looks like neither one of us gets laid tonight."

Chapter 8

"We don't even know what time we're supposed to be here," Riley groused as he, Chick and R&B walked along the sandy drive past the Jekyll Harbor Marina office.

"The Squire never eats till after eight," Chick said. "You worry too much about everything, Chipmunk."

"I really wish you'd quit calling me that," Riley continued plaintively. "None of us like your nicknames."

"Hey, don't try to drag Arbie into your family argument," R&B injected, but with a tone suggesting agreement.

Chick threw an arm around Riley's shoulder as they walked, hugging him.

"Come on, Chipmunk, you know I love you," he mocked.

Breaking away from the embrace, Riley just shook his head, while glancing around to see if anyone else in the marina was watching. It was a relief to see no heads turned their way. Rather the marina manager was standing on the porch of the small office talking to a man who looked like a "live aboard" from one of the sailboats. Riley found that sailboat owners hanging around a marina were always pretty easy to spot. Was it the way they dressed? Not much different from tourists, but maybe it was the way they wore the deck shoes, shorts and tee or polo shirts? Could also be their causal air, or the way they carry themselves.

Up on the patio at Sea Jay's there was the usual complement of diners watching the sun sink over the marsh, and a young couple lounged in the swimming pool that separated the restaurant deck from the shoreline. But all of those folks were also occupied and not watching the trio head to the dock. For a second, Riley considered why it was that he was always worrying about other people watching him and what they were thinking. Instinctively he knew that even if they were watching, they could care less what he was doing. Still, it seemed impossible to shake that deeply embedded bit of self-consciousness that gnawed at him.

As they reached the dock, the creek's surface stretched out beyond the marina in a mirror finish. The afternoon breeze had lain down, almost as though offering a courtesy to the sinking sun to better reflect its fading rays off the sheen. Over the marsh a great blue heron winged its way, low and slow, across the resulting glare, while an osprey cruised high above the waterway on its final search of the day for mullet straying too near the surface for too long.

At the point the men reached the boat lift, they started down the slope of the walkway leading to the dock. The marina had no boat ramp, which is common along the Georgia coast. Instead, smaller boats of up to 24 feet were tied up at the dock permanently, or they were kept in dry dock, and then delivered to the lift by an industrial-sized lift truck to be lowered into the water. It was a more practical set up because this strip of coast endures some of the more exaggerated tides on the east coast, with changes of six to seven feet normal. On extreme spring tides, the water can rise and fall eight or nine feet in a cycle. Also to deal with these changing water levels, the dock floated rather than sat on pilings. The dock was attached by huge rings to telephone pole-sized pilings, keeping the structure stationary as it rode on the tides. Thus the walkway was hinged to swing up or down with the changing flow. The wooden gangway was covered with a rough sheet metal surface to prevent slipping when it was inclined, still all three men felt the need to grasp the hand rails and stare down to assure their footing for the unsteady descent.

    Once off the gangplanks and moving along the main dock, Riley again felt comfortable to raise his gaze to their destination. The white hull of the Marquessa fairly glowed in the late sunlight, turning the tinted windows wrapping around the upper deck and the portholes below into mirrored black surfaces. Above, the silver sheen of stainless steel fittings gleamed from the flying bridge. At the aft of the yacht, hanging from davits, was the small inflatable boat that had picked up Feldman the previous evening. If the detail of the boat was designed to impress, it had the desired effect, practically commanding attention to its opulence.

    "Pretty impressive up close," Riley commented. "Must cost a fortune."

"Two mill plus," Chick offered. "Wait till you see the teak decking. The Squire spared no expense. But I'll warn you now, don't ask how he made his bundle. He's a bit touchy about the fact it's inherited family money."

"I know the feeling," R&B injected, affecting the oppressed weariness of a Mississippi Delta tenant farmer to explain his own burden of unearned support.

"So why do you call him Squire?" Riley asked.

The only reply Riley got was a trademark, and playful Malor smile. Riley immediately wondered what possessed him to even ask the question that just reminded of why those nicknames galled him so. Instinctively he knew there would be no answer, most likely because there was no answer. Yet, Chick's smile and refusal to reply gave the impression of an inside joke or secret, conspiratorially concealed to avoid embarrassment. It was that same behavior that on several occasions after Chick had exited a conversation had left Riley to claim ignorance of where his friend came up with those monikers. Of course, there was some basis for "Chipmunk," though it was not a tale Riley was likely to divulge. And, that fact did leave enough doubt to suggest there might be some basis for creating someone else's nickname? Fortunately, Riley's attention was now distracted from these musings.

Up ahead, standing at the rear of the boat on the dock, dressed in white Bermuda length shorts and uniform shirt, a woman in her early thirties was in animated conversation with an apparently angry younger man who was gripping a duffle bag. With a final flurry he began striding down the dock, obviously headed for the shore. The woman at first stood following him with her eyes, facial expression communicating frustration. When her gaze turned to the approaching trio, her countenance shifted toward unease.

She was five feet, six, maybe seven, but the length of her legs left the impression of being taller, as she stood offering a profile view. Her blonde hair was pulled back, not in a bun, but rather an "s" shaped ponytail held quite close to the back of her head. Riley guessed that this was the captain they had seen in the dory at Saint Simons last evening. Now in the full light of day, he thoroughly agreed with Chick's assessment. She had slender hips, but an even narrower waist highlighted them. The shirt of the uniform was tight across her bosom, which was not exceptionally large, but also benefited from its contour above her waist. The shapely legs suggested activity, exposing no sign of excess bulk.

The face that watched the approach of the men was narrow, framed by petite ears, the upper tips of which were high and extended outward just enough to present a pleasant elfish quality. As the men neared her, the uneasy expression on the woman's face melted into a smile that showed twin ridges of even white teeth and twinkling green eyes.

"And you are the boys from last evening," she announced as the trio reached her. "Thanks again for helping Mr. Feldman. I would not have wanted to retrieve him from the pier alone.

"I'm Captain Carla Mays," she added, extending her hand.

Each of the men in turn accepted the hand and introduced themselves.

The final touch that Riley noticed about the captain's face when she shifted her head slightly to the side and providing a profile view was the strong line of her chin.

"Just glad to be in the right place at the right time," Chick then offered. "Hope Briscoe recovered from the evening."

"As he does regularly," she said wryly, but adding the glimpse of an expression suggesting she was stepping beyond the bounds of propriety in speaking of her employer.

She then quickly shifted the subject.

"I'm afraid we may have a problem for dinner. As you probably noticed, my cook just jumped ship and he had barely begun preparing the meal," she explained apologetically. "Mr. Feldman will meet you onboard in the salon for drinks, but we'll probably have to go ashore in search of a restaurant."

"What got into him?" R&B asked, momentarily looking back over his shoulder in the direction in which the cook had disappeared.

There was something about the way the question was delivered that made Riley wonder if his companion was leery of boarding a vessel from which he had just watched another black man exiting in a hurry.

"Let's just say that at times Mr. Feldman can be sort of testy," she said, revealing a bit of exasperation.

Stepping onto the boat and crossing the small deck at the transom, the group filed up four steps to emerge in the white gleam of the cockpit, then through double doors into the chill of the air-conditioned salon. Riley found that Chick's earlier promise was right on the money. The interior wooden deck planks glinted with a rich yellow-brown luster. At the back starboard corner of the room was a sofa that wrapped around the corner and beyond it a dining table and chairs made of teak to match the deck. The port side of the compartment held a pair of upholstered armchairs. Just forward of those stood Briscoe Feldman. He was at a bar backed by tiny shutters that opened into the galley beyond, and was mixing a drink. As on the prior evening his attire was the epitome of Newport yachting, complete with a blazer.

"Damnable situation," he said upon spying his guests, but making the statement with an incompatible touch of gaiety. "My crew has mutinied. Could stand the loss of the deck hand, but now the cook too. Allow me to apologize with a round of drinks."

The offer was presented with a dramatic sweep of his hand toward the obviously well stocked bar.

"You should find something that meets your approval," he added.

The three visitors helped themselves to liqueurs and mixers, while Capt. Mays joined the social hour with diet soda only. They next followed Feldman as he provided the grand tour of the vessel, which he identified for them as the Sea Prince. Having approached the boat from the bow, so that the name and homeport of Boston, Mass. painted in black block letters were not visible to them, it was the first time Riley and his traveling companions were aware of the yacht's name. They first climbed the exterior ladder to the flying bridge, where Capt. Mays gave a quick and simple overview of the controls and equipment there. While Riley found her explanation mildly interesting, he noted that both Feldman and Chick were mesmerized. It was not, however, the speech, but the speaker that held their interest. The boat owner followed along gazing at his captain with expressions seeming to range from pride to that of a loyal puppy. Meanwhile, Chick made eye contact with the woman as often as possible, but when she turned away his eyes strayed downward, enjoying their own anatomical tour.

Next the sojourn took them below deck. The stateroom in the bow was indicated as the captain's quarters, into which the visitors were afforded only a glimpse of the queen-sized bed. Just aft, on the port side, was a smaller cabin with twin bunks that was identified as the now empty crew's quarters, while across the corridor was a service area, complete with stacked washer and dryer. Also on that side, beneath the stairs they had descended from the salon, was the crew's head. Riley was impressed that even in that area the matching teak trim continued to appear and lavatory counters and basins were made of cultured marble.

They then moved through a narrow passageway between twin engine rooms that the captain said each held a marine diesel. At the end of the corridor the door opened into the master stateroom, of which Feldman gave a detailed tour that bordered on pure braggadocio. The centerpiece of the cabin was a king-sized bed, surrounded by high-gloss wood hanging lockers. Mirrors were attached to the outer surface of each of the locker doors, creating a complete reflective surface both port and starboard of the bed. When the owner opened one of those closets, the odor of camphorwood wafted out. The spacious head that was attached at the fore, starboard corner featured a full bath with tub.

Trouping back up, the tour passed the galley, just fore of the salon and partitioned off from it by a wall formed by a big screen television and the bar. Within the galley were a stove and oven, refrigerator with a through-the-door ice dispenser, and a pair of microwave ovens. On the counter and range were the signs of meal preparations that had ground to a halt.

The last sight on the inspection was the bridge area to the fore of the galley. Here there was a set of controls matching those found up on the flying bridge, only the surfaces and even the wheel were of teak. On either side were doorways leading out onto the fore deck.

"It is a shame," Feldman observed at they again passed the galley on the way back to the salon. "It was an excellent cut of veal we were to have dined on."

"Veal?" R&B said, as he scanned the galley.

"Yes," Feldman replied. "A simple veal Parmesan with a few vegetables was the plan, but I suppose we'll have to make do with restaurant fare now."

"You don't mind, I can whip up this meal in nothing flat," R&B offered. "Looks like all the heavy lifting's already been done."

"You know Italian cooking?" Riley asked.

"I know all kinds of cooking," R&B said with a sly smile.

"The man never ceases to amaze," Chick said, with a wink toward Feldman.

"I really couldn't impose on you," the yachtsman feebly protested.

"No problem," the blues man said, and then snapped, "now get out of my kitchen and let me at it."

Back in the salon, over refreshed drinks, Chick and Feldman slumped into the armchairs and fell into conversation about the Sea Prince and its present voyage. Riley took the opportunity to catch the captain's eye and gesture toward the door leading to the cockpit. With a nod she preceded him out to the deck. On the platform the light of the sinking sun angled in sharply from the west, where a few clouds hung low on the horizon. Shaded from the rays, the facing side of those billows appeared as smoky gray swirls, edged with light so bright it burned away all color. Farther from the edges that crisp aura dimmed, giving way to crimson, scarlet and coral hues.

"Pretty impressive boat," Riley began. "Feldman seems to like showing it off."

"He's quite proud of it."

"Mind if I ask why the crew abandoned you?" Riley said, even surprising himself a bit with the presumptuous question.

Carla Mays stared into Riley's eyes for a moment, as though taking a measure of him. Then with a shrug and wry smile said, "Like I said, Mr. Feldman can be a little testy at times. He fancies himself the master of his domain, and unfortunately that included the galley. You know the old saw about too many cooks in the kitchen, don't you?"

"Yeah. I've noticed that in him already."

"Don't get me wrong," the captain said, tossing her head as she leaned on the rail. "I have had no problems with him interfering with my actual command of the boat, if he would just leave the crew alone. I don't like having to find hands in a strange port on short notice."

"Have you been on the Sea Prince long?" Riley asked, beginning to feel unusually comfortable in his role as inquisitor.

"About a year now," she replied.

"How'd you get into captaining a boat like this?" was Riley next question.

Carla Mays crooked her head to again look directly into Riley's eyes, which made him uncomfortable, but he consciously fought the urge to break away and look down. It was like trying to hold a smile for a camera as a photographer fiddled with settings. The longer their gazes were locked the harder it was to remain natural; rather his facial muscles took on a stilted feel.

"What's your real question? How does a person without a penis get this job?" the woman stated humorlessly. "Or maybe you think that lack of equipment is how I got command?"

The ease he at first felt in talking to the captain was now gone and he knew his demeanor was beginning to give off subtle and defensive messages. Animal instinct was kicking in. It was time to fight or run. Should he boldly strike back defending himself against the implied accusation? Or scurry back from the confrontation, batten down the hatches and meekly weather the approaching storm of criticism? Fortunately he had to choose neither option.

Wondering if his masculinity was being challenged, Riley doggedly refused to lower his gaze, remaining locked on the sharp beryl tint of her eyes. Yet, he still detected none of the hostility or rage that her questions suggested to him. It was more like staring at a blank monitor and waiting for typed words to begin appearing on the screen. As the standoff continued, however, the captain apparently found something for which she was searching. Her features softened with just the tiniest trace of a smile before finally looking back out toward the water.

"That's not what I meant." Riley finally stammered.

"Sorry," she acknowledged. "I can be a little defensive; probably from habit. You get used to hearing some questions.

"My dad ran a crab boat on Chesapeake Bay out of Mattapex on Maryland's Eastern Shore. I grew up on boats, and worked as a mate on fishing charters in the summers during college — different port each year, as far north as New York. Then I got a captain's license after graduation and now have my own boat berthed up on the bay," she continued. "I was working a striped bass tournament out of Montauk on Long Island when I met Mr. Feldman. Then he offered me this job. Gave me a chance to see more of the southern coast.

"Too bad I didn't realize then how tough it would be to keep a crew," she mused. "It's not the first time he's run a man off."

A short silence ensued. The sun had now set, allowing the dull after-glow of dusk to creep in over the marina. The gentle lapping of water against the hull of the yacht mixed with muffled voices carried across the harbor from the restaurant, punctuated occasionally by the sharp splash of a leaping mullet crashing back into the brine.

"Wonder why they do that?" Riley asked, when one of the sleek silver fish combined three such jumps, greyhounding across the surface.

"Who?" the captain asked, looking over at him.

"The mullet; why are they always jumping? Doesn't look like they're chasing or being chased by anything," he explained. "They look like they're just feeling frisky and having fun."

"Your questions sure jump around, Mr. Bright," Capt. Mays noted smiling, again tossing her head with a little shrug as she turned to look at the fading rings created on the water by the fish. "I'm no marine biologist, but have heard that they do it to remove parasites from their gills. I can't imagine a fish living in its eat-or-be-eaten world doing anything just for the joy of it."

"Call me Riley," he said. "Unless you've already put me in the class with your boss."

That merited more scrutiny from Carla Mays, as she again trained her stern, probing gaze his way, challenging him to refuse to look into her eyes.

"I don't discuss my employer, nor do I have a boss," she said coolly with finality, but apparently having made her point, added, "Now let's get back inside, Riley."

Before turning away from the rail she offered a smile, which Riley gladly returned, hoping that he had indeed held his own, and had not wilted in the woman's estimation.

"Good timing," Feldman blurted as the pair came through the salon doors. "The chef informs that the meal is quite close to ready."

Chick and the owner were still seated in the armchairs. Calling on his memories of the previous evening, Riley guessed that Feldman had already made several more trips to the bar. Increased doses of alcohol seemed to bring out corresponding levels of dominating sociability in their host.

The captain excused herself and disappeared down the companionway into the interior of the vessel, leaving Riley to visit the bar, then take a seat on the L-shaped sofa across from Chick and Feldman. In the process, he noted that the table had already been set, complete with a bottle of wine. Could R&B have had the time and been able to find the dining service? It seemed unlikely that Chick or Briscoe Feldman would have done the chore. A fifth chair had also been scrounged, with the matching dinner setting, throwing off the balance and crowding the tabletop.

Carla Mays emerged from below deck, passing through the salon silently on her way up to the flying bridge. Riley noted that both Chick and the boat owner closely followed her passage. In itself that was not surprising. A woman with a good figure passing usually draws the attention of men, and the motion produced by the captain's walk was appealing. It could not be called a sway; her hips did not move enough for that. With each of her steps she produced a movement that Riley could only describe as a twitch.

"She is constantly checking on the condition of her command," Feldman noted, seeming to confirm the fact that all three of the men had ogled her transit through the room. "I do admire her attention to detail."

Riley suspected from the look on Chick's face that they were both thinking that Feldman's admiration was drawn more to Capt. Mays' physical detail, rather than character traits.

"She does seem quite competent, Squire," Chick added.

Riley took note that it was the first time Chick had applied the nickname face-to-face when Feldman was not teetering drunk. But, the owner's countenance betrayed no sign of surprise or resentment, and perhaps just a hint of satisfaction. Apparently he also noted something in Riley's response.

"I do like a collegial atmosphere. Feel free to call me Briscoe," then turning toward Chick with a grin, "or Squire if you prefer."

"Y'all want to help me bring out the food?" R&B called from the galley in his most affected street drawl. "We're ready to eat."

"I'll get it," Riley said rising, leaving Chick and Feldman to freshen drinks and head to the dining area.

By the time the meal was on the table, the captain had rejoined the group. With no room for serving dishes on the crowded surface, Riley brought out the dinner plates two at a time and was impressed with the look of the meal. Not just giving off an excellent aroma, the veal and vegetables were not heaped on the plate, but placed with care to produce a pleasing appearance as well.

"Truly a man of many talents," he said to R&B upon arriving back in the galley for a second load.

"Spent some time in the kitchen back home with the cook," the black man said sheepishly.

In short order the members of the dinner party were all seated and the host had filled each glass with wine. Feldman then raised his glass in the air.

"To the chef who saved the evening," he offered. "I trust his culinary skills match his musical talents."

As the group joined the toast, Chick and Riley exchanged a nervous half-smile. Their reticence proved unfounded, as the flavor and texture of the meat and vegetables were exceptional. As they ate, the Squire regaled the group with some of the same tales he had spun the previous evening at Murphy's, while tossing out a few new ones. Predictably, all his stories were egocentric in nature.

Eventually Capt. Mays was drawn into recounting some stories of her time aboard fishing smacks and charter boats. When she spoke the attention of the three visitors sharpened, but Riley especially noted the way Chick hung on her words, trying to establish eye contact with the woman. He peppered the woman with questions, including a couple that incorporated sexual double entendres bordering on blatant. Chick's interest was so obvious that it made Riley uneasy to watch.

Her narrative too rapped Feldman, who gave the appearance of having never heard any of it before. It was also easy to see that he could read Chick's interest, butting in anytime possible as if defending his domain. During this sparring match Capt. Mays nimbly maneuvered along, maintaining a steady course, avoiding the rocks and reefs of the conversational voyage. Riley suspected she had handled interest like Chick's before and the woman ably walked the thin line between fending off Feldman, while never offending.

After the meal, in the absence of a crew, Riley volunteered to clean up the dishes, only reluctantly getting Chick to abandon the salon and join him in the galley to dry dishes.

"A little obvious aren't you?" Riley asked as the work progressed.

"Just giving her what she wants," Chick stated confidently. "She's interested and you never know if you don't ask."

"I don't know, Chick. Couldn't you at least be a bit more subtle?"

"Just watch and learn Chipmunk," he said with an impish look. "Everything I've ever gotten was because of my silver tongue. I'm not pretty enough to sweep them off their feet, but you can talk women into anything."

When the pair finished up in the galley they moved back to the salon for more drinks, but found Capt. Mays had departed below deck to attend to some unspecified duty.

"Gentlemen," Feldman, by now well lubricated with alcohol, greeted. "Just in time. I have just broached the subject of a sea voyage to your friend Arbie."

That provoked the usual sharp stare from the blues man in the direction of Chick, who accepted it with a blank and blameless countenance.

"In light of his newly revealed expertise in the galley," the host continued, "and your own seafaring skills, I have a proposition for you."

At the mention of seafaring skills, Riley turned a suspicious eye to Chick, recalling Feldman's initial greeting the previous evening at Murphy's.

"I would like you men to fill in for our absent crew for the rest of the trip down to the Keys," Feldman offered. "Though it will overstaff the boat, you two can handle the able seaman's duties and Arbie can man our galley. Of course, you will not be treated as a crew, but as guests, though I will expect to provide remuneration as well as provisions. It will be a grand seagoing party.

"And, it will save Capt. Mays a great deal of trouble in finding a new crew," he added, as if the idea had just come to him. "I believe that you have a couple of more days on your rental on the island, so that will provide time for the captain to familiarize you with the Sea Prince."

"Sounds like a good idea to me, Squire" Chick responded immediately.

Finding it interesting that Feldman knew so much about their situation, Riley looked directly at Chick, who just raised his eyebrows questioningly. Next cutting his eyes over to R&B, the black man yielded an indifferent shrug.

"What about it Chipmunk?" Chick asked.

"Sounds like it could be interesting Briscoe," Riley said. "But you mind if we talk it over a little before deciding."

"What's to talk over?" Chick injected.

Riley just glared at his friend.

"That will be fine," Feldman said with a hopeful tone, but looking a bit disappointed. "But we do need to know soon. Capt. Mays will still need to find some seamen if you don't join us."

"How about in the morning?" Riley asked apologetically.

By the time the trio left the yacht to amble along the planking of the dock, a three-quarter moon had risen to dominate the black veil of the night sky. Surrounding the lunar orb, the ebony backdrop was pinpricked with the varied intensities of white light streaming from stars situated light years away. The evening breeze had long since died off into stillness. The footfalls of the men echoed off the sides of sailboats as they passed, mixing with the rush of water dragging along the side of the vessels as the ebbing tide escaped southward around Jekyll Island and into the Atlantic.

"Come on, Chipmunk," Chick said. "This can be a great trip. Just ask Arbie."

"Don't call me that," Riley snapped, and then looked over to the blues man.

"I got nothing else to do for a few weeks," R&B shrugged.

"How did Briscoe know about when our rental runs out?" Chick asked, turning back to Chick. "You had already talked to him about this trip, didn't you? And what is this with him referring to our seafaring?"

"Yeah, I probably mentioned our flexible situation to the Squire and he could have gotten the idea that you and I have some experience on boats, but there's nothing to running the one he's got," Chick said. "And Carla knows what she's doing, so we just have to do as we're told."

"Carla?" Riley scowled. "You're now on a first name basis with her too?"

"Well, practically," Chick reply with a grin.

"What about the car?" Riley changed the subject.

"Not a problem. We can work something out to leave it here behind the marina office."

The group moved along several more wordless paces.

"Do we have enough time left for this trip?" Riley broke the silence. "I've got only 10 more days of vacation banked after this week. I doubt you have that much."

Finishing this last sentence Riley was again accosted by the image of facing his old boss back at the Amax building, suffering through a lecture about company loyalty and having Seth Wheeler doubting his reliability. Yet, in spite of the distaste he harbored for such a scene, he also felt a longing to go back. It was akin to the homesickness experienced while at camp as a kid. Still, he knew this melancholy was just a manifestation of his personality; even a bad situation is less scary than the unknown.

"We can play it by ear, Chipmunk," Chick countered. "How often will you ever get a chance like this for a free cruise?"

"Are you planning on ever going back to Atlanta?" Riley blurted confrontationally.

Silence again closed in as they walked. By now the men had fallen into a line as they climbed the ramp leading up off the floating dock. The hinges creaked as the structure gave slightly under the counter pressures of their unsynchronized steps.

"Look man," Chick said with an uncharacteristic seriousness, upon reaching the top of the ramp. "If you don't want to tag along, that's fine. Arbie and I can handle it. I want you along for the ride, but if you need to head back you can take the car and hang on to it for me. I'll pick it up later. It's your decision and no hard feelings either way."

In the glow of the night light in front of the marina office Riley paused, slightly puckered his lips and nodded to Chick. He felt a fleeting touch of embarrassment when he met R&B's eyes for a second. Then he led the group off into the darkness in the direction of the parking lot.

Chapter 9

The imposing man strode down the gangway and onto the wharf, turning right to proceed along the low, white painted building at the end of Pier D-2 of the Naval Air Station Annex in Key West. As he moved down the walkway beside the structure that now served as headquarters for Coast Guard Station Key West, he squinted into the afternoon glare. Ahead a single royal palm tree splashed its shadow down on the hot concrete offering the only relief from the mid-afternoon, early fall tropical sun's blaze. Behind him, the empty decks of the cutter from which he had appeared looked hot to the touch as they too sweltered beneath the solar onslaught. Outfitted in the light blue short sleeves, shorts and ball cap of his working blue uniform with chief petty officer insignia, Foster Bork of the USCGC Sapelo appeared impervious to the blistering heat. Whether hot or cold, the chief never showed deference to the elements.

Passing through a doorway into the building, Chief Bork was confronted with the chill rushing from the air-conditioned interior. Before him a seaman sat behind a desk, flanked by a computer monitor.

"Chief Bork to see the captain."

"They're expecting you, Chief," the young man said, looking up from the pile of papers spread on his desk, then adding with a motion of his head toward another door. "In Capt. Andrew's office."

Bork knocked on the door indicated and upon the command, "Come," he entered. Once inside he came to attention, seeming to flow into the rigid stance with the confidence of experience, rather than the snap of trying to impress.

"CPO Bork reporting."

"Afternoon, Chief Bork," said Capt. Thomas Andrews, Group Commander, Coast Guard Group Key West. "At ease and join us in a glass of lemonade."

"Thank you, sir," the chief replied, advancing to take a chilled glass from a tray on the corner of the captain's desk.

Capt. Andrews was in his mid-40s, shorter than the chief, with close-cropped hair and a gruff appearance, but a now smiling countenance. Also standing before the desk were Lieutenant Matthew Jackson, commander of the Sapelo, and the cutter's executive officer, Lieutenant Junior Grade Arlen Tobaris. These other officers exchanged greetings with the chief as well.

"Let's have a seat, gentlemen," the captain said, motioning to the three chairs arrange in front of the desk, then sinking into his own, swivel arm chair. Behind the commanding officer, through the window, the masts of sailboats at the docks of Key West Bight were arrayed to the south. "It amazes me how you can look so cool coming in out of that unseasonable perdition chief. It has to be pushing 90 out there."

"I prefer it to the ice and wind of the Bering Sea," the chief replied.

"Point well made, chief, but I doubt the winds there were any worse than what George just threw at us." the captain chuckled, then plunged ahead into business. "As you know, chief, I like to keep the ranks as informed as possible about operations. That's why I've asked you to join us. I know the crew of the Sapelo will have questions and are more at ease approaching you than the officers with the minor stuff."

The chief nodded in agreement.

"Gentlemen, our ops in Frontier Lance and Frontier Shield that you took part in earlier this year were obviously pretty successful," the officer began again. "Besides confiscating some drugs, we made it a hell of a lot tougher and unpredictable for bad guys to move this direction by sea. But, as you can imagine, they get creative as well. Intel from the DEA says they are going to be trying to do some direct runs to our area of responsibility. It's up to us to stop them.

"The go-fast boats they have been using don't have the range to make the entire run, so we should expect some other method of transport. The Sapelo will spearhead the ops with support from the Nantucket and the rest of the flotilla as needed. For the most part you will be cruising in our home waters for at least several months.

"I've already covered this in detail with Lt. Jackson, chief," he continued. "Have you got any questions?"

"Yes sir," Chief Bork said. "Since we've been on extended sea duty, the crew will have some questions regarding shore leave."

"After this weekend, liberty will depend on what the bad guys have planned," the captain offered, then with a knowing smirk, "but, don't get their hopes up regarding Fantasy Fest. During that zoo would seem like the perfect time to try slipping into the Keys. I suspect we will all be pretty busy."

"Yes sir," the chief acknowledged.

"If there are no more questions, that will be all, gentlemen," Capt. Andrews concluded after a pause. "Let's get the drugs off our home waters."

Chapter 10

The motor yacht Sea Prince glided across Saint Andrews Sound, cutting through the early morning chop coming in from off the ocean and making steady headway toward open water. To the port the sandy spit of Jekyll Point jutted into the surf, lapped by the rising tide. The brink of the water was lined by a menagerie of gulls, skimmers and pelicans standing like the crowd along the route of a parade. Around the edges of the flock, tiny white-bellied sanderlings did their quick step, scurrying like restless children awaiting the arrival of the next float. Up the beach a few yards a pair of birders had a spotting scope set up atop a tripod. One stared through the scope toward the flock, while the other held binoculars to his eyes, training them in the same direction.

Just out from the shore, only 30 feet into the surf, the mast and trawl of a shrimp boat protruded from the surface, standing perhaps 20 feet aloft with some of the rigging still attached. Whiling away an afternoon on the deck as Sea Jay's, Riley had heard the tale of how the vessel reached this resting place. Supposedly two 40-foot shrimp boats had anchored on this spot at the very southern tip of Jekyll Island, tied off to each other and the two crews spent the evening partying. While the beer flowed free, one of the boats slipped its anchor during the night, crashed into the other, opening a hole in the hull that sent the second shrimper to the bottom.

The obvious question was what were the two boats doing so close to shore? At high tide the mast is but a stone's throw from the sand, while a full moon, spring tide can lower the water to the point the spot where the mast protrudes through the sand is high and dry. The situation is the result of the steady march southward of the coastal barrier islands along the southeastern states. Jekyll Island is a prime example of the phenomenon. At its northern extremity, facing on Saint Simons Sound is Driftwood Beach. The shore here gets its name from the tangle of bare trunks and limbs of downed trees littering the shore. Rather than actual driftwood, these are trees from the forest that have been undermined by the loss of sand and soil to the encroaching tides.

Meanwhile at the south end of the island, sand is deposited at a geologically rapid rate. On that end of the island 40 years prior, the main building of the 4-H camp located there had been a Jim Crow era beachfront motel, catering to a black clientele. Now that renovated structure stands several hundred yards back behind the dunes in scrub oaks and palmettos. The same deposition of sand that pushed the motel building into the forest also covered the sunken shrimper out on the point, moving the shore inexorably toward it. The entire process pushes the islands steadily southward. In a few million years, Jekyll Island seemed destined to cross the border into Florida.

Riley Bright, standing at the aft of the flying bridge, shifted his gaze across Saint Andrews Sound, from the mast of the unfortunate shrimp boat toward the old lighthouse adorning the top of the dunes of Little Cumberland Island to the south. The light appeared as little more than a pimple on the high bluff behind the beach, just barely jutting above the tree and palmetto horizon.

"Getting comfortable with your first day at sea?" Capt. Mays asked over her shoulder, but never taking her eyes off the boats course.

Riley did not answer immediately. For the last two days at anchor in the marina the captain had drilled Chick and him on the duties they were expected to perform as the crew of the Sea Prince to the point he felt comfortable with the chores - especially since a single crewman ordinarily handled the work. Still, they had now cast away lines and this sea adventure had actually begun.

"No problem," he finally replied hesitantly. "How far out are we going?"

"Never more than eight to 10 miles," she replied. "Mr. Feldman prefers to keep the mainland in sight at all times. Says he likes to see the lights of shore in the evening."

Thinking of the doses of Dramamine he had taken the previous evening and this morning, Riley too liked the idea of being able to see land.

"How long will it take to reach Saint Augustine?" he asked next.

"It's roughly 87 nautical miles," Capt. Mays explained. "If we had to we could make it in under four hours. But we're cruising at about 10 knots. I expect to make the inlet around five this afternoon."

"That long," Riley observed.

"It's not a race. Mr. Feldman likes to take his time," she said, then added, "If you would, please get Mr. Malor from the galley when he is through there and both of you come up to the bridge. I want to give you another walk through on the controls now that we are actually underway. No need to do it twice.

"Maybe even give each of you the wheel for a while," she smiled over her shoulder in conclusion.

"Aye, aye ma'am," Riley grinned back, then headed for the ladder.

Since there was room for but two bodies in the galley at once, he and Chick had decided to alternate with helping R&B clear away after meals. In one of the few instances that Chick's luck seemed to fail, he had lost the toss of the coin to begin that process after their first breakfast aboard the yacht.

"You about finished up in there?" Riley asked in a low voice from the entrance to the galley.

Inside Chick and R&B were in the midst of washing and drying dishes. A dishwasher was about the only convenience not found aboard the Sea Prince. Though her freshwater tanks held 200 gallons to feed the 20-gallon water heater, between showers and other needs, dishwashing by hand with minimal water use was the rule. And in the mornings doing it in virtual silence was also mandated.

"It'll be a while," R&B said, dead-panning the misery of a sharecropper. "Can't be disturbing the man."

During their two days of learning the boat while at Jekyll Harbor, the three new crewmen had become aware that Briscoe Feldman never appeared from his stateroom until at least 9:00 a.m. He then took a seat in a deck chair in the aft cockpit to down a couple of cups of coffee. By 10:00 a.m. the boat's owner would shake off the effects of the previous evening's alcohol and become fit for human interaction. Prior to that time, the captain had warned them that running silent was more imperative than had they been manning a submarine under attack. The Squire did not like to be disturbed too early.

Riley relayed his message to Chick then headed back up to the flying bridge.

When Feldman finally appeared from his cabin, R&B had coffee waiting and the Squire took up his post in the cockpit. Through their first day at sea, Chick and Riley spent most of the time on the bridge with Capt. Mays, being thoroughly schooled in steering the vessel, manning the controls and radio etiquette. It seemed certain she intended to be at the helm when underway, but she also wanted the two men to be ready in case of an emergency.

When not busy in his sea-going kitchen, R&B headed up to the fore deck with his guitar. Seated on the deck near the anchor winch, he strummed, picked and sang. As Chick observed early on, however, it was fortunate that the hum of the engines and sound of the water breaking on the boat's hull drowned out the music. Thus R&B performed a pantomime out on the deck, no doubt expressing his new station in life as a down trodden galley hand, only to have his misery drowned by boat noise and carried away on the winds.

At 4:30 in the afternoon, as the captain had predicted, Saint Augustine Inlet came into view to the southwest. Riley, Chick and R&B joined Capt. Mays on the flying bridge to watch the gap between coastal islands grow larger as they approached. Making the final turn between markers into the channel, the stone jetties to the south fringed the shore of Anastasia Island and its state park lands. To the inland side of the island across the Salt Run, which stretched to the south, midway down the isle the black and white silhouette of the Anastasia Island Lighthouse poked above the trees to stand guard over the landscape as it had for the last 124 years.

To the north and just inside Porpoise Point, the Francis and Mary Usina Bridge spanned the mouth of the Intracoastal Waterway on the Tolomato River, joining Vilano Beach to the mainland. Known locally as the Vilano Bridge, the new span carried old State Route A1A from the barrier island into Saint Augustine. Only a couple of years old, its gothic arches and cantilevered, half-arch pier caps reflected the Spanish motif of the historic district of the old city.

Directly ahead the trees and buildings of Saint Augustine's skyline completed the view.

"So this is the oldest city in nation?" Chick observed.

"Founded in 1565, Mr. Malor," Capt. Mays pointed out.

"Why not drop the formality?" Chick replied. "My daddy was the gentleman called Mr. Malor in my family. First names seem more appropriate here."

"I'm sure he earned that title," Capt. Mays smiled. "No doubt I would have enjoyed meeting him, Mr. Malor."

"The captain believes in maintaining decorum aboard the ship," Briscoe Feldman stated from behind the group. The owner had slipped unnoticed up the stairway from the salon. He delivered his surprise observation with a smug intonation, also smiling when Chick looked back his way.

Riley was instantly jabbed by a pang of embarrassment for his friend. If Chick shared any such feeling at the put down, he gave no outward sign.

"Ah, she'll come around, Squire," he tossed back in Feldman's direction, coupled with his trademark boyish grin, and then returned his attention to the vessel's blonde captain.

Riley noted that the slightest trace of a scowl passed over Feldman's countenance, before rapidly dissipating.

The group then fell silent as the Sea Prince swung south into the Mantanzas River past the massive walls of the Castillo de San Marco on the inland shore. The ancient Spanish fort's rock walls that had been standing sentinel over the harbor since 1695 were topped by equally old cannons and the flags of the United States, state of Florida and the National Park Service.

Ahead the low span of the Bridge of Lions crossed the river at the city's center. Like almost everything in Saint Augustine it reflected the Spanish influence, from the stylized lion statues that guarded each end and provided its name, to the four guard towers near the center, framing its drawbridge section. Those little enclosures were replicas of the ones that marked the corners of the nearby Castillo.

As they progressed along the channel, Capt. Mays had been on the radio, conversing with the bridge tender. She then turned the wheel, steering the boat to starboard.

"Mr. Malor, would you please go forward and tend the anchor. Seems we have approached the bridge at a bad time."

"What's the problem, captain," Feldman asked.

"As you can see, the old bridge is low. Clearance is 24 feet on this falling tide, which is just about our height. The bridge only opens on the hour, but being Monday and rush hour, they don't open at 5:00 o'clock. We have to wait until six," she advised.

Once securely anchored the sailing party regrouped topside and settled in for the wait, scanning the panorama of the ancient city to the west. Along the river ran a concrete seawall backed by Avenida Menendez, beyond which stood the city's historic district. In the background, the spires of the Cathedral Basilica of Saint Augustine rose above the other structures. Also joining the backdrop was the massive old Ponce de Leon Hotel. The Spanish Renaissance hostel was the largest of the triumvirate of Henry Flagler's hotels in the city that served travelers along his Florida East Coast Railroad as he opened the state to tourism in the late 19th century. On the near side of the waterfront thoroughfare, a couple of horse-drawn carriages sat idle, their drivers lounging on the park benches along the sidewalk. A scattering of tourists meandered along the walkway.

"How long do we plan to be here?" R&B broke the silence, directing the question to Briscoe Feldman.

"At least through tomorrow evening, maybe longer," was the answer. "It depends on how interesting the city proves and how long it takes to explore it."

"Do you want to eat on board tonight," the blues man-turned-cook asked next.

"I believe so," Feldman replied. "It will take a while to get berthed and squared away. By tomorrow evening we'll have a better feel for the dining possibilities of the town."

At the end of the hour, the Sea Prince slipped its anchors, queued up with another pleasure craft and a shrimp trawler to pass through the bridge. Beyond it skirted the pier that housed the Santa Maria Restaurant, and then turned to starboard into the Saint Augustine Municipal Marina. During the passage

Capt. Mays had again been on the radio, this time to the marina. She now eased the big boat into the berth the office had assigned. Once firmly roped off to the dock, the umbilical connections for electricity and water made, the Sea Prince and her crew reverted to life in port.

With the owner occupying one stateroom and the Capt. Carla Mays the other, sleeping conditions were a bit tight on the yacht. The remaining cabin was on the port side, just aft of the captain's quarters. It contained two bunks, leaving one of the Sea Prince's new crew without a bed. Because R&B was to have the most consistent workload, it was agreed that he got one of the bunks, with Riley and Chick to alternate every two nights in the other. The odd-man-out would endure the sofa in the salon. Thus, after a flip of the coin, the first night in Saint Augustine found Riley the loser and ensconced on the sofa.

The next day was one for exploring the old city. With but a single day afloat there was little work to do on the vessel, other than Chick and Riley sharing the chore of washing salt spray from the decks and hull in the morning. Once R&B finished up the breakfast dishes in the galley, he and Riley strolled out of the marina onto Avenida Menendez. They then turned north along the waterfront, skirting the main plaza at the city center and past the carriage stands along the seawall, which they had seen from the previous day's anchorage at the Bridge of Lions. Along the way they passed the two-story Casa Blanca Inn girded with verandas on each level, gleaming white with yellow trim in the morning sun. Upon returning to the boat the duo found that Chick, as usual, had been busy and already knew the staff of the marina as well as the owners of several nearby boats.

Around noon the entire complement shared a leisurely lunch on board, at which time Feldman broached his plan for the evening. The Squire had made reservations for dinner and drinks at the Santa Maria Restaurant. The eatery sat on a pier next to the marina, connected to the shore by a boardwalk that opened onto Avenida Menendez. Afterward Feldman had arranged for the party to be picked up by one of the carriages they had seen on the waterfront. Following a tour of the historic district it would deposit them at the old city gate at the north end of Saint George Street. That thoroughfare was now open as a promenade for foot traffic only as it cut through the heart of the historic district.

"Sounds fine, Squire," Chick said, then added, "the folks two berths down said a good place to finish an evening is on Saint George too. It's called the Mill Top Tavern. Live music every night, but not too loud for talking as well."

"Excellent," Feldman returned. "Then we have a plan. Dinner is at 8:30, so let's all meet here in the salon for an aperitif at 8 o'clock, and then walk over to the restaurant."

Dinner on the pier at the Santa Maria was a mixture of hearty helpings of seafood, pleasant conversation and Briscoe Feldman's usual generous portion of alcohol. As the meal wound down, R&B tossed shrimp tails and other leftover tidbits out through the jalousie windows to land in the water below and disappear amid the swirling fury of a school of saltwater catfish swarming on the surface. Watching the spectacle, the blues man grinned broadly, chuckling to himself.

Emerging from the restaurant, the party advanced along the boardwalk toward a middle-aged black man, his horse and carriage drawn up on the avenida. The driver was dressed in casual street clothes, but his ensemble was topped off by an incongruous stovepipe top hat resting on his head. Darkness had descended on the old city, but nightlights shown all along the waterfront.

Rather than a modern, crisp brilliance, however, the city's face was bathed in a softer glow. Like dim parlor lights the muted radiance smoothed the crow's feet and wrinkles of the aging belle, leaving her mysterious and alluring.

The carriage the quintet boarded had a driver's bench up front, followed by two, padded seats facing forward. Both Feldman and Chick offered their hand as Carla Mays stepped up into the back seat. To Riley the men seemed like a pair of rutting bucks, jockeying for dominance as they then assumed stations on either side of the woman. He and R&B climbed onto the other seat and the carriage moved off down the avenida slowly, the driver beginning a running commentary on the old city, accompanied by the measured clopping of iron horse shoes striking the pavement.

Though not deserted, auto traffic was light and pedestrians few on this Monday night, a good month after the regular tourist season's end. Entering Plaza de la Constitucion the carriage passed Potter's Wax Museum to the west and the entrance to the Bridge of Lions on the east. At the near end, standing atop a pedestal, a life-sized statue of 4-foot, 11-inch Juan Ponce de Leon, discoverer of Florida, dominated the plaza. A steady breeze was coming in off the Mantanzas River, rustling through the fronds of the tall royal palms. Beneath the trees in the park-like setting, other monuments and quaint pieces of ancient artillery surrounded a covered pavilion the driver described as the Slave Market.

"You mean that's where they sold our ancestors, brother?" R&B called up to the narrator.

"Probably not," came the reply from the grizzled figure, "It was actually the city market place in colonial times. You could buy most anything here, but folks were usually sold on the courthouse steps down at the far end of the plaza. The Slave Market name sort of stuck because it's what visitors want to hear."

With the explanation, R&B gazed in silence down past the Cathedral Basilica at the old courthouse as the tour continued out the north side of the plaza. In passing the group heard the history of the Castillo, the old city gates, Ripley's Believe It or Not Museum, the Fountain of Youth and the Mission of Nombre de Dios. This latter shrine, the first Catholic mission in the present boundaries of the nation, began a string of the nation's "oldests" that the carriage passed as it wound through the historic district, among them the oldest house, jail, school house, store and pharmacy. Eventually the narrow streets took them to Henry Flagler's still grand Victorian hotels in the center of the district. The old Alcazar Hotel now housed the Lightner Museum and Antique Mall, while the Cordova Hotel was in the process of renovation, having served as a city hall annex and was now being refurbished to again assume the role of a hostel called the Casa Monica. Finally on King Street at the entrance to the former grounds of the still resplendent Ponce de Leon Hotel that houses Flagler College, a statue of the Standard Oil Company man, turned railroad and hotel baron stood guard over the city he literally put on the map in the 1880s. By the time the carriage disgorged the party at the old city gate at the north end of Saint George Street, they were suffering historic sensory overload.

"Where might this oasis you promised be found?" the Squire asked Chick, while stepping down beside the gate.

"Just a short stroll down Saint George Street on the left was what I was told."

"Shall we then," Feldman said, using his now familiar sweep of the arm to offer Capt. Mays the lead at his side.

The group entered beneath the arch of the gate, which was constructed of the sand, lime and oyster shell concoction known as coquina and is the only remaining vestige of an 18th century defensive wall that surrounded the city. Though paved, Saint George Street now accommodated only pedestrian traffic as it cut directly through the center of historic Saint Augustine to end at the plaza beside the Basilica. At this late hour on a weeknight, that traffic was light. A little more than a block down the street sat a two-story structure with a huge water wheel attached to the north facade. The group cut through a courtyard beneath the wheel, then climbed to the upstairs bar of the Mill Top Tavern. The actual bar was at the end of the space, beneath a roof that also covered a bandstand on which a folk-rock duo was offering its renditions. Back away from this stage, the cover ended, leaving the tables on an open-air deck. It was around one of these tables in the open that the party crowded in, ordered drinks, listened and talked.

As in the carriage, a not too subtle contest continued between Feldman and Chick for the attentions of the captain. In the process, the Squire's efforts at charm were soon awash in the steady stream of old fashions transported his way from the bar. As this interaction played out, R&B seemed oblivious, concentrating on the music, though it hardly resembled his own blues genre. For Riley the puzzling part of the triangle was Carla Mays. He saw her as intelligent and no-nonsense in demeanor, yet she tolerated the testosterone posturing of the men on either side of her. At times she seemed not to be aware of the verbal strutting, while occasionally providing hints that she even enjoyed the attention.

"I don't want to break up the party," the captain offered near the 11 o'clock hour, when the performers took a break, "but I need to get back and see to the boat."

"But captain," Feldman slurred as she stood. "It is early yet and what can the ship require of you at this hour?"

"Duty of command," she replied with a smile.

"I'll walk back with you, captain," Chick offered.

"No need, Mr. Malor,' she snapped. "I know the way and don't need protection."

"Not offering protection," Chick said with his impish grin, "just company."

"As you please," she acquiesced.

Chick rose and joined the woman in heading to the stairway. As they went R&B for the first time turned his attention to them, following their progress across the deck.

"That woman's like a dresser. Somebody always going to be trying to ramble through her drawers," he said in a low whisper.

"That's a pretty good line," Riley observed. "You should put it in song."

"Already been said," the musician replied across the table, "Robert Johnson in *From Four Until Late*."

Meanwhile, the Squire also watched sullenly as the couple disappeared down the stairs.

Chapter 11

The lot near the north end of Caroline Street lay just inland of Key West Bight and close to the corner with Margaret Street. The wood exterior of the building was characteristic of the old seaport area, the frayed and curled remnants of an ancient green coat of paint displaying a degree of shabbiness that is possible only in tropical climes. Scruffy bits of grass clung tenaciously to the sand in the little bit of ground not covered by the old building, while the southeastern corner was shaded by the limbs of a gumbo limbo tree, complete with its peeling red bark. The front of the structure featured double-hung doors like those of a garage in the days before modern overhead versions became prevalent. To the side of these a regular pedestrian door entered a small office space that also had a grime-encrusted window opening onto Caroline Street.

Behind the office, in the single large bay that composed the rest of the building, three bare bulbs hung from the high ceiling, providing a dingy yellow light that bathed the dusty interior. Beneath the trio of glowing orbs a group of five men huddled, inspecting the surroundings. They were all dressed in floral pattern shirts of varying motifs, with slacks that matched each of their color schemes. At the center of the group and conducting the inspection was Macland Garland, a man in his mid-50s, tanned and rotund, his receding hairline tinged with gray. He was wrapped in a shirt featuring yellow parrots amid green palm fronds.

"Oh Mac," one of the group began, "it's so — raunchy?"

"You're exactly right, Bernard," Garland replied, "which is why we can afford it. I'd love to build the float in the Grand Ballroom at the Casa Marina, if you'll foot the bill. Our treasury is not what you'd call flush with cash."

Garland spoke like a person used to leading and providing explanations. Indeed he had been a pillar of Key West's gay community for three decades, having opened his bookstore in the early 1970s in one of the storefronts on southern Duval Street. At the time it seemed a bit of poor judgment. That entire end of the street was being boarded up, with business after business failing as the U.S. Navy wound down its operations and the naval station roster shrank. Simultaneously, the fishing and shrimp fleets were imploding. Surprisingly, in that decade tourism was only a minor part of Key West's economy and many feared that the only thing left to keep the city going was the thriving drug smuggling traffic. For old timers it seemed the southernmost city was returning to the Depression era when the town went bankrupt and most of the inhabitants lived off relief checks from the federal government — as well as the profits from running Prohibition rum from Cuba and the Bahamas.

Mac Garland, however, saw a different future based on the free-and-easy, anything-goes-attitude of the city in which he arrived fresh out of college and fresh out of the closet in the late 1960s. He worked hard in his business, which prospered as tourism took root, attracting visitors and especially an influx of gay and lesbian travelers, many of whom ended up putting down roots on the island. He was also active in helping lay the groundwork for the Key West Business Guild.

With a light-hearted grin he liked to tell visitors this latter group was sort of the "Chamber of Commerce in pastels." Garland even strove to become Key West's first openly gay mayor, but lost out in the effort to Richard Heyman in 1979. Next he threw himself into his love of music, becoming a founding member of the Cayo Hueso Men's Chorale. For two decades the group, which took its name from the island's original Spanish designation, had been crooning and supporting a number of causes in the community.

One of the group's annual efforts was placing a float in the Fantasy Fest parade that coursed down Duval Street during the Halloween week events. This year's extravaganza seemed an especially apt one for the group, since the theme of the festivities was to be "Fright Night on Bone Island." In English, Cayo Hueso translated to Bone Island and was derived from the human bones that supposedly littered the isle when the first Europeans arrived. Thus the steering committee of the chorale found its collective self looking over the dilapidated garage near the waterfront.

"What do you think, Mike," Garland directed to a large framed man, whose sun baked appearance and rough hands hinted at labor in the sun and working with tools. "Can you work in this place?"

"I've worked in a lot worse," he replied. "We should have room to get the truck through the doors. I expect it'll get a bit hot and stuffy though.

"Facilities will probably be better than the sissies you give me to work with," he added as an afterthought, cutting his eyes toward Bernard.

"Bitch," Bernard returned with a coy smile and raised eyebrows.

"Why don't you take it back down to Fleming Street," Mike grinned at the smaller man, as a collective chuckle rippled through the group.

"Ok, ladies," Garland admonished, "let's get out of this dungeon. We can finish the plans over drinks on my patio."

On the street the group loaded up in Garland's car and Mike's pick-up truck. They headed east, made a couple of turns to end up on White Street and cut across the island to the south. Along the way they passed reminders of the recent visit paid to the island community by Hurricane George, as workmen scurried around clean-up sites. At Flagler Avenue they turned east, soon pulling into the drive of Mac Garland's single-story, Spanish motif, white stucco house that was surrounded by a privacy fence. Before them and behind a trellis, the shaded patio looked inviting and once the fans were running, proved quite comfortable. In one corner a large macaw, its blue, red and yellow plumage ablaze, looked down on the assemblage. Drinks served and in hand, the group lounged on the patio furniture.

"Gentlemen," Garland offered, "this year I purpose we get western when we play dress up for the parade."

"As in?" Mike asked.

"I was thinking we might play on our group name," Mac began to explain. "Perhaps give the float a western look like a corral. It would play off of 'chorale.' We can dress as a bunch of wild Indians and rugged trail hands."

"And a cow girl?" Bernard injected.

"If you like, we can put you in the corral with a bull," Mac smiled back at him.

"Oh, any stud will do."

"Seriously, what do you think, guys," Garland asked.

"Sounds interesting," Mike mused. "Maybe get some loincloths for the Indians and chaps for the cowboys."

"And the float?" Garland added.

"Should be no problem. We can put a rail fence around the back of my old flatbed trailer and pull it behind the truck. Scatter hay on the floor — yeah, it should be easy." Mike replied.

"So, does the idea pass muster," Garland tossed at the rest of the group and was rewarded with approval.

"We'll go with it then," he added. "Mike is in charge of the float, and let me add that we do realize and appreciate his time. With the cleanup from the hurricane going on, he is giving up a lot of business to help us out."

Mike acknowledged the kudos with a tilt of the head and self-conscious smile.

"Bernard and Tom will arrange the beads to toss during the parade," Garland continued, "and Quinton and I will plan the after-the-parade soiree."

Mac Garland then raised his glass.

"To Fright Night on Bone Island with the Cayo Hueso Men's Chorale."

Chapter 12

"Damn, the Squire likes to travel slow."

R&B was standing at the shaded rail of the aft cockpit of the Sea Prince as it rode steadily through the calm waters making 10 nautical miles per hour heading south.

"Yeah," Riley Bright agreed, "but it's not like you've got any place you need to get to in a hurry."

"Just because a man doesn't have a destination, don't mean he wants to stand still," the blues man protested. "I just don't like wasting a bunch of time for no reason."

"We've still got a couple of weeks before Fantasy Fest," Riley observed, "and we probably don't want to get there until they've gotten some of the damage cleaned up from that hurricane that just passed through. I'd call that a reason for taking our time. Besides, you got to admit that we're getting to see plenty of the coast."

After leaving Saint Augustine, the Sea Prince had crept steadily southward, stopping in each port that struck its owner's fancy. Along the way the vessel alternated between cruising offshore and ducking into the Intracoastal Waterway for short runs. The anchor had been dropped in Daytona Beach, Cocoa Beach, Melbourne, Jupiter Inlet, Fort Lauderdale and Miami. Now in mid-October they were cutting through southern Biscayne Bay in the late morning, headed for Key Largo.

"Guess I'm just getting restless," R&B admitted. "Been a month since I've actually played a gig. Man like me can't just turn it on and off. Music's in my blood."

Riley leaned on the rail looking at the black man that had his gaze fixed on the passing shoreline of mangroves, backed in the distance by a few taller trees. How could such an obviously intelligent man have such a blind spot on a single subject? Though he and Chick were tolerant of their friend's musical folly, they avoided having to endure it. Even Feldman had caught just enough of R&B's rehearsals on the fore deck that he no longer dropped hints about having the blues man play something. Rather, the entire group left it that they did not want to sap his musical energies during this creative sabbatical; it was better to let him create lyrics and melody lines for the world to appreciate later.

"Ah, gentlemen," Feldman said, coming through the doors from the salon and into the cockpit. "Nothing like the freshened air of autumn at sea."

As he made the statement Feldman inhaled deeply, stretching arms wide to the side. At the sight, Riley was reminded of the southern puffer fish he had seen an angler pull onto the planks of the dock in the marina at Fort Lauderdale. As it had lain there the fish sucked in air, expanding its girth by at least three fold. The added air gave the puffer a more formidable, but illusionary size and appearance. The corners of Riley's mouth curled up as he mulled the comparison of how important a little hot air could be for the image of various specimens.

"Morning, Squire," Riley offered, while R&B only nodded, then returned his attention to the distant shore. "Fine weather and slick seas, all right."

"Indeed," the owner said, looking around. "And where is the rest of the crew?"

"Chick is topside on the bridge with the captain," Riley replied.

"Your fellow crewman seems almost joined at the hip to the captain," Feldman said, casting a glance up the gangway toward the flying bridge.

"He's a lot better at the helm than I am," Riley weakly defended his friend. "Let's her attend to other things rather than watching over my shoulder."

"Yes, I'm sure," Feldman said, still looking toward the bridge, while giving Riley the impression he had hardly heard his explanation. "I believe I'll check with Capt. Mays about our day's itinerary."

"Want me to bring your coffee up to the bridge?" R&B asked.

"If you will, please," the Squire replied, prompting a surprised exchange of glances between Riley and the blues man. It was the first time at sea Feldman had broken his morning ritual of coffee in the cockpit. With a shrug, R&B headed to the galley, while the boat's owner started up the ladder to the flying bridge. For a moment Riley hesitated, wondering if he should ask permission to tag along, but finally just followed Feldman up the ladder.

The two men broke into the full glare of the sun topside. The panorama of Biscayne Bay was more impressive from the height of the bridge. The water extending before them had a different tint from the dark coastal seas farther north or even the deep blue they often rode on in central and south Florida. It now alternated between tropical aquamarine, soft greens and vivid blues, depending on its depth, but also exhibiting gold, tans and yellows over stretches of shallow grass flats. At any point on the horizon where there were no cloud or islands, the sea faded indiscernibly into the azure of the sky. To the port the black silhouette of Elliott Key separated the bay from the Atlantic Ocean, while straight ahead the scattered Arsenicker Keys awaited their passage. Off the starboard, on the mainland, the only breaks in the vista of mangrove shores were the buildings and twin smoke stacks of the Turkey Point Nuclear Power Station rising to the south of Homestead. In the maze of cooling canals around that power plant the warm waters provided the best remaining nursery for the vestige population of endangered American crocodiles. Even if a passing sailor had wanted to venture into that mosquito-infested area, the rangers of the U.S. Fish and Wildlife Service would have been quick to respond. No one is allowed to disturb the ancient reptiles as they try to recover their numbers in solitude.

"How's our progress?" Feldman asked, plopping down to the left on one of the cushioned benches that wrapped around each side of the aft portion of the bridge.

"On time," Capt. Mays answered, obviously surprised by this arrival at an unusual hour. "Is there a problem?"

"Not at all, Captain," Feldman said, switching his gaze from the mainland to Chick, who was standing beside the captain as she steered the vessel. Then he added, seemingly as a defense, "I'm just a bit restless this morning, I guess. About what time do you expect to reach Card Sound?"

"We'll be anchored at the bridge by noon," the woman replied.

"And how are you this morning, Chick," the owner added.

"Just fine, Squire. The weather and water just seem to get better the farther south we go."

"It gets even better in the Keys," Feldman said, and then added with a smile, "Chick, would you be so kind as to run down to the galley and bring me some coffee."

Riley was just at the point of saying that R&B was already fulfilling the request, when Feldman turned his way, providing a look that clearly meant keep silent and mind his own business.

"Sure thing, Squire," Chick said, but obviously also taking note of the unusual situation.

Once Chick was off the bridge, Feldman turned his attention to scanning the horizon. Chick reappeared at the head of the ladder very quickly, having obviously met R&B bringing the coffee from the galley and relieving him of the burden. As he handed the steaming mug over to the owner, Capt.

Mays looked back over her shoulder at the scene and Riley caught what he perceived to be a look of concern on her face. Chick then moved back forward, positioning himself to the right of the captain. A low conversation ensued between the pair, with the woman motioning with her hand toward the port and starboard quarters. All the while Briscoe Feldman sat brooding over his coffee, staring at the black shape of the mainland. Riley felt much like the proverbial fly, but without even a wall on which to perch. Rather, he braced himself against the support of the cover that extended over the fore part of the bridge, but was forced to awkwardly lean over the bench seat that ran along the side opposite of Feldman. After a few uneasy moments, the captain handed the wheel over to Chick.

"Mr. Feldman," she said turning, "will you please accompany me below. There're a couple of details I'd like to discuss."

Though the woman delivered the line with a smile, it held no warmth.

"As you wish," the owner said a bit sullenly.

With that the pair disappeared down the companionway. Once they were below, Riley moved forward, taking the station just vacated by Chick to the starboard of the wheel.

"What was that about?" he asked the new helmsman.

Before Chick could answer, the pair heard the staccato plucking of guitar strings wafting up from the fore deck. Instead of the seeming random notes that R&B instigated when working on his original music, however, there was a more precise direction to these. Intermingled with the noise of the boat cutting through the air and water, the blues man's voice, with an unusual falsetto quality, floated up to the bridge as well.

Riley recognized the song as the first one that R&B had played for them down on River Street in Savannah at their first meeting. It was the first time he had heard him singing anything on deck that was not one of his original works in progress.

It was the *Dead Shrimp Blues*, all about a stranger fishing in a man's pond, where the owner was now posted out.

"I suspect that my presence is growing thin on the Squire," Chick said. "Though she didn't say it, I think Carla is afraid she may soon be looking for a new crew again."

"You could back off her," Riley offered. "At least while we're on board."

"Yeah, I could," Chick grinned over at his friend.

But Riley took the expression to mean, "Not likely." It was the same attitude he has seen back at Amax in Atlanta, as Chick had dealt with Benson Carter III. The relationship between Chick Malor and Briscoe Feldman was no longer acquaintances, or employer and employee. They were now fighting cocks, strutting around the pit, sizing each other up and preparing for the final onslaught that would finish one of them off. While Riley suspected that

Chick was a match for the yachtsman, he also had the gut feeling that Feldman would have his pound of flesh in the end. None of which bode well for the rest of the voyage. All the while this contest was over a woman who, at least in outward appearance, was above the fray. She was a prize neither of the strutting roosters was likely to claim.

"Do you know where it is we're headed for lunch?" Riley asked to change the subject.

"Some dive down at the tip of the mainland that the Squire is fond of," Chick said. "It's called Alabama Jacks. Another of his ritual stops along the waterway. We'll have to anchor out in the ICW and take the dingy in."

For several minutes Chick guided the vessel southward, keeping the green channel markers to the port and the red ones off the starboard side, cruising beneath the warmth of the October sun.

"Just don't push it too much," Riley finally concluded in almost a plea.

About half an hour later, Capt. Mays reappeared on the bridge. Though she maintained her ordinary stoic countenance of command, it was more somber than usual, betraying no hints of a smile. She took the wheel from Chick, seeming lost in thought as she steered the vessel farther south.

"Gentlemen," she finally said rather formally, almost appearing to arouse from a trance, "Mr. Feldman has become concerned about the expense of the present voyage. He feels that Mr. Mann is indispensable in the galley, but would like to reduce the crew by one when we reach Key Largo. And he is adamant that you be allowed to decide who'll leave."

As she made the statement, her eyes never wavered from Chick. Riley could plainly see in her face that she considered both the reduction in the crew and the way it was to be handled to be interference in her job, or perhaps a challenge to her command. Either way she was not happy at being left in the middle of this male posturing.

"The Squire's not man enough to simply throw me overboard himself?" Chick asked sarcastically. "I'm real sorry that having me on board is bankrupting him. But, I'll make it easy for everybody. I'll get my stuff together now."

With that Chick headed for the ladder. Once he was off the bridge the captain turned slightly to look at Riley.

"You know that I'm going too," he spoke first before she could say anything.

"I'd have been surprised if you didn't," she said with a weak smile. "I'm sorry, but you know how difficult Mr. Feldman can be."

Just before noon the arch of the Card Sound Bridge came into view, sitting astride the dividing point where Card Sound, in which they were sailing, and Barnes Sound met. Though they had been cruising just inside the most northerly Florida Keys for most of the morning, Key Largo was now coming up on their port side, stretching southward along Barnes Sound. Not only the largest of these islands, it was the first that was accessible by vehicles and was considered the jumping off point for the string of isles. County Road 905A passed over the bridge to connect the mainland to the northern tip of the big island.

Just to the north of the bridge, Captain Mays slipped the Sea Prince to the extreme western edge of the channel and had called instructions down to the anchor deck, where Chick and Riley secured the boat. The atmosphere aboard had changed noticeably, but the fact that Briscoe Feldman kept to his cabin relieved some of the strain. Once the vessel was squared away, the captain went below to inform the owner, returning with the news that he did not trust the dingy with five people in it. Rather he wanted her to ferry the crew into the restaurant, then return for him.

The small boat was swung out on its davits, and then lowered over the stern into the water. Once everyone was crowded in, Capt. Mays headed toward the western end of the bridge. Nearing the shore, she guided the craft into a canal running along the south side of the road and framed on its southern shore by a bank of mangroves. They passed a boat ramp, then a tollbooth sitting up in the middle of the roadway, coming to a short stretch of docks on the right side. At the near end of these was a narrow strip of patio with several small tables, then a section of thatched roof, fronted by open windows behind which a dining area was plainly visible. Once beyond the eatery, Carla Mays turned the boat into the dock to offload her passengers.

"Mr. Feldman said to go ahead, open a tab and get some drinks," she said as the men exited the boat. "He'll cover it all. Be back shortly."

With that she backed the boat out into the channel and headed back to the yacht.

"Don't think I'd order anything we can't cover," R&B said, watching the boat shrink down the canal. "Probably should have brought my guitar with me."

"You think Feldman will take off without us?" Riley asked a bit surprised.

"I wouldn't worry about it," Chick answered instead. "He probably doesn't have the balls, plus Carla would never go along with it. They'll come on in.

"Let's have a look at this place," he concluded, heading off the dock and around the end of the building.

The restaurant sat on a narrow strip of causeway, approaching the Card Sound bridge, with water visible through gaps in the mangrove limbs lining the far side of the road. Over there was a parking area holding a couple of cars, matched by two more sitting on the near side in front of the building. On top of the restaurant stood a white sign emblazoned across the top in red with "Welcome to Downtown Card Sound." Beneath in the center and also in red was "Alabama Jacks." Passing under the sign and through a gate in the chain link front wall of the diner, the group entered the shaded relief from the noon sun provided by the thatch roof. Ahead a portion of the dining room sat on pilings out over the canal, its shutters thrown up to provide an open air view down an intersecting canal to Barnes Sound. The room was edged on the right by doorways leading into the kitchen, while the opposite end was composed of a square, three-sided bar. On the front of the building next to the bar was a now vacant bandstand. To the waterside of the bar was the open patio area they had passed on their way in aboard the dingy. A clutter of plastic lawn tables and chairs littered the dining area, with several of the tables occupied. Along the rafters and the columns supporting the faux thatched roof was a number of photographs of groups of sky divers doing aerial tricks. A couple of ceiling fans stuck down, whirling lazily, and their shafts painted to look like the propeller-adorned noses of aircraft.

Chick, Riley and R&B picked a table at the windows by the canal, ordered a round of Corona beers with lime and some conch fritter appetizers from the waitress.

"What're all the parachuting photos about?" Riley asked her when she brought out the drinks.

"From a movie that was shot here back in '94," she replied. "Thing called *Drop Zone* with Wesley Snipes and another guy. What was his name? I think somebody said he played Buddy Holly in a movie back in the 1970s."

"Gary Busey," R&B injected, eliciting a look from his companions.

"Yeah, that's him," the girl agreed. "Anyway, it was all before my time here. They did a lot of sky diving in the movie, but the bar scenes were made here.

"Anything else?" she asked.

"No thanks, we're waiting on some folks and will order then," Riley said.

The threesome looked out to the water at the sound of a motor in the canal, expecting to see the dingy approaching. Instead it was an open cockpit boat of perhaps 22 feet, holding a couple of weathered, commercial crab men in tee shirts, jeans and white calf-high boots. The boat and its occupants both displayed the grungy look of hard work in a dirty business. The pair only stared when R&B offered a salute with his beer bottle, continuing their journey on up the canal.

"Friendly crackers," R&B noted.

"Just don't appreciate any of us tourists, Arbie" Chick said. "Probably nothing personal toward you."

Riley noticed that R&B had gotten to the point he no longer bothering with showing displeasure with Chick's corruption of his name.

"Still just crackers," the black man said, punctuating the remark by taking a swig of the beer.

"I guess we need to talk about what we're going to do next, before the Squire gets here," Riley changed the subject. "I've already told the captain that I'm getting off at Key Largo too."

"I appreciate that, Chipmunk," Chick smiled. "Too bad I spoiled the cruise for you.

"Arbie, old buddy," he continued, turning to the blues man, "I hope you're going to stay on board. Carla can run the boat down to Key West by herself, but will need you. With me out of the way, I suspect the Squire will be easier to get along with, and I'd hate to make her have to find a new crew again."

For a moment R&B stared at his beer bottle, but before saying anything, the waitress reappeared with a couple of plastic baskets filled with fritters. Unlike what many restaurants serve, these were not just round hushpuppies with conch meat tossed in during the cooking. These were flatter, reminding Riley of funnel cakes he had seen coming out of the cooker at the North Georgia State Fair out in Cobb County on the northern edge of Atlanta. Bits of red and green chili peppers and chunks of the shellfish were evident in them as well. R&B broke off a piece of the fritter, took a bite and savored it for a moment before speaking.

"What are y'all planning on doing?" was his noncommittal answer, at which Riley turned his attention to Chick as well.

"The Chipmunk and I'll find a way down to Key West. Probably be there before the Squire."

"That's true, the slow ass way he travels," R&B agreed, slipping into his burdened black man persona. "Guess I'll ride it out on the boat. He ain't driving me too hard and I get time to work on some new music. Besides, we might hook up again down there."

"That way you can look out for Carla, too," Chick offered.

"That woman don't need anybody watching her," R&B shot back. "She's more of a man than any of us."

"Not always," Chick grinned, breaking off a chunk of the fritter, then adding, "Think I'll go have a talk with the bartender."

Before his companions could speak, he was on his feet and headed across the room munching on the fritter.

"He'd never make a blues man," R&B observed. "Nothing gets him down."

"That's for sure," Riley chuckled.

Riley watched his traveling companion strike up a conversation with the young man behind the bar, who was incongruously dressed in an ice hockey jersey. But the shirt did bear the insignia of the National Hockey League's Florida Panthers, who make their home in Miami.

"Ice hockey in south Florida?" Riley muttered under his breath, with an ironic cluck.

R&B cut his eyes toward him and squinted as if to ask what he was talking about, but Riley just smiled and shook his head side to side.

Meanwhile, Chick was now in conversation with two other men who were seated at the bar finishing off sandwiches they washed down with bottled beer. When Riley returned his attention to his own table, he joined R&B in leaning out, looking over the low railing into the water of the canal below.

Beneath the surface and around the pilings of the dock was a swirl of marine life. The top layer was formed by schools of Atlantic needlefish, compacted into groups as if someone had sorted them by size. Their pencil-slender, neon green bodies almost glowed as they coursed along the film at the top of the water column. Whenever a patron of the eatery tossed a meal scrap out the window, the fish converged like tiny spears thrown toward the central point of the ripples where the crumb landed. At that vortex the water erupted as they competed for the morsel. From above gulls swooped to the commotion as well, trying to pick off any bit of sustenance that did not immediately sink. From below the attack was also joined by a herd of mangrove snappers that rushed upward from milling about the piling base. These gray shadows ranged from hand-sized up to several pounds each, breaking off sharp turns as they slashed at the food fluttering downward.

The final components of this marine menagerie were several larger fish. Lying back at the edge of the shadow created by the dock's edge and virtually motionless, the foot-and-a-half, elongated shape of a barracuda eyed the proceedings. Yet the smaller fish seemed oblivious to the proximity of the predator, as if they could sense it was not his time to feed and thus safe for them.

Also cruising along from piling to piling, a pair of snook performed an endless patrol, while ignoring the smaller forage fish as well. Anytime that duo changed course, the thin single black line curving along their sides was clearly visible, bisecting lengthwise the gold-tinted sheen of their flanks.

"Those are the boys we're looking for."

Riley looked up to see the men from the bar, along with Chick, standing beside the table and staring down into the water. The speaker was a slender, yet well-built man, probably just under 6 feet tall, with a pleasant open demeanor, his head topped with a tangle of brown hair. Dressed in khaki cargo shorts, the tail of his tee shirt hung down on the outside of his pants, hiding his waist and giving the impression of more bulk than actually existed. The shirt bore the logo and inscription of the Hard Rock Café, Gatlinburg, Tennessee, which struck Riley as a peculiar combination of venue and location, sort of like a mixed metaphor.

"I'm Bart Skier," he said, extending his hand to Riley. "And y'all must be the Chipmunk and Arbie."

Riley tried to mask his gnashing teeth as he returned the handshake, suspecting that R&B might be doing the same. When he looked over at Chick, his friend was still gazing down at the water, smiling nonchalantly. Sometimes Chick could rub him so wrong, without even being actively involved in a situation.

"This is my buddy, Jack Thompson. We're headed down to Key West for some partying and fishing," Skier continued, cutting his eyes down to the water at the mention of angling. "Seems we got something in common. We're from up at Atlanta, actually Marietta. Chick was just telling us you boys are in a bit of a fix regarding transportation."

"Let's have a seat," Chick interrupted, and while speaking waved to the waitress. "Y'all get another beer and we'll order some food. I think the Squire is going to keep us waiting and I'm getting hungry."

With that the five men crowded around the table and the orders were placed.

"At the bar Bart was telling me about the fishing down at Key West," Chick opened, speaking to Riley and R&B, "and Fantasy Fest."

"Hard to beat spending the day catching grouper out on the reefs and bar hopping at night," Skier said with a big smirk, then reached over, hitting his companion on the shoulder with an open hand, rocking the man slightly to the side. "That is if I can keep Jacky here from chasing the half-naked women in the streets all night."

"Not only will I whip your ass fishing," Thompson replied good-naturedly, "but when the girls get a look at me, the only thing left for you will be the sweet boys."

"Yeah, yeah, you the man," Bart laughed back.

"Do you guys have your own boat," Riley asked.

"Nope," Skier returned, and then peered at Riley over the long-necked beer bottle as he took a drink. "We're booked to fish with Capt. Arnie Patranicholas. Folks call him Capt. Arnie. Cantankerous old fart that's something of a legend down there. Good fishing guide and full of stories about guns, drugs and women from his younger days. Don't know if any of it's true, but he can sure entertain you if the fish aren't biting."

"Y'all are welcome to hitch a ride down to Key West with us if you want," Thompson butted in. "Like we told Chick, we're in a crew cab pick-up, with an empty back seat and plenty of room for gear in the bed."

Riley looked over to Chick, who grinned, raised his eyebrows and shrugged.

"Better than walking, Chipmunk," Malor said. "We can get Carla to shuttle our duffels in from the boat after they eat and meet up with R&B when they dock down there?"

"Why not," Riley agreed, raising his bottle in a salute aimed in the direction of Skier and Thompson.

Eventually the little dingy came buzzing down the canal toward Alabama Jacks, the Squire perched in the bow and Capt. Mays at the stern steering the outboard. Feldman was again dressed the part of the yachtsman, complete with a blazer more suited for a trip to the Hamptons than south Florida.

"Damn," Thompson muttered, stretching the word out, eyes glued on the figure at the front of the boat. "What the hell is that?"

Chapter 13

Samuelo Porticia lumbered heavily across the deck of the S.S. Loro, mimicking the sluggish progress made by the fertilizer boat as it plowed through the waters of the Gulf of Mexico. Short, in his late 50s and sporting an expansive midriff that flowed over the top of trousers held up by suspenders, Porticia's gray hair was slicked back, held in place by days of unwashed salt spray acquired at sea. Squinting in the noonday sun, the old mariner made his way to the wheelhouse of the 200-foot vessel.

"How does it go, Hector," he asked, entering the enclosure.

"Well, *capitan*," the younger man at the helm replied, gazing out through the dirty glass. "But I worry."

"I hope it is something new that bothers you."

"No, *capitan*," the helmsman glanced over at Porticia. "We sail through dangerous water here and have no protection. I don't like it."

The captain gave a frustrated shake of the head and shrugged.

"How many times must we cover this?" he offered.

"But the Coast Guard could appear anytime?"

"Which means nothing to us, Hector," Porticia said. "You have spent too much time running the *ganja* for the Jamaicans. We have nothing to fear from the *gringos*. They can board and search all they like. Let them bring their sniffing dogs aboard. We will even let them sniff at our *posaderas* if they want, and we will become great friends with the *perros*, but they will find nothing. They are not trained to find clay and stone. And, with our weapons locked away, they will have no suspicions."

"But *capitan*, what of the competition? They could want the boat."

"We will see they are not Coast Guard, Hector. Even their go-fast boats can't slip up on us so fast in open water. You will have plenty of time to get to the locker and retrieve your guns. They won't test us when they find we are just as well armed as they."

The captain continued to shake his head, pondering the one-track thinking of his crewman, Hector Corro. But, he too had been young once with *cajones* to be tested. The experiences of that time had convinced him there was a better way to earn a living than smuggling drugs. That profession was much too dangerous as a free-lancer, and only slightly less so working for the cartels. Plus, when working for them, the money was not so good. The sailors take the risk, while the big men kept the profit. Granted, that business had earned the cash to buy his ship, but the old scow was very little to show for all the risk he had endured.

Now he plied the same waters, but buried beneath the phosphate in the hold he carried other moneymaking cargo, yet one that was harder to detect by the authorities and of no interest to the other smugglers. The artifacts smuggled out of Peru were easily attained along the north coast of his native Columbia, ideal for transport in his boat and awaited by ready buyers in the United States.

Though the money was not as great as from contraband drugs, the risks of pre-Columbian art were also much lower. That suited Porticia fine. He had so far defied the odds, having never had his long career on the wrong side of the law interrupted by the authorities, and only delayed occasionally as they fruitlessly searched his vessel. Even better, he also had never fired a shot in anger, despite his earlier involvement in a more violent branch of the smuggling business. He had no intentions of having either record changed by the impetuous behavior of any of his crew.

The Loro would continue to crawl northerly across the Gulf, then through the Florida Strait and just out of U.S. coastal waters along the eastern edge of the peninsula. The ship would pause only briefly off the lower Florida Keys to offload the hidden merchandise into a smaller boat for transport to shore. At the present speed and course that rendezvous would occur when the Coast Guard and police would be preoccupied with other matters. Then he could swing back near Jamaica and using forged papers continue on his way. Indeed, he had gotten great mileage out of his single load of phosphate, which had been "picked up and delivered" many times without ever leaving his hold.

Eddie Crawford fidgeted nervously as he hung up the telephone in the office at the back of his used furniture and pawnshop on the south side of Jacksonville. His mannerisms did not denote any concern garnered from the conversation, but were simply part of his restless nature that demanded action, or at least movement. His call had been to the Salvation Army store in Marathon, mid-way down the Florida Keys, to set the time and date that he would pick up the load of worthless dinette sets, worn bedsteads and rickety chairs they had amassed for him. He again reached for the receiver and began punching the buttons.

"Cheap Trucks, this is Donna. Can we put you on the road?"

"You can do more than that for me, sweet thing," Crawford said into the telephone. "It's me Eddie. I'm going to need a truck at the end of the month."

"Hi ya, Eddie," the voice replied. "Been a while. You need the usual?"

"Actually, I think I can get by with a 14-footer this time. How about I pick it up Thursday afternoon, on the 29th?"

"Let me check," was the answer, followed by a silence disturbed only by the soft chatter of a keyboard escaping from the phone. During the pause, Crawford shook a cigarette from the pack on his desk and lit up.

"Round trip?" was the next question.

"Yep, it'll be back on Tuesday afternoon," Crawford confirmed.

"OK," the woman's voice began again, "I've got you down for one of our 14-foot thrifty haul vans reserved for Thursday Oct. 29 through Tuesday November 3. Pick up is after 3 p.m. and return by 6 p.m. The rate is $19.95 per day, plus 39 cents per mile. What else do you need?"

"A date with Donna for the night I get back," Crawford grinned into the receiver.

"And which hospital will you be using when my husband finds out about it?" the woman shot back with a laugh.

"You're breaking my heart, sweet thing."

"Yeah, yeah, take care Eddie. Bye-Bye."

Crawford hung up the phone, leaned back in the swivel chair and sent a stream of smoke into the air.

On the Friday after he picked up the truck he would spend the day chain smoking as he drove down I-95 to Miami, then on to Homestead where he planned to spend the night in the cheapest motel room he could find. The following day the drive would continue down U.S. 1 to Vaca Key and the furniture loading, then on to meet a small boat after dark on a side road farther down the string of islands. There a couple of crates would be added to the load and he would be back in Homestead around midnight. The next day would bring him home to eventually send most of the cargo he picked up to the local landfill, though occasionally some of the furniture was actually saleable in his store. On the other hand, the contents of the crates would soon be turned into cash in hand, and the cargo entrusted to new owners as it started a journey for New York, the West Coast or some other destination that Eddie Crawford did not care or want to know about.

Chapter 14

Briscoe Feldman had eaten a quick lunch at Alabama Jacks and Capt. Mays ran him back to the yacht immediately, avoiding virtually all contact with his soon-to-be ex-crew or their new acquaintances. R&B had remained at the restaurant, sharing beer and sandwiches, then, when the woman returned, joined Riley and Chick in the round trip to collect their gear. By the time the duffel bags had been ferried in from the Sea Prince and loaded in Bart Skier's pick-up truck it was midafternoon.

R&B proved to be about as accomplished at good-byes as he was in his musical endeavors. Offering up a weak handshake he stammered a few words about seeing his departing friends down in Key West. As the truck with Riley, Chick, Bart and Jack headed for the tollbooth at the entrance to the Card Sound Bridge, the blues man standing at the roadside gave them a last wave and turned away to walk down to the shore where the boat awaited him. Capt. Carla Mays, the slight breeze pinning the fabric of her white shirt against her breast, was staring after the truck. Riley cut his eyes over to Chick, whose eyes were lingering on the woman.

"Should I even ask?" Riley ventured.

"That's a good woman," Chick said, raising an eyebrow.

"Maybe you'll see her down in Key West," Riley offered.

"More likely the Squire will chunk Arbie overboard and turn north," Chick smiled ruefully, then turned his attention to the front seat of the big pick-up. "What's next, Ski Man?"

"Some of the best scenery you'll ever see," Bart tossed back. "We've probably got close to three hours of driving over the prettiest water in the world."

"I can see what you mean," Riley said as they topped the high arch of the bridge, with Card Sound to the north and Barnes Sound stretching away to the south. Down below and just north of the bridge a small dingy with two occupants was cutting through the green waters, headed toward the anchored Marquessa yacht.

"You know, I heard that some fool tied himself to the top rail of this bridge during Hurricane Andrew because he wanted to see what it would be like," Jack Thompson, said shaking his head. "Never found him, just the broken ropes."

"I don't think that really happened," Bart injected. "It was just a story from a book or something."

"I don't know," Jack shot back. "Hell, you know how crazy these island folks are. I believe there's somebody down here who would try anything."

"Y'all come down here a lot," Chick asked.

"Try to make it once or twice a year," Skier said with a twist of his head toward the back seat, as the truck rushed off the bridge and past the sign for the Crocodile Lake National Wildlife Refuge. "Can't beat the fishing and it sure does wonders for the attitude. Keep an eye on the water in the creeks and lagoons through here. If you see what looks like a 'gator, you've seen an honest to God crocodile."

With that the party settled in for the ride, making occasional comments about sights along the way. Before they had exited CR 905 onto U.S. 1 at Key Largo, Skier had pushed a CD of Jimmy Buffett music into the player and the cab was filled with his crooned tales of the tropics, the sea and the sun. For the next couple of hours a panorama of palms, coral rock, hotels, dive shops, restaurants, gift shops and marinas blocked out the view of the water, only to have the sparkling aqua expanses suddenly pop into view as they raced across one of the 43 bridges connecting the string of isles. Alongside many of the spans ran the abandoned concrete sections of the old Overseas Railway that first connected the mainland to the islands in the early 20th century. Atop most of these structures the remaining cracking pavement of the first Overseas Highway still appeared. Built after the Labor Day hurricane of 1935 destroyed the rail line with 200 mile-per-hour winds, the guardrails along the roadway were constructed of salvaged track iron. Those aging black strains of steel, spotted with yellow and reddish brown rust, snaked unevenly past, some having corroded loose to hang from one end.

Midway through the ride, just past the town of Marathon where the string of islands that had been running southwesterly from the mainland began their turn to an almost western direction, the truck started the trek across the Seven Mile Bridge. Looking to the left from this longest of the spans on U.S. 1 provided a vista of the Atlantic Ocean, while the view to the northwest was of Florida Bay. Beyond the old bridge paralleling the new one in that direction, the distance was dotted by the uninhabited mangrove keys of the Great White Heron National Wildlife Refuge, each isle squatting like a dark blot on the horizon.

In steady progression the islands of the lower keys slipped past, with signs identifying Bahia Honda, Spanish Harbor, Big Pine, Ramrod, Summerland, Cudjoe, Sugarloaf, the Saddlebunches, Big Coppitt and Boca Chita. Finally the truck crossed the bridge over Boca Chita Channel onto Stock Island.

"Looks like we need to stop for some gas," Bart observed, gazing down at the gauges on the dash, and then looking back at the road ahead. "This place should do."

The truck moved into the turn lane, then angled off the highway to the left into the parking lot of the convenience store perched on the corner of U.S. 1 and McDonald Drive.

"Everybody ready to stretch some legs," Jack asked, throwing open the front passenger side door, allowing the late afternoon heat to rush into the air-conditioned cab, then added. "Man, it's easy to forget how muggy it gets down here."

Bart Skier began filling the gas tank, while Jack and Riley headed into the store. Near the entrance, Thompson paused briefly to look over a big Harley Sportster parked between a battered old pickup truck and a smaller Kawasaki motorcycle, then followed Riley inside.

Chick stood on the passenger side of the truck as the others scattered, stretching his arms, then shaking much like a dog coming out of water to get his circulation flowing. Wandering aimlessly off across the parking lot, at the end of the building he peeked around at the open space beside it. There beneath a royal Poinciana tree a rather large hog lay grunting, pulling against a rope looped around its neck and tied to the tree trunk. Chick stepped past a low pile of lumber scraps and walked over to the animal, which paused its struggle to look up at him suspiciously.

"Looks like they got you tied up awful tight," he said to the pig. "Rope must be chafing your neck in this heat, big fellow."

Chick bent down and began working the knot in the rope to loosen it a bit.

"Ugh, you could use a bath, too," he observed, turning his nose away from the pig. "Guess we're not the only ones that sweat down here."

Once the rope was looser, the man rose and considered his efforts. The hog now lay still, seemingly also satisfied with the handiwork. With that Chick turned and walked back around the corner of the building just in time to follow Bart into the store.

"Think I better go wash my hands," Chick noted, and then headed toward the back.

Bart joined, Riley and Jack, who were still looking over the selection of cold drinks in the cooler that lined the back wall and end of the store. At the counter the clerk was talking with a big man dressed in jeans, chaps, and sleeveless black tee shirt, a bandana covering his head, but allowing a few loose strains of greasy hair to escape. Over on the front glass wall a much smaller, but similarly dressed man was at the news rack, thumbing through a magazine looking at the photos of scantily dressed girls posing with hot rods.

"Ellie, you better get over here!" the little man suddenly burst out.

"I keep telling you not to call me that," the big man from the counter said as he walked over to his smaller companion, who was transfixed staring out the window, a look of disbelief on his face. The big man looked out in the same direction.

"Son of a bitch!" he screamed and made a break for the door, upsetting a rack full of maps as he passed, sending them flying across the aisle.

The smaller man now also began to move, but tripped over the fallen rack and sprawled just inside the door, then picked himself up and followed his companion out.

"Hey, what the hell?" the clerk yelled after them as he started around the counter toward the mess they had created, but once near the door he came to a halt and stared out toward the parking lot. He was quickly joined by Riley, Bart and Jack, who stepped quickly to the front of the store to see what was causing the commotion.

At roughly the same moment, Chick Malor reappeared from the restroom to follow the general exodus toward the door.

"What's happening?" he asked from behind the knot of onlookers.

"Looks like a pig trying to screw a motorcycle," Bart replied incredulously as they all began filing out the door.

Out on the sidewalk in front of the store the group was confronted by the bizarre scene of a large hog, reared up on its hind legs, appearing to try to mount the Harley Sportster. The animal's odd, headless and twisted penis was extended, suggesting that the pig's interest was carnal as opposed to seeking transportation. Riley choked back a laugh at the sight of the hog accosting the "hawg," stifling the accompanying smile for fear the cycle's owner might take offense to it. His restraint was probably a wise instinct.

"Damn it, Joey," the big man in black shouted, "Help me before that pig ruins my bike."

"Sure El," Joey Smatt answered, "but how?"

"Grab something and let's beat hell out of it!"

The little man began a frenzied search for a weapon, all the while moving with what Riley thought was an exaggerated, bowlegged gait, as though his groin area pained him. Meanwhile, Elsworth Score had reached into the back of the old pick up next to the scene of the action, retrieved a tire iron from its bed, to brandish it at the pig.

"Aw, crap," he exclaimed as the motorcycle teetered, then tipped over under the weight of the hog, which continued its single-minded assault on the machine, seemingly oblivious to the activity around it.

Just as the big biker closed in on the hog, the entire group's attention was drawn to the corner of the store.

"*Mi cerdo*," cried a Hispanic man, who had just rounded the end of the building. "What are you doing to him?"

With that, Enrique Gutero grabbed a short two-by-four from the pile of building scraps at his feet, advanced toward the man in black and the two men faced off.

"The bastard is ruining my bike," Score screamed at the intruder. "I'm going to kill the son of a bitch!"

Then the two men began moving in a circle, sizing up each other up and considering their prospects for a successful attack, the store clerk disappeared back inside, while the big pig continued its flirtation with the machine.

"You ever see a pig's pecker before?" Bart Skier asked in the general direction of Jack Thompson, while staring down at the animal.

"Huh," Thompson said, glancing back from the circling men in the parking lot.

The pig's attack on the Harley now slid the bike across the asphalt with a raspy, scraping of metal, at which Elsworth Score turned his attention aside for a split second, his face twisted into a pitiful visage by the sound of the perceived damage to the cycle. Gutero took advantage of the lapse and swung the board in his hand at his adversary. With more agility than one would expect for such a big man, Score avoided the blow. The force of Gutero's effort was so great that the piece of lumber slid from his hand to bounce heavily off the side of the old truck next to the action, while also throwing the Hispanic man off balance. His momentum rolled his body forward to catch Score, who had turned sideways to avoid the blow, with a body block worthy of a Sunday afternoon pro football lineman. The biker's tire iron was knocked from his hand and the two men crumpled into a wrestling, grunting and cursing pile. Around the tussle, Joey Smatt hopped like an excited Chihuahua, yipping encouragement, but apparently unable to decide on giving any real help to his partner.

By this time the sound of an approaching siren was clearly audible, as officers of the Key West Police Department sped to answer the call made by the store clerk. Riley, Chick, Bart and Jack backed several yards away from the fracas, still mesmerized by the action, but also demonstrating their lack of involvement in it.

A big police cruiser lurched to a stop in the parking lot, each side disgorging a uniformed officer.

One was a sergeant in his mid-30s, tall, barrel-chested and hair close cropped like a military man. His uniform was wrinkled and stained with sweat around the armpits. From the other side emerged an officer perhaps 10 years younger, 30 pounds lighter, but his blond hair sported the same military haircut. His uniform, however, was spotless, creased and drawn taunt over a tanned muscular body. The sergeant ambled over toward the two men still rolling around on the ground, trying unsuccessfully to land punches on each other, while the younger officer quick-stepped to catch up.

Towering over the wrestling match the sergeant twisted a baton in his hands.

"You want to break this up, or am I going to have to?" he announced in a loud, no-nonsense voice, punctuating the question by slapping the club into the palm of this left hand.

The combatants both looked up, and simultaneously released each other. They began getting to their feet, red faced and both excitedly making their cases at once.

"He's trying to kill *mi cerdo*," Gutero blurted.

"Look at what the damn animal is doing to my bike," Elsworth Score shouted, starting to move toward the hog.

"Officer!" Gutero yelled.

The sergeant reached out with his club, blocking Score's move.

"Stand down fellow," he ordered. "Both you boys up against the car, hands on the hood and feet apart."

"Mark, call this in and get animal control out here for the pig," the sergeant then said over his shoulder to the younger officer. "Then see what these other boys saw."

"What are you doing letting that critter run loose anyway?" he next asked, as he patted Gutero down looking for weapons.

"He was tied up," the Hispanic man pled. "Someone must have let him loose. I had the knot very tight."

As the man spoke, Chick Malor shrank a bit farther behind his companions in the direction of their pick-up truck.

Meanwhile the porcine paramour had apparently finally come to the conclusion that the inanimate object of its attentions was not responsive to the flirtations and had abandoned the pursuit. The pig strolled over next to the store's front, looked nonchalantly around at the commotion, and then plopped down heavily with a grunt in the shade.

Shortly another police cruiser and a van with Monroe County Animal Control marked on its side rolled up. After a short consultation with the policemen, the two men from animal control proceeded to loop a rope around the pig's neck and the hog then was led placidly into the back of their truck.

"What you want us to do with it?" one of the men asked the big sergeant.

"Take it to the shelter?" he offered.

"We only have dogs and cats there," was the response. "We can't handle anything this big."

"Hang on a minute," the officer said as he completed ducking Elsworth Score, hands cuffed behind his back, into the rear seat of his cruiser. The newly arrived officer and second car were receiving an equally trussed Enrique Gutero.

A short conversation on the radio ensued, before the sergeant returned to the animal control van.

"Take the pig over to the jail," he directed. "They'll take it in the petting zoo until we figure out what to do with it."

By this time Officer Mark Farnsworth had finished talking to the store clerk and made his way over to Riley, Chick and their traveling companions.

"Just need you men to confirm a couple of things, then you can be on your way," the young man said. "Who instigated the incident?"

"Truthfully, I'd say it was the pig," Bart mused.

"OK, but let's just stick to the two guys," Farnsworth smiled. "Did you see who was the aggressor?"

"I guess it was the Cuban," Jack Thompson offered. "He made the first move."

"Do you know him?" the officer asked, turning to Jack.

"No sir."

"Any particular reason you called him a Cuban then?" was the next question.

"I just assumed," Thompson stammered.

"He was just defending his pig," Chick tossed in. "The other guy had a tire iron."

"All the same," Farnsworth said in Malor's direction, "I just need to know which man started the actual fight."

"Looked a lot like they both wanted a piece of the action," Bart observed.

"Look, let's don't make this any harder than necessary. Did the Hispanic guy throw the first punch or didn't he?"

The group reluctantly agreed that he had, with Chick seeming most hesitant of the four to confirm the statement. At that point Officer Farnsworth thanked them and moved back over to his partner at the police car.

A bit later, a flatbed truck arrived, on which the Harley was loaded and as it drove off, Joey Smatt followed it down U.S. 1 astride his Kawasaki bike. A few moments later the parking lot was entirely vacant.

"Never let it be said that it gets boring in Key Weird," Bart Skier stated as the pickup truck crossed the bridge from Stock Island on to Key West.

"What do you think will happen to the pig?" Chick asked soberly.

Riley looked over at Chick, contemplating his friend's unusually serious demeanor.

"Knowing the Keys, they'll probably throw the biker in jail, set the Cuban adrift in a small boat and make barbecue out of the hog," Thompson said with a chuckle.

Riley and Bart laughed at the comment, but Chick only stared sullenly out the window.

Chapter 15

Riley Bright sat at a table by the open shutters facing Whitehead Street, alternately sipping on a beer, scanning a copy of the Key West Citizen and watching the stream of people passing along the sidewalk beside the Green Parrot Bar in the late afternoon. It was an eclectic parade composed of tourists making their way from Duval Street to their parked cars, the older ones bedecked in tropical shirts and Bermuda shorts, while their younger cohorts wore cargo shorts, tee shirts and ball caps. Waitresses, store clerks and busboys joined the flow, headed to or from shifts serving the vacationing hordes. The final ingredients composing this human *calaloo* were the omnipresent hangers-on, hustlers and street dwellers. Some of these latter denizens of the Key West lanes seemed consciously to affect the persona of being "characters," while others wore the mantle naturally, having to put forth no effort to achieve the status. Shaggy and unkempt in appearance, a few moved quickly with darting eyes, apparently bent on some personal mission, but more often they meandered aimlessly with hollow stares toward ill-defined destinations.

After a week in the city, some of the passing throng had become recognizable to Riley. He saw weaving through the flow the ebony-skinned Rasta man, dreadlocks oozing from beneath a knit cap, hauling his Conga drum in the direction of Mallory Square where he would take station in front of the First Union Bank building to create chants and songs about the passing tourists, thus enticing them to reward his creativity with a few coins or bills. A couple of times he spotted a young girl, in her early 20s at most, pedal past on her old bicycle, short cropped brown hair aflutter and faded print dress flowing in her slipstream. She apparently spent most of her day thus cruising the town's byways, before ending up back at the Green Parrot after dusk to hustle vacationing — and usually inebriated — anglers at the pool tables.

It was just after her third pass along the street outside that Riley noticed a small item in the newspaper regarding the upcoming session of the 16th Judicial Circuit Court of Florida to take place in two days just a block down and across Whitehead Street at the Monroe County courthouse. Such a mundane tidbit he ordinarily would have skipped over, had it not been for the headline.

Passionate Pig Incident Comes To Trial.

The fracas that he and his companions had witnessed upon their arrival in town had been out of the ordinary even by Key West standards and prompted a couple of news stories in its wake. Apparently the law enforcement and judicial officials were now ready to put the episode to rest. According to this story, Enrico Gutero, 46, of Stock Island and Elsworth Score, 32, of Fort Payne, Alabama would be going before a county judge to face charges arising from the fight. Since the pig that had been at the center of the controversy had gained a bit of notoriety as well, the piece even mentioned that a decision would be made as to its fate as well.

Unfortunately, since both the men involved had chosen to pick up makeshift weapons during the fight, they has spent the last week in the county jail out on Stock Island, following their initial appearance in court under Florida's new expedited Felony Disposition Project. Riley made a mental note to point the story out to Chick, who had seemed enthralled by everything revolving around the incident.

A sudden outburst drew Riley's attention to raised voices at the bar. A middle-aged man dressed in worn shorts, flip-flops and a tan "wife-beater" tank top from which masses of black hair escaped at the neck and armpits, had turned to face the man on the stool next to him. His apparent adversary could not have been more of a contrast. He was in his 20s, wearing thick black-rimmed glasses and dressed in deck shoes, crisp khaki slacks and a knit shirt. Though Riley was certain the shirt also sported a tiny man on horseback on the left chest, it was obscured by a large white button emblazoned in red with "STAG" and an inscription beneath it that was too small to make out. The only words Riley caught from the younger man sounded like "Nazi carnivore," while the older man's references included observations about faggots and ways in which his young opponent should feel free to make use of his own body orifices.

"I've already warned you before. The sign says No Sniveling Zone," the bartender bellowed at the young man, while pointing to a placard bearing the inscription behind the bar, "and that particularly applies when you start in on politics, religion or philosophy. Now you want to take your ass out of here, or do you need help?"

As the barman added the question he raised an eyebrow toward a barrel-chested form dressed in a Green Parrot tee shirt, seated on a stool by the bandstand and leaning against the wall. The bald man was so stocky he resembled one of the empty kegs that lined the wall near his station. A full beard enveloped his chin and a large gold ring hanging from his left ear lobe punctuated the visage. He smiled across the room at the young man, but it was a cold, grim offering that held nothing but menace. With that the young man turned and walked out the door onto the sunny sidewalk, while his recent foe returned his attention to his beer, with a grunted laugh in the direction of the bartender who was just shaking his head.

In a few minutes Riley looked up from the news again to spot Chick coming along the sidewalk on Whitehead from the south. Ambling beside him was a small man in work pants and a long sleeve black shirt that looked unbearable hot. Protruding from the little man's clinched teeth was an outrageously long cigar that emitted no hint of being lit. Unconsciously, a small smile spread over Riley's face at the sight of his friend and their new found host, Captain Arnie Patranicholas.

Upon arriving in Key West the duo had spent an uncomfortable first night sleeping under a tarpaulin in the back of Bart Skier's pickup truck, which was in the parking lot of the Holiday Inn near the entrance to the isle. The next day the two had showered in Skier's room, then hiked down the North Roosevelt Boulevard incarnation of U.S. 1 to Garrison Bight. Located on the north side, the small harbor protruded into the island and was home to most of the sport fishing fleet. It did not take Chick long to ferret out Patranicholas, who Skier had mentioned was universally known as Capt. Arnie.

His boat, the Rosita, was near the east end of the line of docked fishing vessels and struck a discordant chord in the trim fiberglass and chrome symphony of the surrounding sleek offshore vessels. The boat was a wooden relic of an earlier era. Though clean, it was worn and threadbare. While it may have been washed down after a day on the water, all repairs or maintenance seemed to have been neglected. There was also an air about the vessel that suggested its days on the water were now few and far between. Most of the faded blue paint covering the hull was cracked and chipped.

The Rosita had begun her career as a dragger, pulling trawls through near shore waters in the commercial fishing trade. Once purchased by Capt. Arnie, however, she had eventually been withdrawn from that line of work and impressed into a string of other ventures. Both the history of the boat and its owner leaned heavily on the captain, who over the course of the ensuing days filled in details piecemeal through rambling oratories over libations at the Green Parrot. The old seaman, like his vessel, was of indeterminate age, but the vintage of some of his recollections suggested a very long active life, or a quite vivid imagination. His weathered, tanned and wrinkled skin voted for the former, while the sheer audacity of what he claimed to have done rushed forth like hot air.

Capt. Arnie was a second-generation "conch," as natives of the Keys called themselves, deriving the name from the queen conch that was once abundant and still present in surrounding waters. The pride of association with those large mollusks runs so deep that Key West High School teams even proclaim themselves the Conchs. The captain claimed a lineage from Greek spongers who migrated to the area in the early 19th century. As a young man, Capt. Arnie worked the fishing fleet along the Keys, as well as on the shrimp boats pursuing "pink gold" in the early 1950s. Also in his resume were stints as a harbor pilot on the old naval base, running guns into and people out of Cuba and other Caribbean destinations, along with smuggling a variety of illicit recreational drugs and even boatloads of the Cuban cigars he favored. Other acquaintances Chick and Riley made in Key West who knew Capt. Arnie invariably could not vouch for any of these, but nor would they discount any of it either.

Now the veteran seaman just sat on the stern of his boat at the fishing dock, talked to any passerby who offered or accepted conversation and on rare occasions took groups of gullible or miserly anglers out for some bottom fishing around the reefs.

When Chick first crossed paths with Capt. Arnie he soon discovered that the seaman had a couple of vacant rooms in his house on Flagler Avenue. Due to the reference of being friends of angling client, Bart Skier, he was willing to rent them to Chick and Riley for a small stipend and help with washing down the Rosita after fishing trips. In light of the extreme lack of accommodations in the city in advance of Fantasy Fest, the duo jumped at the opportunity. In the ensuing week they had made the rounds of Key West with their new landlord, gaining entrance to the fraternity of locals via their association with the captain.

Riley continued to watch Capt. Arnie, with his swaggered gait, only slightly impaired by advanced years. He was obviously regaling Chick with some tidbit of knowledge or story of yore, for the younger man only nodded as they approached. So far, Capt. Arnie's most singular achievement, as far as Riley was concerned, was that he was able to dominate a conversation with the usually loquacious Chick Malor. At length the pair entered the Green Parrot beneath the sign bearing its name and its claim of being the oldest bar in Key West - established in 1890 - to end their journey at Riley's table.

"Mind if we heave to at your dock," Capt. Arnie asked Riley, though he was well on his way to being seated regardless of the answer.

"Feel free," Riley returned, "and what've you two gentlemen been up to?"

"Gentlemen, my fine fuzzy butt," the captain scowled amicably. "I've just worked up a thirst strolling your landlubber friend across the island, trying to instill a bit of sea lore into him."

"More like a fast-paced jog through the streets and a barge full of crap," Chick shot back with a glint. "How about you, Chipmunk?"

"Just chilling and reading the paper, but I did get to see a guy get thrown out of the bar a while ago."

"Chrispus J. Attucks," Capt. Arnie swore with a tone of admiration. "Who might that freebooter be and who did he lay low?"

"Don't know who he was, though I've seen him around town," Riley replied, surprised at the old seaman's reaction and interest. "Young guy, glasses, dresses preppie with a streak of nerd. Had on some kind of button. Apparently was on the wrong side of a political debate at the bar."

"They tossed his butt out for talking?" the captain asked incredulously. "Can't be. You'd have to kill somebody to be thrown out of this black hole. In 50 years the only ones I've known to be forcibly removed were drug into the street after the fight."

"Guess you haven't had a run-in with Eric Allen yet," Chick offered.

"Is that the ruffian's moniker?" the old seaman asked.

"Hardly a ruffian," Chick laughed, "but probably worse. Sure sounds like him. I met him a couple of days ago over at the Bull and Whistle. Claims to be president and founder of a group called STAG."

"Yeah, that's what was on the button he had on," Riley added.

"Stands for Stop The Animal Gulag," Chick explained. "He's one of those animal rights kooks. Wants to empty the zoos and give the critters the vote. Let's just say he can be a rather overbearing twit on that subject."

"Ever get him on my boat, he'll go overboard and missing," Capt. Arnie growled, instantly shifting from admiration to disdain for the subject of the conversation. "Probably down here meddling in our business, working to get those marine refuges put in place. Bad enough slowing us down with all these manatee zones, but never thought I see the day when landlubbers would start telling fishermen where they can drop a trawl."

"I wouldn't worry about him, Cap," Chick countered. "He seems pretty harmless to me. So far off the charts that no one would take him seriously. Seems to be his way, though; he has to be out on the fringe.

"For instance, we got to talking fishing," Chick continued. "He loves it, but only fly fishes. Claims it is the purest form of the sport."

"I thought that's something you just do for trout out West?" Riley asked.

"Ought to be," Capt. Arnie scoffed. "You see fools out there flailing the air all around the islands. They don't bother me though. No more fish than they catch, there'll always be plenty out there for the real fishermen."

"Whatever," Chick conceded to get back to his train of thought. "When I said fish were animals too, he got sort of huffy and dropped the subject. Still, basically, if you can keep him off the subjects of animals and politics, he stays pretty sane."

"Still deep six him if I get the chance," Capt. Arnie frowned.

"Yeah, with your anchor tied to his leg, Cap," Chick grinned playfully. "Seems that's your cure for most of the world's ills."

"Don't mock me, Malor," Capt. Arnie spat out, punching the air in Chick's direction with his unlit cigar. "You're playing with fire."

"No offence, Cap," Chick said in a serious tone. "I've heard the scuttlebutt on the docks about how dangerous Capt. Arnie can be. Not to be trifled with is the way it's put."

"And don't forget it," the old seaman snapped, tossing a nod in Riley's direction for emphasis. "The islands are full of salts that let their memory lapse on that point."

It was an exchange that Riley had witnessed several times in the short stay with their aged landlord. Chick gently ruffled the man's feathers, and then just as seamlessly smoothed them back down.

The strange little dance seemed to confirm the old man's reputation in his own mind and seal the bond with Chick for having been the vehicle for acknowledging that persona.

"Oh, Chick," Riley piped up, passing the newspaper across to him, "you'll probably want to see this. Looks like your pig and his friends are getting their day in court."

As Chick stared at the newsprint, a rare look of genuine seriousness spread across his countenance. For some reason that Riley could not discern, his friend was rapt by anything that touched on the brawl they had witness out on Stock Island. The mood was totally out of character for Chick Malor. It was as if the fight and its participants were a personal concern for him?

As Chick read the paper in the last fading light of day, Capt. Arnie had struck up a conversation through the open window with an aged black man who had come walking down the street. Riley sipped his beer and turned his attention to the pool tables at the end of the room. The bicycle girl was standing by a table, having apparently slipped in unnoticed by Riley. She was leaning on a pool cue and flirtatiously chatting with a slender man in cargo shorts and a tee shirt adorned with a print from the brush of artist Guy Harvey. The sailfish on the shirt seemed to swim as the shirt moved when the man shifted his weight. No doubt he was the first of the evening's anglers who would think about seeing what was under her sundress, but was more likely destined to be parted from some of his vacation money after a game or two of eight ball.

Capt. Arnie's attention now turned back to the table as the black man ambled on down the street.

"Who was that, Captain?" Riley asked, staring after the man.

"Only man on the island I'd never fight," the old seaman said, also looking down the street at the retreating figure. "Toughest son of a bitch that ever tread the dock planks of Key West Bight. Name's Kermit Forbes, but prefers to be called "Shine." He was telling me he's going to be in a book and on television too. Some limey came all the way from England to talk to him."

"Just because he's mean?" Riley asked.

"I didn't say mean," the captain corrected. "Shine keeps to himself, and he's never done nothing to anyone that didn't deserve it. It's because back when he was a young stud he cold-cocked Ernest Hemingway in a boxing match on the quay. Only man on the island had the nerve to do it. Not that others couldn't have. It was during the Depression and Hem was one of the few that had any money, so you didn't want to get on his bad side. He might cut you off from picking up money by helping around his boat or house."

"He really fought with Hemingway?" Riley quizzed, watching the man shuffle around the corner and out of sight.

"Laid him low too," Capt. Arnie replied. "I was just a boy, but was right there on the dock to see it. After that Hem used Shine as a sparring partner all the time. Almost like he was proud to show off the only man on the island that kicked his ass."

"Where's the courthouse?" Chick asked, oblivious to the conversation that had been going on next to him.

"Couple of blocks down the street. Why?" Capt. Arnie asked.

"That's where they're having the trial," Chick replied as if it was the most obvious of facts.

"Yeah," the captain returned, "that's where they have all the trials. Which one would this be?"

"You know, the one from the fight we saw our first day in town. Think I'll go watch it," Chick said. "Y'all want to go too?"

"I've officially seen the inside of them courtrooms too often over the years," Capt. Arnie said shaking his head. "It'd just piss me off if the judge turned out to be one of the bastards I'd faced before."

"How about it, Chipmunk?" Chick said, turning to Riley.

"Sure, I guess," Riley agreed. "But I still don't know why you're so hung up on this thing."

"I just like courtroom drama," Chick said with a dismissive, but unconvincingly forced grin.

Chapter 16

As Officer Mark Farnsworth walked into the Key West Police Station on North Roosevelt Boulevard, the early morning pre-dawn gloom was giving way to sunrise over the Atlantic Ocean behind the structure to the east. From the parking lot streaks of gold and crimson were visible, framing the building as they shot up into the stratosphere, rivaling the island's famed sunset colors. But, this was a performance never viewed by vacationing throngs, and only experienced by bleary-eyed anglers headed out on charter boats from Key West or Garrison Bights, or unlucky conchs having to start their day's work early.

For most residents or visitors to Key West it was an ungodly hour. At 6:00 a.m. the bars had been closed for a couple hours and it was still too early for most retail and tourist activity to commence. The rush hour influx of labor from the islands to the east was still a few minutes away, so the streets of the city were in their most deserted condition. This was the moment when Key West caught its breath before starting the tedious grind of another day as a real town, but presenting the facade of paradise. Also falling in this quite interlude was a shift change for the men and women of the Key West Police Department.

This changing of the guard ordinarily consisted of the officers, sergeants and detectives of the shift coming on duty gathering in the second floor briefing room where the watch commander covered the mundane details of the coming day of policing the southernmost location in the nation. Key West famously attracts the eccentric, who bring odd lifestyles and attitudes with them. The resulting culture presents the usual law enforcement challenges, but also throws into the mix other crime waves. Many calls answered by the officers deal with "unwanted guests or undesirable sleepers" as the reports officially list them. In other environs these folks would be "homeless" or "indigent," causing a nuisance to some resident or business owner who finds them snoozing or loafing on a patio or in a doorway. The difference in Key West is that a lot of these people seem oddly complacent with forming the bottom rung of society. While not above performing a necessary amount of panhandling, they rarely display a malcontent demeanor or the anger often thinly masked by street folk of more northern climates. Rarely pushy, even panhandling for change is transformed into performance art on the streets of Key West. Still, even here in paradise, life and commerce must go on, so the police are called several times each day and night to roust the unwanted from their lodgings of opportunity.

Another variety of calls answered by the patrol officers deals with "lost property, or property found." All too often the property in question is a bicycle. In a small island town "borrowing" a two-wheeler carelessly left unattended, then abandoning it at the destination, easily solves the problem of getting from one place to another. Needless to say, police officers new to the force end up handling most of those calls.

Mark Farnsworth faced the prospects of a full day of such duties as he climbed the stairway headed for the conference room. With four months of tenure with the Key West Police Department he was just beginning the climb of seniority. If the duty was dull, mundane or distasteful, he fully expected it to be directed his way. So far in his law enforcement career the most exciting chapter had been teaming with Sergeant Al Hastens to answer a call out on Stock Island that his peers and the rest of Key West had come to know as the case of the "Passionate Pig." The sergeant had gotten great mileage out of recounting the swine's amorous adventure to other members of the force over coffee. On the other hand, since it was Farnsworth's high point in crime busting, his part provoked only jokes and sniggering. Plus, the rookie officer found no comfort in knowing one of the men in the disturbance had hired a lawyer, thus he would be making his first appearance in court tomorrow to testify in the case. It would have been so much better if the men in the fight had simply pled guilty at the arraignment.

No doubt the visit to court would open the door to more ribbing from his comrades in the station house. Having his standing so quickly degenerate into one-liners about "porkers in paradise" was hardly the basis on which Mark Farnsworth wanted to found his reputation as he kept order in the streets of Key West.

Hitting the second floor hallway, Farnsworth also knew this morning's briefing was to be a special occasion. Time was winding down toward the advent of Fantasy Fest, a week of activity that called for added planning on the part of the men and women of the police force. Knowing that week's events would culminate in 60,000 revelers filling Duval Street on the Saturday night of Halloween Weekend was enough to put the city's leaders on edge every year. In the history of the carnival-like frenzy, problems had been surprisingly few. Such a crowd, with more than a fair share well lubricated with alcohol, would seem rife for trouble. Add to that mix the number of females, mostly tourists from colder climes, who chose the Saturday night parade route as the scene of their one night of annual debauchery amid a sea of inebriation and the prescription for trouble appeared complete.

Yet, despite the ladies on the streets dressed in costumes consisting of little more than bikini bottoms and thin layers of body paint on their bosoms, the street party produced no major wave of crimes against persons or property. The crowd of revelers good-naturedly jostled for strings of plastic beads tossed from passing floats, then flooded into the street in the wake of the parade to shift up and down the thoroughfare like the ebb and flow of water on a tidal flat. Small streams of the human torrent occasionally broke off to ooze through the open doors of watering holes, but more people joining the throng as they exited other bars and restaurants replenished the main tide. All in all it was an amazing display of passivity by the human herd.

To make sure that civility continued this year, the city manager, police chief and the entire force were convening during this morning's shift change. Farnsworth's queries to more veteran officers had him prepared for little more than a pep talk from the senior management, with the important part coming afterwards when the shift commanders issued the individual Fantasy Fest weekend assignments. Needless to say, everyone would be on duty during the culminating parade and street party, along with a good portion of the Monroe County Sheriff's Department and any other certified law enforcement personnel that could be spared from corrections or any other source. Though Farnsworth had no great expectations regarding his posting for that coming weekend, he was still anticipating it. It would be his first experience of policing Fantasy Fest and would definitely be better than rousting unwanted sleepers from doorways.

Entering the briefing room, Farnsworth was not surprised to find it sparsely populated. He was a bit early by design and headed to the back wall where a coffee urn and some doughnuts were arrayed on a table. Passing down along the line of folding chairs, from one of the rows he left in his wake he heard a low muffled "oink." In spite of the twitter of laughter that spread to the few officers present, the rookie knew better than to look back. Such a reaction was just what was desired and would open the door to more of the quips he did not want to endure yet again.

Grabbing a couple of the doughnuts and a cup of coffee, the young officer moved to where Sgt. Hastens had just entered the room and plopped heavily into a chair. Since he could not escape his part in the pig escapade, the best refuge seemed likely to be found in the lee of the other participant, whose seniority and gruff wit might deflect some of it.

"Morning, Sarge," Farnsworth offered. "How's it going?"

Never a morning soul, Hastens nodded and grunted an acknowledgment, as the young officer settled down in the adjoining chair to work on the breakfast in his hand.

At a quicker pace the room was now filling with the slightly more than 20 officers and patrol personnel of the Key West Police Department. The faces entering the room were as eclectic as the population of the city itself, reflecting the racial, cultural and gender mix. Caucasian, black, Hispanic, male, female, young to middle age, the men and women in uniform and street clothes sifted in for the meeting.

The final ingredient for the gathering soon appeared in the form of Police Chief John Pollard and City Manager Jaime "Jake" Suarez, who entered together and took a position at a table in the front of the room. Tall, graying at the temples and ramrod straight, Pollard wore a starched short-sleeved, white shirt adorned with insignia of the police force and his rank as its leader. His bearing seemed to clash with that of his companion. Suarez was dressed in a blue, flora-print shirt, the tail of which flowed down over the top of his tan slacks. His round jovial face, capped with a tuft of unruly black hair also differed from the stern stare of the chief's long, horse-like visage.

"Listen up people," the chief opened the meeting. "You all know why we're here. We've got just over a week before Fantasy Fest, and I want us ready when the lunatics hit our streets. You've already been informed that there will be no leave during the week for any certified personnel. We're all on duty.

"Captain Jorgenson will be the liaison with the Monroe County Sheriff's Office, Captain Teller with the Highway Patrol and Lieutenant Small will coordinate with the public works folks. I expect professionalism from all of you and if that's what I get, we'll have another safe and trouble-free event. After the meeting, check with your section commanders for specific assignments.

"Now I'll turn it over to the city manager, Jaime Suarez, who has a few points to cover," the chief concluded.

In contrast to the stiff, no-nonsense lecture of the chief, Jake Suarez hit his feet with a broad grin.

"Good morning, boys and girls," he beamed. "Only amendment I'd offer to the chief's comments is his 'lunatics' are my 'paying guests' that keep us all in a job and we want them to be welcome and have a good safe time.

"You may or may not have been following the debate between the mayor and city council," Suarez began again, "regarding what I guess you might call a dress code for Fantasy Fest. They've heard a lot of complaints from some segments of the citizenry about the number of bare bosoms on our streets the last couple of years."

The manager paused momentarily as a muffled sniggering rippled around the room. Now seated at the table just behind Suarez, Chief Pollard maintained a stony countenance.

"To the disappointment of many of you," the manager finally continued with a grin, "and the relief of the ladies on the force, the council has mandated no nudity at this year's Fest."

A mock groan this time spread through the males in the room, causing another pause during which Suarez chuckled aloud and the chief glared disapprovingly.

"I know, I know," Suarez jibed, shaking his head and mimicking a Bill Clinton voice. "I feel your pain. And it'll add to your workload. While we want the ladies dressed, we don't want to arrest them or make them mad enough to quit spending money. The council has authorized the purchase of a couple of thousand tee shirts with Fantasy Fest logos. These will be issued to all officers."

With the pronouncement he picked up a sample shirt from the table and held it up.

"When you see a woman with exposed breasts, whether painted or not, you give her a shirt and remain on site until she has it on. But, you don't need to help her with it," Suarez added smirking and staring straight at Sgt. Al Hastens, who returned a "who me?" look as the room gave up a round of unbridled laughter.

"That's all that I have, chief," Suarez concluded, turning toward Pollard, who stood up.

"All right then. Break off into groups by division and watch to get your assignments," the chief of police said to end the meeting.

Mark Farnsworth slowly gravitated toward the corner of the room where Lt. Charlie Small was handling the assignments for the uniformed patrol officers of the day shift. He had only recently been assigned to Small's watch after doing his first three months on the swing shift, four to midnight duty. While the young officer had gotten the mundane work until now, he had not yet experienced the graveyard shift of midnight till morning. In Key West that was when most serious crimes occurred and when the island weirdness was at its daily height. For that reason Chief Pollard maintained a policy of getting some time on the streets under new officer's belts before they drew those rotten hours. Farnsworth knew that eventually his time would come and actually looked forward to it. His first three-month tour on the over-night watch would be his coming of age — after that he would join the other patrolmen in hating those hours. Shuffling along behind other officers, Farnsworth finally reached the head of the line and Lt. Small.

"Here you go, Mark," the lieutenant said, handing him a computer generate sheet of paper, which the officer scanned, then looked up at his watch commander quizzically.

"Look at it this way," Small offered with an almost apologetic smile in return, "you're the only one on the force with an island to himself."

"Stock Island?" Farnsworth said.

"The county has pulled most of the corrections folks from the jail for street work, leaving only one jailor and a reservist out there," Small explained. "You'll be the only certified personnel, other than the jailor, on the island. Just patrol in your vehicle, maintain radio contact with the jail and check the Children's Animal Park hourly."

"Animal Park?" the officer asked.

"Yes, the petting zoo," the lieutenant replied, obviously a bit put out by what he read as reluctance on Farnsworth's part to embrace his duty. "They have a high school kid who has volunteered to keep an eye on the animals Friday and Saturday night, since there will be no one else out there. We just need you to check on him to make sure there are no problems."

Another trait of life in Key West is that the odd citizenry that the town attracted brought with those folks some equally odd tastes in pets. Not only did unwanted dogs and cats show up on the island, but a variety of exotic birds, reptiles and other critters from time to time ended up homeless. The Florida

Keys Society for the Prevention of Cruelty to Animals operates an animal shelter for common pets, while exotics were placed with exhibitors when possible. The need for a place to hold this latter menagerie while awaiting transfer, however, led to the opening of a Children's Animal Park in 1994. Located immediately adjacent to the Stock Island Detention Center, the facility became a permanent home to some animals in a complex of aviaries, reptile exhibits, rabbit warrens and holding areas for farm animals. This petting zoo proved popular with local youngsters, but was also used to give inmates at the detention center hands-on experience in animal husbandry. As the primary attendants at the park, it was felt that working with animals in need of compassion might also prove positive in sparking a bit more of humanity in those law breakers.

After a short silent pause, Small spoke again.

"Any questions?" he asked.

"That's where they're holding the pig from the convenience store incident," Farnsworth said, as if speaking to himself.

For an instant a slight smile and look of recognition shot across the lieutenant's face, as though he had just recognized the connection between the young officer and the now infamous Passionate Pig. He was aware of the ribbing the rookie had been enduring from his peers.

"I understand your reluctance," the lieutenant commiserated, "but we all have our duty."

"Yeah, thank you sir," Farnsworth said half-heartedly, then turned and headed for the door.

Small watched his subordinate walking away and when the young man passed out of sight, the lieutenant shook his head slightly.

"Passionate Pig patrol," he said aloud, but barely audible, anticipating the likely abuse Farnsworth was now destined to endure.

Chapter 17

For the second time since leaving Atlanta Riley had been forced to go on a shopping trip with Chick to acquire some clothing. His friend's compulsion to be on hand for the trial at the Monroe County Courthouse made the venture a necessity. Appearing in court, even as a spectator, requires a measure of decorum in attire that is truly rare in the Florida Keys, making their collective wardrobe of shorts and flip-flops woefully inadequate. Thus, they took the opportunity between seeing the newspaper story and trial day to pay a visit to the Searstown Mall on North Roosevelt Boulevard.

The shopping center had been the first in Key West, with its doors swinging open in the late 1960s. As the name implied, it was anchored by the venerable old name of Sears, Roebuck & Company. Through the ensuing years that name had been officially pared down to simply Sears as the company shut down its legendary catalog business and struggled for an identity in modern retailing. Of all areas of Key West, Searstown looked the least like paradise. Rather it was the epitome of mid-20th century shopping mall architecture, replete with concrete, glass and asphalt in copious supply. The mall sat in the midst of what is called New Town, owing to the fact it is located on terra firma that did not exist prior to World War II. The U.S. Navy's need for more space for housing during the conflict led to a dredge-and-fill philosophy that added about a quarter to the island's size. The project, which would never meet environmental standards imposed today, also laid the foundation for postwar expansion of the city that culminated in the arrival of big-store merchandising.

Eventually in the 1970s, Sears was joined by a nearby K-Mart before space became so short of supply that land prices rose astronomically. During the ensuing years these two establishments competed, while both chains struggled for company visions and niches in a new retail landscape. Their competition, however, more resembled two worn out heavyweight boxers lumbering around the ring, occasionally throwing punches that never seemed to land. This half-hearted dance was quite acceptable to both camps, since costs and attitudes on the island seemed to preclude the possibility that the reigning champion from Arkansas would ever be allowed into the arena to challenge their charade of dominance. In the case of Sears, the store's location, much as was the company's good fortune in other cities around the nation, was like an insurance policy. If the store ever failed, the property on which it stood for so many years would prove a financial windfall to the corporation.

Now replete in their new wardrobe of chino slacks, print shirts and deck shoes — ensembles that passed for business attire here in the American tropics — Riley and Chick approached the Monroe County Courthouse on the concrete walkway in the shade of palm and Poinciana trees. The two-story, red brick building dating from 1890 was incongruous amid the tropical setting, looking more appropriate to a city green in New England. At the portico fronting the structure, they passed white columns that supported a balcony on the upper level and the roof another story higher. The double doors through which they entered were trimmed in white to match that around the tall, arched windows that marched down the front of the edifice on both the lower and upper floors.

Once they found the correct courtroom, the pair was quickly ensconced on a bench near the rear. In front of the judge's raised bench, tables were place on either side of the room, while a jury box lined the wall to the left. That fore portion of the room was separated from the six-row gallery by a low wooden railing. Despite the notoriety the case had generated, the room was quite sparsely populated. As with humanoid celebrities chosen by chance, the 15-minutes of fame allotted to the Passionate Pig must have faded.

A couple of bailiffs and a court reporter were up near the bench, chatting with a man in a sport coat and tie. On the opposite side of the gallery a small knot of Latinos were clustered on a bench — a woman in her 40s, a man of similar age and teenaged boy in slacker attire. Just behind sat a young woman that Riley guessed was a reporter from the Key West Citizen.

On the near side of the gallery and seated just behind the rail was the little wiry man that had danced around the edge of the brawl on Stock Island.

He was still dressed in the biker attire he wore the last time Riley had seen him. Next to enter the room was the younger of the two officers who had responded to the fight. The man in the sport coat nodded to him as the policeman took a seat. Finally a tall, dapper man of perhaps 50 years of age entered carrying a brief case. Dressed in a cream-colored business suit, white shirt and yellow patterned tie, he proceeded to where the Latinos were sitting, exchanged a few words of Spanish with them, then moved on to a chair at the table in front of the rail on the right of the room. Momentarily there was a shuffling of people around the front of the courtroom.

"All rise," announced one of the bailiffs. "The 16th Judicial Circuit Court of the State of Florida is now in session. The honorable Judge David R. Kyler presiding."

As the bailiff spoke, Judge Kyler entered the courtroom, seeming to flow in his black robe across the few paces from the door to his lofty perch.

"Please be seated," the bailiff concluded once the judge was in place.

David Kyler was a native conch in his early 60s, dark hair profusely streaked with gray. He possessed the demeanor and physique of a football linebacker, which he had once been. In fact, his performance at that position for Key West High School had distinguished him as one of the island's rare all-state caliber athletes in the sport. It also earned him a scholarship to play for the Tampa University Spartans back when they fielded a football team. He completed his academic work there before moving on to the University of Miami, School of Law.

Forever the athlete, no matter how removed from the glory days of youth and despite his stature in the judicial realm, Judge Kyler maintained his umbilical to the sporting world by refereeing youth basketball leagues. It was that connection and his commitment to officiate a pre-Fantasy Fest tournament taking place at the old Douglass Gym on Olivia Street that mandated a smooth flow of the day's docket. The judge would be pressed for time to get to the gym for the early afternoon tip off, so beneath the judicial robes that signified his position in the courtroom, he was already dressed in the zebra stripes that insured similar authority on the basketball court. There would be no time wasted in Judge Kyler's court this morning.

"Call the first case," the judge instructed the bailiff.

"Case file No. 23-4756, State of Florida verses Elsworth Score," the court officer proclaimed, while nodding to a door on the sidewall, which the other bailiff opened and ushered in the defendant. Riley recognized the man as the big biker whose motorcycle had been accosted by the pig. The man had likely faced a judge before. Though he retained his menacing size that was now clothed in a blue jail jumpsuit, his hair had been cut and he was clean-shaven in an attempt to look as upstanding as possible. The bailiff led him to a spot directly in front of the judge's bench where he stood sheepishly awaiting new instructions.

Judge Kyler finally looked up from shuffling through the case file.

"Mr. Score, it looks like you have waved your right to an attorney. Is that correct?"

"Yes sir, your honor," Score replied.

"And you indicated you would like to change your plea to guilty. Is that also correct?" The judge asked, intently looking over the defendant.

"Yes sir."

"It is always good to see a man own up to the mistakes he has made," Kyler observed. "Did you play any football in high school, Mr. Score?"

The look on Score's face said the question took him completely off guard, leading to a pause and then stammered answer.

"Yes sir, offense line and defensive end," he offered tentatively.

"I suspected as much," Kyler said appreciatively, but Riley suspected the judge was more pleased with his own ability to size up a former athlete than any admiration for the defendant's past.

"Mr. Score, we take public safety quite seriously in Monroe County. The fact that there may have been some provocation involved speaks in your favor, but when you chose to arm yourself in the fight, you lost any sympathy from this court.

"Therefore, with the consent of the District Attorney's Office," Kyler continued, nodding toward the man in the sport coat seated at the table at the left front of the room. "I am finding you guilty of disturbing the peace. However, since no blows with a weapon were landed, I'm reducing the charge of felony assault and battery to one of misdemeanor simple battery. For that reason your sentence will be 14 days in the Monroe County Detention Center. I'll credit time already served against the sentence. So the bad news is, you will miss Fantasy Fest. On the other hand, you will be out just in time to pick up your motorcycle and head home to Alabama."

"Do you have anything else to say?" the judge concluded.

"No, your honor," Score answered while sheepishly looking at the floor.

"Fine," the judge concluded. "Bailiff, escort Mr. Score out and remand him back into the custody of the Sheriff's Department."

As Judge Kyler again shuffled through his stack of papers, signing one of them, the bailiff led Elsworth Score toward the door. As he went Score, looked over his shoulder toward the bench holding Joey Smatt. The wiry man looked at his friend helplessly and gave a shrug of his shoulders, to which Score scornfully rolled his eyes just before disappearing out of the room. At that, Smatt rose and headed out the back door of the courtroom.

Finally the judge nodded to the bailiff at the end of his bench.

"Case file No. 23-4757, State of Florida verses Enrico Gutero," the bailiff pronounced.

Again the door at the side swung open and Gutero was led into the courtroom. As he proceeded to a position facing the judge, the nattily dressed man from the front table rose and joined him.

Briefly Judge Kyler again scanned a file before him.

"Mr. Sanchez, I see you will be representing Mr. Gutero," Kyler said looking up.

"That is correct, your honor," the tall man said in a slightly accented voice, while smiling agreeably.

"Is that your wish, Mr. Gutero?"

"Yes sir," Gutero replied.

"But you are entering a plea of *nolo contendre*?"

"Yes, your honor," Sanchez said, then offered. "If it please the court, our arguments will be confined to the sentencing phase."

"Any objection from the state?" Kyler asked the assistant district attorney in the sport coat.

"None your honor," the man stood and replied. "Nor will the state have a position regarding the sentence."

"Very well, Mr. Sanchez," the judge said. "The court accepts the plea. Your client can have a seat and we will proceed to sentencing. Let's hear your arguments."

As Enrico Gutero took a seat at the defense table where his lawyer had been seated, he looked over his shoulder to acknowledge the members of his seated family. He scanned the faces of his wife, nephew Tommy Arcada, and his brother-in-law, who was Tommy's father. Though the teenager stared stoically at his uncle, the adults smiled hopefully at the defendant.

Meanwhile Miguel Sanchez stood, looking studiously at an open folder lying on the corner of the table. Something about him reminded Riley of a student hastily cramming for an exam, but the man's already exhibited easy manner before the judge suggested he needed no last minute preparations. It was a valid appraisal. Sanchez had been advocating for Monroe County's Cuban community for three decades, battling to get his countrymen into the U.S. and then keeping them out of jail once they arrived. He had particularly earned a name for himself during the Mariel Boatlift.

From the spring of 1980 through fall, Fidel Castro had thrown open the Port of Mariel in Cuba to allow anyone to leave the island country that desired to exit. They were, however, required to leave virtually everything behind, except the clothes on their backs as they fled to the U.S. It was no secret that among the 125,000 Cubans who took advantage of the offer, Castro made sure that the mentally disturbed and criminal elements were well represented, whether they wanted to go or not. Sanchez made his reputation by sorting through the cases of individuals who were detained when they reached South Florida to make sure each got a fair hearing. In the process, he achieved a 100 percent success rate in the courts; everyone he represented was cleared to enter as refugees. It was a record that sealed his hold as the attorney of choice for Cubans in the Florida Keys.

At the same time, Riley noticed that while the judge had been speaking the young officer from the Key West Police Department had a look of relief on his face. From the turn the court proceedings were taking, it appeared the policeman would not have to say anything regarding the case. That view was quickly confirmed.

"Officer Farnsworth, thank you for being here," Judge Kyler announced, "but I don't believe we will be needing any statement from you after all, so you are released to return to duty."

"Thank you, your honor," the officer said, then exited the courtroom's rear door.

"OK, Mr. Sanchez, let's get started."

"Your honor," Sanchez began. "Enrico Gutero is truly sorry for the unfortunate event that occurred on Stock Island. The entire episode was a series of misunderstandings that got out of hand. When he discovered his livestock missing, he naturally assumed the animal had been stolen. Then he encountered a complete stranger in the act of accosting his property. It was only natural that he would try to intervene. Any one of us would likely have followed a similar course. It would be the only manly thing to do."

At this point the attorney paused, turning to scan the faces of his client's family members.

Riley suspected that the barrister's last comments were directed at his present and future clients rather than at the judge. He was reminding his community that he alone stood on the breastworks to defend the Cuban community against the destructive force of American custom and law as it endeavored to ameliorate the character of their men.

"We would also like to remind the court," the lawyer resumed, "that Mr. Gutero has already suffered greatly and out of proportion to any harm done to society, which in fact has also suffered. Not only has he lost time and wages, his employer has been deprived of his experienced services. Additionally, my client was deprived of the warmth of his family during their most important cultural holiday season. While he and his animal were both incarcerated, what would otherwise have been a festive celebration of man's eternal quest for freedom from oppression became a lonely vigil for a saddened family —— a family that lost everything when making that leap of faith to come to this country that now holds their future happiness in jeopardy. "

Sanchez used a sweeping motion of his arm toward Gutero's huddled relatives, who for a brief moment presented a collection of faces featuring blank staring eyes of confused and frightened refugees, just rescued from a homemade, sinking raft and fearing for their future.

The impassive countenance of Judge David Kyler gave no hint as to his reaction to the theatrics. When Riley looked over at Chick, he was taken aback by the look on his friend's reddened face. There was a real appearance of empathy as the man bit lightly on his lower lip. This was hardly the cynical, devil-may-care Chick Malor to which Riley had become accustomed.

"Thus, your honor," Sanchez continued, "we contend that it would be odious to compound the grief in the Gutero household by farther penalizing them of their livelihood through continued incarceration of the head of the family, or by imposing a burdensome fine. Enrique Gutero has had time to contemplate his actions during his detention and now sees the error of his way. Nothing is to be gained by him or by the community at large from more punitive punishment."

"Thank you, your honor," Sanchez ended with a slight bow toward the bench, turned and strode to the table where Gutero sat glumly looking straight ahead.

Judge Kyler leaned forward to rest his elbows on the bench in front of him.

"Quite impressive, Mr. Sanchez," the judge mused. "I'm not sure whether I should initiate an Oscar nomination, or throw a flag for "unnecessary emotion.""

A twitter of laughter rippled the room, starting with the bailiffs, as though they were the court jesters who signaled when it was appropriate for levity to enter the chambers of justice.

"But your points are well taken," Kyler added. "Mr. Gutero, please rise and come face the bench."

Gutero rose and walked to the position indicated by one of the bailiffs.

"Do you, in fact, now realize that it is better to entrust the enforcement of civil order to the duly appointed officers of the law, which is to say the police?" the judge asked.

"Yes sir," the defendant replied, obviously quite uncomfortable with having to endure the present humiliation.

"Very well, in light of this being a first time offense and your standing in the community, the sentence will be time already served in the county detention facility. You are free to go."

"Your honor," Sanchez interrupted, standing at the table. "There is the other matter of my client's personal property?"

"Ah, yes," Kyler smiled, "the Passionate Pig."

Again the bailiffs led a round of sniggering, convincing Riley that they understood and were communicating to all present that joking was allowed, as long as the judge in charge instigated it.

"Your honor, although it is too late for my client and his family to put the animal to the original use in their celebration, in light of his having already been sentenced and paid his debt, there is no reason to impose a further financial penalty upon him through loss of his property."

"Well, counselor," Kyler replied, "the court can appreciate your position, but we also have to take into account the interest of the citizens of Key West. According to the City Code, Chapter 10, Section 4, no animals other than domestic cats are allowed to run free in any part of the city."

"But, your honor, Mr. Gutero did not allow the animal in question to run free. It was restrained on his property. Someone obviously released the animal, for which my client should not be held accountable," the lawyer countered.

"Which could take us into another area of the law, Mr. Sanchez, but it is not one we need to visit," the judge pointed out. "You'll also find that Chapter 10, Section 13 of the code covering livestock prevents the keeping of any such animals in the city, unless specifically allowed on those premises. And, your client's property is strictly residential. He should not have had the animal there to begin with. For that reason I am denying the request for return of the animal, and the defendant will forfeit the hog to the City of Key West.

"Further, since the hog has shown a tendency for aggression, particularly toward technology," Judge Kyler continued, grinning and leading to another chorus of tittering orchestrated by the bailiffs, "the court feels compelled to have the animal permanently consigned to the Children's Animal Park at the Monroe County Detention Center on Stock Island. Finally to make the confinement safe for both the swine and visitors, on the advice of the city's animal control officers, the court orders that the animal be castrated to suppress any future outbreaks of passion."

Riley heard the breath rush from his friend seated next to him. When he turned to look at Chick, he saw a visage drained of all color and framed with a look of near desperation.

"Are you all right?" Riley whispered, but the ashen-faced Chick Malor continued to stare silently straight ahead.

"Mr. Branson," the judge said in the direction of the sport-coated assistant district attorney. "Will your office see to the disposition of the pig?"

"Yes, your honor," he replied. "But the surgical procedure will have to wait until after Fantasy Fest due to a lack of man power."

"That will be fine with the court," Judge Kyler concluded. "Just see that it happens as soon as possible."

"Yes, your honor."

Meanwhile, Miguel Sanchez looked to his client, shrugged as if to say one cannot win every point and began collecting his papers into his briefcase. The small knot of family members in the gallery showed obvious relief with the outcome and Mrs. Gutero had seemed especially buoyant from the instant the fate of the hog had been pronounced. One of the bailiffs now led Enrico Gutero from the courtroom, en route to shucking his county jumpsuit and reclaiming his civilian clothing.

Chick Malor still sat frozen in his apparent agony. Though Riley wanted to again ask what his problem was, he pretty much felt it would be a waste of energy, so he simply sat waiting for Chick to move. Finally, as the bailiffs called another case, Chick rose and began walking silently toward the back door of the courtroom. Riley fell in behind him striding slowly, as they cleared the room and moved down the hallway to the entrance doors. Eventually they exited into the late morning sun and Chick plodded along the concrete walk toward the street. At this point, Riley reached forward and grabbed his arm, bringing the man to a stop.

"Do you expect me to follow you all the way to Key Largo?" Riley asked. "What's going on? You act like you're going to jail."

"Man, I can't believe they're going to cut on the pig," Chick moaned. "It's just not right."

"Come on, Chick," Riley countered. "It's something that veterinarians do all the time. The pig will get over it."

Malor now froze in his tracks, spun and presented Riley with a look that suggested total disbelief.

"They're going to cut his nuts off!" Chick almost shouted, his eyes wide and desperate. "No male gets over that!"

"Is there something you're not telling me?" Riley said, in a lowered voice to try and calm his buddy.

"Yeah," Chick admitted, spinning to begin moving again. "Let's walk down to the Green Parrot. I need a drink. I'll tell you there."

Side by side the duo ambled southeast along Whitehead Street to the next intersection. All the way Chick stared blankly down at the walkway, biting on the inside of his lip. Riley kept silent as well, mulling the fact that it was not quite noon, yet they were headed to a bar for the first libation of the day. In many places it would probably have been hard to even find an open watering hole at this hour, but Key West presented no such complication. He was also mystified that Chick was displaying such a total reversal of character. Gone was any pretense of the man's usual cynicism, replaced by glum remorse. But, what it was that prompted this emotional epiphany in his friend remained unknown to Riley. In the days leading up to the trial, the idea that Chick may have had some connection to one of the people involved had come to mind, but that line of thinking had been put to rest by his outburst on the courthouse steps. It seemed his concern was centered on the fate of the hog. Had his brief association with Eric Allen awakened some latent crusader's gene in Chick? That seemed most unlikely since Chick apparently held Allen and his animal-rights work in low esteem.

In light of Chick Malor's track record and affinity for women, perhaps the situation was just what it seemed. He could not fathom the idea of any male being emasculated, regardless of its species. Still the explanation did not seem quite right to Riley.

There must be more to it. Looking down the block to the facade of the Green Parrot, Riley gave a little shrug. He would find out soon enough what was eating at his friend.

Once in the bar, they ordered a couple of Rolling Rock beers and Riley sat considering that even in the fall, the Key West humidity sent profuse beads of condensation streaming down the cold green beer bottle. Seconds ticked past as they sipped the beer. Chick's expression now suggested that he was no longer wandering a mental wasteland. His eyes had now regained their quickness and he appeared to be wrestling with a problem.

Half a beer later, Riley broke the silence.

"Well?" he asked.

"Huh," Chick said, for the first time since the courthouse actually looking at Riley.

"Are you going to tell me what's bothering you or not?"

"Yeah, it's just not something I want to talk about, but I guess I have to," Chick acknowledged, then with the most serious countenance Riley had ever seen on the man, he continued. "It's all my fault."

"What?" Riley asked, shaking his head slightly to emphasis his confusion.

"You remember out on Stock Island?" Chick put forth.

"It would be a bit hard to forget since it just killed my morning in a courthouse," Riley replied. "You think the fight was your fault?"

"And what is going to happen to the pig," Malor said dejectedly.

"Just how did you come to that conclusion?"

"When we pulled in for gas, the rest of you went into the store," Chick resumed. "While you were in there, I walked around the corner and saw the pig tied to a tree with a rope. The hog was pulling against it. It looked like it was so tight it was strangling him, so I just loosened the rope a little. The pig laid back down and looked fine when I walked off."

"You think you caused the pig to get loose?" Riley interjected.

"I must have," Chick dropped his head and returned in a miserable voice. "And now they're going to lop off his pecker because of it."

"That's not technically true," Riley offered. "Just the testicles."

Chick raised his gaze back up and squinted at Riley as though he just discovered that his friend was a complete imbecile.

"You're just full of useful facts, aren't you?"

"Sorry," was the only thing Riley could think of to say.

"It's just not right," Chick began again. "It wasn't the pig's fault. Couldn't they have just sent him to a farm?"

Though Riley kept quiet, the idea of saving the hog from castration by sending it to a farm where the animal would eventually end up as bacon struck him as ludicrous. It again also sparked his fear that

Chick was leaning toward Eric Allen's philosophy. So often the alternatives coming from such animal-rights ideas were on the surface compassionate, yet totally unsound in review. Sort of like break-ins at mink farms to release the animals and save them from becoming fur coats. Yet this pen-raised stock is so ill prepared for the natural world that instead of growing to maturity before entering the fur trade, they end up suffering a slow, premature death from starvation in the wild. Where was the compassion in that? On the other hand, this was not a point of view that he suspected Chick wanted to hear right now.

"We have got to do something," Chick concluded resolutely.

"Maybe we could just buy the hog from the city?" Riley suggested.

"And I'm sure that by the time we concluded the deal the pig would already be oinking a couple of octaves higher," Chick dismissed. "It will have to be little more direct action and done in a hurry."

Riley did not particularly like the direction that Malor's musings were taking. All of the enthusiasm that his friend had lacked after the court decision had now returned. As impetuous as Chick could be, Riley was now getting concerned as to where the man's thinking might lead. Suddenly the idea of heading back to Atlanta and trying to reconstruct a normal life once again seemed very appealing. Even if there was no job waiting at Amax — and looking for work was definitely Riley's idea of a truly tasteless task — he could still see the possibility of even more odious circumstances arising here in the tropics. He took another mouthful of the cold beer.

"Maybe you should just let it go," Riley offered. "We'll hang around and enjoy Fantasy Fest, then head back north and forget the whole thing."

"I wish it worked that way," Chick said, staring straight ahead into space for a moment, then adding, "but it would haunt me forever. Can you imagine what it would be like to have your manhood whacked off? Especially if it was somebody else's fault?"

"You're assuming a pig can reason and think such a thing through," Riley pointed out. "We're still talking about an animal here."

"Yeah, I know all that, but I still can't get over the idea that I'm dooming another creature to never again experience passion," Chick said dejectedly.

With that Riley shifted his tongue to the right side of his mouth and gently bit down on it. All he could think about was the moniker he had seen in the newspaper several times – the Passionate Pig. It seemed so illogical to him, yet it was clear that whatever Chick came up with as a plan, there would be no deterring his traveling companion from the action. But the part that was really unsettling was the knowledge that thoughts of returning home or not, Chick would so easily talk him into being a part of it. Even worse, Riley knew a part of him would cherish the scheme. Come what may, Chick Malor had definitely put adventure into Riley's formerly sedate existence.

Chapter 18

Capt. Samuelo Porticia leaned heavily on the rusty rail of the S.S. Loro, watching the widening wake of the go-fast boat approaching from the northwest. His old freighter rolled slowly in the gentle chop that ruffled the surface of the Ciacos Passage. In the distance the dim outline of the landmass of Mayaguana Island at the very southwestern end of the chain of the Bahamas was barely visible in the direction from which the small boat was approaching.

"How does it look?" Porticia asked the man standing beside him.

Still gazing through a pair of binoculars, Hector Corro replied.

"Two men in the boat. No guns showing."

"*Bueno*. They still have several miles to cover. Now, my Hector, it is time for you to visit the cabinet. Get Caesar, and the black one. Arm yourselves, but stay back out of sight. And send me the boy," Porticia said, never taking his eyes from the approaching wake.

Hector lowered the glasses smiling, turned and disappeared into a companionway. For a couple of minutes Porticia continued to watch the progress of the approaching boat. Finally he turned his gaze upward. High over the water a pair of frigate birds were circling, riding the air currents. The straight, forked tails and long pointed wings formed stark, prehistoric silhouettes against the cloudless blue backdrop.

"You look strangely at the birds, *capitan*."

The boyish voice roused Porticia from his trance and he looked down at the Miguel Assaya. The youngster's frail frame was hung with a tee shirt and loose shorts and betrayed his pre-teen age.

"It is a bad omen, Miguelito," the captain replied, "to have those bullies hovering around. They pass up no chance to steal the catch from other sea birds."

Then cutting his eyes back toward the boat speeding nearer, he added.

"And they may share that disposition with our approaching visitors. When they come along side, throw the rope down to them, and then pull up what they tie to it."

As he finished speaking, Porticia glanced back behind him. In the passageway Hector crouched, lovingly clutching a Heckler & Koch MP-5. The look of pleasure on the man's face sent shards of worry piercing through the captain's composure. Hector was all too happy when armed. In other nooks of the freighter's superstructure he saw the sailor, Caesar, to the right and a huge black frame to the left. Each of those men also held matching little submachine guns.

"Good day to you, captain," called a grinning black man standing beside the driver of the go-fast boat as if finally came alongside the tramp freighter. "If you be Captain Porticia, we have a delivery for you."

Rearing up as straight as his rotund physique allowed the Loro's master peered down at the two Bahamians.

"I am Capt. Samuelo Porticia," he called down forcefully after a pause, yet mirroring a bit of caution in the response. "What size is the delivery?"

Still grinning the black man raised a small brief case above his head. As he did, both Capt. Porticia and little Miguel Assaya clearly saw the automatic pistol protruding from the waistband of the man's trousers. From the shape of the handle, the captain's seasoned eye guessed it was a Glock 22 or perhaps 23, probably in .40 caliber.

"Very well, we will drop you down a rope on which to tie the package," Porticia instructed, motioning for Miguel to do the deed.

The boy tossed the coiled rope over the rail and it unrolled downward to the waiting men. Never relinquishing his grin, the black man tied the rope to the handle of the case, and then made a sweeping gesture to indicate it was free to rise.

"And do we get nothing for our trouble in bringing it so far out to you, captain?" the grinner shouted as Miguel hoisted the leather case up toward the deck.

Porticia eyed the man for a long moment.

"I am not your employer," he finally spat down at the boat's occupants. "I pay your boss too much for your time already. If it is money you want, ask him for it."

At that the grin faded for a moment from the black man's face. His right hand also moved slowly toward his waist.

At a signal from Porticia, Hector and the other two sailors were at the rail in an instant, the stubby barrels of their automatic weapons trained on the men below.

"And what is this, *mon*?" the black man asked, his hand now stilled and the grin again covering his face.

"It is a signal that our business is ended," Porticia said, "and it is time for you to go."

The grinning man nodded to the driver beside him and the go-fast boat came to life. As it spun to leave, the grinning black man turned his head back toward the Loro and dipped his head in a parting gesture that seemed to transmit respect for a situation well handled by the captain.

"Shall I shoot them, *mi capitan*?" Hector asked.

"No one will be shot today, Hector," he replied, watching the small boat speed away back toward the Bahamas.

"I never trust the Bahamians," the mate offered next. "It is no good dealing with them."

"It is well that we don't trust them," Porticia returned, "but necessary to use them. Once at sea you never know when the *gringo* is listening if you throw your plans to the wind on the radio. This way he cannot know what passes between us."

Once the go-fast boat was out of gunshot range the captain turned to Miguel, but spoke again to Hector.

"Now return the guns to the locker."

"*Si, capitan*," Hector said, turning to go.

From the boy the captain took the leather case and opened it. Taking out a single sheet of paper he scanned it quickly.

"It is well, *capitan*?" Miguel asked with an air of boyish innocence.

"Yes, Miguelito," the Loro's master smiled down at the youngster. "It is very well."

Capt. Samuelo Porticia now had the coordinates at which he would soon launch his own small boat off the coast of the Florida Keys.

Chapter 19

The afternoon breeze was just picking up off the Atlantic Ocean as Riley sat in the shade on Flagler Avenue. The location was far enough inland on the island so the atmospheric stirring was as yet almost imperceptible. But, the protection from the sun provided by the old carport, which now served as a patio on the side of Capt. Arnie Patranicholas' house, was enough to make the spot bearable. Around the old wicker settee on which Riley lounged were several other unmatched pieces of lawn furniture, mixed with a clutter of nautical and tropical junk of which the captain said he was sure to someday find a use. Amid this jumble was a stand topped by a birdcage.

Riley was eying the feathered creature pacing back and forth on the perch spanning the metal enclosure. At one time it had apparently been an African lovebird of the genus *Agapornis* or at least that was what the captain claimed. Riley had now been a lodger with the old mariner long enough to realize the man was prone to tell the truth only enough to keep a listener off balance and unable to simply dismiss his stories. Not being versed in ornithology, and since the question had no apparent relevance to their relationship, Riley gave Capt. Arnie the benefit of the doubt on his bird's identity.

It was for certain, in its present condition, the little parrot would need a trained eye to categorize it. Standing only about six inches high the bird lacked most of the usual green with red and yellow highlights common to its breed. In fact, it was missing a large amount of covering, sporting several completely bare spots where its grayish skin showed. Also among its missing plumage were all of the tail feathers, making it look quite tiny. Capping the bedraggled look was a dark, lifeless hole where its left eye should have been.

The fact the captain kept the bird around should have hinted to a long acquaintance that the man felt unable to relinquish. Capt. Arnie, however, had revealed that one afternoon only a couple of months earlier he found the miserable creature perched on the low cinder block fence surrounding the shell-covered space that served as his front yard. Apparently the two worn relics of the pirates' life formed an instant bond.

A few years earlier Riley had read a feature in the Sunday travel section of the Atlanta-Journal Constitution extolling the virtues of Key West as a vacation destination. He recalled the main thrusts of the journalism were that the island was becoming more family friendly, and how safe the area could be for visitors. In the process the writer pointed out that the most frequent crime on the island was the theft of bicycles and the only modern serial criminal had been a parrot-napper, who absconded with several of the brightly colored birds that had been left unattended on porches or patios. Gazing at this bird, Riley felt confident it was safe from the miscreant, even if he was still at large and terrorizing pet owners.

Riley's attention was drawn to the street out front by the high-pitched, squall of a horn. Standing, he looked out over the block wall at the street's edge to a big three-wheeled bicycle. The horn was mounted on the handlebars and had a rubber ball that the driver was squeezing to produce the bleating. Some Key Westers referred to the contraptions as pedal-cabs, while others called them rickshaws. Either way the back of the vehicle had an open compartment with a padded seat large enough to accommodate two passengers. Up front the driver sat on a regular bike seat and provided pedal power.

Commonly seen along Duval Street in the Old Town section, it was unusual for one to travel this far to the east on the island. The sight, however, did not surprise Riley, since he had summoned it a bit earlier with a phone call. From his first sighting of this mode of conveyance, he had harbored the desire to ride in one. In a few minutes he was due to meet Chick and Capt. Arnie at Captain Tony's Saloon on Greene Street between Duval and Whitehead. It seemed like a good chance to kill two birds with a single stone, so he ordered the rickshaw ride. Capt. Arnie had left to walk downtown earlier, despite Riley's offer to let him ride along in the pedal-cab. In fact, the old seafarer's exact words had been, "I'd march down Duval Street bare-assed with a mackerel sticking out of my butt, before I'd get in one of those damn things."

Riley walked out to the curb, checking his pocket to make sure he had the cash for the fare, which was not cheap. At a dollar a minute, rickshaws were tourist luxuries in Key West, not normal modes of travel. With all the traffic lights along Duval Street, it could push 30 bucks to go from one end to the other on a busy weekend. Riley had already calculated the route downtown for the most scenic value with the fewest traffic lights.

"What's shaking?" asked the cabbie when Riley reached the street.

The young man was lean, barefooted and dressed in cargo shorts and a sleeveless tee shirt, his blonde tresses long and stringy hanging down to his shoulders.

"Headed down to Captain Tony's," Riley stated. "But let's swing down Bertha and along the beach, then down Simonton. You can drop me at Front Street."

"It's your nickel, boss," the driver replied. "I can give you the usual speech with the ride, but guessing from the fact you're coming from Capt. Arnie's, you're probably not a tourist. I was pretty surprised when dispatch gave me the address."

"You know Capt. Arnie?" Riley asked, smiling slightly at the prospect of having been mistaken for a local.

"Not bosom buddies," came the answer, "but I see him around and have heard all the stories."

"No," Riley finally reacted to the earlier question, "No need for a speech. The ride will do."

With that the driver began peddling west along Flagler Avenue, past Key West High School to take a left onto Bertha Street. When he next turned back west on Atlantic Boulevard, the street's namesake ocean came into view, edged by a strand of sand, dotted with some palm trees and a few afternoon sunbathers.

During the ride down U.S. 1 in Bart Skier's truck, Riley had been taken aback by the lack of beaches along the string of islands. Since the isles are no more than chunks of ancient coral rock jutting from the ocean bed, their fringes were more likely composed of mangrove stands or bare jagged marl formations. Other than Anne's Beach on Lower Matecumbe Key, Veterans Park on Little Duck Key and at Bahia Honda State Park, he had seen nothing along the chain of isles that resembled a beach, and even those three had been poor imitations of the strands of sand found on the state's main peninsula. Some of the hotels along the way had resorted to hauling in sand to create tiny faux beaches, while the city of Key West adopted the same idea on a grander scale. Thus, Smathers and Monroe County beaches appeared on the southwestern edge of the island facing the shallow flats of the Atlantic Ocean. A further improvement was cutting a trench in the marl rock along the shore to provide water deep enough for swimming. Now staring out over the stretch known as Rest Beach, Riley had to admit it was the closest thing to a traditional beach he had seen in the Keys.

Splitting Rest Beach from the other portion of Monroe County Beach to the west stood the old

White Street Pier, jutting from the end of the cross-island thoroughfare from which its name was derived. A long, wide stretch of concrete, reaching out into the Atlantic with a couple of wings set a few steps lower and running out from each side, the pier had a couple of stories attached to it, with which Capt. Arnie had already graciously regaled the travelers several times. The main two dealt with a former mayor of Key West, Sonny McCoy. He supposedly once landed a small airplane on the structure, but more famously, it was the jump off point he used for a trip to a mayors' conference held in Havana, Cuba. In September of 1978, his honor the mayor made the journey in just over six hours on water skis, entering Havana Harbor escorted by two Cuban gunboats.

Whether the stories were true or not, Capt. Arnie's renditions of the tales served up an unmistakable hint of admiration for the renegade mayor, before ending the dissertation about the quay by rather sadly pointing out that it is now used only by fishermen and as the launch site for the town's 4th of July fireworks displays.

Completing the sweeping curve of Atlantic Boulevard along the waterfront, the pedal-cab turned inland on Reynolds Street. Quickly the balconies of the old Casa Marina Hotel reared on the left of the street, and then gave way to the front courtyard of the building, facing the corner with Seminole Street. The hotel and Overseas Railway had been the final stars in the galaxy of success forged by Henry Flagler in opening up Florida to its first tourism boom. Flagler created the railroad for that purpose and knew the visitors from northern climes would only come if they had adequate lodging. So along his rail line he strung some impressive Victorian hostels from Saint Augustine's Ponce de Leon Hotel, to the Breakers in Palm Beach and ending with the Casa Marina at the end of the line in Key West. Soon after the completion of the building and railroad, Flagler died in 1913, but almost a century later his shadow still lingers in the form of his painted visage on the front facade of the building.

After connecting to the west via South Street, the cab turned north along Simonton, heading toward the heart of Old Town, Key West Bight and Mallory Square. The farther along the street the driver pedaled, the more pedestrian traffic appeared. Already in the midst of the Fantasy Fest week activities, it was just two days prior to the main event on Saturday night, culminating in the parade down Duval Street that runs parallel and a block to the west. A scattering of walkers was already warming up for the weekend, dressed in costumes mirroring the year's theme of Fright Night on Bone Island.

Capt. Arnie had warned Riley and Chick to expect the levels of revelry and lunacy to increase as the week worn along. Each night the parties increased. First had been the Goombay Celebration centered in the Bahamas Village area, followed yesterday by the Pet Masquerade Parade and celebrity look-alike contest at the La Concha Hotel.

Tonight would be the annual Toga Party at Sloppy Joe's Bar and a costume bash at the Green Parrot. Tomorrow it was the Duval Street Fair and the Masquerade March down that thoroughfare at dusk. Then on Saturday Duval became the uncontested center of attention with the Masquerade Promenade, followed by the parade. In every instance the events were simply preludes to huge street parties that erupted all over Old Town.

Finally just short of the street's end at Key West Harbor, the cab turned left off Simonton and traveled one more block along Front Street before stopping at the intersection with Duval. Riley stepped down, paid the fare and watched the pedal-cab turn up Duval, looking for more riders. He then gazed diagonally across the intersection at the brick building now housing the First Union Bank. According to Capt. Arnie the structure's previous incarnations had also centered on the banking business and it had been the model for the bank robbery scene in Chapter 18 of Ernest Hemingway's novel "To Have or Have Not." As Riley stared it occurred to him that almost everything he knew about the town had been courtesy of the old commercial fisherman. For a moment he considered how much of that history might actually be true.

Still standing on the corner, Riley was alerted to a change. Often, though a person's senses may register everything going on around them, it is as though the brain is only informed of significant changes, rather than being bogged down with every aroma, touch or sound encountered. Thus it was that Riley suddenly realized that the sound of a conga drum and chanting that had been emerging from a knot of tourists across the street at the bank building had ceased, followed by what sounded more like an argument. Like a moth lured by a bug zapper, he jaywalked through the intersection toward the commotion.

Nearing the scene, the circle of bystanders parted to reveal the familiar sight of R&B Mann, dressed in his signature dark slacks, dress shirt and tie, with guitar in hand. The blues man was toe-to-toe and nose-to-nose with the Rasta man with flowing dreadlocks. Surrounding them on the sidewalk was a conga drum, a guitar case and R&B's battered valise.

"*Mon*, time to move along," the Rasta man hissed at R&B. "You be bad for the business."

"Just a brother trying to help out and make you a dime," R&B countered.

"No brother of mine ever make such a howl," Rasta man replied, while cutting his eyes to the thinning circle of onlookers. "You move now *mon* or I be moving you."

With that R&B indignantly gathered his gear and turning, came face to face with Riley.

"Still tough to find a gig?" Riley greeted.

"Hey man, good to see you," R&B lit up, and then scowled back in the direction of the Rasta man. "He must be afraid I'd get all his tips. Just stopped to add a bit of soul to his drumming. Wasn't even going to put my tip hat out. Island trash probably sneaked ashore anyway."

"What are you doing back on the street?" Riley asked.

"We just got here yesterday," R&B explained, slipping easily into his street jive persona. "Spent over a week berthed up at the Ocean Reef Club on Key Largo watching Feldman hitting on the captain and trying to impress the other rich folks. Got so I had all of him I could take. Hated to jump ship and leave Capt. Carla in a bind, but a man can only take so much. Besides it was time to get back to the street and my music."

"How's the captain doing?" Riley delivered his next inquired in rather guarded manner.

"Rolls with the punches," Mann said. "Don't see how she puts up with that ass though. Whatever he pays her to run his boat can't be worth it."

"Well, great to have you back among the living," Riley offered. "If you got nothing else to do, I'm headed down to Capt. Tony's. Chick's there and he'll be glad to see you."

"Got nothing else on my dance card at the moment," the black man smiled as Riley grabbed the valise and they headed up Duval Street.

As they walked Riley recounted the tale of his and Chick's entire sojourn in the Florida Keys. Shortly they had turned onto Greene Street and were crossing toward Capt. Tony's Saloon.

"So exactly what is it that you're meeting about in this bar?" R&B asked.

"Beats me," Riley confessed. "Obviously has something to do with the pig and the fight, but who can guess what Chick's got on his mind? We'll know soon enough. Fact is this will be new to me too. Since we got here I haven't been into Capt. Tony's."

The two-story building they were approaching was painted yellow, with one-level wings jutting from either side. The front sported a sign topped with a huge carved grouper hanging over the main doorway. The bottom of the sign noted that the drinking establishment was the original site of Sloppy Joe's. Two other white signs lettered in black decorated the facade as well. One scrawled banner-like across the building's width, while the smaller one was to the right of the doorways. Both bore the establishments name and the epitaph proclaiming it the oldest bar in Florida. That smaller sign also displayed a drawing of an aged, world-weary man that Riley assumed must be Capt. Tony. The final, hard to miss feature of the bar was a rather large tree sticking up through the roof in the left wing of the structure.

Besides the double doors at the center of the building, another set of doors was on the left wing. Both sets stood wide open, leading into the dimly lit recesses of the bar. The duo passed through the left hand entrance toward the tree. To the left along the wall was a counter displaying Capt. Tony's merchandise and memorabilia for sale. To the other side a horseshoe-shaped bar extended two-thirds of the way back through the room, with its near ends anchored to the front wall between the sets of doors. At the back of the cavern-like area was a small bandstand, while a waist-high railing beyond the bar partitioned off another room to the right that held a couple of pool tables.

For a moment Riley and R&B stood adjusting their eyes to the semi-darkness, inspecting the dingy walls and ceiling, which were thickly covered with tacked-on yellowing business cards or old auto license plates. Interspersed with the clutter were a few bras hanging from the ceiling as well. Along the bar were plain wooden stools, but the seat of each one had a name inscribed upon it, with virtually all those monikers visible since early afternoon patrons were scarce. Riley scanned down the empty row of stools, seeing Bob Dylan, Eric Clapton, Jimmy Buffet, plus several movie stars' names.

"Arbie! I can't believe it!" Chick shouted from near the back end of the bar, where he was seated next to Capt. Arnie. "Get yourself back here, man."

R&B flashed a smile, obviously happy to get a friendly welcome and the pair strode back to join Chick and the captain. After introductions and ordering a new round of beer, Chick quizzed R&B with virtually the same questions Riley had earlier posed, while breaking in to offer some explanatory notes of his own in Capt. Arnie's direction. To each of those the old seafarer nodded knowingly, though Riley was not sure the man was really paying any attention to the conversation. He seemed to be absorbed in thought, wrestling with a problem or idea that he could neither solve nor turn loose.

"Man, this is one funky bar," R&B observed, looking around once Chick had gotten up to date on the blues man's journey down. "Guess it has some history with it?"

"And you have the man present to recount it," Chick winked in the captain's direction and used his elbow to nudge the older man's arm.

At the touch, Capt. Arnie revived from his pondering.

"Damn right, I know all about this place and the imposter that owns it," Capt. Arnie assured in a surly voice.

"Capt. Tony Terracino is not one of the Cap's favorite people," Chick added with a grin in R&B's direction. "Seems they are too much alike. Plenty of smuggling and shady dealing in both their backgrounds, though I can say in Capt. Arnie's defense that at least he has never sank so low as to get into politics."

"What?" Riley asked.

"The bar owner, Capt. Tony, was once elected mayor of Key West," Chick said. "Which tells you the town can't be all bad, if they've got the good sense to elect a bartender to lead them."

"Nothing but a wannabe," Capt. Arnie snapped. "He'll come wandering in here telling everyone stories that he stole from me 30 years ago. Course, the difference is I actually lived through them."

"Why don't you tell Arbie about the bar," Chick changed the subject, nodding knowingly and rolling his eyes in Riley's direction.

With that the old man launched into a rambling history of the watering hole, touching all the high points dating back to the 1850s. Besides its stints as a bar, the building had served as an icehouse and the city's first morgue. Capt. Arnie pointed out that the tree in the back of the room was left there because it was the city's original hanging tree and 75 black hearts had met their fates over the years dangling from its limbs. During that portion of the tale, Riley noticed the uneasy look in R&B's eyes as he inspected the trunk rising up from the floor.

"Don't make for very good karma," R&B muttered, still staring at the tree.

"You're not going to go New Age on us again, are you," Chick asked.

"Ain't New Age," the blues man glared at Chick, as he now fully reverted to his street persona. "Just never liked messing with the dead. This is the kind of place that don't turn loose of them."

"Nor do they turn loose of it," Capt. Arnie injected. "There's one old biddy that killed her whole family and was hung from the tree. Number of folks have seen her at this end of the bar sitting on a stool in a nightgown. Happens pretty regular."

"Come on, Cap?" Chick said, but looking at R&B who grew more restless with Capt. Arnie's last statement. "The freak show that regularly passes through here? The ghosts of Black Caesar and his pirate crew could walk through the door and not seem out of place, let alone a woman showing up here in a nightgown."

The old man rested a hard stare on Chick, his face blank, but Riley felt that it was still registering disdain at Chick's light-hearted disregard for the tale. He also thought that R&B was about to bolt for the door.

"So what it is you wanted us here for?" Riley tossed out to change the mood.

"Not quite yet," Chick answered, looking toward the door. "We're still waiting on one more."

"Who's that," Riley asked.

"You'll see, but let's move away from the bar," Chick replied, the final part delivered with a conspiratorial cut to the eyes toward the two bartenders at work half way down the bar.

With that Chick rose and led the group around the end of the horseshoe then back toward the front. As they went, Riley realized that there was a small sunken room down at basement level on this side of the bar. It was like an open pit with stairs at each end leading down to a pool table. Once past the pit, the wall forming the front of that sunken space and separating it from the front entrance revealed itself as actually a chimney with the fireplace facing the opposite way toward the open doors. Perpendicular and on either side of the hearth were rough wooden backless benches. Between them was a low table made of what appeared to be an old, thick wooden hatch from a boat. The men filed onto the benches on either side of the table.

"Aye, this is better," Capt. Arnie scowled at Chick, apparently not turning loose of the perceived skepticism regarding the apparition. "Only one can hear us here is young Elvira."

"Who?" Riley asked,

The captain, who was seated beside Chick with their backs to the bar and facing the main poolroom that was separated by the wooden rail running behind R&B and Riley, motioned for them to look down through that railing.

"Elvira, the coroner's daughter," the old man said matter-of-factly. "When she died he buried her beneath the morgue floor, and there she lies today."

Riley sensed R&B going stiff beside him on the bench as they both twisted to look down through the slats of the railing at the floor of the poolroom. Just below and behind them was a slab set in the floor.

ELVIRA
Daughter Of
Joseph & Susannah
EDMONDS
Died Dec. 21
1822
Aged 19 YRS
8 MS & 21 DS

"Sweet Jesus," R&B moaned lowly. "Is there really a dead body under that?"

"They don't bury live ones," Capt. Arnie replied with a wry smile. "Don't worry, son. She's not known to join the murderess at the bar."

As the old fisherman added the last phrase he cut his eyes disapprovingly at Chick, who returned a sheepish, rather apologetic dip of his head in acknowledgment.

"Gives me the willies," R&B said.

"Having another New Orleans flash back, are we," Chick jibed.

"Not good to make light of the dead," R&B tossed back seriously. "This ain't a place for a grave. Just inviting her spirit to roam around in here."

As he delivered the last part of the statement, R&B's eyes were sweeping over the memorabilia cluttering the ceiling and support posts of the bar, as though he were trying to catch the disembodied spirit of the coroner's daughter hiding in the cups of one of the faded brassieres dangling by their straps.

"Enough of this," Capt. Arnie announced, and then demanded of Chick, "Whatever we're here for, get on with it."

"Need to wait a few more minutes, Cap," he answered. "Still waiting for one more. But it is good Arbie made such a timely entrance. We can probably use some more help.

"There he is now," Chick added raising a hand to wave toward the door.

The group turned their collective gaze toward the double doors at the front on the near side of the bar. Stepping across the threshold, dressed in khaki pants, oxford shirt and sporting a button emblazoned with STAG in red was the bespectacled visage of Eric Allen.

Chapter 20

As the moving van emblazoned with the logo Cheap Trucks on its side plodded along the last dozen miles on the southern end of the Florida's Turnpike, the flat terrain on either side composed a vista of mixed tract housing and agricultural fields. The boxy, single-story houses stood shoulder to shoulder, glistening in the late afternoon sun from which they found no refuge in their treeless neighborhoods. Abutting the residential developments, however, were open fields of truck farms, crossed by precise lines of planted produce. Moving slowly through some of these fields were tractors towing trailers adorned with plastic tanks of liquid fertilizer that was being sprayed onto the plants and the grayish, sandy soil.

Interspersed in this checkerboard landscape were thick stands of palm trees, too perfectly aligned to be natural growth. Each such field with its thicket of fronds was also composed of trees that were all exactly the same height. Invariably, somewhere along the perimeter of the palm ranks was a small billboard identifying the landscape company to which the trees belonged.

Eddie Crawford barely noticed this panorama where the southern edge of Miami's expanding suburbs blended into the city of Homestead. After a five-hour drive down I-95 that culminated in a turn onto the West Dade Expressway to connect to the turnpike and avoid Miami's traffic, his only concern now was reaching his hotel.

"Damn!" Crawford muttered, as a red, convertible Mitsubishi Eclipse ripped past the truck, and then swerved into the lane in front of him. "Ass hole must be doing 85. No wonder you never see just a fender bender in this town.

"Would be a shame if she tore up the car and herself, though," he reappraised, following the progress of the car and the blonde hair fluttering in the wind as it shrank into the distance ahead.

"Be nice if she was staying at the same place," he smiled, still speaking aloud, though alone in the cab of the truck.

"Probably fat or got a face like a horse," he conceded to himself, "but it wouldn't matter tonight and I still got another day to waste."

At that he glanced self-consciously at the cars around him, as though they might have inklings that boredom and fatigue from his long drive had him giddily conversing aloud with himself.

Finally passing the last sign identifying the double ribbon of concrete as the Ronald Reagan Turnpike, the truck began the sweeping turn to the east and over a slight man-made hill to then drop down and meld into U.S. Highway 1 at Florida City.

"No wonder everybody looks lost down here," he mused, looking at the sign. "Can't make up their mind what they want to call the road."

After inching through a couple of cycling traffic lights and intersections, Crawford turned left across the on-coming lanes, steering into the parking lot of a chain motel. Immediately his eyes locked on the red convertible sitting beneath the covered portion of the drive in front of the office.

"Maybe this is my lucky day?"

In the dimly lit room within the bowels of the USCGC Sapelo a sailor leaned forward, outlined by the fluorescence emanating from the monitor before him. The man's eyes were glued to one of the several images on the screen that were glowing against a black backdrop. Each image had some identifying lettering and Global Positioning System coordinates beneath them. The one absorbing the operator's attention was marked with S.S. Loro and that vessel's position. Signals were being emitted by the Coast Guard cutter's radar that reached over the horizon to find the old and slow cargo craft, while other transmissions were bouncing off satellites hundreds of mile above and returning to the Sapelo. The cutter's array of computers then crunched the combined data to instantaneously tell the sailor exactly where on earth both his own ship and the Loro were located.

"Still on course, Matson?" the muffled voice of Chief Foster Bork drifted out of the gloom of the room.

"North by northwest 310 degrees, but she has slowed to only 6 knots," the sailor replied, also speaking in a low tone, as if afraid the quarry might hear him. "Sort of like she's biding her time. Thirty-five miles off the starboard bow."

"Keep a close eye on her and make sure we know of any course corrections," Bork said, opening the hatch to exit.

"Aye, Aye, Chief," the radar man replied without looking away from the monitor.

A few steps down the passageway and Bork cleared another hatch onto the aft deck of vessel. To the starboard the sun was sinking low on the horizon, preparing its daily show for the tourists back at the Sapelo's home base in Key West. The chief paced over to the rail and peered to the northwest at the unseen vessel they were shadowing.

"Still out there, Chief?"

Bork stiffened ramrod straight at the sound of Lieutenant Matthew Jackson's voice.

"Sorry, sir," he offered. "Didn't realize you were on deck,"

"That's fine, chief," the Sapelo's captain said, raising his hand to the brim of his cap to acknowledge the chief's salute.

"She's still there, sir," Bork offered. "Same course, but slowing. Any chance she knows we're trailing her?"

"Your guess would be as good as mine on that, chief," the officer replied. "Even if she knows we're here I think we're far enough off to keep from appearing too interested. She doesn't seem to have made any visual contacts and I would imagine that Group is monitoring radio transmissions. They'd let us know if someone has given us up that way. Still, between small boats and air traffic, they could have some low tech signals they pass along."

"In which case, she would probably be steaming north or doubling back," the chief mused. "Slowing down makes me think they're synchronizing their timing with a pick up boat."

"Very well could be right about that, Chief," the captain said, running a hand across his chin, then continuing on to rub the back of his neck. "The intel we got on the Loro and its master says they are not on a pleasure cruise. This Capt. Porticia has been boarded before and never caught with any contraband. But if he's up to something this time, we'll be on him like feathers on a duck."

"Guess we'll find out soon enough, captain," Chief Bork replied.

"Looks pretty good to me, Mike," Mac Garland said, standing in the recess of the warehouse on Caroline Street. "Are the rails good and sturdy?"

"It's not a real corral, if that's what you mean," replied the carpenter. "But we can get everybody on the trailer and unless they all suddenly fall against one side, those rails will hold them in. Yeah, it would pass D.O.T. inspection."

"Who'll be driving the truck to pull it?"

"That'd be me," Mike quickly pointed out, provoking an amused look from Garland. "It's my truck, so I'll drive."

"You know, Mike," Garland observed. "You may be out of the closet, but why do I get the feeling you're not overly fond of consorting it public with your peers?"

Mike nodded across the cramped warehouse floor to two men approaching around the flatbed trailer.

"You can look at those two and seriously ask why I'd rather keep a low profile?" he replied.

One of the approaching pair consisted of a figure dressed in boots, leather chaps over a pair of thong bikini briefs, a faux cowhide vest with no shirt and the outfit was topped by a cherry red cowboy hat with white trim around its edge. His companion was adorned in moccasins with red and white feather anklets, a loincloth that hung over a thong and nothing above the waist but a headdress of more red and white feathers.

"What do you think?" the cowboy asked.

"I see your point," Mac Garland said to Mike, then replied to the approaching cowboy, "Quite macho, Bernard, and with a bit of war paint Tom could look fierce."

"Don't you think the hat is outrageous?" Bernard said, and then pirouetted. "And these chaps are so cheeky! I originally thought of having all the bass section be the cowhands, but I just had to wear the chaps."

Mike just rolled his eyes.

"I trust you two have already rustled up the beads," Mac asked, chuckling along with Bernard and Tom at his own play on words.

"Boxes and boxes of them," Tom, the Indian, said. "Red and white to match the color theme."

"Then I guess we have all the bases covered for Saturday night," Garland concluded. "The float, costumes, beads and Quinton and I have the spot picked out and the wood stashed for the bonfire afterward out on Boca Chita Beach."

"Yeah," Mike smirked, "nothing left to do until Saturday when we don our gay apparel and get the party underway."

Chapter 21

"What the hell is he doing here?" Capt. Arnie snarled when he realized that Chick was waving Eric Allen over to the group.

"Relax, Cap," Chick said soothingly. "I'm afraid we're going to need him for this little caper."

"Who's he?" R&B asked in a low tone, while giving Riley a bewildered look.

"I've been led to believe he's an overbearing prick," Riley replied, all the while directing a wry smile at the approaching man, "and I suspect we're about to find out if that's true."

"Gentleman," Allen greeted the group solemnly with a nod, then spoke directly to Chick. "I'll not be having a drink and we need to get right to business. I have a newsletter to get out this evening."

Capt. Arnie glared so intently and savagely at the young man that it reminded Riley of a focused beam of sunlight through a magnifying glass. He almost expected Allen to suddenly ignite into flames from the withering heat of the gaze. Riley knew, however, it was par for the course with the old seafarer. He made his judgments of character quickly and often from second-hand information, yet was reluctant to give them up once formed. It was obvious Chick's description and Eric Allen's passion for his chosen crusade had already molded an impression that created a chasm between Allen and the captain.

"Well at least sit down while we lay out a plan," Chick said, exhibiting a bit of irritation. "Just remember we're saving one of your animal brethren."

"A plan for what?" Riley blurted, as Capt. Arnie continued to glare at Allen, and R&B scooted back from the table slightly, as if to get out of the way of imminent danger.

"Your friends don't seem like they want me here," Allen said glumly, glancing around the table.

Chick rolled his eyes in exasperation before answering.

"Look, will you just sit down," he said to Allen. "No, we're not a happy family here, but we need to just skip over any differences for the next day or so and then we can part company after a job well done."

"By damn," Capt. Arnie snapped at Chick, "just what the devil is this all about?"

Then he turned his gaze back to Allen and smiled evilly.

"And will it mean that our new friend will be boarding my boat?"

"Pardon me for asking," R&B broke into the conversation. "But I got no idea what's going on here. Does somebody want to do a little explaining?"

Eric Allen stared across the table and into space, while Capt. Arnie slouched backward onto his bench and Riley cast a questioning look to Chick. Riley could not decide if Chick looked more like a felon caught in a lie by interrogators or a teenager confronted by parents when slipping in after curfew.

Either way, it was obvious he would prefer to talk about his "plan" rather than the circumstances that made it necessary. A long pause ensued, with no one seemingly willing to break the silence. Finally, Chick took a long drag on his beer.

"I guess everyone here except Arbie knows about the pig," Malor eventually stated.

"Riley told me the basics on the way up here," R&B offered.

"Well, that's a start," Chick began again. "But what he may or may not have told you is that they're going to cut the pigs nuts off to keep him from menacing society in the future, and it's all my fault."

At this pronouncement, Capt. Arnie turned a studious eye on his younger protégé, as if trying to ferret out some hidden meaning to this confession. R&B also looked at Chick blankly, waiting for more of an explanation. As for Eric Allen, his stony gaze continued to wash over the far wall.

"You might as well go ahead and explain it," Riley said. "Tell them what it was we didn't see out on Stock Island."

"Yeah," Chick admitted with his eyes cast down. "When the rest of them went in the store, I walked around back. The pig looked miserable tied to a tree back there, pulling on the rope and making it tighter around his neck. I just felt sorry for the hog and loosened it a little before going in. Next thing I knew, everyone was headed out the door to watch the Cuban and biker slug it out in the parking lot."

At the end of the confession the group sat silent, each one seeming to contemplate how to react to the tale.

"Which explains why you were so interested in the news stories and the trial," Riley help out.

"It wasn't the animals fault," Chick muttered, looking up at his friend.

"It never is," Eric Allen stated with authority, but no compassion for Chick. "Humans inflict more pain in a year on animals than all the misery in 200 years of slavery and the Holocaust combined. Do you know how many pigs are slaughter every day?"

At that proclamation R&B looked at Allen with narrowed eyes and his nose wrinkled up as though a foul odor was escaping from the young man.

"You comparing my people to a chunk of bacon?" he hissed in Allen's direction.

"No offence intended," Allen returned, but unapologetically, "animal cruelty knows no color or racial boundaries."

"Belie me," Capt. Arnie piped up with an incongruous lilt to his voice. "Chick, my young mate, you have touched me."

Then turning to look at Eric Allen, he added.

"Whatever your plan may be, I'd be much pleasured if it includes me and my old scow in some way being of aid in transporting this entire crew."

The old man's bland delivery of the final portion of his statement was free of menace, but the fisherman's cold monotone presented itself like the stellar abyss of a black hole, offering to suck life and light from its surroundings. Barely perceptible, Eric Allen shuddered, and Riley Bright thought that perhaps the worst of the tales he had heard of the captain could actually be true.

"I appreciate that, Cap," Chick said, trying to regain control of the situation. "I can use your help and your boat, but we won't all have to be aboard."

"*Que lastima*!" the seaman said with a smile and raised eyebrow directed at Eric Allen, then turning his attention back to Chick, "So why don't you just tell us what you have in mind."

"I guess if you cut to the chase," Chick offered, "we need to plan a jail break."

"A what?" R&B said.

"Well, it probably doesn't actually qualify as a jail break," Chick corrected. "We just need to steal the pig from the petting zoo out at the county stockade. Next week is when they're going to cut him up, so we have to act fast."

"Exactly how fast?" was Riley's question.

"How about Saturday night," Chick answered, cutting his eyes to each of the conspirators, apparently trying to gauge their reactions.

"During the height of Fantasy Fest?" Riley stated to no one in particular.

"What're we going to do with the critter once we got it?" R&B asked.

"Arbie," Chick said, "I'm glad you're taking an interest. Since you're the late-comer to this drama, I was afraid you wouldn't want any part of it."

"Hey, you ever heard of a blues man that stayed on the right side of the law?" R&B said with a smirk. "Just a way of paying my dues. But, I still want to know what happens once we spring the hog."

"That's where Eric comes in," Chick said, looking over at Allen with raised eyebrows, encouraging him to supply his own explanation.

"I have a truck arranged that'll transport the swine up to Highlands County. There's a farmer up there who has helped out STAG with rescued animals before."

"STAG?" R&B said.

"Stop The Animal Gulag," Allen replied matter-of-factly. "An international foundation dedicated to protecting and gaining rights for all sensate beings on the earth."

"What kind of beings?" Capt. Arnie asked with the insincere smile still painted on his face.

"Any creature capable of sensing its surroundings," Allen replied, only cutting his eyes slightly in the seafarer's direction to avoid making eye contact. "They feel pain and suffer just like humans, but don't have the law or capacity to defend themselves."

The captain narrowed his eyes into a squint as he continued to gaze at Allen, who shifted nervously in his seat.

"So we are going to just walk in to this zoo, take the pig and put it in the truck?" Riley asked incredulously.

"There'll need to be a bit more to it than that," Chick conceded. "I've thought out a plan that should work and keep us all out of trouble."

"Glad to hear it," Riley said, betraying a bit of concern.

"It's probably not a good idea to have the truck anywhere near the jail," Chick explained. "All the local police are going to be in town on the streets during Fantasy Fest, but the Florida State Patrol covers the stretch of U.S. 1 pretty heavily from Stock Island out to Boca Chita. Probably figuring that with the kind of partying going on in Key West some of the revelers are going to try driving drunk up the Keys afterwards.

"That's where Cap's boat comes in," Chick continued. "After we've got the pig, we take it the opposite direction down to Mallory Dock, put it on the boat and run it up to Boca Chita Beach. From there the road runs across to Geiger Key and hits the highway on Big Coppitt. That's well west of where the state patrol will be monitoring. Eric can meet us out on the beach, where we off-load from the boat to the truck."

Chick delivered the final portion of the explanation with a rather wide-eyed hopeful expression that Riley thought betrayed more uncertainty than confidence. Glancing around the table he suspected that Eric Allen was the sole member of the conspiracy that had heard any of the plan beforehand. The icy stare that Capt. Arnie now turned from Allen to Chick Malor seemed proof of that suspicion.

"So I'm to take this pig for a bit of a sea voyage," Capt. Arnie scowled, but then lightened up as he looked over at Eric Allen again. "At least it's the lesser of the evils."

"Are you sure this man can be trusted to deliver the animal?" Allen blurted suddenly in Chick's direction. "How do we know he won't cut it up for fish bait or barbecue it?"

"You damn prissy lubber," Capt. Arnie snarled, leaning forward.

"Excuse me," R&B offered, getting up. "Think I'll see if I can borrow a razor on the way to the john, so I'll be ready when this fight starts."

Riley snickered at the comment, despite the potential for actual fisticuffs. The captain, in fact, reminded him of a yard rooster about to pounce on an adversary.

"Calm down, both of you," Chick implored, then said to Allen. "You can trust the captain's word, period. Now do you want to make your political statement by saving the pig or not?"

Allen sat ramrod straight staring between Chick and the captain.

"Just tell me where to have the truck," he finally said, then looked at Capt. Arnie. "And make sure the animal arrives."

With that the young man stood up.

"The rest of your plans don't concern me and I have work to finish," he said. "Just provide me with the location and the time."

He then headed for the door, Capt. Arnie staring after him.

"By God, given my druthers, he'd be the one to get castrated," the fisherman spat the words in the slipstream of the departing man. "Don't need him procreating any more of his ilk."

"I know he's a pain in the ass, Cap," Chick said, "but he's also a necessary evil."

As Allen exited the bar, R&B rejoined the group.

"What happened to your pig lover," he asked, but before getting an answer added. "I thought I'd run into every kind of fool out on the streets, but he was one I missed."

"Yeah, sorry about that Arbie," Chick apologized.

"You want to tell the rest of us how we figure in this?" Riley asked.

Chick ran his left hand through his mop of blonde hair and smiled at his friend. "I'm hoping that you'll go with me out to the jail and help me with this dirty deed."

"And what then?" Riley prompted.

"We take the pig down to Mallory dock to meet Capt. Arnie."

"So you plan to just walk a stolen pig all the way across the island on the busiest evening of the year and no one will notice?" Riley complained.

"You obviously never been here during Fantasy Fest," Capt. Arnie offered with a snort. "I could walk Hillary Clinton naked on a leash down Duval Street Saturday night and no one would notice. Oh, the damn fool tourists would take a lot of pictures, but it'd just be business as usual. There ain't nothing that surprises people during that night. You'll just look like part of the craziness."

"Exactly what I'm counting on," Chick chimed in. "We'll take a mask or something and strap it on the pig and just blend into the background. I'm even thinking of maybe getting on the Bone Island Shuttle bus to get to the dock. We can wrap the animal up, pay the fare and the driver will probably just think it's a drunk friend of ours."

Riley could just shake his head pitifully in reaction to the plan, all the while feeling it was a disaster waiting to happen, but still suspecting that Chick would go ahead with it regardless of any protest he made.

"What about me?" R&B said. "Where's a blues man fit in this picture?"

"Yeah, Arbie?" Chick said, biting his lip and pondering the late edition to the crew. "Haven't got the details ironed out, but we can use you for back up in Old Town. Sort of scouting and running interference as needed — won't hurt to have some eyes down there ahead of us watching for problems."

After a moment of silent thought Chick added.

"You can set up early, sing a few songs and be the street musician you are. But, all the while keeping an eye out for potential trouble. We can get some cell phones from our belligerent animal hugger and use them to keep in touch. We'll be state of the art pig-nappers," he grinned. "We can get one for you too, Cap. That'll keep us off your radio, which I'm guessing can be monitored."

"Aye," the old man agreed. "Having the Coast Guard and DEA listening in has come close to ruining me before."

"So, what do you think Arbie; you too Riley? Is this something we can do?" Chick concluded.

"Piece of cake," R&B grinned.

But Riley was slower to respond.

"Chick, is this really something we should be doing?" he finally said. "This thing with the pig was not your fault. It was just coincidence and bad timing. Besides, the hog is slated for an easy existence in the zoo. He won't be the first boar to be neutered."

"I can't let it happen," Chick responded. "I just can't."

Riley threw his head back and exhaled a long audible breath between his lips.

"We're all complete idiots," he said, "but I'm in."

"Then it's settled," Chick said with finality. "We'll scout the route tomorrow, plan and time everything, coordinate everyone and then be ready on Saturday. What do you say we drink to our escapade with another round of beers?"

With that Chick rose and moved to the bar to place the order.

"What are we getting into?" Riley asked rhetorically.

"Pretty much in the pork business," R&B jibed.

"Be damned if I ever thought I'd be ferrying contraband hogs," Capt. Arnie observed. "I've smuggled people, guns and grass, but it'll be my first time with livestock."

Chick returned with the long-necked bottles of Corona and passed them around. Taking his seat, he raised his beer.

"To the Cerdo Grande Conspiracy," he toasted with a grin, as the others raised and clinked their bottles together.

Chapter 22

It was just after noon when Chick, Riley and R&B set out for Old Town. The morning was starting so late because the final toast to their coming venture had actually been only a prelude to a long night of bar hopping, as the group had given R&B a taste of the island after dark. From Capt. Tony's they had walked through a maze of narrow streets lined with conch houses to end up in a residential area at Catherine and Margaret streets. There on the corner one of the houses bore a sign identifying it as El Siboney. The family-owned Cuban restaurant proved every bit as good as Capt. Arnie had promised, as they downed roast pork dishes with black beans and rice.

Later the crew dropped in at the Bull and Whistle, the Hogs Breath Saloon, Rick's, Margaritaville and even a brief walk through Sloppy Joe's, though Capt. Arnie was adamant that he would wait outside at the last three. Apparently the places were so "touristy" that he had sworn never to set foot inside them again. He made it clear that he was especially disgusted that Sloppy Joe's had taken that turn over the years. In his view it had at one time been a respectable watering hole that had sold its soul to the Chamber of Commerce. The final stop of the night had been at the Green Parrot.

In the heat of the early afternoon, the previous evening's revelry was hanging heavy on the trio as they turned onto Duval Street, heading toward Mallory Square. Easing along in front of the old

Strand Theater's lavishly ornate baby blue and white facade and its new life as the Ripley's Believe It or Not Museum, the foot traffic was heavy along the sidewalk and all headed in the same direction. Soon the barricades on Duval were in view, where the thoroughfare was closed to vehicles for one more of Fantasy Fest's many personae - the Duval Street Fair. Street vendors and performers lined the pavement beyond the barricade, hawking their wares or talents, as the crowd milled about in a dress rehearsal for the next day's festivities. Costumes were almost as evident as they would be on Saturday evening, but were a shade less risqué.

    Later at dusk the Masquerade Promenade would take place down the street, mirroring the Saturday night parade minus its elaborate floats. It was another chance for the revelers to show off their costumes, adding a bit more spice to them in the fading light, thus honing interest in just how far these librarians from the Midwest and Junior Leaguers from the Piedmont South were prepared to go to expose themselves on the final night of debauchery.

    Riley glanced over to Chick occasionally as they moved down the street, weaving through the crowd. His friends eyes were darting about, obviously studying the scene, much like a general surveying the terrain where he expected his army to do battle. It was a studiousness that seemed so out of character for the devil-may-care Chick Malor. Yet, there had been little about Chick that seemed normal since the fracas out on Stock Island.

R&B on the other hand was lost in the sensory tropical *calaloo* that swirled about them. His eyes were darting from homemade, spur-of-the-moment costumes designed to press the envelope of decorum, baring as much as was allowed during daylight. Other eye catchers, however, were outfits that had been invested with a great deal of planning — lavish spectacles of feathers and shimmering materials reminiscent of Carnival in Rio. As often as not those gala affairs adorned men, reinforcing Riley's impression that the gay community particularly embraced the festivities.

"Will you look at that?" R&B said, probably louder than he meant.

Just ahead of the men a couple was walking the same way down Duval, the man dressed inconspicuously in shorts and tee shirt. At his side was a woman dressed in a thong bikini outfit, made entirely of a rainbow of colored gem clips. Riley scrutinized the woman's derriere, but quickly chastised himself for taking such a technical view. He was thinking of the mechanics of how she got a lining in the thing. Of course, that was assuming there was a lining. Almost together, he and R&B increased their speed to get in front of the couple. Chick, still absorbed in his scouting, matched their pace, but seemed oblivious to the focus of his friends' attention.

As the group passed the woman, Riley and R&B both cut their eyes to the more private portions of her physique. But, not wanting to be too obvious,

Riley just as quickly retrained his eyes back to the street ahead. His quick glance resolved none of the mystery. Though there were no blatant signs of complete nudity beneath the office supplies, he could not swear whether there was a lining or not. Maybe some flesh colored material, but he could not be sure. There had not been any in the back, of that he was sure. He turned to look over his shoulder, chancing one more glimpse to resolve the mystery. This time he peered at her chest, figuring the areolas of her nipples might give away the answer. In swiveling his head, he noted that R&B was also turning his head and Chick was still lost in his thoughts.

With a sudden thud, Riley came to a halt, having walked solidly into someone on the street ahead of him. Momentarily stunned, a wave of embarrassment swept over him, as though he had been caught peeping through a keyhole at the woman undressing.

"I'm sorry," he began to stammer an apology even before looking up, feeling sure that the glare of the sun was highlighting the hue that he knew was spreading over his face, creating a veritable blaze of red.

"I can't believe it," a female voice cut Riley off in mid-sentence.

"Capt. Carla!" R&B acknowledged, as Chick quickly emerged from his trance, snapping his attention to the woman.

"Wasn't watching where I was going," Riley smiled sheepishly, hoping she did not know what had distracted him.

"That's OK," she replied. "I'm glad to see you boys. To tell the truth, I was hoping I'd run into you."

At that moment, it registered on Riley that this was the first time he had seen Carla Mays out of her sailing uniform. Rather she was dressed in shorts and a ribbed top that accentuated the lines of her torso.

"So what are you up to?" Chick asked, making eye contact with the woman. "And where is the Squire?"

"I'm taking in the sites," she began, "and I don't know or care where that obnoxious old prick may be."

All three men reacted with slight signs of surprise at the woman's description of her employer, of whom she was always quite careful in choosing her words.

"We have finally parted company," she clarified, aware of the looks her comment had elicited.

"You mean you finally quit," Riley asked.

"Yesterday," she admitted.

"What new frontier did the Squire cross to prompt that?" Chick grinned.

"Nothing really new," she said, then turned her gaze to R&B. "It was more the blues man's fault."

"Me?" R&B said. "Don't recall having done any such thing, but can't say that I am sorry to get the credit."

"One more good deed added to Arbie's account," Chick agreed.

"It was a song you were singing out on deck your last day aboard. Something about a devil dog, I think. Anyway, part of it kept running through my mind."

At that R&B broke into an a cappella street performance that turned heads in the passing crowd, along with provoking winces on a few faces. The song was *Hell Hound On My Trail.*

"Yeah, that's the one," Carla smiled at R&B. "It really had nothing to do with my situation, but every time I looked at Feldman, I thought of him as that hell hound nipping at my heels. I know it was just finally getting fed up with the whole thing and deciding being captain of that boat was not worth the headaches, but I guess the song was the straw that was need to break my back."

"And let me guess," Riley said toward R&B. "Robert Johnson?"

"Man was a philosopher," R&B said solemnly.

"And we all have something to thank him for now," Chick added, looking at Carla. "What's your next move?"

"Really don't have a plan, but in fact, this is a perfect start," Carla observed. "Now we can check out Fantasy Fest together and make a real party of it."

Riley and R&B looked at each other, while Chick stared down at the pavement for a moment.

"Did I say something wrong?" the captain asked. "Do I get the impression that I am intruding? You boys already have dates for the big party?"

"Nothing like that, but a rather long story," Chick looked up and offered. "But if you'll walk on down to the waterfront with us, we can fill in the blanks."

As they moved off down Duval Street, Chick and Carla led the way, with R&B and Riley trailing behind, again people-watching the odd throng along the avenue. At least on Riley's part, he was trying not to listen to what was being said up ahead. It would be too much like listening in on what the priest hears at confessional. Eventually they ambled between the La Concha Hotel and Saint Paul's Episcopal Church, then past the oldest house in Key West on the left. As they passed the intersection with Greene Street, flanked by Sloppy Joe's and Rick's bars, Riley studied a pair of skeleton's approaching down the middle of the street. One was a rotund male, primed completely black with the bones painted in white. The costume included black face and his baldpate also glistened with paint and sweat.

The female skeleton beside him wore a black thong, the rest of her torso also camouflaged in black paint with bones added. Riley found it rather hard to draw his gaze off the white of the breastbones, however, probably because of the small mesas formed by the bare, but painted nipples that rose amid them. After she passed, he scolded himself again for being so anal. The question that coursed through his mind was whether the couple would, or even could, remain painted until the following night, or would they need a fresh coat?

The group came to a halt, their attention drawn to the sudden approach of a couple of uniform police officers. Both Chick and Riley instantly recognized one of the policemen as the burly one from the brawl on Stock Island. As he passed close Riley noted his name tag — Hastens — and his rank of sergeant.

"Afternoon, ma'am," Sgt. Hasten addressed the semi-nude skeleton. "Enjoying the city?"

"Well — yes, we are," she stammered in reply, obviously taken aback by the patrolmen.

"Glad to hear it," the sergeant nodded, "but we're going to have to ask for your cooperation. We have a nudity ordinance in effect. Unless you have something to put on, we'd like you to wear this shirt compliments of the City of Key West."

With that the other officer, a young Hispanic man offered a white tee shirt to the woman. Instinctively, but with hesitation, she accepted the shirt and just stood holding it for a second. In the knot of people that had stopped to watch the proceedings a male dominated moan arose, mixed with muted laughter.

"Afraid we have to wait until you have it on," Sgt. Hastens smiled, and then glanced around at the crowd good-naturedly, adding slightly louder. "All part of the job, ma'am."

The skeleton slipped the shirt over her head, trying not to smear her paint job. Emblazoned across the front of the white shirt was the logo "Fright Night on Bone Island" and below it "Fantasy Fest '98."

"Hey, I want one of those, too," a middle-aged woman on the periphery shouted.

Handing a cup — that no doubt was fueling her outburst — to a red-faced man that Riley supposed was her husband, she grabbed her blouse and in a single motion raised it and her bra up to her chin. The ensuing mammary cascade that bounced and jiggled down was accompanied by the click of camera shutters and another round of laughter.

"Maybe we should read her rights?" Hastens grinned over at his fellow officer, as he reached over, took another shirt from him and handed it to the woman, then addressed her, "Just put those away before you hurt somebody."

With his final comment the surrounding crowd erupted in more laughter and applause.

Once the crowd dissipated back into a moving tide on the street, Riley looked back to see the skeleton taking the tee shirt off as she moved in the opposite direction away from the policemen.

"What a pig!" Carla was saying as Riley refocused on the direction they were traveling. "Did you see that fat cop never took his eyes off her boobs?"

"Funny you should choose that description," Riley observed, which drew a glance from Chick.

Once their march down Duval restarted, Chick and Captain Mays were again engaged in their conversation.

Upon reaching the ticket kiosk for the Conch Train at the corner of Duval and Front streets, Chick and Carla came to a halt. It was hard to tell what was going through the captain's mind, since her face hinted at a battle between sympathy and the turmoil of trying to stifle the need to bust out laughing.

"So you think you're to blame for the pig's dilemma?" she addressed Chick.

"One hundred percent," he said.

"And you two are going to help him break the critter out of the slammer?" she added, turning toward the two other men and finally giving in to the need to chuckle out loud. "What is this, a Three Stooges at Fantasy Fest episode?"

"If it is, I want to be Larry," R&B grinned. "Always liked his hair."

Riley just added an almost apologetic smile, as if to say he really had better sense, but was involved anyway.

"You know you could actually get in trouble with this scheme, don't you?" Carla continued to ply them with what she had to know were little more than rhetorical questions. "Are that pig's nuts really worth it?"

"I don't have any choice about it," Chick offered. "It's my fault."

"A man's got to be a man," R&B chimed in solemnly.

"Yeah," Chick added with his most engaging grin. "Arbie's got the hell hog on his trail."

"What a bunch of imbeciles," the captain said breaking into another smile. "So what's next in our plan?"

"Our plan?" Chick asked.

"If I don't keep an eye on you boys and you screw it up, I'll end up feeling just as guilty as you do about the pig," she conceded. "And it's short notice to find another date by tomorrow night. So how can I help?"

"If you're sure about it," Chick began. "Let's mull that over as we walk on out to Mallory Dock. I figure that's where we can meet Capt. Arnie with the pig."

With that the group began walking on down to the end of Duval Street, left on Wall Street, then ambling through the open-air Sponge Market toward Mallory Square. As they passed through R&B and Carla looked the part of tourists as they eyed the souvenir monkey- or pirate-faced carved coconuts, wooden parrots and chunks of sponge. Chick's eyes were again displaying his conspiratorial side as they darted about checking every aspect of their route. Riley followed the group, displaying a seeming resignation worthy of a condemned man walking off his last meal on the way down the longest mile. At the far end of the market they emerged into the vast, paved expanse of Mallory Square, which they continued to cross toward the dock facing on the Gulf of Mexico. Just offshore, to the south of Tank Island a center console fishing boat was visible, lines taunt behind it, watched by anglers as they trolled. Above a small Cessna outfitted with pontoons for landing on water passed over, headed west toward the Dry Tortugas and old Fort Jefferson.

"We're going to walk this pig across this square in front of everyone?" Carla Mays directed the question to Chick.

"Yeah, I know," he replied, "but Capt. Arnie says it's not a problem. Nobody will find us at all out of the ordinary tomorrow night. He assures us it gets quite crazy down here."

She just shook her head as she surveyed the dock.

"We'll fit in perfectly then," she said and added. "Have you noticed just how high the dock is?"

Chick's face screwed up into a semi-scowl as he considered her question, at the same time striding over to the edge to look down. When he did, the concern became evident in his face. It was a good 25 feet or more from the top of the concrete quay down to the water. He stood staring at the water's surface for a few moments then turned back to face the group.

"Let me work on that for a little while," he said, then added lightly. "Hey, if we got the Squire down off the Saint Simons Pier, it shouldn't be too much different handling this hog."

"You're right about that," R&B agreed. "Not much difference at all"

Chick now began walking back off the dock, headed toward Old Town.

"When do I get to meet this Capt. Arnie anyway?" Carla asked after him.

"We're headed back to his place now. Eric Allen is supposed to meet us all there with some cell phones."

"And unless we want to lose one of our conspirators to murder, we better get there before those two meet alone," Riley cautioned, about half seriously, which provoked a questioning look from Carla.

"You'll see," was Riley's only reply to her.

With that the party retraced their steps back to Duval Street and headed up the thoroughfare.

"Holy crap," R&B muttered as they approached a couple of men coming from the opposite direction. One was dressed in boots, leather chaps, and a cowhide pattern vest, topped with a cherry red cowboy hat trimmed in white. His companion shared the red color scheme, but sported only a loincloth, moccasins and a feathered headdress.

In passing R&B looked back at them.

"I didn't need to see that," he moaned, snapping his head back around at the sight of the cowboy's butt shining from beneath the chaps, covered only by a bikini-thong back strap.

Now moving on down Duval, the group — even including Chick — took in the full flavor of the street party atmosphere. Alternately eyeing and commenting on their costumed fellow travelers on the avenue or pausing briefly before street vendors and performers the quartet slowly found its way back to the intersection with United Street. From there they continued a slow stroll back to Flagler Avenue, eventually approaching the masonry block wall that separated Capt. Arnie's gravel and weed front lawn from the sidewalk. Riley led the way as they walked up the drive and onto the carport turned patio with its tropical, nautical, thrift store theme furnishings.

"What happened to that poor devil?" were Carla's first words upon sighting the scraggly little lovebird in its cage.

"Not a thing," Chick replied, standing before the cage, looking at the bird as it rocked back and forth on the perch and watched him in return. "Matter of fact, he's looking rather chipper today."

"That has to be the most pitiful thing I've ever seen," the woman added, wrinkling her face in disgust.

"And you probably think my quarters are a garbage scow as well?" Capt. Arnie Patranicholas boomed as he came out of the house to join them, scrutinizing Carla Mays from head to foot as he moved, then adding to no one in particular, "Who's the chirpy?"

The offense taken at the remark was thinly disguised as Carla turned to face the older man, who was several inches shorter then she.

"Capt. Carla Mays," Riley said, emphasizing the title in starting a formal introduction, hoping the similarity of position might ameliorate the seeming immediate dislike that had appeared between the two seafarers, "meet Capt. Arnie Patranicholas."

"Captain is it? And what might you be captain of missy?" Capt. Arnie said with obvious undertones of bullying to gain the upper hand.

"Late of the Motor Launch Sea Prince out of Boston," she replied sternly, giving no ground, her green eyes flaring as she locked them onto the old fisherman's eyes.

"And what is your vessel?" she took the offensive.

"The trawler Rosita," he snapped back, adding, "a working boat in the fishing fleet."

At this point Chick physically stepped between the two who were edging closer to each other in what promised a toe-to-toe confrontation.

"Why don't we all grab a seat? We have some details to iron out," he suggested, then turning his head added, "Arbie, I bet you and Riley can find us some cold beers in the kitchen."

Jumping at the chance to exit the scene of the uncomfortable standoff, Riley moved so quickly that he seemed to be bolting for the door, trailed by R&B.

Still faced off on either side of Chick, the two captains were locked in a staring contest with neither willing to flinch.

"I supposed you've added her to our little enterprise as well?" Capt. Arnie complained to Chick, but never diverting his eyes from Carla. "There's only room for one master on my ship."

"That's OK, Cap," Chick soothed. "Capt. Carla will be working with us on the island."

At that pronouncement it was obvious that Carla wanted to tear her gaze from Capt. Arnie's eyes and question Chick on what he had in mind, but the woman could not and would not give the old man the pleasure of having outlasted her.

"I'm picky about my sailing accommodations anyway," Carla injected as Riley and R&B reentered the scene, beer bottles in hand.

"Come on, guys," Chick pleaded soothingly. "We don't need a pissing contest here. Everybody has their part to play and won't be stepping on each other's toes."

Almost as if at a cue from a stage director, both captains broke eye contact at the same face-saving instant.

"Exactly what is my role in this little melodrama?" Carla Mays then asked.

As the group took seats around the patio, Capt. Arnie made it a point to be last to grab a chair, as if it was his last act of defiance before dropping the confrontation with the woman.

"The trickiest part of the evening is going to be getting the pig through Old Town to the docks," Chick began explaining, directing his comments to Carla. "We'll have R&B down there early doing some street singing and keeping an eye on things. But, since he'll be tied down with his gear, maybe you could stay close and help him until we get past there. Of course, we're all going to be pretty much winging it, except for the timetable. We'll just need to be synchronized on that."

As Carla was nodding, Capt. Arnie broke in.

"And here comes the final piece of this disaster," he noted, gesturing toward the entrance through the masonry fence out front, where Eric Allen was striding toward them carrying a plastic grocery-type sack.

Dressed as always in his khaki slacks, a button-down oxford shirt and loafers without socks, it made Riley hot just to look at him in the tropical afternoon sun.

"We're all here, then," Allen announced when he reached the carport, then squinted through his heavy black-rimmed glasses at Carla Mays. "Who's she?"

"An old and trusted friend," Capt. Arnie snapped at the younger man. "And good day to you too."

Allen shifted his gaze to the old fisherman and just stared blankly at him for a moment.

"This is Carla Mays. She's going to be helping us downtown," Chick jumped in. "Have you got the phones?"

"I didn't know you were adding anybody this late in the game," Allen replied. "I only rounded up four."

"That will be plenty," Chick said. "She and R&B will only need one."

"Just make sure I get them all back in working order," Allen cautioned. "These are all borrowed from STAG, and we need them back."

Then reaching into the bag, he brought out several sheets of paper and added.

"These are copies of the numbers for all the phones, so nobody has to trust their memory."

As he made his last comment, Allen cut his eyes toward Capt. Arnie.

"Prick," the old sailor cocked his head slightly and muttered, glaring back from under his gnarled brow.

"Are you speaking to me?" Allen reprimanded, then instantly rethought his impetuosity as the old man began to rise.

Allen backed up a couple of steps.

"I have to go to another appointment," he quickly added, not taking his eyes from Capt. Arnie, then turned and tossed over his shoulder. "Just be where we agreed and don't be late."

With that Allen headed down the drive and out onto Flagler Avenue.

"Charming fellow," Capt. Carla observed, "perfect for this happy family."

"Serves his purpose," Chick assured, and then leaned forward in his chair. "OK, let's get this thing ironed out."

The last shards of the fading sun had disappeared completely from the western horizon, leaving the lights of the docks and the boats returning to marina slips to brighten Key West Harbor as Chick Malor and Capt. Carla Mays walked out onto Mallory Dock. Around them swirled a mass of revelers, filtering back from the quay in the opposite direction toward Old Town and Duval Street, leaving behind the fire-eaters, acrobats and musicians whose acts had accompanied the ritual setting of the sun but moments earlier. Passing a Rasta man collecting his tip hat and slinging his conga drum strap over his shoulder, the couple reached the brink of the concrete pier. Chick hoisted one foot to prop on the raised rim of the structure, peering out over the water.

"You really think this is going to work?" Carla asked softly, almost in a whisper, while snaking her hand into his and squeezing it gently.

At the touch, Chick turned his eyes toward her and smiled weakly.

"Who knows," he admitted. "I've probably done dumber things that have turned out OK. I'd just hate it though if I get any of the rest of you in trouble – that is except for that twit Allen. I think Capt. Arnie and Arbie would both think of it as a badge of honor, but it wouldn't do you and Riley any good."

"What about you?" she asked next, then observed. "You need to think about yourself too."

"No, I have no choice," Chick repeated the phrase all the conspirators had heard from him often throughout the days. "Riley is the one that really worries me. If I thought I could handle the part out at the jail alone I would. That's where something is most likely to go wrong."

Then changing the subject, he asked.

"Any problem getting the car?"

"No," Carla replied. "They still had a couple out at the place by the airport. It's all set."

Chick again stared out over the water at two sets of lights, far out in the dark and suggesting large vessels. One seemed headed toward the city, but away to the southeast the lights of the S.S. Loro were swinging their way around into the Florida Straits.

"Let's head on back and make it an early evening," Chick suggested.

"We can sleep in tomorrow and have a late omelet," Carla added with a pixie grin.

"We?" Chick smiled back.

Chapter 23

The sun was arcing across the western sky, making its inevitable slide toward the horizon. Officer Mark Farnsworth watched through the windshield of his patrol car as the spreading streaks of gold, magenta and red crept outward from the glowing globe that was preparing to dive into the hazy blue of Florida Bay to the west. Now into his second day of watching the steady stream of vehicles inching along U.S. 1 across Stock Island into Key West, he was finding it hard to stay focused. His assignment was proving far more boring than anticipated. Ordinarily a weekend on the city's back stoop here on Stock Island provided a number of disturbances to break the monotony. The small, shabby houses and trailer courts provided plenty of blue-collar vigor on Friday and Saturday nights. Mix that with a good dose of payday beer money and arguments, fights and general tomfoolery kept the force occupied.

The previous evening had offered none of that. A good portion of Stock Island residents were probably in town working extra shifts for Fantasy Fest, while the rest had fled up the islands to get away from the craziness. Those not working or escaping were probably just as rowdy as usual, but were no doubt in Key West joining the revelry. Whatever the reason, Stock Island, with the exception of traffic on the main highway, had been as quiet as a tomb so far. About the only entertainment he had was listening in on the radio traffic from in town. The 10-

51 calls, which meant an officer was dealing with a subject that was drunk, were frequent. Most of the others bore the code 10-59 for security checks or malicious mischief. Another 10-51 generally followed those, when the officer investigated. Fantasy Fest was progressing as usual, with lots of alcohol, minor disturbances and plenty of revelry.

While the Stock Island patrol was proving quite easy duty, it got off to a bad start. On Friday afternoon when he picked up the patrol car, hanging on the steering wheel he had found a plastic pig nose, complete with elastic strap and scrawled note identifying it as his Fantasy Fest costume for the Passionate Pig Patrol. Determined not to let the needling work, he had strapped the thing on his face as he pulled out of the lot at the precinct, adding a big — though forced — grin to go with it.

Checking his watch, Farnsworth double checked the frequency on his radio, and then keyed it.

"Stock Island Detention, this is Unit 17, are you 10-8."

"10-4 Unit 17, if you mean am I sitting here, while the rest of the town celebrates, then, yeah, I'm in service," a voice crackled back.

"I know what you mean, Delmar," Farnsworth replied. "Are you 10-25 with Stanley?"

"Hell, boy," the voice answered. "Why don't you just speak English instead of numbers? You know we're the only two on this frequency."

Farnsworth could just imagine crusty old Delmar Spence, feet kicked up on a desk and watching the security monitors out at the detention center.

"Because I'm not old as the hills with a vested pension, like some folks," Farnsworth smiled as he keyed the radio again. "Have you been in contact with him or not?"

"He's got the phone number over here and knows how to call it if there's a problem. Acne-faced young punk is probably out there trying out one of the sheep right now," Spence shot back.

"OK, I'll check in later," Farnsworth said, then added with a grin. "You know this could be 11-58 and your transmissions are not 10-30."

"And I got a size 11 on my foot just waiting to be shoved up your ass," Spence offered gruffly, then finished, "10-4?"

"10-4," Farnsworth concluded.

He also thought it was a good thing that Stanley Marks, the high school kid that had volunteered to baby sit the petting zoo, was well away from the old jailer. When the officer met the youngster on Friday, the boy had professed an interest in a law enforcement career. Spending some time around Delmar Spence might have stanched that desire.

The last gasp of the day was now giving up its hold as the light faded quickly in the west. The passing procession of automobile headlamps sent an eerie glow up along the north side of the road, bouncing the light off the trees that swayed in the breeze and separated the asphalt from the fairways of the Key West Golf and Country Club beyond.

Glancing down at his side view mirror, Farnsworth noticed that one of the few cars heading out of Key West had drawn to a stop not far behind him and on the other side of the road. It looked like a rental. Two men emerged from the passenger side and walked toward the nearby convenience store, but dressed in dark clothes, their outlines were quickly lost in the gathering gloom.

The sudden blaring of car horns drew his attention back to the highway in front, where a red SUV had inexplicably come to a halt, blocking traffic and impeding the slow progress toward Fantasy Fest. The officer contemplated whether to get out and walk up there to see what the problem was, when a back door opened, a figure leaned out and vomited on the road.

"Geez, and they haven't even gotten to the party," he mused.

At the corner of Southard and Whitehead streets, the Cayo Hueso Men's Chorale members were queuing up to fill small hand-held bags with strands of plastic beads. The posse of cowpokes clad in a red-and-white motif of chaps, vests and hats mingled with Indians featuring a similar color scheme in their breech clothes and feathers. At the back of a flatbed truck, which bore a railing painted to look like a corral fence, a couple of large cardboard boxes filled with similar trinkets were being hoisted aboard.

"All set then, Mike?" Mac Garland asked.

Standing dressed in the full regalia of the leader of a Native American war party, Garland inspected both the truck and the assembled ensemble.

"Ready as rain, chief," the carpenter replied.

The chief's gaze then came to rest on Mike's outfit.

The carpenter sported the same red cowboy duds as his fellow revelers. But beneath the chaps his denim jeans, which should have added some western authenticity, seemed out of place against the backdrop of chaps over thongs that surrounded him.

"A bit shy tonight are we?" Garland suggested.

Mike squinted at the Indian.

"Hell no, but if you think I'm putting my cheeks on that leather seat for a couple of hours in this heat, you're crazier than that queen," was his snorted reply.

As he delivered it, he gestured toward Bernard, who was climbing aboard the truck and in the process revealing that he had decided to forego the thong with his chaps.

"And you better climb up there too," Mike continued, "so I can get this rolling barnyard into line for the parade."

"That was close," Riley stated for the third time as he and Chick rounded the end of the convenience store on Stock Island.

"Will you quit worrying," Chick Malor admonished him again. "The cop is just watching traffic. He's not looking for a couple of pig-nappers who have not even struck yet. He probably didn't even notice us."

"I don't know, Chick," Riley hedged. "I think, I could see him watching us in his mirror. And we are dressed like a couple of burglars."

"Good Lord," Chick muttered. "We're just dressed in black. Look more like couple of Goth punkers in town for the party than criminals on the loose! Just chill out, man, and we'll get through this."

Finishing the sentence, a flourish of auto horns out on the highway prompted Chick to sneak a look back around the corner toward the patrol car parked on the side of U.S. 1.

"Just follow me and don't get in a hurry," he told Riley, then moved back out into the lot in front of the store, headed for the ribbon of asphalt lined with traffic.

Riley bolted out in his companion's lee, then caught himself and slowed to a normal walk. Quickly they were across the empty northbound side of the road and slipped between a couple of cars in the stalled far lane. Casting a glance up the road, Riley saw a uniformed policeman walking up beside a red vehicle that had the stream of cars blocked. From the passenger side a young man was hanging out the back door and barfing on the ground. The cop stopped short, probably to avoid getting splattered.

In an instant, Riley disappeared into the dark recesses of the hedge of bushes that squatted beneath a line of palm trees. With his eyes adjusting to the loss of light provided by street lamps and auto headlights, he could not make out even the outline of Chick in front of him, but simply followed the sound of his friend busting through the bush row. Quickly the foliage opened on to a flat plain formed by one of the fairways on the golf course. Overhead the moon glimmered, just past its first quarter phase, adding enough light to make traversing the open stretch of mown grass easy. The two figures rushed headlong, instinctively adopting the posture of a slight crouch, as do all commandos in the movies, whether or not there is any surrounding structure or objects to conceal their movement.

Along the far side of the fairway another line of palms and some scattered bushes outlined the break, beyond which another of the links offered more open space. Now running side-by-side in their duck-walk posture, Chick and Riley parted as they passed on either side of a small clump of waist high vegetation that was unidentifiable in the lunar half-light. From the far side of the bushes, Riley heard a distinct, surprised gasp, which maintained his attention for just a split second. By then all his facilities were diverted to his own precarious situation. The Earth seemingly had opened, dropping its reassuring presence from beneath his feet and sending Riley hurling into the void of the eerily lit tropical sky. As he hung there suspended, his ears rang with a self-generated verse of Jimmy Buffett's "Jolly Mon," and he pictured himself being swept up into the stars on the back of a dolphin. That revelry quickly dissipated as he crashed face down on a bed of loose sand. The length of rope and small sack he carried careened out of his grasp, spreading out before him.

"Sand trap," he heard Chick's voice from nearby, strained through his companion's efforts to spit sand from his mouth as he spoke. "You OK?"

"Seem to be," Riley replied. "You?"

"Yeah," Chick acknowledged, already gathering up his gear. "Let's get moving, but take it a little slower in the shadows."

Riley nodded his agreement as he dusted the sand from his clothes and retrieved his load, and then realized the useless nature of the gesture since his friend could not have made it out in the gloom.

"Right behind you," he offered instead.

The duo crossed three more fairways at a slower pace, before reaching a heavier band of foliage, much like the one they traversed along U.S. 1. Once into the pitch-black pall cast by the bushes and trees they halted, squatting low. Chick reached forward with both arms and parted the vegetation, poking his head through the created crevice. As he did, Riley followed suit and both their heads protruded from the hedgerow like prairie dogs popping from their burrows to scan the surroundings.

Before them stretched Junior College Road that lapped around the north side of Stock Island, providing access to Florida Keys Community College, and the Stock Island Detention Center and Children's Animal Park. Most of this asphalt strand was illuminated only by moonlight, though just down to the left a streetlight did glow at the entrance drive to the detention center.

"Ready," Chick asked without turning his gaze from the road.

"Sure," Riley sounded back as they sprang up together and raced across the road and into more bushes that spread down toward the 8-foot chain length fence, topped with concertina wire and surrounding the entire complex of the jail and animal park. As the pair inched through the bushes, brushing spider webs from their faces as they moved, Riley was at least thankful that the ground was solid and they did not have to crawl through a mangrove marsh. Beneath the low-hung canopy of the semi-tropical under story, the outline of their figures was lost as the black shirts and jeans they wore melted into the dark void around them. Long sleeves provided a bit of mental security for Riley by keeping his arms protected from the unseen, but readily imagined, creeping and crawling denizens amid which they were passing. At the same time, that extra bit of material was producing a prodigious amount of sweat that drenched his entire frame. Another hundred yards of crouched duck walking brought them to the perimeter fence.

Beyond the chain link barrier a single night light, near what appeared to be an office, offered some relief from the dark, aided by a bit more illumination escaping through a window from the interior of the building. Spread around what could pass for a farm barnyard were several sheds with fenced gates closed, obviously to keep animals within. The entire scene was silent, save for the occasional wheezed sound of breathing or a muffle grunt coming from the sheds. Most of the grunts were originating from the shed closest to their location along the fence.

"That's it," Chick whispered. "The hog's in that closest shed."

With that Malor produced a pair of hand-held wire cutters.

"What about an alarm attached to the fence?" Riley whispered back with a tone of panic, as he reached out and blocked the path of his companion's hand toward the wire.

"Not likely," Chick shot back. "With all these animals getting loose and bumping it, they'd spend all their time with sirens going off. It wouldn't make sense to tie it into the jail security.

"At least, I hope not," he concluded, pushing past Riley's blocking hand and making the first cut of the wire.

Riley began breathing again when he heard the slight click of the wire parting. The fact they were not instantly bathed in the glow of a searchlight operated by armed guards eased his misgivings a great deal, dispelling the image from old prison movies of George Raft or Humphrey Bogart framed against a wall in such a circular glow as bullets blasted out small spurts of dust from the bricks.

Quickly Chick made a series of such clips that created a circular four-foot diameter hole through the fence. All the while, Riley's eyes never left the door of the lighted office on the opposite side of the zoo. Still watching that portal, he followed Chick in crawling through the breach in the wire, pulling his bag of gear along behind. Carefully, the duo crept to the side of the shed Chick had indicated from the perimeter, taking refuge on the side opposite from the office. Riley squatted, leaning against the rough-hewn boards, listening intently for the sound of a slamming door and approaching footfalls. To his relief, the only sounds were coming from the animals; chief among those was steady, heavy breathing emanating from the opposite side of the wall against which he cowered.

Next, staying close to the ground and almost slithering through the dim light like reptiles, the two men rounded the end of the shed, unlatched the gate and slipped into the darkness within. Chick clicked on a small pen light that cast an eerie green glow to reveal the hog lying on its side, one eye half open staring at the duo and its mouth curled in what Riley though looked like a smirk. The large beast, however, made no move, but simply retained its slouched position.

"Get the rope around its neck," Chick ordered, to which Riley rummaged through his gear bag to produce the strand that would serve as their pig leash. Riley then tried to put the loop over the pig's head and onto its neck, but the swine would not cooperate, keeping its head firmly bolted to the straw on the shed's floor.

"It won't raise up," Riley complained, prompting Chick to turn back from peeking around the open end of the shed and watching the office.

Chick shuffle back from the entrance and ran his hands under the pig's head, as the critter proved remarkably pliant, but seemingly uninterested in aiding the effort either. Eventually the hog apparently tired of this fondling, however, then raised and shook its head, causing Chick to lose his grip as the massive ears flopped against his wrists. Fortunately, Riley had been ready and looped the rope over the animal's head.

"Pig slobber!" Chick grimaced and wiped his hands on his pant legs.

"What if he won't come with us?" Riley asked, betraying a new round of uncertainty.

"There's an easy way to find out." Chick impatiently returned, grabbing hold of the rope that Riley already had in hand. Still in squatting postures to keep low, although their position in the shed made that unnecessary, the two men began pulling on the rope in the direction of the building's open end. To their great relief, the huge hog rose to its feet, muttered a guttural sound and allowed itself to be guided out through the gate and around to the concealed side of the structure.

"I'll go first and pull him behind me," Chick announced, then moved over to the hole in the fence and crawled through. As he began putting pressure on the rope the swine walked easily toward the hole, but just in front of it balked. Chick strained at the rope, but to no avail.

"See if you can give me some help here," he whispered to Riley, who was carrying their gear bags just behind the pig.

"How?" he shot back.

"Put a shoulder to his rump, I guess," Chick hissed back uncertainly.

"Do pigs kick?" was the hesitant reply.

"Legs are too short," Chick assured him.

None too comforted by that assertion, Riley nevertheless placed a shoulder against the surprisingly firm haunch of the hog and leaned heavily on the beast. Rather than movement, he was rewarded with what sounded like a much muffled explosion, followed by several seconds of the rustling of air escaping near him.

"Good Lord, what a smell," Riley blurted louder than he would have liked, as he jerked his body away from the source of the stench.

As though on cue, the hog stepped on through the hole in the fence. Riley crawled through next, still shaking his head and holding his breath to escape the scent. He was sure that as he cleared the wire, he saw the pig look back at him, its face painted with that same smirk, but perhaps a bit amplified now. Within a few more seconds they had the animal into the dark recesses of the undergrowth and headed away from the children's zoo.

Officer Mark Farnsworth strode along the sandy fringe of U.S. 1 on Stock Island headed back to his patrol car. Fortunately, it had taken only a few minutes to get traffic flowing again toward Key West. When he had approached the red SUV causing the tie up, the officer discovered the back and front passenger seats filled with 20-something aged men who were all at least tipsy and roaring with laughter at their companion who was hanging out the back door and gagging violently. It was a relief also to discover a designated driver who was stone cold sober and a bit embarrassed by the scene. That at least avoided the problems of having to wait around for another unit to transport drunks to the station.

As the patrolman reached his car, the portable radio attached to his shoulder came alive with the voice of Spence Delmar.

"Farnsworth, are you there," spilled out of the radio.

"Unit 17, 10-4," Mark replied.

"Have you talked to the kid at the petting zoo?"

"Negative on that 10-25," Farnsworth grinned as he replied, already anticipating the response it would draw.

"You and those damn numbers again," Delmar growled. "He called me a few minutes ago. If you ask me he's seeing his own shadow, but was all worked up over some noise out there. You better go by and change his diaper."

"Got it, I'll 10-42 the children's zoo," Farnsworth needled the speaker.

"And while you're at it, why don't you show him how to bugger a 10-91h?" Delmar concluded.

"Didn't realize they even had a horse out there," Farnsworth shot back, still grinning. "10-4."

Sliding into the driver's seat, the patrol car came to life as he flipped on the blue lights and hit the siren for a couple of seconds to gain a break in the traffic for a U-turn across the westbound lane. He then steered toward the eastern end of Junior College Road, just beyond Mile Marker 5. In all likelihood, for once old Spence was probably right. Could have been a raccoon foraging along the fence that got some of the animals stirred up, but checking on Stanley and the menagerie would at least break the monotony of watching the traffic on the highway.

Just before reaching the lagoon and road fill that connects Stock Island to Raccoon Key, Farnsworth flipped the blinker for a left turn and again hit the blue lights to create a gap in the oncoming westbound traffic. Though this was the long route to reach the detention center, it would be much quicker than having fought through the westward migration to Key West. To his right the freshly risen quarter moon glistened a pale bone color off the surface of the lagoon at each break in the mangrove shoreline, seeming to have adopted the color to coordinate with the year's Fantasy Fest theme. To the left the tree line and hedges hid all but an occasional glimpse of the flat fairways of the country club golf course. Before reaching the big bend around the north end of the island at the college campus, at the very fringe of the reach of his headlights Farnsworth detected a figure scampering across the ribbon of black asphalt. The trailing, banded tail identified it as a raccoon out for its nightly forage.

"Probably you or one of your cousins that have Stanley spooked," the officer said aloud with a muted chuckle.

A half-mile farther along, he turned right into the drive leading up to the detention center and children's zoo. Parking the patrol car, as he got out he subconsciously reached for the big flashlight from behind the passenger side seat and dropped it into the loop on his utility belt. At the office, Farnsworth tapped on the door. The blind in the window next to it parted as Stanley Marks peeked through. Then the lock on the door could be heard disengaging.

"Mr. Farnsworth," Stanley blurted when he swung the door open. "I'm glad to see you. I think there's something been going on out in the pens."

The boy was tall, slender and dressed in a tee shirt and baggy jeans that seemed intent on dropping down over his hips.

"You don't need the mister," Farnsworth corrected. "Officer will do. Officer Spence says you heard some noise?"

"Yes sir, it was out toward the far side at the fence."

"Exactly what was it, Stanley?"

"Mostly just real quiet rustling," the boy replied. "But then one of the peacocks got all excited. The way they call, it gives me the willies."

"You want to point me in the direction of the noises?" Farnsworth asked.

"If it's OK, I'll go show you where it was," Stanley offered, having apparently found a new measure of courage supplied by having the officer as backup.

"That'll be fine," Farnsworth said, gesturing for the boy to lead the way.

The pair walked across the open space from the office toward the fence, bathed in the artificial glow of the night light beside the office. They moved in the general direction of one of the sheds that housed the animals in the evening. As they neared the structure, Officer Farnsworth clicked on his flashlight to illuminate the entrance, since it was set at an angle to keep the nightlight from shining directly inside.

"Gate's open," the boy in the lead yelped, as he quickened his step to peer over the fence into the recess of the shed.

Farnsworth raked the inside of the building with his flashlight beam.

"The pig must've got out. Bet that's the noise I was hearing," Stanley continued, obviously pleased that he could prove something had happened and also relieved that it was only a minor inconvenience. "Better find him before he hurts himself."

With that Stanley started around the shed on the lighted side to begin his search.

"Probably no need for that," Farnsworth said from the other side of the shed.

The boy quickly retraced his steps around the front to join the officer on the darkened lee of the building.

"Why not?" he asked, but fell silent when he saw the beam of the patrolman's flashlight playing on the ragged edges of a large hole cut through the chain link fence.

"You say it was the pig that was in this shed?" Farnsworth grimaced as he asked the boy, already anticipating the answer and his new entanglement with the swine that had already caused him so much grief.

Chapter 24

Riley Bright and Chick Malor made much better time crossing the expanse of the Key West Country Club golf course on their return trek, mainly because the swine they were spiriting away had a better feel for the darkened terrain than did the two men. It was difficult at times to tell who was leading who back across the island. As the trio crossed the links they were silhouetted in the argent glow of the moonlight, then swallowed by the foliage lining the rough at the edge of each fairway. Along the route the men were again stooped and creeping to maintain a useless, but comforting sense of stealth as they progressed. Angling their path just a bit to the southwest, they finally reached the last line of tropical undergrowth lying beneath the row of palm fronds swaying in a light breeze. The conspirators were near the corner of U.S. 1 and the western end of Junior College Road when they halted before emerging onto the shoulder of the roadway.

Squatting in the gloom, Riley peaked out at the traffic on the highway, which was now moving at a slow, but steady pace toward the bridge over to Key West. Just back in the bushes, Chick had dropped the small backpack he carried and began rummaging through it. Quickly he had a multicolored *sarape* draped over the pig's back, clipping it in place with safety pins under the neck and beneath the animal's belly. As a finishing touch he slipped a Halloween mask awkwardly over the head of the hog, sighing with relief when the critter simply emitted a soft grunt and accepted its costume. Next Chick put on a mask, while handing another to Riley.

"OK, buddy, now for the risky part," Chick directed at Riley, as they rose and stepped out onto the shoulder of the road to form a procession of presidents Jimmy Carter, Ronald Reagan and a four-footed Bill Clinton.

In the planning stage the entire group of plotters had recognized the slightly more than a quarter-mile walk along the Overseas Highway and over the bridge into Key West as the most dangerous portion of their scheme. This was the one section of the escape route in which the two men and the pig were most likely to standout, since they would be the only pedestrian traffic and there would be a lot of eyes on them from the passing cars. Hopefully they could pass for revelers with a large, costumed dog.

Their expectations about drawing attention proved true. Several cars honked horns, passengers waved and a couple of indecipherable shouts containing references to interns were hurled their way. Chick, in the lead with the hog on the rope leash, led the way, keeping his focus on the concrete span over Cow Channel.

Riley brought up the rear in his President Reagan mask, weakly acknowledging the shouts and waves from the vehicles with a half-hearted raised hand, much like the semi-wave Queen Elizabeth offers to crowds during public appearances. Rather than providing any measure of comfort, closing the gap between themselves and the bridge only made

Riley more nervous. Any second he expected to hear sirens and turn to see a patrol car skirting the traffic on the roadway, as it raced headlong after them along the shoulder with blue lights flashing. He yearned to be across the bridge and out of the spotlight he felt was being focused on him, all the while perceiving that he was not cut out for espionage.

At long last reaching the center of the Cow Channel bridge, Riley Bright had to fight back the urge to break into a sprint and cover the last few yards to reach the anonymity of the next island. Finally the concrete underfoot ended and they turned across the manicured lawn of the Holiday Inn Beachside, fading back into the shadows cast by more palm trees. Riley shot a glance past the building itself to the channel of water beyond, once again ponder the question of why it was "beachside," when its location was so remote from the sandy strip that lay across the island facing the Atlantic Ocean. He entertained the thought for only a moment before returning to his fears of discovery, in spite of the camouflage offered by being off the roadway.

Standing around the entrance to the motel was a knot of people, some in standard tourist dress, but others decked out in homemade or more commercial costumes. As Capt. Arnie had predicted, some of the costumes related to the Fantasy Fest theme of Fright Night on Bone Island, but others, particularly those of the women, seemed no more than an excuse to display cleavage and other assorted skin. This assemblage, however, appeared to be folks not ready to head to Old Town. But, out by the edge of North Roosevelt at the bus stop marked for the Bone Island Shuttle, stood a lone couple.

Chick led the way with the pig and Riley in tow to join that duo. Stopping just short of the couple, Chick reined in the hog, while he and Riley planted themselves between the animal and the man and woman awaiting the shuttle. The woman was dressed in a full length, black body suit, tipped at the derriere with a long tail of a matching color. Though she appeared to be in her late 40s, the tightly fitted costume stretched over the curves of her still sculptured body, accentuating the rounded protrusion of her rear and fullness of heavy bosoms. Atop her head, bobby-pinned into her hair were two triangular, black fabric ears, finishing off the illusion of a black cat.

Her companion was also in costume, but one that seemed to Riley to hardly fit the Halloween theme of the present incarnation of Fantasy Fest. Rather the man was dressed in Bermuda shorts, socks and running shoes, all in similar shades of gray. His white tee shirt had two large eyes drawn on the chest, apparently using a black marker pen. Strapped on each arm was more gray cloth. When he extended his arms to the sides, the fabric hung in the shape of elephant ears. From the crotch of his shorts, a gray, crinkled, tubular snout extended out, and then drooped toward the ground to complete his metamorphosis into a pachyderm. His movements and speech also suggested that whether it was part of his intended persona or not, he was well on his way to imitating an inebriated elephant. The body language of the black cat in his company also hinted that she was none too fond of the intoxication of her faux animal companion.

Shortly the Bone Island Shuttle arrived and Riley was relieved to see that they would be the first passengers for this run toward Old Town. Conveniently, it was also a coach like the ones used at many airports, having its door half way down the side, as opposed to next to the driver. That promised to make it easier to spirit the disguised swine aboard. Although the driver did turn to check out the form of the black cat as she entered, he next turned back forward, hardly paying attention to the drunken elephant. The pachyderm at first stumbled on the entrance steps then lumbered a few steps forward to pay their fare.

Once the festooned drunk had passed back to join his companion, Riley quickly leapt aboard and moved up beside the driver. He also endeavored to make his Reaganesque appearance as wide as possible in order to block the driver's view of the rear of the bus.

"How much for three?" Riley asked.

"Six bucks a head," the bus driver replied, paying no attention to Jimmy Carter apparently helping Bill Clinton crawl up the steps onto the vehicle. "It's round trip, but lose the stubs and you'll have to pay again to get back."

"Thanks," Riley said, handing the man the money and checking over his shoulder to make sure Chick and the hog had arrived in a pair of seats.

Then as he turned to walk to the back a chill ran down his spine and he froze in position as the driver spoke again.

"And make sure your drunk friend that crawled aboard doesn't throw up in my bus," the driver warned. "Bad enough having to work half the night, I don't want to spend the rest of it cleaning up after him."

"Sure thing," Riley agreed with some difficulty in maintaining a normal voice as he again moved rearward to take a seat just in front of his two traveling companions.

Jimmy Carter leaned forward over the backrest of Riley's seat.

"Need to change your shorts, buddy?" Chick sniggered. "I could see the panic on your face clean through that mask you've got on."

Before Riley could reply, the cell phone in his pocket that Eric Allen had issued to him began to ring. As he reached in his pocket for it, the shuttle bus jerked to a stop and its horn bleated querulously.

Officer Mark Farnsworth was now standing in the control room of the Monroe County Detention Center, facing a bank of electronic gear. In front of the console, lounged back in a swivel chair was the jailor, Delmar Spence. Farnsworth spoke into his portable radio as the other man looked on with a wicked grin of delight on his face.

"Dispatch, this is Unit 17," he said.

"10-4 Unit 17, this is dispatch, what's your 10-20?" came back a no-nonsense female voice.

"I'm at the Stock Island Detention Center," Farnsworth replied. "Looks like we have a 10-59 situation out here."

"Unit 17, what's the nature of the situation?"

"We have an apparent break-in and burglary."

"Unit 17, 10-9 that. It sounded like you're reporting a burglary at the jail!"

"That's exactly what I'm reporting," Farnsworth restated, a bit miffed. "Request Code 8 so I can investigate."

"Unit 17, what was taken in the burglary?"

"Only thing we are sure of so far is a missing pig," Farnsworth reported, to which Spence let out a guffaw that caused his chair to roll backward a few inches.

A short pause followed during which Farnsworth shot a glance at the jailor, suggesting he did not appreciate the background mirth. The older man meekly smiled back, still having trouble keeping a straight face. At last the silence was broken.

"Unit 17?"

"10-4 dispatch," Farnsworth replied.

"Farnsworth," the voice resumed, but now sounding far less official, and more like a mother imparting some helpful advice. "To begin with, even if you really need back up, it would take a murder to get anyone out there. The entire force is down at the waterfront policing the crowds. And assuming you're not just playing a Halloween prank on me, think about what you're doing, honey. Do you really want to report that somebody has stolen your Passionate Pig right out from under your nose? Don't think you'd ever live that one down."

Delmar Spence now broke into uncontrolled laughter in the background.

"You're the only one out there," the female voice reminded. "Off the record, if I were you, I think I'd go find that pig before it made me the laughing stock of the force."

For a moment Officer Mark Farnsworth stood mutely pondering the advice, as his face reddened. Meanwhile, Spence rubbed tears from his eyes, then dabbed the front of his uniform shirt with a handkerchief to remove his mirthful slobber.

"Dispatch, Code 4," Farnsworth finally said, as he headed for the door.

Eric Allen cautiously eased the truck out into North Roosevelt Boulevard. It was not the first time he had driven a vehicle this size, but it was such an infrequent event that he initially needed to get used to it. Having little in the way of a hood up front and sitting high over the surrounding traffic took some adjustment in perspective. At first, he did not feel completely in control when behind the wheel of one of these 14-foot moving vans.

Just arranging this rental had taken some planning. Calling ahead by a couple of days, he then had to come by earlier in the day and pick up the keys, since he did not have a place to park the van. It took a while to plead his case and overcome the hesitation of the rental manager at Cheap Trucks. Allowing the van to be picked up from their parking lot after hours on the evening of Fantasy Fest was an unusual request. Allen had to admit that in the manager's situation, he too would have been leery of the timing of the transaction.

Allen's route up U.S. 1 from the lot beside Searstown Plaza offered the least battle with traffic to get off of the island. He did not want to have to traverse much congestion while driving this monster. Though only creeping, the traffic was at least moving as it inched eastward toward the exit from the island. As he came abreast of the Bayside Courtyard Resort on the right, the line of cars came to a complete halt, giving Allen the chance to peer across the opposite lane to the water beyond. To the west the lights of the naval base on Salt Pond Keys glowed, while the darker bulk of Stock Island anchored the vista on the east. The void between the isles was filled by the blackness of Florida Bay. Streaked across that black sheet of water and seemingly tossed toward the highway on Key West was the ivory reflection of the moon, a bit more than half full and shimmering brightly.

Just before the traffic in his lane broke loose again, Allen glanced ahead in the oncoming traffic, attracted by the bleat of a horn. The squeal came from a Bone Island Shuttle, similar in size to his own truck and piloted by a driver unhappy at being cut off by a car bullying into his lane in front of him. As he edged on past the stopped bus, Allen looked down to see a mask of Bill Clinton, apparently worn by a fat man slumped in a seat on the bus, peering up at him.

Eventually, the line of traffic reached Holiday Inn Beachside, where Allen and his truck were able to break free as he steered east off the island, and over Cow Channel onto Stock Island. At the end of the bridge he saw the blue lights of a police squad car flashing at the intersection with Junior College Road, as it forced its way into the west bound lane that was now a sluggish inchworm of vehicles. As the van passed the road junction, Allen slowed momentarily to stare down at the young officer in the patrol car, who appeared to be quite frustrated by the slow progress. Emitting a slight smile, Allen accelerated up the roadway, headed to his rendezvous point.

Far up the Overseas Highway Eddie Crawford looked down at the black dial with luminescent numerals on his inexpensive wristwatch. Having just passed through the village of Islamorada on Upper Matecumbe Key, he judged that he was ahead of schedule.

"Better here than there," he reasoned, then pulled the small moving van off the road on the coral and sand shoulder of Indian Key Fill.

The narrow band of man-made land that carried the roadway blocked most of the channel between Upper and Lower Matecumbe keys and had originally been filled in by crews building the Florida East Coast Railway almost a century earlier. Crawford parked at the eastern end of the third of four bridges that allow the water to pass through the breaks in the fill. Stepping out of the truck and stretching his arms over his head, he first looked back across the road to the southeast at the lights of the single house occupying Teatable Key at the end of a little causeway off the highway. Almost due south he could also make out the unlit, turtle-like hump of Indian Key on the water's surface.

The man now casually strolled around the van, beneath the lettered "Cheap Trucks" that emblazoned its side. To the north, up Indian Key Channel a couple of lights also seemed to flicker on Lignum Vitae Key, probably getting that appearance from palm fronds or tree limbs swaying in the breeze in front of them, Crawford surmised. Just ahead of him, at the side of the public boat ramp, a small electric lantern suddenly lit up to reveal a man fiddling with some fishing tackle, while two additional rods and reels were leaned against big coral rocks, their lines creating arcs out into the dark of the boat channel.

"*Que pasa, amigo*," Crawford asked, walking in that direction. "What's biting tonight besides the mosquitoes?"

The last part of his question was emphasized by a slap to his left arm to squash one of the insects.

"Lot of grunts and a few mangrove snapper," the young man in his late twenties replied.

"Fishing shrimp?"

"Yeah, live ones" the angler offered. "Having to keep them off the bottom to avoid the hardhead cats."

With the moon glowing over Lignum Vitae, its black back drop dotted with a supporting cast of brilliant white star points, Eddie Crawford launched into a discussion with the young man of the relative merits of live bait versus dead for nighttime fishing.

His little freighter rolling softly in a calm sea, Capt. Samuelo Porticia stared momentarily up at the lop-sided oval of the alabaster moon aglow to the north. Lying in Rock Channel, south by southeast of Boca Chita on the north edge of the Intracoastal Waterway, the night was much brighter than the veteran smuggler would have preferred for the work at hand. Anyone to the south of his position would easily see the stationary ship framed against the lunar glow, but that could not be helped.

He next cut his eyes down to the smaller boat that hovered alongside. The last of four small crates was just being lowered into the craft. Hector Corro and a large black man wrestled the box into place beside the other three, all of which were still coated with phosphate dust from their former hiding spot.

"Ready, *capitan*," Corro called up to the deck above.

"*Bueno*. Send the boy up."

At the command Miguel Assaya began scurrying up a rope ladder onto the large ship, while the two other men readied to cast off.

"At least one pistol?" Hector now pleaded.

"No guns," Porticia said in a voice rimmed with the steel of authority. "You will not need them. They only invite trouble. Say no more of the matter."

"*Si, capitan*," the sailor replied, accepting defeat.

"Now away with you and good luck," Porticia offered with a wave.

The outboard engine of the little boat revved up and the craft inched away into the darkness as the old seafarer and his cabin boy watched.

The crane at the aft of the USCGC Sapelo swung slowly around, easing back into place over the deck of the ship. The ridged hull 19-foot inflatable boat it had just delivered over the gunnels was now roped alongside its mother ship and the last of a party of half a dozen sailors were scurrying down a rope ladder into the smaller craft, M-16 rifles or shotguns on slings over their shoulders. Lt. Matthew Jackson stood grasping the Sapelo's rail with both hands, steadying himself against the gentle rocking of his command.

"All set?" he shouted down to the smaller boat.

"Aye, captain," Chief Foster Bork called upward.

"Group intelligence has the Loro over the horizon and standing to just off Boca Chita Naval Air," the officer said. "Looks like he's planning some shenanigans right under the Navy's nose. You know your orders, Chief. Observe from a distance, when they offload, report and move in."

"Aye, captain," the Chief Petty Officer replied.

"Lines away," the Chief next called.

In the fore of the small boat, Seaman Andrea Livingston tossed the line up to a sailor hanging from the rope ladder and the motor of the inflatable came to life.

"Stow the lights," Bork next ordered as the small craft moved off into the night.

The two hand-held, one million-candle power spotlights were quickly stowed and the boat increased to moderate cruise speed.

"All secured, chief," Livingston reported, moving to amid ship where the petty officer stood.

The older man looked down at the young woman, as she peered out over the black water.

"First away party," Chief Bork stated, not as a question, but to confirm to her what he already knew.

"Yes, Chief," she replied, her right hand nervously fiddling with the strap that held the rifle over her shoulder.

"Should be a piece of cake," he assured. "I've read the background on our Capt. Samuelo Porticia.

He's a smart cookie. Been stopped often, but never resists. I don't expect any trouble."

Seaman Andrea Livingston turned a hopeful smile up at the Chief, but it was one he did not see as he braced himself against the helm console and gazed ahead.

Behind the wheel of the heavy-duty pick-up truck, the driver scanned the intersection he approached, while also glancing at the rearview mirrors extending from either side of the cab. The trailer behind the truck would not ordinarily have presented a problem in making the turn off Front Street and south onto Duval, but the crowds packed in on both sides and spilling into the roadway made the maneuver more difficult. When he checked the mirrors, Mike also caught sight of Bernard, hanging on the trailer railing and flinging beads off the vehicle to the crowd with a girlish limp wrist.

Almost too late the driver's attention returned to the path ahead to spy a couple cutting across the street through the parade traffic. The tall blonde easily darted past, but the retro dressed black man with a cell phone glued to his ear and carrying a guitar case, seemed almost oblivious to the approaching truck. As a result, Mike had to brake quickly, which sent the cowpokes and tribe of savages in the trailer tumbling forward. The roar of the surrounding spectators at the sight of the Old West tossed across the trailer drowned out the shrieks and protests of the Cayo Hueso Men's Chorale members doing the tumbling.

Mike hit the horn on the truck. The black man in the street flashed a sheepish smile and melted into the throng along Duval Street.

Chapter 25

Chick Malor was more correct than he had guessed. After the scare Riley had gotten from the driver's comment about the Bill Clinton disguised swine, the cell phone ringing and bus suddenly jerking to a halt finished unsettling his companion's nerves.

"Sorry folks," the driver tossed over his shoulder to no one in particular, as he straightened himself in his seat, and then glared down at the car that had cut in front of the bus.

Chick peered over his backrest at the hog, sprawled across the next row of seats, still wrapped in the shawl and sporting the presidential mask. In turning back around, he was also surprised to catch a glimpse of Eric Allen staring down from the seat of a small moving van passing alongside as it inched eastward.

"Hello?" Riley finally managed to reply to the insistent ring of the cell phone.

"Riley ... God almighty!" he heard R&B shout from the receiver.

"What's going on?" Riley asked, as Chick hung over the back of the seat, trying to get close enough to also hear the conversation.

"Some gay *caballero* cracker about ran my black ass down with a parade float," R&B described, fading into his street persona, but obviously a bit winded from either a quick movement or simply being surprised.

Riley and Chick squinted their confusion at each other.

"How about Carla?" Riley said. "Is she all right?"

"Yeah, she wasn't distracted by this phone," R&B replied, only adding to Riley's perplexed look. "But, hey man, we got to have a change of plans."

"What?" Riley blurted, louder than he intended, to which the drunken elephant man across the aisle and a row in front turned to look over his shoulder with a sodden countenance in the direction of the exclamation.

"Yeah, there's cruise ship tied up to Mallory Dock," R&B explained. "No place for Capt. Arnie to get his boat in there. That mother's big as a hotel."

Then after a pause during which Riley looked up and back at Chick, who had obviously also heard what had been said and now had the familiar distracted look on his face that indicated he was formulating a new scheme. Chick next reached over and took the phone from Riley.

"Arbie," he said, "go ahead and set up as planned. We'll call Capt. Arnie and get back to you."

"It's always something," he next grinned down at Riley, while hitting the button to cut off the call.

"I hope you have an idea," Riley said.

"Maybe," was the reply, "what's Capt. Arnie's number?"

"Just hit three. It's set for speed dial."

During the pause as the telephones made connection, Riley stared out the window to the north and over the water of Garrison Bight toward Florida Bay. The feeling of disquiet that welled up from the pit of his stomach left him yearning for the boredom of staring out his office window back at Amax Publishing in Atlanta. That scenario, however, seemed years in the past rather than just a month.

"Capt. Arnie?" Chick asked into the receiver.

"Who the hell else would have this phone?" the answer was growled back.

"It's me, Chick."

"And I was expecting a call from somebody else?" Capt. Arnie said. "You think I'm a damn fool?"

"Sorry, Cap," Chick cooed into the receiver. "We got a problem."

"Am I surprised by that?" the cantankerous seaman retorted.

"There's a cruise ship taking up all of Mallory Dock. Must have come in last night," Chick explained, and then waited through a moment of silence.

"Should've thought of that possibility," Capt. Arnie stated, but as though it was meant for himself rather than Chick. "All right, only other dock we can use is the White Street Pier. It's got a marked channel and the depth."

"But we're almost down to the Greene Street drop now," Chick pointed out as he glanced out the window toward Key West Bight.

"So walk the pig up Duval Street," the captain ordered. "Nobody's going to notice, since it's already a zoo there. I'll need the time to get around the west end of the island anyway."

"You think it will work?" Chick asked hopefully.

"Hell, easier than when we used to land square groupers there," Capt. Arnie assured him dismissively.

"OK, I'll be in touch," Chick ended the call.

Just as a small moving van accelerated past in the left lane headed east, Officer Mark Farnsworth flipped off the array of blue lights on top of his cruiser after he had forced his way into the traffic creeping westward. There was little reason to keep the flashers on, since there was no place for the cars in front of him to go to get out of his way. The bridge over Cow Channel constricted the flow of vehicles moving over the span into Key West, slowing progress to a crawl. Even if he could have bullied through, he had no clear idea of where he was headed.

His only clue was obtained before he got into his patrol car, when he asked a guy hanging out the window of one of the cars inching along if he had seen anyone catching a ride along the highway. Though the answer had been negative, the man did point out that two or three people in costumes had walked along the shoulder of the road toward the channel bridge earlier. Even if those folks were the pig-nappers, which way would they head once they got into Key West? Call it a hunch, instinct or intuition, the officer suspected that if those folks were the perps, their costumes indicated they must be headed for Old Town. Down there they could blend in and get lost in the party crowd. Still, they had a head start on him and he would need luck and some help to find them.

Farnsworth first reached for his radio, and then had second thoughts, remembering the dispatcher's admonition. Did he really want to make it official that the Passionate Pig was on the loose and had been stolen under his watch? Instead he reached into his pocket for his personal cell phone. Circumventing department policy could get him in real trouble and maybe even cost his job. On the other hand, if this whole episode became general knowledge, the enhanced derision he was likely to endure from his fellow officers would be intolerable. It seemed he could take his choice of getting fired or resign, with the only other option being to turn the tables by quietly locating and arresting the thieves while recovering the pig. That way his superiors would have to acknowledge his initiative during a short-handed situation and the accomplishment would cut short most of the jokes from his peers. Yet he was still stuck with the need for some support, but no official backup.

Farnsworth punched some numbers into the pad of the cell phone.

"Yeah, who is this?" Sgt. Al Hastens' voice demanded in return.

"Sarge, it's me, Mark Farnsworth."

"Did you lose your radio, kid?" the older officer asked, but now in a jovial tone, then added. "You're still on duty, aren't you?"

"Yes, but I have a situation out here and need some help," Farnsworth replied hesitantly.

"So call for back up."

"There's not any available, Sarge," the younger man offered, "and it's kind of a touchy situation. I need some eyes down in Old Town."

"What the hell are you talking about, kid?" Hastens demanded.

"Somebody stole the pig from the kid's zoo," Farnsworth said sheepishly. "If I don't find it and get it back they'll laugh me off the force. I'm on the perps' tail and I think they're headed your way. Keep an eye out for a couple of guys in costumes with the pig, though they may have it disguised as a dog or something."

After a snort of laughter, Hastens finally replied.

"Hell, kid, you got more balls than I've given you credit for," the veteran said. "If they come through here, I'll find a reason to hassle them and let you know. Good luck with this stunt. I hope you pull it off."

The conversation ended just as Farnsworth's patrol car reached the east end of the Cow Channel Bridge.

As the Bone Island Shuttle now crept nearer to the celebration rolling through Old Town along Duval Street, Riley Bright's apprehension about the coming venture grew. The original plan of spiriting the hog three blocks along the periphery of the Fantasy Fest carnival had now morphed into a trek along the parade route that spanned the width of the island. After talking with Capt. Arnie, Chick had phoned R&B to alert him of the shift in plan and to expect the trio to pass his lookout point at the intersection of Duval and Caroline streets. Instead of skirting the throng of revelers, the trio would become very much a part of it. But, he knew the scheme was past the point of no return. Laws had been broken and snarled traffic in the town demanded they walk the swine to the White Street Pier. That knowledge did nothing to ease the gloomy feeling of inevitable disaster that was closing quickly upon him.

On a completely different vane, Riley's companion seemed to grow more animated with each complicating factor that arose. Chick was no longer lost in the planning and vigilance that had characterized his demeanor since the plot was first hatched. Rather, he was falling back into his normal persona of the impish and sociable extrovert. During the final couple of blocks of the bus ride he even struck up a conversation with the drunken elephant man. All of which prompted Riley to wonder if he was witnessing the same kind of epiphany through which Japanese soldiers passed in the Pacific theater of World War II. Having dedicated themselves to die for the emperor, they had no future, no further worries and could act recklessly. The thought that he may have joined Chick in a figurative banzai charge accompanied by a rather large pig was not a comforting one.

When the bus finally jerked to a halt at the end of Williams Street where that thoroughfare met the dead end of Greene, Chick, Riley and the pig followed the black cat and elephant to the door of the bus, Chick and Riley crowding to the left to try to block the driver's view of the hog clambering down the steps and off the vehicle. Their effort was an exercise in futility, for the man could have clearly seen that their friend Bill Clinton was on all fours. The ruse was not only futile, but also unnecessary; this was Key West on the night that culminated Fantasy Fest. It would take more than a fat tourist in a costume crawling off a shuttle bus to arouse any interest from a jaded veteran of the city.

Once on the pavement the trio headed west along Greene Street, the pig now controlled by the rope leash and, though still in costume, any attempt to disguise its true nature abandoned. The din of the crowd along Duval Street was now audible, mixed with music emanating from the parade, but also from the open doors of every bar along the route. The resultant cacophony seemed a siren song, for the two men and the hog were joined by a growing band of folks drifting toward the lights and sound. Drawing still nearer to the avenue along which the parade traveled, a human barrier of spectators closed off Greene Street, but behind the four or five deep crowd the sidewalk was clear enough to make the turn at Sloppy Joe's Bar and shuffle along Duval to the south. Because of the hog's size and low-slung stature, several people coming from the opposite direction while watching the passing floats rather than the sidewalk, came close to tumbling over the creature. Those episodes elicited some good-natured jibes from the off-balanced pedestrians regarding the truly fat and ugly dog the duo had on their leash.

As the trio of masked presidents neared the intersection of Duval and Caroline streets the last float in the Fantasy Fest parade passed them, heading south. As though sucked in by the slipstream of the procession, the crowd imploded from the sidewalks into the street behind the last vehicle, to begin edging along in the same direction. Following the path of least resistance, Chick, Riley and the swine were carried with the throng. In fact, unless an individual exerted a great deal of effort to forge some chosen path, the human current picked up everyone in its path and added them to its glacial flow down the street. Just before entering the intersection, the crowd parted just enough that at virtually the same instant Chick and Riley spotted a burly Key West policeman finishing a cell phone call at the far side of the street junction. The officer then turned, apparently saying something to his younger Hispanic partner.

Although more revelers were falling in behind the parade vehicle up ahead, some people were also splitting off to left and right down Caroline Street, heading to bars, parties or their parked cars. This lightened the congestion in the intersection and also gave the patrolmen a better field of vision. The two officers were now scrutinizing the passing mass of tourists, witches, skeletons, vampires, hobgoblins and other costumed fantasies that flowed past them.

As though sharing thoughts, Riley and Chick both edged to the left of the street, putting as much distance and as many people as possible between themselves and the policemen. Unfortunately, having the pig as their companion necessarily created a slight open area to their front as the critter ambled and grunted along. Still Riley was sure that the prying eyes of the lawmen had not fallen on him and Chick. That luck seemed destined to hold, but just after they passed the policemen's location, the crowded opened for an instant, leaving a new gap directly to where the pig pulled them along.

Riley felt the bottom fall out of his stomach and panic begin to scramble up toward his brain, when the burly older cop locked his gaze on the two upright presidents and the third one crawling along in front. Riley quickly looked to Chick for some suggestion of what to do, but saw only a hopeless set of eyes peering out from the toothy grin of the 39th U.S. president. The recognition that his companion had no ready plan completely drained Riley of life. He felt as though it was time to simply slump into a heap and await the sound of handcuffs clinking closed. Time slowed as he envisioned himself in a jumpsuit with hands and feet shackled together and shuffling into a courtroom toward certain ruination. Slowly he turned his gaze back across the street with the intention of meeting his fate head on.

At that moment, for the first time, he became aware of the black man dressed in jeans, white dress shirt and the worn suit jacket, holding a guitar and speaking to the tall blonde woman. Attired in khaki shorts and light blue pullover blouse, her hair hung freely in a ponytail. The pair was just to the right and a dozen paces in front of the two law officers. For a second, R&B Mann glanced past Capt. Carla Mays and acknowledged Riley with eye contact.

Meanwhile, Sergeant Al Hastens had begun deliberately walking across the intersection toward Riley, Chick and the hog, his eyes firmly set on the trio. After covering only a few steps, however, his path was suddenly blocked by Carla Mays. Not directing her action toward the Key West policeman, she instead faced a group of revelers that were also milling about at the crossroads. Riley instantly recognized two of the little knot of onlookers as Jack Thompson and Bart Skier, the anglers who had given him and Chick a ride down the Keys. The duo was dressed in angling clothes and sported deep tans earned by some extended hours under the tropical sun. Like most of the other partygoers, the men's hands were clasped around plastic cups, the contents of which seemed to be fueling this gala in the streets.

Just behind them and holding his conga drum was the Rasta man with whom R&B had the confrontation upon arriving on the island.

Once disrupting Hastens' line of approach, Carla shouted something inaudible above the din, then reached down and grabbed the bottom of her shirt. In a single motion she yanked both the shirt and her sports-style bra up over her head and off. The display was directed at Bart, Jack and the others standing nearby, but she was strategically turned so that Sergeant Hastens would get a full dose as well. From his vantage point behind and slightly to the side, Riley could still tell from the oblique angle that she was also adding a bit of motion to her performance.

Panning his surroundings, Riley first looked over at Chick, but was rewarded only with the constant, winning smile of Jimmy Carter. When he switched his gaze to Bart Skier, the angler was also grinning broadly and staring at Carla Mays chest. For an instant, Riley was a bit jealous of the man. Circumstances were handing the angler a gift to ogle, and though the show probably impressed him, Riley knew Bart could not truly be appreciating the magnitude of the boon provided so freely to him. Mixed emotions shot through Riley as the several surrounding revelers grasp the opportunity and the flashes of their cameras added light to the scene. Though envious of the position Bart held at that moment, Riley also had a feeling of sadness at such a jewel going to waste. He smiled behind his Ronald

Reagan mask, remembering the Biblical admonition from Sunday School during childhood about not "casting pearls before swine." It was advice that Capt. Carla Mays was ignoring in a most fortuitous way.

Next Riley eyed the approaching police officers. The young Hispanic one brandished the inoffensive, good-times smile so prevalent of the men along Duval Street. On the other hand, Sergeant Hastens offered up a crusty, almost lecherous grin, his leer pinned tightly on Carla's display. And the show obviously paid dividends, for the lawman's resolute advance across the intersection wavered and halted before this shield of feminine assets. Though the crowd noise drowned out the words, Riley could see the sergeant's lips moving as he addressed both Carla and the now more tightly knotted spectators. Also, while watching her, Hastens was rather slowly and deliberately brandishing a tee shirt he got from his partner.

At that point Riley felt the pull of Chick's hand on his arm, urging him on down Duval Street. Turning to go he cast a last look back to where Carla was being reluctant to replace her clothes and Hastens appeared only half-heartedly trying to make her comply. Finally shifting his gaze back to the direction they were walking, Riley next eyed the gyrating rear of the hog as it wobble along Duval Street on the leash in front of Chick. Shaking his head a bit sadly, Riley Bright slowly fell in line behind them, contemplating the actions to which the "gang" was sinking on its behalf.

Duval Street was now completely filled with the flood of mankind that formed the residue along the parade route. The bars on the avenue continued to have their doors thrown wide, with people wandering in and out. On the street, two-way foot traffic had formed in the separate lanes, no doubt instinctively mandated by the automobile driver hidden within every American. However, down the middle of the thoroughfare the streams of revelers seemed to periodically clash like cross current waves in the surf. Momentarily one stream or the other would falter, breaking on a small stationary group, then reform and again advance along the asphalt.

Joining the southward migration along the west side of the street, Chick, Riley and the pig melded into the chaos. At virtually every intersection, one or more police were evident, but none of them exhibited even slight interest in the passing trio. Still, when possible the group sidled across the flow to get as far as possible from the law at each encounter. There was no point in trying to hurry through the throng; it was simply not possible. Like a stream finding its way along a broken course, this flow trickled, hesitated or rushed as the terrain allowed and demanded.

A couple of times the trio's flight was interrupted by revelers wanting to pet the "dog." The true nature of the beast brought one such encounter to a quick halt when a woman dressed like Morticia

Addams dropped her drink in disgust at the realization she had her hand on a hog. The second such incident took more time, for the drunken man in a pirate costume never seemed to comprehend that he was hugging a swine. Once past the old La Concha Hotel, the crowd began to thin a bit, allowing Riley, Chick and the pig to gain some speed. Finally reaching the junction of Duval and United Street, the trio turned east on that latter avenue, passing back into a residential section.

The change of direction also brought an end to glaring streetlights along Duval, but some pedestrian traffic continued to flow along both sidewalks. A few of the houses were also well lit by parties that would no doubt continue far into the evening and morning. Beneath a huge banyan tree that created almost pitch black conditions under its spreading girth Chick halted the group and got the cell phone from Riley's pack.

"Cap," he quizzed after dialing, "where are you?"

"At the helm of the Rosita," was the groused reply from Capt. Arnie. "Where the hell else would I be? But if you're interested in where she might be, we're rounding Fort Taylor and should be at the quay in another 15 minutes."

"We're on United now," Chick informed, "It'll probably take us a bit longer to get down there. We'll be coming down McReynolds, past Higg's Beach and then along Atlantic."

"Aye," the old fisherman acknowledged. "Even and old sea dog like me should still have eyes enough to spot two fools and a pig on the beach. I'll lay to just off the pier till I see you."

"Thanks Cap," Chick ended the conversation.

The next call was to Eric Allen.

"Allen, how's it going?" he quizzed.

"I'm ahead of schedule and cooling my heels in a convenience store parking lot on Big Coppitt Key," came the smug reply from the parked van. "Will you be there for the pick up?"

Eric Allen delivered the last line in a sinister tone, as though trying to imitate a covert agent.

"It's looking good," Chick said, "but we've had a slight change of route in town. We should be on the water in about half an hour. We'll call from the boat and tell you when to move to the drop point."

"I'll be there," Allen concluded simply and cut off the call.

Chick then dialed a final number.

"Arbie," he said into the receiver, "How'd you make out?"

"Like a charm," R&B Mann answered, and then added in a lowered voice, "thanks to Capt. Carla's charms. Man, did you get a look at the hooters on that woman. That cracker cop sure took his time enforcing the law on her. Suspect you'll see her all over the Internet before the night is over. She showed some nerve with all those cameras flashing."

"So you're in the clear?" Chick asked.

"Yeah, he finally made her put the tee shirt on that he gave her," the blues man reported. "But right afterwards he got out a cell phone and called somebody. Don't know what that means? Cops usually use radios."

"Your right," Chick agreed. "But either way, you bought us the time we needed. Now it's time for the two of you to clear out. Are you still on Duval?"

"Headed over to Greene Street now to pick up the car."

"Good," Chick said, "see you after while."

"Luck to you and your pig," R&B ended the call.

"What do you think?" Riley, who had caught the gist of the conversations, asked.

"Our luck does seem to be holding," Chick offered. "The cop's call bothers me though. Hopefully it was just to brag to a buddy about Carla's boobs. If not, there's nothing we can do but keep moving, which I think we had better do right now."

Quickly on the move again, the trio headed east along United, then turned south on McReynolds Street. Now freed from the Fantasy Fest crowds, their porcine companion was bent upon stretching its stubby legs. Riley was breathing a bit faster than normal trying to keep pace with Chick, who was holding the rope leash like a water skier as he streamed along in the pig's wake.

At the end of McReynolds the group rounded a bend onto Atlantic Boulevard and came abreast of the sandy southern fringe of Key West. The moon was now high in the sky behind them, shining across the island to fall on the black sheet of water stretching off toward Cuba. Along the distance horizon the blinking beacon of the light off the southern tip of Fort Taylor flashed intermittently, marking the reef that skirted the Intracoastal Waterway and the Hawk Channel. The running lights of a single large tanker or container ship were also visible out there as well. Much closer to shore and not far off the end of the White Street Pier, the running lights of a smaller boat glowed.

The two men and the swine quickly covered the remaining beachfront to turn right out onto the long quay. Walking out the concrete structure, they passed the first of two sets of wings branching out to the sides. Connected by a set of steps, these were several feet lower to the water than the main level. At the last set of these they climbed down to the right, just as the bow of the Rosita nudged in against the concrete.

"Get the hell on board and let's get moving," Capt. Arnie demanded.

The old man's face was slightly lit by the console lights on the helm. At the sight of him, Riley imagined that not all the illumination was coming from gauge lighting. The seafarer's eyes were so bright and animated that it was not hard to guess he was enjoying being in the nefarious role so often presented in the yarns he spun. Whether dangerous or benign, smuggling guns or a hog, such adventures were obviously what the captain considered his element.

Combining their efforts, Riley and Chick quickly, but wordlessly, had the hog off the pier and over the gunnels into the fishing smack's rear cockpit area.

The diesel engine then roared loudly into gear as the vessel backed away from the dock. Making a wide turn the Rosita headed out to the dark, deeper waters before turning east.

Officer Mark Farnsworth was still bogged down in traffic, having just reached Garrison Bight on North Roosevelt Boulevard, when he got the call from Sergeant Al Hastens. The sergeant had seemed uncharacteristically apologetic in relating that he was fairly certain he had spotted the perps with the pig, but they had managed to elude him in the crowd. At least, however, Farnsworth knew they were headed south along Duval Street. For the first time since he left Stock Island he had a direction to travel with some purpose.

When he finally crept up to the intersection with First Street, he again used his blue lights to speed a turn through the oncoming left lane. Though still congested, the traffic lightened considerably and kept moving as he drove south across the island's narrow waistband, headed toward the Atlantic Ocean. Crossing Flagler Avenue, where the throughway changed its name to Bertha Street, Farnsworth was mulling his situation. In a few more blocks he would have to decide whether to cruise east on South Roosevelt along Smathers Beach or west past Rest Beach toward the White Street Pier on Atlantic Boulevard. The hopelessness of his predicament was closing on the young policeman. Not only had he lost the hog and most of his hope of recovering it, but it could be construed that he had left his assigned post as well.

For no precise reason, he made the turn west onto Atlantic Boulevard. His options for the moment and the future were coming into sharper focus as he edged his cruiser into a parking space on the right of the road. With no idea where to turn next, his best bet appeared to be a return to Stock Island and make an official report of the hog heist. If he did not get fired for chasing off into the city, he knew his job would still become intolerable in the sarcastic hands of the rest of the officers on the force. For the first time the offer his uncle Art had make to get him to come up to Fort Lauderdale to work for him in the home security business began to sound appealing. Maybe he would give his mother's brother a call on Monday morning.

Reversing his course, Officer Mark Farnsworth swung the police car across the highway to head back east. In pulling away, he glanced past the trunks of a couple of palm trees and out over the water to his right at the lights of a small fishing boat fading into the Atlantic's black night.

Chapter 26

Once shrouded in the darkness and out of eyeshot of the shore, Chick, Riley and the hog shed their presidential disguises. The pig then unceremoniously plopped down against the transom at the back of the cockpit, seeming to take the whirlwind of activity to which it had been exposed in the last hours in stride. Now away from the crowded island, Riley too was a bit more at ease.

After a few minutes he was drawn to staring at the furrowed wake the Rosita plowed through the calm surface of the night sea. Attached to a rope, they were towing a small skiff that erratically zigzagged as it skipped back and forth across that churned water. But, it was the phosphorescent glow trailing in the wake that held Riley's attention. Dredged up from the forgotten depths of high school or college reading, he recalled that the glow was produced by millions of *protozoan noctiluca* being churned by the spinning propeller. The disturbance of their microscopic world induced them to give off a "cold light" — one that science could not fully explain.

Riley glanced up at Chick, standing beside the captain and peering ahead into the darkness that the boat was penetrating. The similarity of situations struck him as ironic. Just as the passing of the Rosita was setting the world of the protozoans a churn, the passage of Chick Malor through Riley's settled existence had knocked normality off center, producing a whirl of confused activity.

He also wondered if the tiny animals in the boats slip stream were so dazed by the light they gave off that they simply fell in with the path of least resistance, awaiting calmer water. If so, they were sharing his fate. Riley felt a bit helpless as he considered the last couple of weeks and his own ride on the currents that had swirled around him.

A soft snort emanating from the swine near his feet drew Riley's attention back into the boat. The hog was looking up at him, and for a second there seemed to be some intelligence behind the piggish snout and its constant faux smile. Riley shook his head slightly, clearing his mind of this reverie. It was no time to start commiserating with small animals, or communicating with greater ones. Better to stay alert to their venture, which could still end up a disaster just as easily as a success.

The diesel engine of the fishing boat hammered away, pushing the craft through the dark water to the east as Riley now gazed toward the sparkling lights of the islands along which they plied. Directly north the sky was bright above Key West, swallowing the glow of the town's lights that streamed up from the parties that would continue all night. Along the shore they now skirted, the row of streetlights on South Roosevelt Boulevard formed a string of pearls edging the end of the land. Ahead to the northeast, Stock Island from which they had so recently fled, presented a subtler vista. The lights of that isle were fainter as they shined over the low dark silhouette of undeveloped Cow Key. Farther in the distance the sweeping lights of the flight control tower on Boca Chita Key hinted at the presence of Naval Air Station Key West, which lay very close to their destination.

Riley took a few paces toward the bow to join Chick and Capt. Arnie at the helm.

"How much longer?" he asked the old seafarer.

"You should have you're lubber feet on dry land inside the hour," the old man said, glancing over at Riley with an appraising eye, seeming to measure the man's fitness for handling covert endeavors. "If you don't get lost between the ship and shore."

"The toughest part's over now," Chick assured, also looking over at Riley. "All we have to do is row the pig ashore and turn it over to Allen."

For the next half hour the trio ran into the night in silence, the old fisherman's gaze locked on the dark water ahead, while Chick and Riley scanned the lighted horizon to the north.

Finally Chick broke the calm, turning his attention to the captain.

"Sure appreciate your help, Cap," Chick said. "We couldn't have pulled it off without you."

"You ain't ashore yet," the old man chided, and then softened. "Too bad you're not coming back to the town."

Then, as though catching himself in a weak moment he reverted his tone.

"I was getting used to the rent you paid," he snapped.

"Yeah," Chick said, throwing an arm around the smaller man and squeezing him.

Capt. Arnie shook him off with a scowl, reminding Riley of a terrier shedding water after a bath.

"No time for sentiment," Capt. Arnie said. "Like I said, you're not off the boat yet."

"You're right, Cap," Chick agreed. "Hand me the phone, Chipmunk. It's time we get Allen moving."

Riley dug into his gear for the cell phone, realizing it had been a while since Chick had used that nickname on him.

On the second ring Eric Allen answered.

"It's time to move," Chick said, sounding much like a character in the old "Mission Impossible" television show. "Give us a call back to confirm when you are in position."

As he finished the instruction, he could hear over the phone the grind of the van's starter turning over as Allen complied.

"I should be there in about 10 minutes," he replied.

"Take your time," Chick added. "We're at least 30 minutes out."

"Just don't dawdle," Allen snapped back as he cut the call off.

"Dawdle?" Chick said with a bemused smirk, first looking at the phone and then over at Riley. "What a perfect prick."

"This is it," Capt. Arnie announced, then addressed Riley. "Time to get the skiff in."

Riley moved to the stern and began pulling the rope that towed the small boat in their wake. Once alongside, he lashed it to a cleat on the gunnels. Immediately Chick had the hog roused and the pair struggled to get it through the portal in the rail and down into the smaller craft. Once accomplished, Riley addressed the captain.

"Is this as close as we can get?" he asked, surveying the dim rim of backlit land in the distance.

"Without going aground," the old man replied. "Nothing but a bonefish flat between us and the shore. If the tide wasn't in you couldn't even row the skiff over it."

"What's that glow down to the left," Riley added.

"Looks to be an open fire," the old man said after peering in that direction. "Probably some Cuban's on an all-night fishing and beer party."

Chick had already climbed down into the small boat, but reached a hand up to Capt. Arnie who had moved over to the railing.

"Thanks again, Cap," he said, taking the little man's strong hand. "Maybe we'll get back down to visit again."

The older man just nodded and smiled, then released the grip and offered his hand to Riley.

"You two lubbers take care," he concluded.

With that Riley climbed down into the skiff and pushed it off from the larger boat. He offered

Captain Arnie a last wave, as Chick leaned into the oars to pull the small boat away into the gloom.

Eric Allen did take his time getting out onto U.S. 1 on Big Coppitt Key, seeing no reason to wait out in the dark mangroves rather than where he was now stationed. Since he was the one that would be stuck with the stolen pig all night, the rest of the plan should now revolve around him. In fact, he decided to walk inside the convenience store and get a Dr. Pepper before leaving. There was plenty of time because they were coming ashore in a rowboat, which would take forever. That made no sense to him. Why not use an outboard? Who would hear it out there anyway? All in all, to him the venture seemed poorly planned and contorted. Certainly not up to STAG standards of operations.

And the place they had picked for the rendezvous out at the end of the road on a gay, nude beach in the middle of the night? Did they really expect him to be hanging around out there waiting on them? If it were not for his commitment to the cause he would never have gotten involved with that crazy, old Neanderthal fisherman and a couple of tourists. They probably did not even know anything about Boca Chica Beach and what goes on out there. That is exactly the reason he had been adamant that they meet at the Geiger Creek bridge. If someone was going to be traipsing around out there in the "gay friendly" bushes at night, it would not be Eric Allen. The fact his co-conspirators had not protested spoke volumes to him as well, further proving their ignorance of the area. He would be a good half-mile from anywhere they could land along the beach area.

In fact, it would not surprise him if this whole thing was a trap to discredit his organization. The local, state and federal agencies would dearly love to catch him on that beach. He could see the headlines all over the east coast. "STAG Goes Gay And Nude!" They would do anything to stop the movement. But by only venturing as far as the bridge, if things did go badly he could claim he had heard what was going down through the grapevine and was only worried about the welfare of the pig. Thus he was conducting a covert operation to monitor the situation.

Finally, after what he considered a sufficient amount of time, Allen got back in the van and pulled out on the highway, traveling a little to the east before turning south onto Old State Route 941. The road made a long loop out across the southern arm of Big Coppitt, then across small Geiger Key and finally onto Boca Chica. At one time the road had almost circled that latter island, but was now washed out and closed just a short way east of the end of the Naval Air Station's southeast runway. Driving south along the roadway, Allen passed through the residential developments of Big Coppitt Estates, Boca Chica Ocean Shores, then a small Navy radar tracking station reservation and finally through more houses in Tamarac Park. Crossing the bridge that connected Geiger and Boca Chica, he pulled off onto the shoulder of the road into the area used by locals when they fished from the bridge. Again, he congratulated himself on his own resourcefulness as he got the spinning rod out of the back of the truck, walked out on the bridge and dropped the bait less line down into the water. He was now just a guy trying to put a mangrove snapper on tomorrow's dinner table.

He had hardly gotten in position, however, when headlights came sweeping down the road from the east. He watched them grow in intensity and as the vehicle passed, Allen's face twisted with concern. Could it be just a coincidence that a van just like the one he was using had driven past? It even bore the same "Cheap Trucks" logo on its side. He had only a few moments to consider the situation before three more vehicles came rolling down the road. Two were full-sized sedans, and the third was a big SUV, all packed with occupants.

Allen watched the procession, trying to fight back the sensation that they must be law enforcement and looking for him. Relief then flooded that concern away when the vehicles rolled across the bridge and kept moving toward the beach. He watched them passing on down the highway, then felt fear welling up again. The cars and truck stopped a couple of hundred yards down the road, with the SUV firmly planted in the middle of the highway facing west toward the beach. The cars were turned out like wings to either side, completely blocking the roadway and shoulder between the mangrove swamps on either side.

Eric Allen swallowed hard and reached for the cell phone in his pocket.

To the east of Boca Chica Beach and due south of Pelican Key and Saddlebunch Harbor, the USCGC Sapelo lay rolling gently in the one-foot swells sweeping down the Hawk Channel. Though appearing dead in the water, the 110-foot craft's dual diesel engines idled with the twin props turning just enough to hold her position. At the rail on the bridge level and just aft of the cutter's helm compartment, Lt. Matthew Jackson stood in command, surveying the stern deck. The derrick had just been withdrawn to its normal position, having earlier launched the 19-foot rigid hull inflatable boat by swinging it over the side. With the away party in that craft absent, the cutter's complement was reduced to 10 officers and crew, all of whom were at station ready to put the craft in motion or man armaments as needed.

The officer next cast his gaze southward at the sea glistening beneath the quarter moon. A few lights glowed from boats in the distance, but he knew that the single ship on which he was concentrating was not among them. He was still keeping close watch on it, but rather electronically, as the cutter's powerful radar swept the water to monitor every move of the S.S. Loro, though the two craft were not within easy eye contact of each other. Finally satisfied with the deck situation, Lt. Jackson turned and entered the wheelhouse.

Once inside he took the radio handset from the console and keyed it. Rather than transmitting on one of the three VHF marine channels reserved for Coast Guard use, however, the transmission was scrambled and secure. He had little doubt that aboard the Loro, lying just outside the 12-mile limit of U.S. territorial waters, Capt. Samuelo Porticia was monitoring all those normal frequencies.

"Chief Bork, what's your status," he quizzed. "Do you still have contact?"

"Aye captain," was the reply from his senior petty officer. "We have visual and the target's still moving toward Boca Chica and giving no hint he knows we're here."

"OK, chief," the officer noted. "All assets are in place. The DEA has the land route blocked and the helicopter is hovering just north of the naval air station. On your call they'll come in and light up the beach. Good luck and stay safe."

"Aye, captain," Chief Petty Officer Foster Bork replied, then handed the radio to Seaman Andrea Livingston.

The CPO and other five members of the team crouched in the small boat as the 60-horse power outboard pushed them easily through the water. Dressed in black long sleeve shirts, pants and baseball-style caps and running with no lights, the crew and their boat were nearly invisible. Strapped around Bork's head was a set of night vision goggles through which he peered to the south. Through the eye gear he was locked on the surreal green glow of a small skiff containing three men running parallel to their own craft, but many yards off their port.

"Just hold her steady," he said to the man at the helm, who also sported the night vision gear. "Don't want to get too fast or close and goose them."

Livingston and one other member of the party were armed with M-16 rifles, while the rest clutched Coast Guard 12-gauge combat shotguns. The chief sported only a 9-millimeter pistol holstered to his belt. Additionally, the young woman held a large pair of binoculars.

"We'll just hang with them until they are about to land," Bork concluded, as though talking to himself.

The flames of the bonfire leapt skyward, filling the tropical night with a spray of glowing ash-embers each time another section of scrap two-by-four board was tossed into the inferno. The blaze was centered in a small section of sand, amid the scrub brush and coral rock of what passes for a beach in the Florida Keys. Spread around the fire were several blankets on the ground, some low beach chairs and several small coolers. The chairs and blankets were inhabited by a collection of men ranging in age from their mid-20s on up into middle age, the bulk of whom were attired in the gaudy western wear recently displayed on the Cayo Hueso Men's Chorale float in the Key West parade. The scarlet and white clad cowboy and Indian entourage put up a continual din of laughter and conversation to compete with a portable cassette tape player that provided a background of Jimmy Buffett crooning "A Cowboy In The Jungle."

"That should hold it for a while," Mike said, as he chunked a piece of the scrap lumber onto the fire, then glanced over to Mac Garland, "and makes a useful end to the float."

"You're a veritable environmental wonder," Garland shot back, already showing the early results of having visited the surrounding coolers. "Recycling one of our escapades into another. I can also assure you that there's enough libations to hold us for a while too,"

A raised plastic cup in one of Garland's hands accompanied the last part of the line, while the other held an open bottle of Chateau Saint Michelle chardonnay.

"Will someone please change that music?" Bernard shouted across the sand from the opposite side of the fire ring. "I'd like to have something that I can dance to. It's booty time!"

Finishing his plea, the man was on his feet, still dressed in vest, cowboy hat and chaps, doing his best impression of a buck dance. Garland just grinned, as Mike shook his head in mock disgust. Then as the music shifted to a beat more suited to a big city dance club, Bernard began to gyrate to it, joined by several other men rising from the shadowy flicker of the light. Their movements around the bonfire, silhouetted against the moonlit sea offered an aboriginal quality to the scene.

"Gentlemen," Mac Garland shouted, raising his cup in the air, "I give you a successful Fantasy Fest and an evening in the men's corral!"

As Riley took his turn at the oars, their little rowboat drew nearer to the beach of Boca Chica Key. Chick sat in the bow of the boat, alternately peering shoreward or looking down at the hog that, as usual, had immediately plopped down in a heap between the seats of the skiff. Besides claiming the oars, Riley had progressively recovered his uneasy with their situation as well. Above the splash of the oars hitting the water he was sure he had heard the buzz of at least one and possible more outboard motors in the distance, though there were no boat lights visible. The music and scrambled voices drifting up the beach from the now clearly visible bonfire did not help either. Though never stated, he had assumed they would be landing on a deserted strip of shore, not one where a party was in progress.

"You think we should aim farther down the beach from them?" he asked over his shoulder.

"Who?" Chick replied, almost as though he had not seen the fire, but then acknowledged, "No reason to, Chipmunk; probably just some kids drinking beer. Good sign; means everything is normal out here. Few more minutes and we'll have the hog in the van."

Riley physically started from his seat, when the ring of the cell phone in the pack cut through the sea air. His companion quickly had it out and to his ear. Before Chick said a word, Riley could hear an excited voice rushing through a message.

"Yeah," Chick finally said, "it does sound like a problem? So it is just on our side of the bridge and not a problem for you?"

After a pause he continued.

"Is there dry land and underbrush to the north of the road? OK, just hold on where you are. When we get ashore, we'll cross over the road and come up along through there, between the pavement and the fence. And you've got no idea who it is that has set up the road bock?" then he concluded. "Just don't panic. Keep fishing and we'll be there as soon as we can."

"Road block? Fishing?" Riley blurted as Chick ended the call. "I gather we have a problem?"

"Nothing we can't work around," Chick grinned through the darkness at his companion.

Fortunately, having his back to Chick and bending to the oars, Riley could not see the concern that next crept over his friend's visage.

With a few more strokes of the oars, the little skiff covered the final approach through the almost imperceptible swelling of the water reaching shore. Still 20 feet from dry land, the bow of the rowboat jammed against the shallow sand and rock bottom. When the boat made that landfall, Chick, Riley and their contraband swine lumbered over the side, the men's feet marring slightly in the soft sand bottom. The pig splashed heavily as it plopped over the gunnels into the shallows. As the trio turned to cover the last couple of yards to the beach, the air was suddenly shattered with a thunderous whacking noise. At the same instant, both the sea behind Chick and Riley and sky above erupted with streams of brilliant white light.

Chapter 27

The complement of Coast Guardsmen was tense in the small inflatable boat. Once the other launch they had been tracking from the S.S, Loro made land fall, Chief Foster Bork had made the call to bring the HH-65A Dolphin short-range recovery helicopter with its twin gas-turbine engines thundering over the beach from the inland side. From beneath its fuselage the glaring spotlight - ordinarily used for search and rescue missions in the dark at sea - swept across the shoreline of Boca Chica, locking in on the spot where Hector Corro and his two crew mates from the Loro were just planting their feet in the shallows and off-loading the first of several small crates.

From the Sapelo's away boat, two hand-held, one-million candlepower spotlights were added to the illumination, both to brighten the scene and impress the intruders with the fact they were hemmed in from sea and air. The final prong of their dilemma would also quickly arrive in the form of agents of the federal Drug Enforcement Administration moving down the only road along this part of the island.

Sitting just offshore, CPO Bork had almost forgotten to remove the night vision gear from his eyes before the light came on. Three other members of the crew nervously grasped their weapons, alert for the first hint of resistance. Next to the chief, Seaman Andrea Livingston held the binoculars to her eyes sweeping up and down the shore.

"Holy crap!" she blurted, then momentarily and sheepishly averted her gaze up to her taller superior. "Sorry, chief."

"What is it, Livingston?" Bork asked,

"I've got our target and they're unloading, chief," she replied. "But there's another boat just down the beach too."

"Another boat?"

"Yeah, and what appears to be a couple of men with," she hesitated, "a pig on a leash?"

"Let me see those," Bork ordered reaching for the glasses, then quickly surveying the shore himself.

As described, he spotted the Loro's motor launch sitting on the shallow water just off the beach, while Corro, Caesar and the huge black seaman were wrestling with boxes in the shallows near the sand. But also to the right and some yards down the shore there was a rowboat, and struggling toward the beach what did look like two men with a huge hog on a leash. The chief's survey of the shore also revealed a couple of other discoveries, one of which was expected, but the others were additional surprises.

Parked back behind a low tangle of bushes that separated the sand from the road, a small moving van was visible. On its side was stenciled "Cheap Trucks" and beside the vehicle a man stared slack-jawed out to sea. He and his van were the expected find, since the Loro crew would need a pick up connection. But down the sand to the left the chief spotted a pick up truck with a flat bed trailer attached, along with more commotion,

"It can't be?" he muttered aloud as though doubting his own eyes.

"What've you got, Chief?" the young woman at his side asked.

"Damned if it doesn't look like the bushes are full of half naked cowboys and Indians scattering every which away!" he described, and then lowering the glasses glanced to the helmsman. "Get us in there."

Riley, Chick and the pig stood on the sand bottom in water up to the men's ankles. Their clandestine landing in the dark had suddenly been illuminated by the rays of brilliant white light streaming in from the sea and above. The noise of a clattering helicopter hovering low provided a deafening soundtrack to the activity on the ground. As Riley looked down the beach to the west, it was as though time stopped. The entire area that was lit by the spotlights and the bonfire farther down was alive with moving figures.

Closest to Riley was another small boat beached in the shallows. Three men were lumbering toward the sandy shore, laden with small crates that were obviously quite heavy from the way they were moving. The last of the three men dropped his load as Riley watched and began running toward the beach with a high stepping motion through shallow brine. When the other two followed suit, the middle of them stripped off the white tee shirt he wore. A large black man, once free of the light colored fabric he would have disappeared in the night, had it not been for the sweep of the floodlights playing back and forth across him to create a silhouette.

In the direction the men fled, Riley next became aware of a single man standing beside a van. At the sight, his heart virtually stopped beating for a moment, fearing the individual to be Eric Allen. Riley's dread from earlier in the evening about being apprehended and incarcerated swelled anew.

While he watched, that man suddenly swung around as if to get into the truck, but again froze when he spotted headlights now slowly approaching along the highway from the east. With that, the van driver too joined the mad scramble along the beach. He began running west toward the bonfire.

The confusion now became complete as those fleeing men intermingled with a flood of others running from the direction of the blaze. Riley stood mystified at what seemed a scene from a psychedelic western movie. In what appeared to be sheer panic, several dozen figures were rushing up the shore from the west. Some wore cowboy hats, while other sported Indian headdresses. As the lights played across them, red and white reflections appeared on their bodies, from chaps, loin clothes and vests, but some lacked portions or even all of those coverings.

Indeed, Riley might have simply held his position just at the edge of the lapping waters of the Atlantic Ocean and let the tide of approaching humanity sweep past, had not his moment of suspended senses been abruptly halted by some much closer activity. For the first time since he and Chick had spirited their porcine companion from the children's zoo, the creature's animal instincts succumbed to the surroundings through which it was passing. The combination of moving lights, thundering din and frantic activity jolted its most primitive motivations — it was time to fight or flee. The hog chose the latter.

At the sound of a splash, more perceived than actually heard, Riley spun to see the pig in full stride making for the beach heading into the oncoming crowd. Showing for the first time its strength, the pig had caught Chick completely off guard, yanking him face first in the shallow water and proceeding to drag him out on the beach. Whether from sheer surprise or determination, the man did not release the rope leash and was being dragged out on the coral and sand shore. The hog with Chick in tow made quick work of the beach, crossing the narrow band and disappearing into to scrubby brush row beyond. But, before dragging Chick into that dimly lit region, one of the figures running down the beach from the bonfire tripped over the rope connecting man and animal. As the man flipped and rolled wildly past, Riley noted that he was dressed like a cowboy, though it did register that such western attire ordinarily included some kind of pants or jeans under the chaps.

Finally breaking free of the lethargy, Riley set off at a run in the direction the swine and his friend had disappeared. Upon reaching the line of underbrush separating the beach from the paved road, he looked back over his shoulder to see armed men exiting yet another small boat. It reminded him of a scene from some Navy SEAL movie. While single members of that force made directly for each of the two stranded skiffs, the rest joined the confusion on the shore. Feeling the hard, but very broken pavement now underfoot, Riley glanced to his right and could see outlined by lights coming down the road that a barrier was across the highway, effectively ending any vehicle passage farther down to where he was crossing.

Picking a spot to get back into the undergrowth presented a moment of puzzlement for him, since the thrashing of the pig and its towed cargo had now subsided. But figuring the pair had so far traveled in a straight line, Riley saw no reason to expect a change and charged straight into the foliaged edge beyond. He quickly discovered that this side of the roadway was actually a mangrove swamp. The first set of trailing roots he reached tripped him up and he pitched face first into the slime. Rising up on his hands and knees, both of which sank several inches into the soft muck, he spotted Chick and the hog just ahead, the rope tangling in the short mangrove bushes having halted their mad rush. The pig was grunting loudly trying to pull the rope free.

Never regaining his feet, Riley crawled through the mud to the where Chick lay.

"You all right?" he asked in a whisper, staring at his buddies scratched and scraped visage.

"No need to whisper," Chick replied. "Nobody could hear you for the helicopter and this animals bellowing. Don't think anything is broken. And why don't you answer that telephone?"

At the question Riley became aware for the first time that the cell phone in his pack was ringing. He had no idea when it started. It could have been sounding since the first lights appeared for all he knew. Scrambling to get the daypack off his back he finally got the cell phone out and instinctively answered it.

"Hello?" he said.

"What's going on out there?" Eric Allen's voice literately hissed from the phone.

"Where are you?" Riley shot back, rather than answering the question.

"With the truck where I'm supposed to be. But if you don't get up here soon I'll be in it and gone in a hurry," he warned.

"But I saw you run away from it?"

"Unless you're up here at Geiger Creek there's no way you've seen me, dick head. Let me talk to Chick," Allen demanded.

Riley sullenly stuck the phone out in Chick's direction, who sat up to accept it.

"OK, what's going on?" Chick asked,

"I have no idea," Allen returned. "The road block is still here, but one of the cars and a bunch of men did head down to the beach."

"Looks like we just stepped into something," Chick said. "We've got helicopters over the beach, landing parties and a bunch of really weird dudes running up and down the shore."

"You better have a good plan on the tip of your tongue right now," Allen growled crossly, "or you two and the pig are in for a long stroll up the islands."

Chick only paused for a moment.

"What's the inland side of the road look like up there?" he asked.

"A dark, wet, smelly swamp as far as I can tell," Allen said.

"We're already on that side of the road," Chick explained. "We're coming up through the swamp, so just hold what you got until we get there."

The phone connection fell silent for several moments, and Chick guessed that Eric Allen was pondering whether it was time for him to just beat a retreat and leave the rest of them stranded.

"You there, Allen?" he finally demanded.

"Yes. You have 20 minutes and not a second longer," then he hung up.

"Let's move parallel to the road," Chick said turning to Riley. "That bastard will leave us for sure."

Immediately, Riley's stomach soured again. Despite his cynical nature, that was the roughest assessment he had ever heard Chick render regarding anyone. He suddenly felt any hope of escape slipping out of his grasp. Still, he crouched low and followed Chick and the swine through the sulfur smelling muck. They labored through the mud, making their way around the descending roots of the mangroves, thrashing in the water and getting marred in particularly soft spots on the bottom. The hog had once again calmed down and seemed quite happy with their route and its condition. Fortunately the continued presence of the helicopter over the scene provided plenty of background noise to conceal their passage. The aircraft was now hovering higher above the beach, still sweeping its lights back and forth.

After about 50 yards of the slogging, lights were visible to their right on the roadway. Halting, both men peered through the dark mangroves at the glow of headlights illuminating the van Riley had spotted earlier. The vehicle bore the Cheap Trucks logo and was a dead ringer for the Eric Allen was supposed to have parked up at Geiger Creek.

Flashlights were also playing in the dark around the truck, revealing two men spread-eagled and hands rooted on the hood of the vehicle. One appeared to be Hispanic, while Riley had the gut feeling the other was the individual he had earlier seen next to the van. Around them were several men in windbreakers marked with the initials "DEA," plus a man and woman clad in black. The woman casually clasped an automatic rifle, muzzle pointed to the ground. Also visible standing nearby was a couple of the band of cowboys and Indians, apparently being questioned by more of the DEA agents. Riley recognized one of them, who had a DEA jacket wrapped around his waist and wearing it like a skirt with the chaps protruding below, as the man who had taken the tumble over the pig's lease on the beach. Sitting askew and crushed, but still clinging atop his head was a red cowboy hat.

Chick reached over and tapped Riley on the shoulder, then made a hand signal indicating a desire to move deeper into the swamp away from the road. With a final glance toward the lights, Riley complied.

Chief Foster Bork stood in the glare of the headlights, silhouetted with another man dressed in a jacket emblazoned with the Drug Enforcement Administration initials.

"Chief, I'm lead agent Jeff Seymour," the man introduced himself to Bork, and then shook his head with a quizzical look on his face. "You ever been involved in a goat roping like this one?"

"Foster Bork," the chief returned the introduction. "Doesn't fit the text books does it? What'd you find in the crates at the beach?"

"I'm no expert, but it appears to be some kind of pre-Columbian artifacts. We'll have it tested to make sure of the composition. Could have something concealed, but then they probably wouldn't have been coming in here at night with it," Seymour surmised. "Best guess is we just busted some art smugglers that will get turned over to customs. Rest of these characters appear to have been having a pretty raunchy party in the wrong place at the wrong time. Just going to take us some time to sort out who's who."

"We'll help round them up," Bork offered, "and leave the rest to you. By my count, we're still missing two of the Loro landing party."

"Only one," Seymour corrected. "My guys have another of them just up the beach and bringing him in now. A big black guy."

With that, Bork turned his gaze out toward the dark swamp.

"Any word on two men with a pig?" he asked.

"Yeah, chief, that one's a puzzler. The guys in the chopper reported seeing them on the beach, but nothing since then. What do you make of that pair?" the agent wondered.

Chief Foster Bork gestured over toward the knot of men in western wear, where Bernard now stood in his makeshift skirt next to a very glum looking Mike the carpenter.

"With this crowd, I'd just hate to be the pig." the chief replied humorlessly.

Squatting in the dark shadows beneath the mangrove leaves, Hector Corro silently cursed to himself in Spanish, while his mind also raced to come up with a plan of some type. From the moment the lights had come on down on the beach his mind had not functioned. Rather, primal instincts had driven him inland away from perceived dangers. Just before plunging into this filthy hell of a swamp he had seen Caesar taken at gunpoint, but knew nothing of what had happened to the black one. Indeed, he cared little what became of either of the men. His own survival and escape were driving his actions.

Now catching his breath, he began to consider his options. Alone, illegally in an unknown country and unarmed he felt helpless. Had that *cabra viejo* of a captain allowed him a gun he would have felt more confidant. As it was he must hide like a timid *raton*. Should he simply sit still, hide and hope not to be found? Or which way to move to escape?

Falling back onto another basic human trait, now confronted with a problem for which he had no solution and was unprepared to deal, he chose the comfortable assumption that action would denote progress. Slowly he slipped through the shallow, stinking water, moving away from the road and deeper into the muck surrounding the mangrove bushes.

Chick, Riley and the pig were now fairly creeping through the shallow water and sticky bottom beneath it, balancing the need for stealth with the certain knowledge that up at Geiger Creek, Eric Allen might at any moment turn rabbit and scurry for cover. Adding to the ordeal, the helicopter was now slowly working its way from west to east, sweeping the black waters with its searchlight. Riley assumed that meant the beach and road had now been cleansed of confused individuals running amok in the darkness. Like a medieval executioner wandering the field after a battle to finish off the wounded and stragglers, the clattering aircraft searched for its prey.

Having retreated inland before turning east, the trio had come to what resembled a moat edging a raised levy topped by a chain-link fence. Though the little channel of water was only four or five feet wide, it proved to be quite deep, probably having yielded the fill material from which the opposite embankment was created. On both passes the helicopter made over them, the men had sunk down into the dark water until only their heads were exposed and those shielded beneath the bows of the mangroves. There they clung with their hands to roots at the waterline to keep from putting their feet and weight down into the abyss of muck on the bottom of the channel. Meanwhile the hog simply stood under the canopy amid the roots with its usual amused look on its snout. After the last transit of the copter, Chick and Riley sloshed back up out of the water and moved as quickly as possible to the east. Another hundred yards along, however, they again froze, and slipped back into the water. Down the fence line a pair of flashlights were approaching from the east.

The two figures moved cautiously down the levy, just within the fence that surrounded the perimeter of Naval Air Station Key West. In the lead was a young, slender boy in fatigues carrying a flashlight and 12-gauge shotgun, his uniform bearing the insignia of the base's marine security detail. Behind him also casually sweeping the edge of the fence line with a flashlight was a slightly older black man bearing the stripes of a gunnery sergeant. On his belt was slung a holster containing a side arm, the flap holding it in place loosened for quick action.

"Check on down the line, Anderson," the sergeant instructed, coming to a halt and looking through the fence across the canal.

"You see something, gunnie?" the young man asked.

"Just need to take a whizz," he replied. "Keep moving and I'll catch up."

With that the younger man proceeded along the fence line.

"What do you think's going on out there?" he asked back over his shoulder.

"Only know it's some kind of security operation," the gunnery sergeant answered, "and we're supposed to make sure it doesn't spill over onto the base."

Now a good 30 yards ahead of his superior, the enlisted man kept sweeping the far bank of the ditch with his flashlight. In one of the passes of the beam, he found it illuminating a pair of close-set eyes separated by a seemingly smiling snout. Frozen for an instance, he then looked back toward his companion.

"You better get down here, gunnie," he yelled in a voice tinged with puzzlement. "I got something."

The sergeant came along the levy at a double-quick trot, his hand on the butt of the pistol in his holster. But, when the younger man looked back to the canal, the visage he had seen was gone.

"What is it, Anderson," the sergeant asked, looking across the water at the tiny circle of light playing along the mangrove edge.

"It's gone, gunnie," he answered. "But it looked like a wild hog, except I'd have sworn it was smiling at me?"

Both men continued to play the beams of their flashlights along the far shore, revealing nothing. Slowly they moved a bit farther west along the levy.

"Damn, Anderson, there ain't no wild hogs on this island," the sergeant finally said sternly. "This better not be some kind of your cracker crap."

"Honest, gunnie, it looked just like a pig looking out of the bushes at me," he pleaded.

At that moment both lights struck movement just ahead of them on the far shore. Immediately, the water in the canal erupted in a huge splash as a man lunged across the narrow waterway. Quickly reaching the levy side, Hector Corro scrambled out the dark water and began running along the high ground on the opposite side of the fence from the two guards.

Instinctively, the younger security man raised his shotgun, but the gunnery sergeant stuck out a hand to restrain him.

"Just let him run," the sergeant said, while reaching for his radio. "We got a detail coming from the other direction and the beach is covered."

"Base security," he called over the handset. "Notify the Coast Guard that we've got one of their subjects on the run to the west along the outer wire."

For the first time in what seemed to be several very long minutes Riley Bright finally felt able to breath freely. From the moment the flashlight's beam had crossed the face of the stolen pig, both he and Chick had been motionless, with just their faces above water under the hanging foliage. Fortunately, the hog had moved a step or two back into the mangroves, out of the spotlight. Then, when the man had burst from the same shore not far from their position and began running away, the guards' attention had been diverted from where they were hiding.

As the two armed men moved off at a trot following the fleeing figure, Chick, Riley and the pig were once again on the move, heading east toward Geiger Creek. Throwing caution to the wind on the knowledge that the security detail was headed in the opposite direction and knowing their window of opportunity to meet Eric Allen was closing fast, they now plowed through the mangroves.

Quickly they passed the barely visible lights of the DEA roadblock out on the street, and then reached the spot where a paved road from the inland cut across their path. After crossing the asphalt, the trio turned and hurried to their right to the junction with the main road. To the east they could now see the Geiger Creek bridge and Eric Allen preparing to climb into the van in the parking area. Breaking into a run, they covered the hundred yards quickly.

"About time," Allen snapped, looking a bit startled at their sudden appearance.

"We're here," Chick shot back. "Get the back open and let's get the hog in there."

Quickly moving to the rear of the van, Allen swung the doors open, then he and Riley slid out the loading ramp. Chick led the purloined animal up into the van.

"Christ, you people stink," Allen said, twisting his face into a scowl. "You're not riding up front and smelling up the cab. I'll have to be in it most of the night."

"Climb in," Chick said to Riley, but casting an exasperated look Allen's way in the process.

"Just get us out to the highway to Mile Marker 11," Chick then demanded of Allen, as he and Riley pulled the loading ramp up into the back of the truck.

With that Allen pushed the van doors closed, leaving the two men and the pig in darkness. The vehicle quickly swung out on the road and began bumping along.

"He's right," Riley said in the pitch black.

"Who's right about what?" Chick asked, in a voice tinged with crossness.

"We do smell pretty bad."

"Just give me the telephone," Chick muttered after a brief silence.

When Riley finally fumbled it from the soaked pack, Chick took it, but when he hit the buttons, nothing happened.

"Looks like the saltwater made quick work of this thing," Chick groaned.

The little moving van covered the six miles north to Big Coppitt Key very quickly, but the traffic streaming out of Key West and up U.S. 1 made the right turn onto the main highway a slow one, only possible when the traffic light eventually halted the line of exiting cars. Another mile and the truck came to a halt on the road's shoulder just short of where the fill connects Big Coppitt to Shark Key. Another moment and the van's back doors swung outward.

"This is it," Allen announced in a matter of fact tone.

"How about dialing up Carla and getting her moving," Chick said as the pair climbed down. "Water killed our phone."

From his pocket, the truck driver produced the phone.

"Be my guest," he said, handing it to Chick, then closing the doors and adding," I expect you to replace that phone. It's STAG property."

Riley's last view of the contraband pig was the swine lying on its side in the dim light seeping into the back of the truck. The animal's now familiar snout turned toward him, still painted with its permanent amused look. Then the door was closed.

Chick finished the call and glared at Allen for a moment. Then quickly he heaved both the cell phones off into the tangle of foliage along the roadway. When Allen started to protest, Chick simply grinned at him.

"Bill me," he said.

Without a word Eric Allen was back in the cab and at the first break in traffic, wheeled the truck onto the highway and headed east.

"Do you think we're in the clear?" Riley asked Chick as they watched the van fade into the stream of traffic and dark of night.

"It would appear so," Chick mused, as he led his companion back off the shoulder of the road to stand in the shadows of the roadside bushes, "assuming our ride appears."

In roughly 10 minutes a sedan did pull to the side of the road beside the little Mile Marker 11 sign. Chick and Riley approached as a window rolled down.

"My, my, you two sure look a mess," R&B Mann observed.

"Glad it's a rental car and not mine," Carla Mays added from the driver's seat. "You boys care for a ride."

The duo tumbled into the back seat and the car pulled away, also headed east up the chain of islands.

Chapter 28

"Double-wide," Eric Allen mumbled to himself, "It figures."

As he completed the phrase he brought the van to a halt beside the structure, which had several sheds out behind it. Opening the door, he exited the cab, stretched his arms and walked around the front of the truck. The mid-day sun was bright and it was surprisingly muggy for fall in Highlands County.

Across the yard a wiry man in overalls approached, accompanied by a teen-aged boy in denim jeans and a dingy white tee shirt.

"You must be Allen," the man said with a broad smile, offering his hand.

Allen looked at the outstretched arm as if deciding whether to grasp it or bolt backward a few paces to avoid the grizzled and dirty appendage. Reluctantly he chose the former, shaking it weakly.

"Yes, from STAG," he said, releasing the grip. "I've got the rescued animal in back. I suppose you have a home prepared for it?"

At the word "home," the young boy looked up quizzically at the older man in overhauls, then turned his face to Allen with a squint.

"Yes sir," the man replied, "First rate accommodations for him to live out his natural life. I'm always glad to open my farm to save one of our animal brethren. Let's have a look at the fellow."

With that the trio walked around to the back of the truck and swung open the door.

"Where'd you say he came from?" the farmer said looking in at the hog.

"He was in Key West and about to suffer a cruel fate," Allen said, and then added, "had not our organization mounted a covert operation to save him. We risked a lot for our sensate brother."

"Ain't nothing but a pig in there," the teenager observed.

"Quiet boy," the farmer said sternly. "Help me get this ramp down."

Sliding out and lowering the ramp, the farmer strode up into the truck and brought the hog down to the ground, leading it by the rope leash still attached around its neck.

As he reached the ground, the farmer spoke again, as the boy slid the ramp back up and closed the van doors.

"I hope you didn't forget the rest of the bargain," he directed to Allen. "Costs a lot to maintain an animal this size. Feed and trips to the vet and all."

"As we agreed," Allen said, handing a wad of currency over to the older man and concluded. "Now I have to get back to the islands."

With that, Eric Allen climbed quickly back in the cab and immediately headed down the drive to the washboard dirt road that would then take him to Florida State Route 70 and on north to Lake Placid. From there he would drive east to pick up the Florida's Turnpike for Miami.

After the truck was gone, the man and boy walked the hog around behind the mobile home and through the gate into an open-ended shed. Closing the gate, the pair leaned on the rails looking at the hog.

"You really going to just keep this pig here?" the boy said, looking up at his father.

"Son, this is a working farm. Nobody or nothing gets a free ride," he explained.

Then taking the wad from his overhaul pocket, he began counting the money and straightening the bills as he added.

"Every animal on the place is for sale."

The boy gave his father a knowing look of admiration, then turned his gaze back on the hog, which lay in the dim light of the shade, bearing a constant amused look on its snout.

"You know, Pa, there's something awful familiar about the look of that critter?"

Mark Farnsworth, late of the Key West Police Department, had driven north to Fort Lauderdale, consuming most the morning in the process. After grabbing a sandwich at a place on Commercial Boulevard, he found his way to the glass storefront emblazoned with Farnsworth and Spade Security across its door.

He was now sitting in an uncomfortable, metal frame and fabric office chair across an equally cheap desk from a short balding man in his late 50s, who was dressed in a tropical shirt and tan slacks. The older man lounged back in a more expensive padded chair, his right hand draped at the end of the armrest with an unlit cigar clutched between his index and middle fingers. He was smiling across the space to where Farnsworth sat.

"So," the older man began, "your momma's going to be really happy, Mark. She's been talking about wanting you to get into something safer."

"I know, Uncle Art,' Farnsworth agreed. "She's mentioned it more than once."

"She didn't tell me why you decided to quit the force," the older man noted.

"You know how it is," Farnsworth fumbled. "You get to a point where you just know you're not going to move up very quickly. I'd learned the ropes, still love law enforcement, but wanted more. Thought I should see another side of it. Sort of get the private sector view."

"It's going to be a sweet set up, too," his uncle said, leaning forward with a twinkle of delight in his eye. "Your police background brings something to the table. Add a little prestige and expertise to the business."

"Glad to hear it," Farnsworth smiled slightly, wondering how much prestige it took to install a security alarm.

"I know I just skimmed the surface in covering the operations," his uncle noted. "But have you got any questions so far?"

The younger man bit his lower lip, then with a shrug asked.

"Yeah, do you have a partner? Who's the Spade in the company name?"

With a muffled snort of laughter, a wicked little smile turned up the corners of his uncle's mouth.

"Doesn't exist. That's for your Aunt Annie," he explained. "She loves old Humphrey Bogart movies — especially the Sam Spade mysteries. Fact is, she likes to dress up in old clothes, looking like Mary Astor in the Maltese Falcon."

Then with a wink he continued.

"At least at the beginning of the evening. Really gets her off, if you know what I mean."

Farnsworth forced a grin and nodded his understanding; all the while trying his best not to imagine what went on between his uncle and aunt.

"So you ready to start right away?" Uncle Art shifted gears, as he leaned back in his office chair.

"It'll only take me a day or two to get my stuff moved up here," he answered. "It's pretty easy to sublet anything in Key West, so the lease was no problem."

"Already got a place to stay?"

"Plan to move in with mom until I find something," Farnsworth admitted sheepishly.

"She'll like that," Uncle Art grinned. "Understand though, I'm not cutting you any slack because of blood. You're going to have to learn the whole business from the ground up. Any problem with that?"

"No, sir," Farnsworth offered blandly.

"How about you start next Monday then. That'll give you an extra day or two to settle in. I'm going to start you off in the sales end first. You'll spend the first couple of months out there learning to root around for new accounts."

The use of the word "root" struck an unpleasant associative chord in the young ex-officer's mind, sending a slightly pained look across his face.

"I know it's not very glamorous, but it pays the bills," his uncle offered apologetically, mistaking the source of his nephew's reaction.

The mid-afternoon sun at the beginning of November was warmly bathing the open yard in front of Sea Jay's Restaurant and the boatlift of the Jekyll Harbor Marina. Yet a few steps away in the shade the chill of the season applied its crisp hold. The stiff 20-knot wind blowing down from the northeast was evident as it played with the tips of marsh grass across Jekyll Creek, producing a vista reminiscent of Kansas wheat ruffling in a strong breeze. The location on the inside of the island, however, provided plenty of live oaks to break that wind, leaving the grounds pleasant, at least where the sun was finding them.

In the drive behind the restaurant and in front of the marina's huge dry storage building a rental sedan and an SUV sat side by side, with a small knot of people standing together.

"Are you sure you won't go with us, Chipmunk?" Chick Malor asked, exhibiting a regained playful mischievousness that had so recently been missing from him. "Capt. Carla will show us the Chesapeake area. Who knows, she might get a crab boat and we can crew it."

"Don't think so," Captain Carla Mays interjected lightly, with toss of her blonde hair that hung loose over her shoulders. "I think I've learned my lesson about sailing with this crew."

"Sorry, Chick, but I'm not cut out for this life," Riley Bright declined. "I'm headed back to Atlanta. I'll drop your car and pick mine up at your apartment."

"Then what, man," Chick asked a bit more seriously. "Go back to Amax to romance old Bennie and beg forgiveness from Seth Wheeler?"

"I'll go by there," Riley said with a little wince, "but probably just to pick up a box of personal stuff, if they haven't thrown it away and will still let me in the door."

For just a moment the group stood silent with Chick shaking his head with a rueful look on his face as Riley appeared a bit forlorn at the prospect of his next journey. Finally Chick again broke the silence.

"How about you, Arbie?"

"A ride into Brunswick and the bus station will be just fine," R&B Mann grinned. "I been hanging with you white folks too long already; losing touch with my people and the streets. Need to seriously get back to my music. Thinking about heading down to Mobile and check out some crossroads in that delta."

"Well, I guess this is the break up of our pig-napping ring then," Chick concluded.

The men shook hands all around, while Riley and R&B also got hugs from Carla Mays. Three of them then climbed into the rental car and waved out the windows as they departed down the sand driveway.

Filled with a hollow feeling, Riley Bright walked over and got in Chick's SUV. He followed the settling dust of their departure along the drive, and then turned left onto the paved street. At the next intersection he headed the vehicle west on Georgia State Route 520, passing the toll plaza and onto the bridge linking the isle to the mainland's causeway. Climbing up the span, he could see the sheen of the sun's rays glistening in either direction as they reflected off the bare black mud flats of low tide. Beyond, the rippling marsh grass stretched to the north and south horizons, broken only by the raised outlines of islands and hammocks.

For the first time he noticed the cassette tape jutting from the face of the car's stereo system. Absently, Riley reached down and shoved it in. After a few seconds of grinding away, and just as he topped the center span of the bridge, a mix of guitars and drums began to flood from the speakers. A smile spread over Riley's face as he listened to the Grateful Dead and Jerry Garcia singing *Truckin'*.

It was a line about a long strange trip.

Made in the USA
Columbia, SC
15 February 2023